Z E T A K. P I E R C E

The Crimson Knight

Book 1

CONTENTS

CONTENT WARNINGS

The Crimson Knight is a dark fantasy intended for an adult audience. It contains elements and tropes that are commonly found in the genre, including but not limited to: graphic depictions of violence, death, blood, gore, torture and dismemberment, alcohol use, child death, animal death, one mention of domestic abuse (largely implied, no actions described in detail on page), and kidnapping.

CHAPTER 1

The Illinizan Mage Academy stringently taught their students the foundational principle of healing: all life was sacred.

No longer a child under their tutelage, Haizea disagreed.

Sanctity implied a certain inviolability. It reduced life to a mere sacrosanct entity, only meant to be honored with godlike reverence and never to be touched or tampered with.

Instead, Haizea believed in the principle that all life had purpose. Even the loss of life itself had its place. Moreover, it gave her the ease of mind regarding her intentions with the small rodent caught in the trap outside of her home.

If the animal's life was sacred, then she had an obligation to protect it.

But if it had purpose, then that purpose should be fulfilled regardless of whether it lived or perished.

Rays of sunlight reflected off her blade as she pulled it from her sheath. She crouched and caught the rat's tail, which hung outside of the trap, and nicked it. A few drops of blood emerged, and Haizea allowed her magic to rise to the surface. Her honey-brown eyes turned cinnamon, slowly taking on a brownish-red hue with the trickle of her powers, but she would have to reach further to achieve what she came here to do.

With ironclad control, she loosened her grip on the gate that kept the brunt of her magic at bay, and the vitality in the rat's blood blossomed before her eyes.

When Haizea killed the rat, she made it quick. Painless. One moment the animal teemed with life and the next Haizea had taken that life for herself. Its body withered to nothing more than a shriveled husk beneath the weight of her magic.

With the dam broken, her powers flooded through and gave her a feeling of much needed release. She let out a long, shaky breath as her body rewarded her with a rush of ecstasy. Her heart raced, and a light buzz invaded her mind. She retained just enough of her composure to halt the smile threatening to creep across her lips.

Although the release paled in comparison to what she would have felt had it been a human, Haizea closed her eyes and took a few moments to bask in the feeling, with a pleased hum rumbling from the back of her throat.

When she opened her eyes once more, her irises had deepened into a crimson red, and her vision tinted with a shimmering vermillion hue, signifying that her body had fully absorbed the rat's vitality.

Vitality was the force that lived, breathed, and gave life to the Human Realm. It coursed through the tiniest insects. It emanated within the largest mountains. It existed as deep as the realm's core and rained down from the heavens.

Mages possessed the ability to sense and manipulate the vitality around them.

Usually when Haizea used her magic, she healed herself and others. But at this moment she had a different objective, a darker one.

More than a simple healing mage, as an omen and a master of the Cosmic Arts, Haizea wielded the power of the Cosmos to twist and warp her abilities into blood magic.

Only once had she ever used that power on another human being and she'd nearly killed them. Afterward, she had vowed to never use blood magic on another human being unless in necessary defense and veered from the path of most blood mages by choosing to sacrifice animals.

But she could not abandon Cosmic magic completely; omens who refused to continue using the Cosmic Arts suffered from magical wasting, a fatal disease.

The intoxicating high vibrating through Haizea served as an addictive lure, specifically to prevent such an outcome.

Still, Haizea used her blood magic sparingly. Just enough to stave off the same illness that had killed her father. Taking the life of rodents kept her magic from bursting at the seams and eating her alive with it. With her father's untimely demise as a constant reminder, Haizea paid the price willingly. And at times, eagerly.

Her eyes fell to the rat's corpse once more and a small voice in the back of her mind wished that she could rewind the hands of time so that she could do it all over again. Haizea stopped short, realizing the dark path her thoughts had taken.

Those weren't her genuine feelings. Her corrupted magic had momentarily taken the reins. *She* didn't enjoy it.

Haizea's fingernails dug into her skin as she clenched her trembling fists. She sequestered those wretched desires in the recesses of her mind, locking them away in the same manner she kept her Cosmic power at bay.

There was a slight haze clouding her reddened vision as she climbed to her feet. It would take another hour or so for her eyes to return to their normal brown and the vitality of the Human Realm would turn invisible once again—enough time for her to get ready before paying a much-needed visit to her grandfather in Von Stein.

Von Stein didn't have nearly as many people as where she lived in the Capital, but it had a fairly sizable population and the people lived in comfort.

A familiar, rhythmic clopping sounded through the air as horse drawn carriages traveled along the paved roads. One of the horses whinnied as the rumble of a steam powered engine grew closer.

The lone vehicle zipped past the numerous carriages rolling down the street. When one of them didn't get out of the vehicle's path quickly enough, the driver waved their hand out of the window and a swell of magic pushed the carriage out of the way.

Haizea glanced after the scene with a small frown, standing on her grandfather's doorstep. When his frail frame appeared at the door, a wave of guilt washed over her. She bit it back before he could see it in her eyes. Grandfather Harzel might be old and physically weak, but his youthfulness continued on in his mind, astute and sharp.

While not quite the mirror image of her grandfather, Haizea shared many features with him. They both had rich brown skin. Haizea had dense, shoulder-length honey-blonde coils whereas her grandfather had a short gray afro, once blond in his youth. Just two inches shy of six feet, Haizea stood at eye level with the average man.

She had light brown eyes, just like her father's—and by extension, Grandfather Harzel's. She shared mother's austere countenance, and around her neck hung her mother's pendant: the last gift she'd ever given her.

Grandfather Harzel waved her in as he hobbled inside and made his way into the kitchen, returning with a tray holding a steaming kettle and two cups. Haizea tried to take it from him, but he silently gave her a stern glare. She sat down in one of the soft chairs in the living room.

"So, what brings you here unannounced?" His hand trembled as he poured her drink.

"The Guard will be departing in a few days for a diplomatic trip to Olysseus and Llyr. I'll be gone for a few weeks, so I wanted to make sure you have everything you need before I leave."

"I'm fine. I can take care of myself," he huffed, peering up from his task.

She shrugged. "I know, but it's good to have someone check on you every now and again."

Handing her a cup of tea, he gave her a pointed look. "And yet when I express the same sentiments to you, I get a mountain of resistance."

Haizea snorted. "Not a *mountain*, Grandfather. You convinced me to let you move here, didn't you?" she replied.

"Only because I couldn't get you to change your mind altogether. But we all make mistakes, and it's better to have someone who loves you nearby to pick up the pieces. Life is fragile, Haizea, even yours. I hope when I'm no longer in this realm, you'll allow the people who love you to look after you."

Chastised, Haizea fell silent. Grandfather Harzel mixed ground mirwort into his cup, his hands trembling with each motion.

Haizea reached over and held his hand. As the mirwort potion slowly spread through her grandfather, she aided the healing process with her magic. Without her blood magic activated, she couldn't see the vitality, but Haizea felt it responding to her touch as she mended the warped and damaged particles. The tension in her grandfather's body slowly melted away.

After a few moments, Harzel cleared his throat. His sharp eyes took note of Haizea's fingers running along the pendant around her neck.

"Something's on your mind," he remarked. "What's bothering you?"

Haizea dropped her hand and hummed softly to herself as she gathered her thoughts before speaking. "What if I arranged a carriage to take you back to Illiniza while I'm gone?"

"Haizea," he chided, "I'll go back to Illiniza when you decide to resign from that bastard's Guard and return home. Not a second sooner."

They'd had this conversation several times now. When Haizea learned of the trip a few weeks ago, she tried to convince her grandfather to spend some time back home in Mount Illiniza. It had been nearly two years since they'd left.

"This knight business is beneath you," he went on. "You aren't meant to serve any ruler. Not as a mountaineer and certainly not as a warrior." He raised a hand when she opened her mouth to rebut him. "You won't admit it, but I know you feel it deep in your veins. Otherwise, you wouldn't be here trying to convince me to go home."

She blew out a frustrated breath. "I just want you to be somewhere safe."

"Is Arcelia not safe?" A challenge echoed in his tone.

"That's not what I said. You know what I mean, Grandfather," Haizea sighed.

"What you don't say holds just as much weight as what you do. In either case, I don't think my body can take another trip like that, Haizea. If I leave now, I won't have the energy to come back. I'm eighty years old, you know. I'd love to spend my last days in the mountains, but not without you there.

"I'll be fine while you're gone. I've lived more than three of your lifetimes. I've seen some things—much more than you can fathom at your young age. I'm still a healer. And even if I don't look like it, I'm still a blood mage." He shrugged with a wink.

Back in the mountains, they didn't have to hide the true nature of their magic. The mountaineers had a common saying: *Cosmic magic is only as vile as the mage who wields it.* Unfortunately, the kingdoms didn't share that sentiment, and not only did they strictly forbid the Cosmic Arts, but they also punished omens by death.

Because of that, Harzel adamantly vocalized his disapproval of Haizea's decision to move, but his words went unheeded. The mountains carried whispers of her loss everywhere she looked, and Arcelia offered a change of scenery that her homelands couldn't provide.

Grandfather Harzel remained a constant at her side. Her trip would be their first time apart and the first time Haizea would be truly alone in her twenty-four years.

Her expression did not waiver, but her stinging eyes threatened to betray her thoughts. She blinked, intent on maintaining her composure. Harzel gave her hand a light squeeze.

"You don't have anything to worry about. Your trip with the Guard will be fine. And if it isn't, your blood magic makes you more dangerous than any other Cosmic Arts practitioner in the realm. You learned from the best there is. Trust in me. I can handle myself," he said. His eyes crinkled as he gave her a small, smug grin.

Haizea didn't quite smile back, but her gaze softened considerably.

She sipped on the warm tea, and in the few minutes of silence that passed, Grandfather Harzel fell asleep, his light snores filling the room.

Haizea took the opportunity to take inventory of everything he had. His bare pantry needed more of his usual staples. The handrail that helped him get in and out of the bathtub looked about ready to fall off the wall. On her way home, she would put in a request for a delivery service as well as a work order.

She didn't know how much longer he'd be able to live on his own, but she would do everything in her power to help him maintain his independence. He did not have much time left in this realm, but she wanted his final days to be happy.

Her parents hadn't left this realm with dignity, a fact that haunted her even now. She refused to let the same happen to her grandfather. Haizea grabbed the blanket on the couch and draped it over him. Then she gave him a light kiss on the forehead before making her leave. For now at least, he was alright.

Chapter 2

A messenger hawk landed in Haizea's window as she sat on her bed and folded clothes for her upcoming trip. She opened it to find a summons from King Rhys ordering the entire Guard to report to the Royal Palace immediately, even those off-duty. Something urgent must have arisen.

Haizea quickly donned her knight's armor: white with streaks of cerulean, representing the colors of the Arcelian flag. It covered every inch of her body with a helmet and cape to match. Next, she fetched her swords and slid them into the sheaths on her hips.

She lived close enough to walk to the palace, as did the rest of the Guard. Her hair shifted slightly from the gust of air caused by a steam-powered carriage speeding by on the cobblestoned street. During her few years in Arcelia, the newly developed technology quickly took hold amongst the elites. Having grown up in the mountains, the sight of vehicles still felt foreign to Haizea, but she understood the general concept of how the carriages worked. They could only be operated by telekinetic mages, who used their magic to move the turbines that created the steam which then propelled the vehicles forward.

When Haizea arrived at the palace, she ran into Zander first. His tan skin paled in comparison to her warm brown tone, and he stood roughly an inch taller than her. His straight brown locks laid flat down his neck, and the bright blue of his eyes complimented the streaks in his armor.

"Looking lively this morning, Haizea," he said, smiling warmly as she approached.

Haizea gave him a dutiful nod as she took her spot beside him, mindful to keep a respectable distance.

"Any idea why King Rhys summoned us early?" he asked.

"No, but it must be something troublesome if he wants the entire Guard here," Haizea retorted, glancing around for the last member of their trio, Jirina, who should have arrived by now—and was better suited to answer Zander's question.

Zander moved closer and bumped Haizea with his elbow to reclaim her attention.

"Where's your optimism?" he mused. "I bet five coins he wants to treat us all to a nice meal for all the hard work we've done so far before we leave."

Haizea let out a long exhale. As she resisted rolling her eyes, Jirina's form approached in the distance.

"Fashionably late as always," she murmured, pointing her chin in Jirina's direction.

Jirina's brown hair hung past her shoulders, and her skin was much paler than either Haizea's or Zander's. In addition to a single sword, she carried a scepter attached to the hilt on her back.

"Haizea and I were just taking bets on why the king summoned us. You should throw in your lot too, Jirina," Zander said.

"I'll pass. You two have your fun."

Jirina pulled her scepter from her waistband and closed her eyes. Her vitality surged, and waves of energy rolled off the scepter.

Haizea suppressed her blood magic when it tugged in response, keeping the true magnitude of her power buried beneath the surface. Her pendant buzzed against her chest in muted vibrations.

After her mother passed away, Grandfather Harzel always made a fuss about maintaining the necklace's quality and demanded that she give it to him for cleaning every few months. Haizea didn't mind, but he would not have taken no for an answer even if she did. Right before they left Mount Illiniza, her grandfather borrowed her pendant for about a week and when he returned it, Haizea sensed a change within, like the metal teemed with life.

Around the time he'd taken the necklace lined up perfectly with his annual practice of consuming human blood to stave off magical wasting.

He explained that he'd placed a curse on it to help hide her forbidden power. It could prevent another mage from sensing the undercurrent of her blood magic that always flowed beneath her healing abilities. It wasn't foolproof, but so long as Haizea kept her corrupted magic suppressed, the necklace would assist in shielding her from exposure.

Grandfather Harzel's words at the time still stuck with Haizea:

"Blood magic is your heritage, your identity, and your legacy. My mother taught me. I taught your father. He foolishly refused to teach you, but I will. You have more vitality coursing through you than I've ever sensed, and you deserve to know how to use it properly. It's better to know it and never use it than to find yourself wishing you learned when you need it the most."

Beside her, Jirina's vitality calmed. The call in Haizea's blood diminished, and with it the threat of discovery.

"He's in the king's suite, standing in the window while he waits for us," Jirina said.

With the three of them finally together, Zander opened the palace gate. His blue eyes took on a faint glow as his magic allowed him to manipulate the vitality in the objects around him. A loud rumbling and creaking sound reverberated in the air as the gate swung open to allow them passage.

They entered the castle and passed by the training room, where the prince and princess studied under the tutelage of their private tutor, Grand Magister Ophelia.

Prince Felix was a boisterous seventeen-year-old, with brown hair and blue eyes like his father and a face that strongly resembled the queen's. Princess Sage was the impressionable age of fourteen, with a head of blonde hair unlike the rest of her family, but otherwise was a mirror image of her father. Haizea paused at the entrance to watch their telekinetic lesson.

Prince Felix held his arms outward, concentrating intently as he used his hands to guide a cluster of darts toward the target across the room.

Beside him, Princess Sage maintained a collected demeanor. She stood with her arms relaxed at her sides, and her darts blurred as they barreled through the air, each landing perfectly on the center bullseye.

Prince Felix's darts landed a moment later—some of them missed the target entirely while the rest scattered across the board.

"Solid form, Prince Felix. I can tell you've been practicing, so keep at it. Princess Sage, you performed perfectly, as always. The vitality has blessed you, just like your father," Grand Magister Ophelia complimented, earning a demure smile from the princess.

Then Sage caught sight of Haizea in the doorway, who gave her a small nod, and she beamed in return. Behind her, Prince Felix stared at his sister with his lips downturned into a scowl. When he glanced up to see Haizea watching him, his face blanched, and he quickly turned back toward his tutor.

"Are you done? We've got work to do," Jirina whispered behind her.

Haizea turned away from the practice room.

"Prince Felix will be king someday, and his sister will also play a supporting role during his reign. There's no harm in checking in on their progress. The more competent they are with their magic, the easier our jobs will be," Haizea responded with a shrug.

Zander offered an agreeable nod, but Jirina had already turned her back to walk away; Haizea's words had flown into one ear and out of the other.

Jirina's mind was most likely on more pressing matters, like the upcoming trek to the neighboring Kingdom of Olysseus before a joint meeting with the King of Llyr. They aimed to strengthen ties with Llyr who, at best, held lukewarm ties with Arcelia. King Rhys said it was a solid future investment to address any strained relationships Arcelia had so that eventually his son would have a peaceful transition into power.

The trio made their way towards King Rhys's suite. Despite the castle's own enormous size, the first time Haizea had glimpsed the suite, she wondered how something so expansive could possibly fit inside. It was painted with Arcelia's colors—white and blue.

A portrait of the royal family hung on the wall above the king's study. Along the opposing wall hung portraits of the two dozen knights currently serving on the Royal Guard.

King Rhys stood before one of the tall windows that took up the entire height of the room, from floor to ceiling. He'd clasped his hands behind his back and wore his dark, gray-streaked hair pulled back into a half bun, while the rest of his hair fell down his shoulders.

When the doors slammed shut after the trio stepped inside, it was the result of his own telekinetic magic. Three chairs levitated in front of the knights before dropping to the floor, signaling for them to sit.

The king turned around to face them, towering over their seated forms. The long-healed scar that spanned from his cheek and down his lips glinted under the sunlight that beamed in from the window.

"Jirina. Haizea. Zander." He looked pointedly at each of them. "You three are the last of the Guard to be briefed. There's an execution scheduled this afternoon. We discovered a mage using the Cosmic Arts. We have their family in our custody, as well."

Haizea's stomach dropped at the mention of the Cosmic Arts. Although her expression remained neutral, she froze in her seat. In reality, the moment had been fleeting, but it felt like an eternity passed while she thought someone had seen her use her blood magic earlier and reported it to the king.

But she knew that King Rhys would never let that happen.

He wouldn't knowingly allow corrupted magic within the walls of his castle. Nor would he knowingly expose his family to it, either. Haizea would have been apprehended long before she crossed the threshold.

Although the king tried to be fair in his dealings, he had no tolerance for the Cosmic Arts.

The punishment for corrupted magic was death, and King Rhys was the judge, jury, and executioner.

He sighed, "I know it's a tough job, but it must be done. This will be open to the public, so the rest of the Guard will help prepare. I need to make an example out of them." The welcoming expression he'd had when they entered now melted into one filled with rage and disgust.

Haizea hid it well, but the shift in his demeanor made her skin crawl. Even if she wouldn't be the one dealing the lethal blow, she would have to assist with and witness firsthand the killing of a fellow omen.

It wasn't lost on Haizea that all it would take was one slipup and that could be her.

The execution took place in the colosseum. The king's order for the entire Royal Guard to be present—despite many of them being off-duty—made more sense to Haizea now. He wanted this to be a public spectacle for every person in and near the Capital City of Ravaryn to see.

Queen Mireille had insisted that Princess Sage was too young to witness such an event. The king conceded, but in turn, he did not relent on the young prince's attendance. Prince Felix was nearly the age of adulthood. He could not shy away from kingly duties, no matter how unpleasant they may be.

King Rhys then charged Haizea, Zander, and Jirina with guarding the queen and the young prince. Queen Mireille wore a golden crown on her head and carried with her a gleaming scepter, though unlike Jirina's, it was simply a royal artifact rather than a tool for magic. She wore a dress that had a white bust with intricate plaits down the center. The skirt portion flowed down her legs in a mix of white and Arcelia's cerulean. A soft white and blue mantle draped over her shoulders and flowed past her ankles, brushing against the ground.

She took her seat in a huff, barely acknowledging the presence of the royal knights nearby. Prince Felix stole a few nervous glances at Haizea as he took slow and deliberate steps to join his mother.

Situated high up in the stadium in a private booth, they had a clear view of the platform below where other members of the Royal Guard prepared the stage for the incoming execution. They placed several stakes in the ground and chained bonds to them.

One person was already tied down, presumably the omen. A dark cloth covered their head. Ser Bren, the most senior member of the Guard, stood next to them.

Haizea narrowed her eyes, noting several other knights huddled close to the walls where the shadows obscured their features. In fact, one of the silhouettes looked very short in stature—much too small to be a knight. If Haizea didn't know any better, she'd say it was a child.

King Rhys had said that they'd taken the mage's family into custody. Surely, that didn't mean he intended on slaughtering them all. Maybe he merely wanted them to witness the consequences firsthand, in the same way he commanded Prince Felix's presence. Still, that thought didn't bring her much comfort.

The Royal Guard finally brought the prisoners from the shadows. Once chained in place, the knights removed the covers from their heads, revealing two young girls.

Haizea stole a glance at the queen, who had stiffened into stone. Haizea had been around the woman long enough to sense the queen's displeasure, even if she did not give voice to her opinions. Ultimately, regardless of anyone else's feelings—including those of his own wife—King Rhys had the final word: the decision to carry out this execution rested entirely on his shoulders.

The cover lifted from the omen's face next. They began to wail once they realized who stood next to them on the platform. Haizea did her best to block it out.

She turned to Zander, who had preoccupied himself with Prince Felix, likely to help keep the young man at ease. As telekinetic mages, their subtype was much more common among the Physical Class than healing mages. In fact, telekinesis was the most common magic of all mage classes, whereas healing was the rarest.

Zander's sword floated in the air before doing a quick twirl.

"Careful, now. Remember, the sword is a weapon. Even if it's not in your hands, you can still hurt somebody with it," Zander warned.

Prince Felix responded with a calm nod, though a bead of sweat trickled down his forehead. He put both hands up, and the sword drifted toward him in the air. Then, very gingerly, he grabbed onto its handle.

"Very good. At this rate, you'll be an even match with your father," Zander said.

Jirina snorted.

"King Rhys is the most powerful telekinetic mage in the land. It's going to take much more than a few sword tricks to surpass your father."

The boy's face deflated.

"...What I mean to say is, sword tricks are beneath you. Powerful magic runs in your family. Zander ought to be showing you the more advanced techniques," Jirina amended.

Queen Mireille hushed them, her eyes fixated on the scene unfolding down below. King Rhys had finally entered, wearing similar garb as his wife. He paused in front of the prisoner with a deep frown that creased his scar.

His hand clutched the sword on his hip before he turned to address the crowd.

"Today, our prisoner is guilty of the highest crime a mage can commit: meddling with the Cosmic Arts."

Murmurs ran through the masses, and Haizea repressed a shudder.

"And it was not just *any* corrupted magic either. This man is guilty of the crime of transmutation, a bastardization of telekinesis." The king's tone dripped with acid, and his teeth gritted into a vicious snarl.

The queen visibly flinched at his words. Haizea kept her countenance even, although her insides withered.

"There is only one path to justice for this man. The penalty for practicing the Cosmic Arts is death." King Rhys turned to the two girls next to him.

One was truly a child while the other seemed to be around Prince Felix's age. He put his hand on the older one's shoulder.

"The call of justice must be answered regardless of age. If you're old enough to defile the gift that vitality gives you, then you're old enough to face the consequences of your actions. This young woman recently celebrated her eighteenth birthday. She is guilty of aiding and abetting an omen attempting to flee from justice."

His sword flashed. One moment, the teen was standing there trembling. The next, her head fell to the ground, decapitated with a single swipe. When the child next to them cried out in despair, King Rhys forced their mouth shut with his telekinetic magic.

"Regarding this child, today I will show mercy. She will be sent to a correctional center for juveniles," he addressed the crowd before turning to the child.

He projected his voice so that everyone could still hear.

"If you were just a year or two older, you'd face life imprisonment for your involvement. A few more years older than that, and you'd share your sister's fate," he warned.

More murmurs rushed through the crowd, but King Rhys spared them no heed. Haizea had assumed that the knights would carry the girl away, but the king had other plans. He raised a hand, signaling for silence.

Haizea forced herself to stand still as a statue. Her eyes flickered to the queen and the prince. The boy's face had paled and now held a tint of green. Haizea took a step to the side, putting more space between them.

Down below, King Rhys had a feral, blind rage in his eyes. He looked nothing like the king that Haizea knew. By the expression on Queen Mireille's face, she likely felt the same way.

Unlike his son, King Rhys did not need to raise and wave his arms to utilize the full force of his telekinesis. With a small, simple twist of his fingers, the omen's neck snapped and turned and pulled until his head finally tore away from his body.

The little girl cried out once more and, without so much as a glance in her direction, King Rhys quickly silenced her with a snap of his fingers.

The man's screams echoed in Haizea's mind, burning into her memory. She would never forget what it looked like for the king to kill a person in cold blood, especially someone just barely at the cusp of adulthood.

Murder, assault, abuse—crimes of that nature surely warranted violent retribution. She'd known of the death penalty for practicing the Cosmic Arts, but up until this point, there hadn't been one during her tenure on the Guard. All this time, it had been an abstract possibility. A pit settled deep in her stomach. The risk suddenly felt all too tangible.

Prince Felix retched a few feet away from her. The queen reached over and gently rubbed her hand along his back. Swallowing, Zander escorted the boy away. Future king or not, this event was no place for a teenager. Even Jirina held an apologetic expression.

The three women stared down at the platform where blood pooled around the omen's body. Yet Haizea wondered why the man hadn't fought back.

As a Cosmic Arts practitioner, his power should have eclipsed King Rhys's. Perhaps the man had been a nascent omen and still didn't have a full understanding of his abilities yet. It was the only explanation Haizea could think of that made any sense.

"Being an omen was bad enough alone. But having the gall to attempt transmutation of all things under the king's nose is about as foolish as it gets," Queen Mireille murmured, getting to her feet and finally directly addressing the two remaining knights.

An uncomfortable silence followed. Neither Haizea nor Jirina knew what to make of her remark.

"See to it that this mess is cleaned up, will you?" The queen pointed at the puddle Prince Felix had made on the ground.

The two knights exchanged a glance. *That* would be a job for the servants.

Chapter 3

The Drunken Maiden was far enough away from the palace to evade King Rhys's scrutiny, but close enough that the Royal Guard could return to a call of duty in a reasonable timeframe.

Although no one dared to say it out loud, the king's display of violence unsettled the entire Guard. They in turn decided to decompress with alcohol.

Haizea removed her knight's attire in favor of her civilian clothing. Her mother's necklace hung loosely around her neck. The absence of her armor left her shape visible; she had prominent curves filled out by dense muscles, sculpted by a lifetime of training. She wore her hair in a braided style, with two cornrows on either side of her head which fed into a broad ponytail that rested against her shoulder blades.

Zander and Jirina had also discarded their armor before arriving. In fact, the entire Royal Guard had packed into the tavern along with its regular customers.

They'd already earned a few dirty looks for bumping one too many times into the patrons, but the knights paid the civilians no mind. To the naked eye, they blended in seamlessly, but anyone with even the smallest connection to the vitality would be able to sense the intense magic emanating from the members of the Royal Guard.

Only a fool would pick a fight with them; the Royal Guard were not only the strongest mages, but also the best fighters in Arcelia.

"I'll have the Devil's Serge. Two of them," Haizea said.

It was said to be the most potent whiskey in the kingdom. She'd need that much after what they'd witnessed today.

"Starting off strong, I see. I'll take a Twilight Blaze," Zander remarked, opting for an ale instead.

"A River Mocha for me," Jirina ordered, preferring mixed drinks.

Minutes later, the trio had their cups in hand. Haizea knocked back her first shot without even a flicker of a grimace.

Jirina sipped from her glass while Zander gulped his drink. The sight of blood pooling on the platform after King Rhys had beheaded the man flashed before Haizea's eyes. She tipped the second shot into her mouth.

As the alcohol seeped into her system, she let the music in the background come to the forefront. Some of the other knights must have had the same idea, because one of them came over and asked Jirina to join him, leaving Haizea and Zander alone.

Haizea didn't dance much, but she had a few moves in her repertoire. She timed her steps to the beat of the drum as she did the Pavissa—a dance the mountaineers performed during times of celebration.

When Zander failed to stick with the rhythm, she giggled, the alcohol unveiling her rare smile. Zander stalled, thrown off at the playful change in her demeanor.

"Like this," Haizea grabbed his hands and guided him along to the beat.

Zander cleared his throat and found his voice again after a few moments. "I can tell those shots are getting to you. You're already cutting loose."

She snorted. "Stop talking. It's making you lose the beat."

She pointed down at their feet, where Zander stepped off rhythm, a slight stagger in his movements. He rolled his eyes and opened his mouth to retort, but a server interrupted them, offering Haizea a glass.

"Someone put it in for you," the server said, pointing toward the bar, but too many people crowded around the area for Haizea to figure out who. Zander's brows rose as Haizea downed it in one go.

"You're not gonna try to find your secret admirer?" he asked with a laugh.

Haizea shrugged. She'd long grown used to the way people admired her from afar but seldom approached. She didn't have the patience to hunt them down; anyone worth her time would come find her. Either way, a free drink was a free drink.

The omen's cries of pain assaulted her ears once more. His screams combined with the buzz of the alcohol. It reminded her of the first time she'd used her blood magic on a human being and the Cosmic high that followed. Only human suffering could bring about that all-consuming euphoria, intense and unraveling.

Warm bodies surrounded her in every direction. Their heartbeats pulsed against her vitality. Her breathing quickened. It would take no effort to drain them and feel the high once more.

Haizea shook her head and shoved the thoughts to the back of her mind where they belonged. Something, or someone, caught Zander's eye and he wandered off. Haizea sighed and made her way toward the bar.

The free drink had solidified her buzz, but another shot would ensure it stuck around for a while. She wanted just enough to relax but still retain some of her wits: a prescient decision, because as she made her way back to the open floor, of course someone bumped into her.

Her drink spilled on her clothes, but she let it go. The man in front of her did not.

"Watch where you're going, bitch,'" he growled.

Haizea blinked in disbelief, too drunk to be certain she'd heard him correctly. "Excuse me?"

He looked her up and down before leaning in closer. "I said, watch where you're going. *Bitch*," he sneered.

She narrowed her eyes at him, annoyed at his words, but let the insult roll off and moved to walk away. The man grabbed her arm.

"You need to apologize," he demanded.

Haizea didn't bother arguing the fact that *he* bumped into *her* and between the two of them, she was the only one wet from a spilled drink. She wrenched her arm free. The man yanked her back. Her light brown eyes met his blue ones.

"Put your hands on me one more time and I won't be responsible for what happens to you," she said, freeing herself once more.

The man threw his head back and cackled. If not for the active crowd and loud music, it would have been disruptive.

"I'd like to see you try," he said, balling the fabric of her shirt in his fists and pulling her close enough that she could smell the beer on his breath.

Haizea did not warn him a second time.

With the way he currently held her shirt, he'd left his front wide open. Haizea reached up and wrapped her hand around his neck, purposefully placing her fingers on top of his arteries.

She applied pressure, just enough to make him lightheaded without choking him out completely. He released his grip on her clothing and wrapped his hands around her arm, but his fingers clutched uselessly against her musculature.

She brought him in so that his cheek brushed against hers, almost as if they were dancing to the music and wanted to close the distance between them.

"What did I just say?" she spoke low and even in his ear.

Haizea monitored his vitality with her healing magic. She suppressed her first instinct as a warrior, which told her to go for a quick and efficient kill. She didn't intend to hurt him, but rather bring him close enough to the brink that it would scare some sense into him. As the vibrancy in his vitality diminished, he began to sag against her.

Haizea let him go, her expression remaining impassive as he dropped to his knees. His hands trembled as he rubbed his throat, now red with the imprint of her hand.

She crouched down in front of him and knotted her fingers into his hair. He resisted when she yanked his head to look her in the eyes, but she overpowered him with ease.

"Consider this a light warning. If you try me again or if I see you causing trouble for anyone else tonight, someone will have to carry you out of here. Now, I think you owe me another drink."

He wobbled as he got to his feet. Haizea kept a firm hand on his shoulder while he threw a few coins at the bartender.

Most patrons were too inebriated to have really paid them any attention, and unless someone had been watching them already, the subtlety of her retaliation would have gone unnoticed.

She ignored his labored breathing and the tremors running down his body. He'd gotten off lucky. Compared to the brutality she could have inflicted on him, she spared him.

Back in the mountains, attacking a warrior in such a manner would have turned deadly, but here in Arcelia she was a knight with a king to answer to. Any healer worth their salt could fix him up just fine. But given her magic's rareness, actually finding one would be a different matter. That wasn't her problem.

Across the floor, Zander danced—entirely off beat, of course—with another person, and Haizea couldn't find Jirina anywhere in the crowd, guessing she was probably long gone by now.

Haizea decided to fraternize with the rest of the Royal Guard instead, making rounds through the various teams and catching up with everyone. By the time she reached the last group, it was well into the night hours. Dawn would creep up on her before she knew it.

Saying her farewells, Haizea took her leave and went home. There was still their upcoming trip to prepare for, after all.

Only half of the Royal Guard traveled with King Rhys, while the remaining dozen tended after the royal family. King Rhys wanted Jirina and the utility of her scepter by his side, so he assigned Haizea and Zander as part of the traveling crew.

They rode in the steam powered trolley that had multiple cars: one for the traveling Guard and one for their equipment.

"Olysseus has looped me in on their correspondence with Llyr regarding the appearance of Beasts in one of their cities. This is a unique opportunity for us to work together and warm up relations with them," King Rhys said. His voice was even, but he bristled as he divulged the information.

Beasts came from the Beast Realm. Most humans could not traverse the realms, much less wield the power to bring living beings back with them. Only an omen could accomplish such a feat, specifically a realmdrifter. Within the Spiritual Class, realmdrifting corrupted the vitality of mages gifted with astral projection.

The information piqued Haizea's interest. Bringing those creatures here would only incite chaos and confusion. The only alternative culprit to a realmdrifter would be a Demon, but that seemed even more peculiar given that the Demons had not visited the Human Realm in centuries.

"As you all know, we will be taking a detour through Olysseus prior to the meeting with Llyr. We should arrive just in time for their Festival, which is good for maintaining our alliance."

Haizea didn't know much about Llyr other than that the kingdom rested along Arcelia's northern border. The same went for Olysseus, who shared Arcelia's eastern border. In fact, until she joined the Royal Guard, Arcelia hadn't been rather noteworthy to her. Mountaineers didn't typically concern themselves with the surrounding kingdoms unless they tested their boundaries.

They would have to pass by the Bayeux Mountain Range to reach Olysseus. The range consisted of five major peaks: Mount Niaby, Mount Illiniza, Mount Haligus, Mount Valdare and Mount Cortara. The latter three were volcanic.

Although their trip would only involve traversing the base of the range, Haizea naturally served as their guide since she was familiar with the area. So long as they remained at the base, the Bruvian warriors would let them pass unharmed. When the first peak came into view, she pointed.

"The northernmost mountain is Niaby. Illiniza is my home and is directly south of this formation, but with our current path we won't get to see it," she explained.

King Rhys stood next to her to get a closer look. Haizea stiffened at his proximity, but given her naturally stern demeanor, the subtle change went unnoticed. Memories of what he'd done to that omen and his family—his *children*—resurfaced. She bit back the sour taste in her mouth.

"I'm sure you miss your home," the king said after a moment.

She gazed at the passing villages across the mountain, some close and some far. Haizea was twenty-two when she left Illiniza, and nearly two years had passed.

During her time as a royal knight, she'd never used her leave to return home. It brought back too many memories. The last time she'd been here, her mother had fallen ill with a deadly disease, and her father killed himself trying to heal her. Even with the distraction of training with her grandfather and the newfound closeness in their bond, the wound in her heart caused by the death of her parents still gnawed at her.

She'd needed something different, at least for a little while.

"Some days I do. But I'm grateful to have found a place in Arcelia," she said.

King Rhys unleashed his boisterous laugh. The sound grated her ears, and she resisted curling her fingers into fists.

"No need to be modest. I remember reading the details of your application like it was yesterday. Your mother was an esteemed Bruvian warrior. Long ago, they bested the greatest mages of the realm with nothing but the swords on their backs. I know you take pride in your heritage."

Joining the Royal Guard was no small feat. The king received thousands of applicants whenever an opening arose. Knowing that her status as a Bruvian warrior could be as much of a deterrent as it was enticing given the bloody history between the mountain range and surrounding kingdoms, Haizea only shared the minimum information necessary with when she submitted her paperwork for consideration.

King Rhys wanted an elite group of fighters to protect his throne. After meeting Haizea in person, he'd found her to be genuine. Confident that the generations of peace between the mountain range and kingdoms would continue, he invited her as a permanent resident in Arcelia's borders.

She shrugged. "Carrying on my mother's legacy means everything to me. It's the same for my father's, as well."

"Yes, if I recall correctly, he was an incredibly gifted healer. It's a shame he died so young. I am sure your parents would be proud of your accomplishments," King Rhys said with a thoughtful look.

She nodded. Her father would have more than mixed feelings about her decision to learn blood magic. But he would have been elated that she'd found a way to make a good and honest living. As a knight, she protected the king and his family, which helped maintain stability and peace in the kingdom. In a different lifetime, her father might have followed a similar path.

"Is it really true that mages from the mountains have stronger magic?" Zander asked.

"Yes. The concentration of vitality is strongest in the mountain range, so the people born here have a stronger connection to it than those of the kingdoms."

Haizea didn't bother saying why. Outside of the mountains, the facts rubbed many people the wrong way. Centuries ago, the Demons came to the Human Realm and restored humanity's magic after it had been lost for millennia. When they did so, they arrived in the mountain range.

Accounts from that time didn't have much to offer regarding an explanation. A golden being with the face of an Angel had introduced herself as Aaryn. She said that she was returning righteous power to humanity. Described as strikingly beautiful, Aaryn claimed to be Queen of the Demon Realm. On that fateful day, she'd brought not only her fellow Demons, but Titans and Beasts had joined her to bear witness.

Reliable records stated that none of them lingered afterward to explain their actions. Aaryn and her followers had simply arrived, restored the vitality of the Human Realm to its original state, and departed, never to be seen again.

Believing their actions to be benevolent, some mountaineers worshiped the Demons, but Haizea didn't go so far. No Demon would help humans out of the kindness of their heart; there had to be a reason, some sort of benefit to them.

In the same vein, that was why the mountaineers did not view the Cosmic Arts as taboo. In fact, according to their oral traditions, prior to the loss of magic, many mages possessed abilities akin to what they called the Cosmic Arts in present time. In contrast, kingdom dwellers believed that the Demons corrupted humanity's magic upon returning it to the realm, resulting in the Cosmic Arts.

Due to the scarcity of written records from the period before the disappearance of magic in the Human Realm, neither side had any way of verifying the veracity of those claims.

"Yes, there is a reason why Haizea's healing is so thorough. Her bloodline expands generations, where the mountains are the foundation in the vitality that connects us all," King Rhys said, still standing uncomfortably close to Haizea.

Zander cast Haizea a soft smile while Jirina only nodded quietly. With the odd exception of Ser Bren, powerful mages made up the entirety of the Royal Guard. As such, they appreciated the strength the mountains represented.

Haizea glanced out of the viewing window again. A shape caught her attention off in the distance: a woman, camouflaged against the backdrop so that she almost missed them entirely. A Bruvian warrior. Face paint streaked across her forehead and cheeks, signifying her status as a non-mage. Two swords hung from her hips, sheathed in the same position Haizea carried hers.

She wore long pants and heavy boots—essential to trekking through the mountains. But even from this distance, Haizea could see the denseness in the woman's form: muscle packed on top of muscle. Warriors rarely ventured this far down the mountain's slope, but given Arcelia's passage through the area, she'd likely been sent to keep watch.

A feeling of longing overcame Haizea at the sight. Although she didn't grow up in Mount Niaby, she considered any and all mountaineers her kin.

There were so many people she hadn't seen and old friends she'd lost touch with since she'd left Windhaven, her home village. Grandfather Harzel would be more comfortable there, too.

Yet Haizea's thoughts took her by surprise. For the first time in a long time, she did not feel a pang of sadness at the idea of returning home.

CHAPTER 4

The sight of stone roads and brick architecture greeted King Rhys and his Royal Guard as they crossed into Olysseus. A few years had passed since he last visited, but the inhabitants seemed just as well off as he remembered. As they made their final approach to the Capital, paper lanterns attached to strings decorated every home as far as the eye could see.

The Olyssean Guard awaited them at the city entrance. Their armor mimicked the color scheme of the Olyssean flag: a gentle sea green with streaks of soft white. One of their knights boarded the trolley and offered a brief yet polite salutation to King Rhys before instructing the driver on how to reach the palace. As they rolled through the Capital City of Vadronia, the sounds from the festival followed them; laughter and chatter and horns blaring through the air.

Intricate paint design patterned the walkway, along with celebratory decorations—from ribbons to balloons and even fireworks, ready to be set off.

Sovereign Jasver waited for them at the palace gates, dressed in sea-green pants and a white shirt. A similarly shaded mantle draped over the sovereign's shoulders, long enough to brush against the ground. A crown rested atop their head, adorned with jade gemstones that sparkled under the beaming sunlight. The sovereign had styled their dark brown hair in braided plaits that hung down to their hips, with light brown skin and topaz eyes to match.

A knight of distinction stood next to Sovereign Jasver who wore solid green armor as opposed to the white streaks like the rest of the guard.

His position beside the sovereign reminded King Rhys of Ser Bren, his most senior knight and the only one he trusted with the knowledge of how to properly subdue omens. For those reasons, Ser Bren was among the Guard members he'd commanded to remain in Arcelia.

King Rhys had charged him with leading the remaining members of the Guard in protecting his family. With Ser Bren nearing the age of retirement, this trip served as an opportunity for the younger knights in his Guard to prove themselves capable of replacing him.

Closing the distance between them, King Rhys shook Sovereign Jasver's hand. In his peripheral, he took note of each of their respective guards silently standing by. They kept a respectable distance, far enough to reflect the amicable nature of the alliance but close enough to intervene at a moment's notice should the need arise.

"Thank you for traveling all this way to visit us," Sovereign Jasver said warmly.

"I should be thanking you. Though I must say, it would have been quite difficult to say no to a chance to experience your festivities," King Rhys remarked, his lips quirking into a grin.

"Well, the bad news is you're a bit too late for the first few days. But the good news is you've arrived in time for the last day, which is undoubtedly the best of all."

Sovereign Jasver quietly regarded the Arcelian knights. Each one offered a small smile and a steep bow, that is, until the sovereign's eyes met Haizea's. Rather than bending at the waist, she bowed with just a slight dip of her head, her expression cold and unyielding like steel.

King Rhys knew she meant no offense, but the sovereign's eyebrows rose in surprise. Their vitality increased; a sign of them using their mediumship magic.

It took a larger toll on a medium's vitality to read the Souls of the living than it did to commune with the dead. Regarding the dead, there was no living body or conscious mind that could cause interference.

The blood drained from the sovereign's face and their brown skin paled as they read Haizea's Soul. King Rhys couldn't help but wonder what they'd found.

In her few years of service on the Guard, Haizea had always been honest and hardworking and fulfilled her duties as expected—bare minimum qualities required to join his Royal Guard. But moments like these, with her harsh glare bearing down on the sovereign, it reminded King Rhys of Haizea's roots.

He could not allow himself to forget that she'd grown up training in the ways of a Bruvian warrior. And although the warriors only ever attacked when provoked, their reputation preceded them.

They went beyond merely killing their enemies; they went so far as to mark the mountain range's territory by putting the heads of their enemies on spikes.

Some might recoil at the thought of interacting with them, but with a warrior serving on his guard, King Rhys had the power to direct that type of ferocity with a single command.

Even with every person in the room training their focus on her, Haizea's expression did not waver as she held the sovereign's gaze. Between her half-hearted bow and sustained eye contact, proper etiquette called for King Rhys to apologize to Sovereign Jasver on her behalf, but he decided against it, at least not with so many observers.

Bringing a warrior into his Guard meant turning a blind eye to certain behaviors deemed crude by the kingdom's social etiquette.

Unsurprisingly, the sovereign averted their eyes first and turned back to King Rhys, offering an innocuous smile.

"I believe our discussions would be best facilitated in private. Our castle is secure and well-guarded. I would be remiss if I didn't offer your knights the chance to rest and enjoy the festivities while we determine the best course of action regarding Llyr," the sovereign said.

"Of course," King Rhys quickly agreed, eager to maintain the semblance of trust.

Sovereign Jasver nodded. "I don't foresee this taking the entire day, but if it does we can take a reprieve to enjoy the nighttime festivities," they said as they led King Rhys away.

Once in the privacy of the sovereign's quarters, they handed King Rhys a sheet of paper containing an intricate drawing.

The devastation in the portrait immediately jumped out at King Rhys, depicting a building that had collapsed down to its foundations with rubble strewn, trapping people underneath. The artist had even gone so far as to color the ground bright red, stained with blood.

As King Rhys held the paper, it quaked in his hands, and a vision overtook his mind.

The brick building stood about four or five stories high, restored to its normal state. Numerous glass windows made up the façades with a central door allowing people to enter and exit.

A small family of four made their way toward it. As they crossed the threshold, a shadow enveloped the entire building, casting them in darkness.

A paw came rushing down from the sky, its massive size dwarfing the building as it slammed down on the structure. The building crumpled beneath the weight and force of the blow, and cries for help quickly sounded moments later.

One of the children struggled against the fallen stones and in turn crushed their bottom half. As they strained, a second paw crashed down on top of the rubble, finishing off anyone who had survived the initial collapse.

King Rhys blinked, and his mind was his own once more. An enchanter had imbued their magic into the paper, it seemed.

"Well… either Llyr is expending much effort to tell a very elaborate lie about the Beasts, or they are truly in dire straits." His words came slowly as the effects of the enchantment wore off.

"It's the only tangible evidence Llyr has sent thus far. I agree, it could very well be a trap, given that they've never taken kindly to our kingdoms. But it's a risk worth taking. If it's true, then there's nothing stopping whatever, or whomever, has brought the Beast to our realm from releasing it in our borders as well."

"Did they mention the extent of the damage? How many cities have been affected?" King Rhys inquired, brow furrowing in thought.

"So far, just Zariya. Oddly enough, Zemira has been unaffected."

Zemira was the Capital City of Llyr. If they intended to topple the kingdom, it seemed odd to leave that untouched. Based on the vision within the enchantment, Llyr's rulers could have easily been wiped out with a single swipe of the Beast's paw.

It led him to think that a Demon had perpetrated this act of violence rather than an omen; a human would understand the political structures of the kingdoms and would have known the most harmful location to attack. Unless…

King Rhys tilted his head, and a frown spread across his face.

The sovereign nodded. "I made the same face when I saw the vision. We could very well be leading our Guards into a trap. But, in my opinion, the fact still remains that whether this is a ploy or not, a Beast in the realm is a threat that cannot go ignored. It's worth investigating. If we erroneously ignore their pleas for help, we risk letting more innocents die in the same fashion as the letter showed us."

The image of Felix and Sage flashed before Rhys, both crushed by rubble in a similar manner as the child from the enchantment. His throat tightened. He would never allow such a date to befall his children.

King Rhys gripped onto the hilt of his sword. If an omen had unleashed the Beast, he absolutely could not allow a threat of this magnitude to go unchecked.

"I have a clairvoyant mage in my Guard. I will instruct her to verify the validity of the enchantment before we proceed." The floor rumbled beneath his feet as he spoke, his magic rising with his emotions.

King Rhys inhaled deeply and exhaled slowly to regain his composure and keep his power in check. Despite his efforts, calm eluded him. He had only just exterminated an omen a few days ago. They were like roaches—vermin that kept intruding on his life no matter how many he stamped out of existence.

He ground his teeth and let go of his sword, his hand clammy and slick with sweat. Depending on what they uncovered in Llyr, he may very well have to kill another.

CHAPTER 5

A tense lull permeated the room in the absence of the two rulers. Haizea didn't so much as fidget. Eventually, one of the Olyssean knights broke the silence.

"We can show you all the sleeping quarters so you can change. No need to wear a full suit of armor to enjoy the festival," they said.

The knights led them around to the back of the castle to the visitor's suite. It held an abundance of rooms, providing ample space to accommodate twelve knights plus King Rhys. Based on its cozy setup—large beds, servants standing in wait, lavish decorations—it seemed geared more toward extended family rather than a visiting monarch and their Guard.

Haizea and Jirina roomed together, while Zander found a room with another man in the Guard. As they changed clothes, Haizea felt Jirina's eyes on her. She braced herself.

"What was that about with the sovereign?"

She blew out a slow breath. "The sovereign is a medium. That subtype is prone to being caught off guard by wandering Souls. There's no telling what they saw or heard," Haizea said.

Jirina pursed her lips and narrowed her eyes. An energy sparked low on Haizea's chest where her pendant rested. A vein in Jirina's forehead pulsed and her expression pinched, as if in pain. Haizea maintained an even expression. Jirina had tried to get a reading on her and delved too deep, prompting the curse magic within the jewelry to forcibly kick her back.

"The sovereign seemed... uneasy. Frightened, even." The vein still pulsed in her temple.

"Well, we're here because there's a Beast terrorizing a neighboring kingdom. That's enough to rattle even the bravest of people," Haizea replied, feigning a casual air.

Jirina looked at Haizea with a dazed expression. Several beats passed before she rubbed her forehead and let out a huff.

"What about the Beasts again?" she wondered.

"Nothing. Never mind," Haizea sighed, relieved for the conversation to end.

Jirina would undoubtedly investigate it further if given the chance, but with the curse interfering, she had no choice but to drop it for the time being.

Yet Jirina's suspicion was warranted. More than a tense look had passed between Haizea and the Sovereign; they clearly felt *something* within her Soul and had not liked what they found. Haizea laced her boots as she mulled it over.

If the vitality was the heartbeat, then the Soul was the breath of life. When a medium felt a person's Soul, they unveiled the very core of their being.

If Haizea's Soul made the sovereign uncomfortable, she wondered what about it had made it so. Then again, it was possible that it hadn't been her Soul at all. Perhaps with the stress of being in an unfamiliar environment, she hadn't suppressed her blood magic as well as she did normally, and the Sovereign caught traces of her true power.

The latter indicated inadequate control over her power, which concerned her. But the former had nothing to do with her magic and instead reflected the type of person she was on an intimate level. The implications of that chilled her to the bone.

A knock on the door interrupted her thoughts.

She opened it to find Zander waiting for them. They made their way out of the palace and into the city streets of Vadronia, eager to experience the festival.

A man walked by wearing a sea-green headdress. Metal pieces fanned upward in an arch on each side. Each arch had feather-like shapes on them, like wings. A halo rested between the wings, supported on thin wires to give the illusion that it levitated in the air. It reminded Haizea of the Angels.

As the man ambled along, he played a flute—speeding through a melodious tune, with each note full and rich and supported by an expertly executed vibrato.

Behind him, a group of dancers tossed flags into the air as they moved. They performed an energetic choreography, fast paced and filled with various elaborate flips, which matched the song he played. The Arcelian Guard watched the display before splitting off into their typical groups, with Haizea, Zander, and Jirina sticking together.

As the trio made their way through the grounds, a jolt ran through Haizea. Zander must have felt the same, because he pivoted along with her. Across the way, a woman sat in the booth advertising magical tricks. She had emerald-green eyes, wavy dark tresses, and her skin was a few shades darker than Haizea's.

"Come on," she beckoned, waving them on. The words gripped onto Haizea's mind, and her legs moved to bring her closer to the woman of their own accord.

Enchanter, she thought. The mage's words had caused the jolt in her vitality.

Enchanting magic made up one part of the Mental Class. Whereas clairvoyance magic bestowed an internal enlightenment, enchanting magic imposed a user's will on the people around them. This was the case with all three classes: an internal and external element made up two complementary subtypes.

The Physical Class had healers, whose powers worked within the body, and telekinetics, whose powers affected surrounding objects and the environment.

The Spiritual Class had mediums, whose abilities let them hear a Soul's calling, and astral projectors who could separate their own Souls from their bodies. A medium's magic operated in their own mind, whereas an astral projector impacted the world around them.

Going by Zander's broad smile, he hadn't noticed the woman's magic influencing his behavior. Jirina's eyes narrowed.

"Careful, Zander," she cautioned, but the mage had captivated him.

"Have you ever met an enchantress before?" she purred. When Zander shook his head, the mage smiled.

"I'll go easy on you then. You're going to give me half of the money you have right now."

When Zander actually reached for his pockets, Haizea put her hand on his arm to halt his movement.

"Stop," the mage said. Again, the woman's words reverberated in Haizea's mind. She faltered in her tracks, but so did Zander.

"She can only do one enchantment at a time," Jirina said, her tone even with confidence and certainty; every time the woman used her magic, she gleaned more information through her clairvoyance.

"Calm down. You're sucking the fun out of this. Just watch. As I said, empty your pockets," she said, rolling her eyes. This time Zander complied, and Haizea and Jirina silently waited.

She counted the money, grabbed the largest coin and pushed the rest back to him.

"When the clock strikes midnight, you're going to flip this coin in the air. Heads, you'll clap three times. Tails, you're going to come back and give me everything that's on this table."

"How can you be sure I won't just ignore it?" he challenged.

"We'll just have to see," she said with a flippant shrug.

Zander's expression landed somewhere between dumbfounded and awestruck. Enchanters did not typically display their magic so openly, because people tended to keep their guard up, leery that their minds may be overtaken in the span of a breath.

They often found employment as spy masters or shop owners, since their abilities gave them an edge with anything that involved dealing with information or money in general.

"How about you?" the enchantress said, looking at Haizea.

She bristled. "No thanks."

"You look like you hold your cards close to the chest. I've got a good one. It's easy. Tell me, what's your worst nightmare?"

Before Haizea could refuse, the mage's power catapulted her thoughts into her past and her mother's face appeared before her.

Haizea was a fifteen-year-old girl again in the middle of a growth spurt, and just a few inches shy of her adult height. Her hair hung much longer, coming all the way down to her hips, and she styled it in braids to protect her curls against the harsh mountain wind.

She wiped her brow with her arm, removing the beads of sweat. Her mother had put her through a series of sword fighting drills. For the last drill, Haizea had demonstrated her skills against a practice dummy. It had a small hole in the center of its chest where her blade had impaled it.

Her mother inspected the dummy before waving her closer.

"Your blade sliced clean through the heart, but your blow lacked adequate power. This tiny hole you made should be the size of your arm. You see how the spine and rib cage and vertebrae are still identifiable? A perfect strike will shatter them upon impact," her mother said.

The material of the dummy's bones adequately mimicked the proper structure and density of a human being.

"Yes, Mother. I'll keep practicing."

Her mother's lips tightened in a stern expression, but she nodded and gently stroked Haizea's hair.

"The technique is there, but your strength will come with time. Your body is still growing. You'll be ready for your mastery test within the next year if you keep this pace. You always perform very well; I just want you to reach your full potential."

As they walked back to their home, her mother winced and clutched her abdomen. She'd drank a potion earlier that morning before their training. It must not have worked. Her mother mentioned being in pain to her father as soon as they crossed the door.

Haizea's brows knitted with worry. For her mother to outwardly show her discomfort, and much less verbalize it, alarmed her. Her father pressed his hands on her mother's to take a closer look. The brown skin of his face blanched, and the sight made Haizea's heart gallop in her chest.

"Haizea, sweetheart, I need you to prepare a few potions for me. One for pain, and one that aids the body in replenishing vitality. You've learned that in mage school by now, correct?"

"Yes, Father," she said.

While Haizea prepared the potions, she eavesdropped on her parents' hushed whispers. Her mother had contracted a disease; Father had found a growth in her body that weighed as much as a newborn infant.

Haizea's throat tightened, but when she returned with the potions, the determined look on her father's face steeled her. He got right to work and used his advanced healing techniques to excise and remove the growth. Surely, with two healers by her side, her mother's recovery was a foregone conclusion, and the illness that afflicted her would be quashed.

How wrong she had been.

The growth returned with disturbing swiftness.

Her father repeated the same treatment. Again, the growth came back.

The cycle repeated for months and months with her mother withering away and her father doing the same as he dragged her back from the brink of death. Nothing he did brought her comfort.

Haizea was a few months shy of eighteen when, one day, she heard her father and Grandfather Harzel shouting outside of the house in a heated argument.

When her father crossed the threshold, she struggled to breathe as his vitality swept the entire house. When father stormed up the stairs and passed by her bedroom door, her hands trembled.

Splatters of red stained his clothes, the stench of blood followed in his wake, and his eyes shined a vibrant crimson. She went back to her window and saw Grandfather Harzel walking away from their house. He turned back only once, revealing a face streaked with tears. Haizea inhaled sharply in surprise and crept out of her room just as her father entered her parents' bedroom.

Although he shut the door behind him, Haizea opened it slightly so that she could see. Her mother lay in the bed, her once vibrant brown skin steadily becoming paler with each passing day.

Her father took her mother's hand in his. He had always been slight of frame, while her mother had always exuded strength. Haizea bit back the sting of tears at how frail and thin both of her parents' hands were as they held one another.

A slow evolution unfolded before her eyes. With each second, her mother grew livelier, and her father became frighteningly feeble.

Back then, Haizea assumed that her father utilized a healing technique he'd yet to teach her. In hindsight, she knew better. At his wit's end, and after many years of nonuse, her father reached for his blood magic.

When the high hit, it gripped onto his mind and body and refused to let go. Her father's eyes glimmered red for weeks, with an ever-present grin on his face. Most days she came home from the academy to find him rocking back and forth, wringing his hands together as he muttered to himself.

"Not again. I can't do this again," he would say, day in and day out.

For a while after that, her mother seemed fine. More months went by without any signs of her illness. But when it returned, it came back with a vengeance. It invaded every cell and desecrated every ounce of vitality in her entire body. The extent of his sickness overwhelmed her father, so he turned to his blood magic once again.

But years of non-use had dulled his abilities, and he utilized an imperfect and imprecise technique. Perhaps Mother might have lived had he been stronger.

Haizea's mother died in agonizing pain and a few months later, her father followed. While his blood magic had replenished the vitality he'd lost, it was too late. Magical wasting had eaten away at his body for many, many years and he'd long passed the point of no return.

The sudden influx of vitality put an overwhelming burden on him. He spent his final weeks bedridden and too weak to even feed himself. Grandfather Harzel came by every day to help until one morning, Haizea woke up to her grandfather sitting by her bedside.

He held her hand and told her that her father had passed away in his sleep the night before.

Haizea's mind snapped back to the present and her eyes met the enchantress's. She blinked and a few tears fell from her eyes and slid down her cheeks.

"Well?" the enchantress asked.

Haizea didn't answer. Instead, she put her hands on the stand and leaned forward, looking the mage in the eye. She tried to find the right words to express her anger, but they escaped her. The woman had forced her to relive the anguish she'd spent so much time running away from, and yet Haizea could only manage a glare, filled with disdain and contempt.

However, that alone seemed to be enough because the mage's hands trembled as she smoothed her shirt down.

"I suppose rather than a possible future scenario, my question brought up past memories. You've already lived a nightmare. Poor wording on my part." Her emerald eyes flickered to Haizea's pendant, which had slipped out from her collar when she leaned forward.

Haizea stood upright, tucked it away, and turned to leave.

"That's a beautiful necklace," the enchantress commented as Haizea joined Jirina, and Zander, who clutched his head.

Haizea paused and briefly looked back at the mage. With more distance between them, the woman looked more relaxed. She gave Haizea a brilliant smile and waved. Haizea scowled in return, her lips still curled downward when she turned back to her comrades.

"Hey... you never answered her question," Zander said as they walked away.

"An enchantment is like a very strong suggestion. All it takes is a strong will to break it," Haizea answered with a snap.

"Ouch. I think she just called you feeble, Zander."

Haizea rolled her eyes, but Zander let Jirina's words roll off.

"I wish I'd known that. I sure as hell hope I get heads later."

"I swear, the line between enchantment and curse magic is paper thin. It ought to be banned," Jirina huffed.

"You're just jealous. I bet you can't see through a curse like you can an enchantment, huh? You don't like your magic being useless," Zander teased, and Jirina bristled.

"I'm not jealous, I'm appropriately cautious. It's bad enough that enchanters can invade your mind and influence your actions. But at least you can break through it if you try hard enough. Curse mages make the warped vitality bleed from their victims and bend reality itself. All it takes is a single word and you've already lost, and there's not a damn thing you can do about it."

Haizea remained silent as Jirina and Zander went back and forth. The weight of her pendant bounced against her chest as she walked. She knew the way to break a curse: kill the mage who cast it.

You either had to be blindingly fast or clever enough to find the gaps in the curse, but it could be done. An astute curse mage used more than just their words. They knew they could leave a curse lurking anywhere, like how Grandfather Harzel had done with her necklace, which made it difficult for others to identify them.

Haizea kept that information to herself, not wanting to bring too much attention to her own magic, or her mountaineer heritage, where the Cosmic Arts did not carry the same social stigmas.

After leaving the booth, the trio agreed they didn't want to do anything that involved enchanting magic again. Instead, they stopped by one of the food vendors and more dancing performers passed by. A telekinetic and astral projecting mage did a combined performance. The telekinetic mage held a torch and used their magic to manipulate the flames.

They watched in awe as the other mage formed a projection with their Soul. First, it appeared in the form of their body and then molded into a flame-like shape. The two fires intertwined in a captivating dance, one red and one a translucent blue.

The two mages circled one another, and the shapes they created with their magic shifted. The flames and astral projection each took on a human-like figure, except a pair of massive wings protruded from each of their backs. Again, it appeared to pay tribute to the Angels, beings of the Celestial Realm.

The flames and astral projection twirled in tandem with the mages controlling them. Their movements started slow and hesitant, with noticeable distance between the figures before they came together.

As the mages spun and intertwined, so too did their projections. At the end of the performance, the flame Angel appeared to absorb the astral projected one, consuming it until it disappeared. When the show ended, the knights clapped with the rest of the crowd.

Beside her, Zander dabbed tears from his eyes. Even Jirina seemed captivated. The Olysseans had put on a nice performance, but as a mountaineer, the Angelic references didn't resonate with Haizea; she couldn't think of a single thing the Angels had done on behalf of humanity that warranted such a display of reverence. The reason they could showcase such a colorful display of magic to begin with was because of the Demons.

A ringing clock chimed in the background, disrupting the crowd's cheers. Zander's expression went blank, and he pilfered through his pocket before flipping the exact coin the enchantress had told him to.

Both Haizea's and Jirina's eyebrows rose as it tumbled in the air. The trio let out a collective groan of annoyance when it landed on tails. Zander made his way back to the enchantress mage's booth, only to find it empty.

He still put the money on the table and let out a loud sigh. "I think that's enough for tonight."

They made their way to another food vendor who sold a variety of delicacies. The choices ranged from smoked meats to baked pastries. Zander's mouth watered at the sight, but he lamented when he pulled at his empty pockets.

Fortunately for him, Haizea took pity and bought him a few selections. As they pondered over the choices available, a hush fell over the festivities before erupting into voracious applause.

In the distance, King Rhys and Sovereign Jasver enter into the fray. They walked with their hands clasped together before raising them high above their heads.

"Guess they wanted a united front for the people," Haizea said.

Zander nodded. "Not a party until the king shows up."

The trio made their way toward their king. Meeting in private with Sovereign Jasver was one thing, but they would not allow King Rhys to enter the festival area without protection.

The remainder of the Royal Guard must have had the same train of thought, as they also interspersed in the crowd. Sovereign Jasver's Guard followed suit as well.

"My subjects," Sovereign Jasver began with a warm expression. "This is King Rhys and his Royal Guard. Please welcome our friends and allies from Arcelia. Let us show them the hospitality of Olysseus through our grand festival."

The crowd cheered again. Haizea, Zander, and Jirina clapped along with them. A charge sizzled in the air, and the sensation ripped through Haizea's veins, threatening to ignite the blood magic she kept hidden beneath the surface.

She looked around, curious as to what had nearly set her off. More mages gathered nearby, putting on dancing displays of astral projections and telekinesis. Musicians joined together and the once cacophonous, individual sounds of their instruments weaved together in a harmonious melody. With so many people and so much energy, perhaps the vitality had increased to match the crowd's tangible excitement.

With King Rhys here, the knights largely focused on keeping him within their sights. Although they did not have their armor or weapons, most of them could wield magic—a weapon in its own right.

But as Haizea watched Sovereign Jasver lead the king through the crowd and visit the various booths, she suspected there would be no need for their protective efforts here.

Olysseus had welcomed them with open arms and displayed nothing but hospitably.

The true obstacle would be Llyr, who had requested help with the Beasts in their cities despite their icy relations. Haizea wondered how they would go about addressing that ongoing threat and what the lurking danger that the Beasts' presence meant.

CHAPTER 6

HUMAN REALM, KINGDOM OF LLYR, CAPITAL CITY OF ZEMIRA

The trip to Zemira was just a day's journey north from Vadronia. Haizea sat in the aisle of the trolley to stretch her long legs while Jirina gazed out the window to take in the passing scenery.

When Zander came by and tried to squeeze in between them, Haizea glared at him. He sheepishly changed course, opting to sit directly across from her rather than sandwich himself like he'd originally intended.

As they approached Llyr's Capital City, a rich, deep purple flag greeted them. Unlike Arcelia and Olysseus, who used white as their complementary color, Llyr had chosen black to interweave with their purple base, projecting a darker aesthetic by comparison.

Haizea sat up straighter as she leaned around Jirina's head to get a better look out the window. Because Llyr did not share a border with the Bayeux Mountain Range, she knew the least about this kingdom. Generations ago, after magic had returned to the Human Realm, Arcelia and Olysseus led an assault against the mountaineers, eager to expand their borders. The inhabitants swiftly beat them back; average everyday people formed together to protect their homes.

Unwilling to accept defeat, the Arcelians and Olysseans licked their wounds and returned later, after years of training in the new-found magical abilities. The mountaineers similarly did not mistake the period of silence for peace and the Bruvian warriors formed in response to the first war.

During that time, Llyr hesitated to support an unprovoked attack, but they also did not want to attract the ire of their neighbors who, combined, were double their size. Unfortunately for them, the kingdoms ultimately strong-armed them into the war effort and sent Llyr's knights to the frontlines as fodder against the mountaineers.

When the kingdoms lost yet again, Llyr suffered the most casualties, and they still had not forgiven their neighbors for their past actions.

Now, with Llyr calling for help regarding Beasts in their lands, an opening to mend the rift and right the wrongs of the past lay before Arcelia and Olysseus.

The trolley came to a stop at the palace gates, and the knights quickly donned their armor. Haizea wrapped her leather holster around her waist and slid her swords into the accompanying sheaths. Llyr's Royal Guard escorted them into the castle, where Llyr's reigning monarchs, King Johan and King Consort Arlo waited for them.

With the looming threat of Beasts and contentious history between the kingdoms, the Royal Guards remained close to their respective rulers as they gathered in the castle's entryway.

Jirina took her place directly beside King Rhys with her scepter in hand. Haizea stood just a few feet behind them with Zander by her side, holding his spear. The ceilings arched high overhead, with a glass chandelier chiming softly as it swung.

"King Rhys. Sovereign Jasver. We appreciate you coming to our aid. It is our hope that with your assistance, we'll be able to slay the Beasts in our lands," King Johan said.

His husband stood quietly beside him. While they both had pale skin, King Johan had topaz eyes and hair of a similar shade, while King Consort Arlo had dark brown eyes and jet black hair.

"The presence of the Beasts poses a threat to us all. It is only natural that we should provide assistance with this." Sovereign Jasver smiled warmly.

"Agreed. Arcelia will use every resource available to bring the person responsible to justice," King Rhys added, puffing his chest out slightly as he spoke.

Haizea bristled at the arrogance in his tone. King Rhys truly believed he could circumvent the abilities of a realmdrifter, who could phase through the physical world in the blink of an eye, rendering his abilities as a telekinetic null and void.

It would only take a single misstep for his life to be extinguished.

As Haizea contemplated this, her blood began to hum. In front of her, Jirina stiffened and a second later, her scepter glowed with the use of her magic. Before Haizea could worry about whether Jirina had sensed the unintended spike in her blood magic, a whisper of air brushed past and a blurred form flew by at impressive speed.

It was both physical and spiritual. Tangible and intangible. Visible and invisible.

A realmdrifter.

Jirina's head jerked left and right, trying to find the source of the disturbance, but she could not see like Haizea could. An omen would always know the presence of another omen.

The realmdrifter's presence carried a weight to it, like a heavy blanket draped over one's body.

Instinctively, Haizea dug deep within herself, searching for the gate that locked away her own Cosmic magic, but she stopped short. Once again, the image of the execution platform in the colosseum came to mind.

No. Using her corrupted magic here, with so many eyes and ears watching, would undoubtedly put a target on her back. Haizea suppressed her warrior's instinct, which told her to go for efficient kill by delivering a quick defeat with her own Cosmic magic. Instead, she would approach this like a knight and take the honorable route.

Haizea's hands hovered over her hips, hesitating to unsheathe her swords. Despite wanting to protect her secret, every fiber in her being bucked against approaching this battle like a fair fight. She took a calming breath. Instead, she would wait and see how it played out and hopefully find out what the omen wanted. If they could be appeased without her having to intervene and expose herself, all the better.

The unmistakable click of the entrance door locking shut sounded behind them.

King Rhys drew his sword, as did Sovereign Jasver. Even Kings Johan and Arlo joined, a pleasant surprise given that no one had fully ruled out that this was all a ploy on their end.

"This was too easy."

They all turned around to see a woman standing behind them.

Haizea's eyes narrowed as she absorbed her features: emerald-green eyes, smooth dark skin, and a head full of jet-black hair. The enchantress.

Only two days had passed since their encounter at the festival.

King Rhys did not waver as he stepped forward. With his mind alone, his telekinesis held the omen in place, and he closed the distance between them, his sword at the ready to strike.

"Drop your weapon," she said smoothly.

This time her voice brought a blistering pain as it echoed in Haizea's mind. Everyone in the room had no choice but to comply.

Haizea breathed a sigh of relief at her earlier hesitance, as with her swords remaining in their sheaths, she did not hold anything to release. Zander's spear clattered to the ground and Jirina's scepter did the same, but as mages, that alone did not subdue them.

The knights circled around the woman, and she smirked, her green eyes alight with amusement. Another breeze brushed against Haizea, instantly reminding her of the realmdrifter's presence. The omen took physical form behind Kings Johan and Arlo before picking up their fallen swords and slicing open their necks.

Meanwhile, the curse mage closed in on King Rhys.

"The great and revered King Rhys. Well-known for his hatred of the Cosmic Arts," she drawled with a sneer.

"And for good—" King Rhys began.

"*Quiet,*" she snarled. His mouth snapped shut.

The woman patted King Rhys's cheek. She bent over to pick up his sword before pressing the blade against his neck.

"Good boy. *Now, stop breathing.*"

It did not take long for King Rhys's face to start turning red.

As King Rhys suffocated himself in front of Haizea, the grunts of dying knights filled her ears, slain by the realmdrifter that they could not see until she'd already plunged a blade into their bodies.

The metallic tang of blood wafted through the air, infiltrating her nostrils and coating her throat. She would be able to heal some of them, but not this many. And even for the few that lived, she would have to take out the mages first before she could even think of helping them.

With all three rulers of the major kingdoms currently standing in the same place, the scene before her reeked of strategic maneuvering on the omens' parts.

They clearly intended to take out each ruler simultaneously, wreaking havoc and bringing about instability throughout the realm. Haizea's hesitance from earlier evaporated. She would not allow this slaughter to continue just for the sake of keeping her secret.

Her father crossed her mind then. How he'd died because he refused to accept his heritage. He would have been able to heal her mother. He *should have* been able to save her. Though she loved him, Haizea decided years ago not to follow in his footsteps.

Grandfather Harzel had implored her to ignore her father's warnings about Cosmic magic and spent years teaching her to perfect her abilities, from surgical precision to overwhelming might. She would not roll over and die when she had inherited a power that could bring any enemy she faced to their knees.

Her grandfather's words echoed in her mind:

"It is better to have it and not need it than to find yourself wishing you had learned when you had the chance."

Haizea honed her focus on the spilled blood that teemed with vitality and tore open the mental gate that safely locked her blood magic away.

Her brown eyes became richer, first a muted brick-red, then a luminous crimson.

The vitality she had merely sensed before unveiled itself to the naked eye once again, tinting her vision with a shimmering red. As she absorbed the life forces around her, Haizea's strength doubled, then tripled.

The potency of her vitality emanated from her body, permeating the air and revealing the true nature of her power.

The curse mage in front of King Rhys stopped in her tracks as she sensed the sudden surge of magic. She jerked the blade she held against King Rhys's throat, but Haizea closed the distance in the blink of an eye, her form blurring in a streak of blue and white.

She drove one sword into the curse mage's back, straight through the chest, while the other blade seared through her neck. With her healing magic, she sensed the curse mage's spinal column collapse, and her ribcage shattered upon impact.

Haizea put all her magnified strength into the blow, the sheer force of it thrusting the mage's still beating heart outside of her body, impaled on the sword.

Haizea yanked her blades back. The omen collapsed in a heap in front of her. King Rhys fell to his knees gasping for air. Blood poured from his neck. The mage had managed to slice him in those final moments.

Haizea extended a hand out to heal him and pressed against the wound. She focused on weaving his vitality together to speed up the healing processes. It took every ounce of her willpower to ignore the call of her blood magic, which told her to drain him dry.

"Haizea, behind you!" Jirina's voice brought clarity amidst the chaos.

The realmdrifter still lurked in the shadows.

Haizea flung the blood off her swords, squinting against a light-headed fog as the high slowly settled in. Never before had she absorbed this much vitality at once, let alone from a human source.

Her mental acuity gradually slipped, and her magic had a mind of its own, reaching out around her to deplete every open source of vitality. It had been difficult enough to resist the call from a single person's blood, but she did not possess the willpower to escape the lure that dozens of people presented.

Any wounded person lying on the ground who had miraculously survived the realmdrifter's onslaught perished under Haizea's power, which reduced their corpses to brittle husks.

When Haizea attacked this time, she moved faster than any human eye could track—no longer a blur, but completely undetectable. The vitality she'd absorbed came from all sorts of mages, giving her access to their magical abilities in addition to her speed and strength.

When the realmdrifting mage tried to attack, Haizea raised her hand and stopped them in their tracks with telekinesis. Then she pulled them toward her like a magnet, directly into her blades.

At the very last possible moment, the realmdrifter entered the astral plane, rendering their body intangible.

Because none of the fallen mages had the ability to realmdrift, Haizea did not possess any vitality that would let her enter that form herself. But she got a good look at the omen's appearance as she disappeared from sight.

The realmdrifter was a woman with skin much darker than hers and cloudy eyes. She had long, dark blue hair that fell down to the middle of her back. Fine jewelry adorned her body: bracelets, a necklace, rings on multiple fingers, along with several earrings—one set of them dangled low with sparkling gemstones.

"You are... incredible," the woman whispered.

Haizea's eyes landed on the hollow shell that was once the curse mage—her blood coursed through her veins. That power momentarily belonged to Haizea now.

The realmdrifter followed her line of sight, and a tense silence passed between them when their gazes met. Haizea could not follow the realmdrifter into the astral plane, but with curse magic, she could wrest control of her mind.

Haizea inhaled and infused the weight of a curse into her words.

"Come back here," she commanded. But her movements had given her away and made her intentions too easy to see. In the time it had taken her to breathe, the realmdrifter disappeared into the void.

Haizea dropped to her knees. Her body pulsated with the corrupted vitality coursing through her veins so that it enveloped every inch of her being. Haizea's mind drifted away on a cloud and her usual austere expression evaporated as laughter bubbled up in her chest before erupting out, the unsettling sound carrying through the air.

In the back of her mind, shrouded by the euphoria, was a sinking, dreadful feeling at what she'd done. At how many knights she'd just sacrificed. So much blood... so much power... so excessive. And even worse, it was the high coursing through her and not the fact that she'd saved her own like that that made it feel like it was worth it.

The vitality took Haizea then. The last thing she saw were her trembling hands on the ground before she collapsed, unconscious.

CHAPTER 7

To a realmdrifter, distance was nothing. The vitality within enabled them to blur the lines between spiritual and physical. For mages who could astral project, they left their bodies behind while their Souls wandered.

But for a realmdrifter with corrupted astral projection magic, they could bring their body *with* them.

For those blind to such vitality, a realmdrifter moved about beyond their visible perception. Only another omen could see them, and even then, those bound to the physical world could not lay a finger on them.

As such, realmdrifters danced between two planes of existence: visible and invisible, tangible and intangible. They possessed the ability to traverse between the realms, and therefore, getting from one mere city to the next was child's play.

Only a moment ago, words of admiration for the blood mage's display of power had left Kallistê's lips. Seconds later, she stood in Zariya where her Beast wreaked havoc.

Things had gone... awry in Zemira. The objective had been to wipe out the reigning monarchs and replace them with omens.

Maybe if they'd had a seer, a corrupted clairvoyance mage with the ability to peer into the minds of others, they would have snuffed out the blood mage's presence before she violently disrupted their plans. Now, Kallistê was grappling with the loss of the two mages she'd brought into her fold.

First, she lost contact with Cyrus, who she'd planted in Arcelia. She'd instructed him to spy on King Rhys during his time there and trail him as he traveled to Llyr, but Cyrus never showed up. With an infamous arrogant streak, Kallistê imagined Cyrus carelessly let it get the better of him. Despite her warnings, he brought his family with him from Kestramore, believing their victory and his installation on Arcelia's throne was inevitable.

His absence likely meant that King Rhys's forces had snuffed him out and killed him. Cyrus's indiscretion ultimately led to the loss of Tarja, the cursed omen: another deep blow that Kallistê had not anticipated.

Had things gone to plan, Kallistê and Tarja would have handled the monarchs while Cyrus rendered the knights harmless with his transmutation magic. An easy, simple, straightforward strategy. There should be three dead monarchs right now, three open seats on the throne, prime for the taking by her Cosmic Arts coalition.

But everything currently lay in shambles, and now Kallistê had to meld the pieces back together. Still, an opportunity existed within the calamity.

What once would have been a power sharing arrangement could now consolidate under her. But the image actively shifted before her, a portrait easily erased and redrawn. If Kallistê could have accomplished her goals by herself, she would have never involved the other two to begin with. Now, she needed allies in a place where they were few and far between.

Arcelia and Olysseus shared the same stance on the Cosmic Arts, so she didn't expect to find someone like minded so easily. It was for the same reason that Kallistê never even considered the prospect of failure: she never imagined a blood mage, the rarest of all, to appear during the attack.

Too shocked to feel anything else, anger and grief eluded Kallistê.

A blood mage. In King Rhys's Guard of all places, she thought.

Kallistê couldn't help but laugh, a mixture of her own humor and the oncoming high from realmdrifting. The sound floated through the air like wind chimes.

Her eyes lost their cloudy appearance and now gleamed a rich, deep sapphire as they twinkled with whimsical mischief. The bracelets around her wrists bangled as she reached up to fluff her hair, making the luxurious tendrils roll in long waves down her back. Though her mind steadily climbed toward the skies, Kallistê anchored herself to concentrate on her next move.

Only through blood magic could a mage access every class, every corresponding subtype, and every Cosmic Art known to mankind.

A blood mage could be her largest obstacle yet.

Or her greatest asset.

A burning curiosity settled in Kallistê. How had she slipped under the king's radar? Or had he known it the entire time? Did she know other blood mages?

With the level of skill she displayed, someone had to have taken her under their wing.

In any case, Kallistê would have to watch her back regarding the blood mage. Until she knew where her loyalties lied, or if they could be swayed, Kallistê would approach with caution.

Any omen working for King Rhys, regardless of their reasoning, was a walking red flag.

Fortunately for Kallistê, so was she.

She would focus her efforts on the other, more pressing tasks that needed tending to. With the deaths of her comrades, handling business in Llyr fell solely on her shoulders.

She'd slain the rulers of Llyr, but she decided against attacking King Rhys and Sovereign Jasver so soon. With an omen in their ranks, only a fool would charge forward without a new plan of attack.

Kallistê walked through the corridors of the abandoned home she had taken over. The owners had fled the destruction of her Beasts. Or perhaps they'd perished. She wasn't sure which.

When she reached the study room, she sat down to think. She hit the chair like a lead weight, and the sudden jolt sent vibrations through her body. Kallistê sat motionless for several seconds as she tingled from head to toe. The high would overtake her soon. She could feel it.

Given that King Rhys and Sovereign Jasver lost most of their knights in the attack, they didn't have the manpower to stay and guard over Llyr. With a realmdrifter after them, the shrewd course of action would be to return home and get their affairs in order.

They wouldn't retaliate right away, which left Llyr wide open for the taking. By the time Arcelia and Olysseus sought vengeance, Kallistê would firmly hold the throne in her grasp.

Kallistê giggled again, and a white haze clouded her vision as lightheadedness settled in. An involuntary, lopsided smile spread across her face as the corrupted vitality coursed through her, catapulting her into a state of sheer bliss.

Her entire essence thrummed with energy, from her mind to her body right down to her Soul. Her grip on her own Soul ebbed and flowed, and the different realms flashed before Kallistê's eyes.

Her hand, which rested on the desk, slowly drifted through the solid structure. Her vision split into two—one of the room before her and another that turned pitch-black as tendrils of the Cosmic Realm wrapped around her.

Within that second image, two massive feet slammed down beside her, and the ground quaked, rolling in a massive wave. She craned her neck to see a Titan towering overhead. It screeched out an ear-shattering battle cry as it tackled another to the ground.

Kallistê closed her eyes and breathed. She did not panic, as this wasn't the first time the vitality had called her in this way, but she didn't have enough control to safely traverse the realms.

If she allowed the Cosmos to pull her in now, while intoxicated by the Cosmic high, she may never find her way back. In an effort to keep herself grounded in the Human Realm, she leaned forward to rest her head on the desk, but instead she slid out of the chair and onto the floor.

Kallistê let out a startled yelp. When she moved to get up, her arms quivered beneath her weight. She sat back down on the ground and decided that she would give herself an hour to let the brunt of the high wear off. In this state, she wouldn't get anything productive accomplished.

She leaned her head against the back of the chair and closed her eyes.

It felt odd to be back on the continent, so close to her home. Kallistê was born and raised in the Three Corners, an independent city located at the intersection where Arcelia, Olysseus, and Llyr met, and operated outside of the jurisdiction of the three Kingdoms.

The city was largely a black market, run and operated by merchants. Ironically, her parents were shoemakers who made a simple, honest living.

Nothing bored Kallistê more.

The black market always carried whispers of untoward secrets. Kallistê was a young teen when she learned about the existence of the forbidden Cosmic Arts and Kestramore, an island across the ocean that not just tolerated but also openly endorsed such practices.

She left home at the age of seventeen, dashing all hopes of inheriting her parents' shop.

Kallistê had sailed north, with the sun shining on her face and winds whipping at her back. She arrived at the island of Kestramore with nothing but the clothes on her back.

Her time in the black market, where dealing with hecklers and underhanded merchants was a quotidian occurrence, proved useful. It didn't take long for her to find her place among the inhabitants. She batted her long lashes at any wandering eyes; useful for luring in men, who showered her with gifts and money in hopes of garnering her affection.

She sweet talked any listening ear, her words like poison wrapped in candy, and an elderly woman took pity on her and set her up with lodging.

Kallistê never went without a meal. She acquainted herself with any mages she could find. Eventually word got to one of the council women who took a liking to her ambition. She quickly connected Kallistê with a mentor who took her under their wing and taught her the Cosmic Arts. Now as a fully realized omen in her mid-twenties, not a single realm in existence could bind her.

Naturally, once she mastered the Cosmic Arts, Kallistê's life in Kestramore became more routine and less vibrant. She wanted—no, she *needed*—volatility. Thus, she plotted the assassinations of the kingdoms' rulers. Kallistê had a vision for the realm. A Cosmic one.

And due to Kestramore's contentious relationship with the continent, it took little effort to find and gather likeminded mages.

She'd brought Tarja and Cyrus back with her back to the continent while other loyalists remained in wait on the island. To kill all three monarchs at once would throw the kingdoms into chaos. But with a massive wrench thrown into her plans, Kallistê could only imagine how the fallout would have unfolded.

She'd used the Beasts as bait to bring the rulers together in one place, making their elimination that much easier. But she could adapt. The Beasts still remained here in Llyr. Surely, Kallistê could make use of them, whether it be to keep a safe distance from the blood mage or to protect herself from the backlash by Llyr's inhabitants. Now that she thought about it, that was a solid idea. At least one portion of the original plan could still proceed.

Kallistê would secure her place as Llyr's new ruler. She would take stock of all the resources available and leverage her position against Sovereign Jasver and King Rhys.

As her plan formulated, the high finally began to lessen, and her wits slowly returned. Kallistê raised to her feet, cemented in this realm once again. She had a continent to overthrow. And she'd be damned if a bump in the road got in her way.

CHAPTER 8

*"**G**randfather, I'm not sure if we should be doing this. Isn't there another way?" Haizea asked.*

He stood in front of her and put each hand on her shoulders, his grip firm and unyielding despite the gray hair on his head.

"The most powerful blood magic comes from the vitality flowing through your fellow man, Haizea. You'll never understand the depths of your power if you're too afraid to delve deeper. I'm a blood mage, so I'm hardier than most. I can take it, I promise. If you tried this on anyone else, you'd kill them. Using me is the most humane option you have," he said.

Haizea had already taken a life once before. Part of her final initiation into the Bruvian warriors cohort required joining them on a cull. A woman had reached out to the warriors, severely beaten and battered. She breathlessly told them her husband inflicted the wounds on a daily basis and she'd finally managed to escape.

As an all women group, the warriors took crimes of that nature seriously, and because it was Haizea's initiation, she led the charge.

She'd employed a seer in their ranks to assist her in interrogating the woman's husband; with crimes severe enough to warrant a cull, the warriors preferred to ensure absolute certainty regarding the culprit's guilt or innocence.

They visited the couple's home, swords at the ready. With each question Haizea asked, the seer saw through the man's lies, cuing Haizea in with a simple shake of her head. Haizea killed him with a single blow. By doing so, she not only delivered justice by ending his life, but also eliminated a threat to her people.

Grandfather Harzel's suggestion felt different. It served no purpose other than attaining more power.

Up until this point, they'd used small animals for her blood mage training. Haizea still hadn't quite figured out how to balance draining the vitality from another being without killing them.

The thought of using her grandfather as a test subject made her heart clench in her chest. What if he was wrong?

Even now, Haizea searched his unwavering features.

Although she still lacked precision in her blood magic, she made up for it in raw power; her connection to the vitality was stronger than even her grandfather's. Harzel had no troubles with training her father, but would that still be the case with her? Her father never wanted his blood magic to begin with.

His final days played out before her. His hollowed cheeks. The prominent bump of his joints beneath his paper-thin skin. How his once thick and voluminous blond coils had lost their vibrant sheen. The same fate lay ahead of her if she followed in his footsteps.

Now that she'd opened the gate to the Cosmic Arts, it could not be shut.

The time for vacillation had long since passed.

Haizea took a deep breath and steeled herself. If she faltered and let her control slip, she would only do more damage than she'd intended. She could do this without hurting him. She would do this without hurting him. Haizea nodded at her grandfather.

He cut the palm of his hand with a blade. Blood oozed out, and Haizea closed her eyes and focused. She'd spent years training in the healing arts at the Illinizan Mage Academy, so sensing the vitality came as naturally as breathing.

It took more concentration to fall into the world of vitality, where she could do more than simply sense it, but see it, touch it, and drain it out of another being.

Her brown eyes melted into a warm burgundy. The vitality revealed itself to her. Another deep breath. Calm. Focus. The world began to shimmer. The sparkling emanated most brilliantly in her grandfather's hand, where his blood pooled. Haizea willed the vitality that made up his life force to flow into her.

First, it trickled, then it poured out of him. A giddiness came crashing into her mind like an avalanche. This felt good. Incredible. A smile played on her lips, and she chuckled to herself at the sensation.

Why had she been so worried? This was fine. This was—

Grandfather collapsed in front of her. In her stupor, he fell in slow motion. She watched him sag to his knees before he tumbled forward, falling face-first into the ground.

Her mind dragged along at a sluggish pace, and it took her several delayed seconds to register that this was her *doing. She fought her way through the haze and willed herself to stop draining his life force.*

Vitality continued tumbling toward her, caressing and collecting across her skin before melting into her body. It only took a few moments for the flow finally to decelerate, but it felt like an eternity. By the time she had forced the gate in her mind closed, Grandfather looked like an entirely different person.

Just a few moments ago he had been a strong, healthy-looking older man. Now he wallowed on the ground, frail and thin and fragile. His muscle mass had withered away. His cheeks sunk into his face, the same way her father's once did.

And yet, to her bewilderment, Harzel smiled at her.

Haizea helped him to his feet. He cupped her face in his hands and kissed her on the forehead.

"I can tell you are frightened, but this is a lesson you should never forget. Balance is difficult to master. Imagine how you would feel if you had used someone without our power; someone who could not have survived. With me, there is room for error while you learn control. I lived because I am a blood mage. And you will live through your blood magic, too. The vitality has blessed you. This is a gift from the realm itself. Always remember that."

Haizea's words escaped her as her grandfather pulled her into an embrace. Her heart broke at his brittle arms. But he looked so happy. Elated, even.

A mix of relief, apprehension, and fear shook her to her core. Haizea hated that she'd hurt him, but the ecstasy terrified her just equally. Using her blood magic released a pent-up energy she never realized existed within. Draining his vitality had felt as natural as breathing.

After that day, she better understood why her father had turned his back on the Cosmic Arts. But even then, her mother's death gnawed away at her. She might still be here had he never abandoned his magic.

Haizea committed herself to the path before her, determined not to fail like he did. From the ages of eighteen to twenty-two, she studied diligently under her grandfather's tutelage. She didn't know if a power required her to drain the life of others was truly such a blessing. But if someone she cared about ever needed her, she could at least use it to aid and protect them.

Haizea groggily opened her eyes. A fuzziness lingered in her vision, but the delirium no longer affected her. Rather than bright red, her eyes had dulled to a warm ginger. She tried to move, only to find her wrists bound together and her ankles chained. Her bottom rocked and bumped in her seat from the forward momentum of the trolley car.

Her eyelids drooped heavily as she looked around. The trolley car was empty. Well, not entirely. Zander sat on a metal case directly across from her. When their gazes met, his fingers clenched tighter around his spear, and his eyes hardened.

Haizea's heart sank as memories came rushing back.

"Where... are we going?" she asked, her words came to her slowly.

Zander shrugged.

"How long have you been a Cosmic Arts practitioner?" he asked. The distrust in his eyes cut deep.

Despite wanting to answer, she couldn't bring herself to. It would only confirm that she had lied to them for years. It didn't matter that she stopped the omens and saved him as a result.

The cost of her intervention came at a price: the sacrifice of her fellow Guard members.

No wonder she'd woken up chained and caged like an animal.

Haizea tore her gaze away from Zander and quietly pondered her own question. The Beasts' presence in Llyr had been proven to be the work of omens in a plot to assassinate the rulers of the three kingdoms. Haizea failed to kill the realmdrifter, which meant Sovereign Jasver and King Rhys needed to tread carefully. A realmdrifter could show up anywhere, anytime, across any of the seven realms without any warning.

The omen's parting words echoed in her head. Words of admiration. Haizea didn't know what to make of that, but she knew the conclusion King Rhys would have drawn. Revealing her blood magic was akin to digging her grave. When the omen who tried to assassinate the king praised her, it *built* the coffin.

King Rhys had undoubtedly deemed her a danger to the surviving Guard members. But why not simply kill her while she was unconscious? She remembered how her control slipped toward the end, killing all those knights to bring power to herself.

Anyone who'd witnessed that sight would likely refuse to come near her, too afraid her magic would intervene to protect her if they attacked. Tying her down from a distance with telekinesis would avoid direct contact altogether.

A voice nagged in the back of her mind. A puzzle piece that she was missing, something important. An image flashed of the execution platform, but as quickly as the thought formed, it escaped her grasp. The clouds of the Cosmic high had not yet fully evaporated.

Haizea hoped that she would be able to put it all together when she finally came down and fully regained her senses.

Zander's blue gaze chilled on her as he observed her movements. Despite the tumultuous storm brewing within, Haizea maintained an even expression. She shifted slightly and realized she no longer wore her knight's armor. They'd stripped her down to the form-fitting pants and sleeveless top she wore underneath.

She tugged at the chains, and the metal creaked in protest; at least some of her enhanced strength still lingered. She could break them herself, but she needed to be quick and clandestine about it. Physical strength alone would not be of much help against Zander's telekinesis.

A fluttering motion outside the window caught her attention. A messenger hawk. It landed in the trolley in front of them. The wheels in her mind turned.

If the hawk was arriving instead of departing, did that mean they had called ahead? King Rhys probably wanted the colosseum ready for her execution. But it didn't seem plausible for enough time to have elapsed to both send and receive a response all the way from Arcelia. A shorter distance made more sense. Perhaps Sovereign Jasver?

The memory of her healing King Rhys while struggling to keep her blood magic at bay came rushing back. Haizea's heart dropped into the pit of her stomach. Her control had slipped with the knights... what if she'd killed him too?

"King Rhys... how is he faring?" Haizea asked carefully.

"That's no longer any of your concern."

Haizea blinked. One of her coils fell in her face as she looked away from him. Her breath hitched in her throat at what his coldness meant, of what their intentions were. She focused on holding back the tears that threatened to come forth and maintained her composure.

Above all, she needed to escape before they reached their destination.

Her wrists chafed against the chains that bound her. Outside of the window, the base of the Bayeux Mountain Range steadily entered her view, an auspicious development after a sudden string of turmoil.

Haizea settled her eyes on Zander: glacial and yet piercing despite her inner worries. When his face blanched and he shifted away, she suppressed the twinge of guilt. He was a fellow knight and a friend. She didn't want to hurt him, but she couldn't stay here.

The gift of persuasion had never been her strong suit, so the chances of convincing him to willingly untie her were slim. She braced herself for violence. Haizea reminded herself of what helped her get through her warrior's training and what eased her conscience whenever she used her blood magic:

Life was not sacred. It couldn't be, when her own life depended on her ability to drain the vitality of an innocent being. Zander's life was no different. Her first choice of action would be to escape without bringing him harm, but Haizea would not underestimate him. Zander's telekinesis allowed him to move any object with his mind, putting her healing magic at a great disadvantage.

With that type of power imbalance, she could not demur at the thought of hurting him... of using her blood magic against him. Not if she wanted to make it out alive.

CHAPTER 9

"We've received correspondence from Sovereign Jasver. They've made it back home," Jirina said, handing the missive from the messenger hawk to King Rhys. He crumpled it in his fist.

"A coordinated attack on all three kingdom's rulers. By fucking omens of all things," he snarled.

His mind still reeled from what he'd witnessed. One moment, he stood in the center of a tense but cordial meeting. The next, he, the other monarchs, and their Royal Guards were fighting for their lives. Dozens of knights disarmed themselves, their wills overtaken by a curse mage who forced them to drop their weapons. Then, an invisible force raised those same blades in the air before plunging them into their bodies.

The weight of corrupted vitality that blanketed the room still bore down on King Rhys even now. The sensation sent him reeling back to a far distant memory from when he was just a teen, no older than his own son, Prince Felix...

King Rhys stopped short. If he let himself return to that dark place, he would not be in a state to lead. He shoved the memory back and tabled his rage for later. First, he needed to ensure the surviving members of the Guard returned home safely... all two of them.

In the aftermath of the attack, Sovereign Jasver offered to escort them back home, but King Rhys declined. Instead, he requested an enchantment for Haizea to send her into a deeper slumber, hoping that she would sleep for the entire trip. Should she rouse while still in transit, she could slaughter them all. Only Sovereign Jasver's words of caution stopped him from ending her then and there:

"King Rhys, I hope I am not overstepping the boundaries of our friendship when I speak now. I understand and share your apprehension regarding the Cosmic Arts. But this knight just saved our lives. Though your anger is righteous, I believe it may be a more judicious course of action to listen to what she has to say when she wakes."

King Rhys remained silent as he contemplated the Sovereign's words.

"Sovereign Jasver, you took an interest in Haizea when we first arrived. You felt her Soul with your medium magic. And you felt something you didn't like." *Jirina stepped closer, and though her tone quivered with a hint of fear, her words rang with the absolute conviction that came with clairvoyance.*

"Yes, what I felt made me uneasy, but what I sense in a person's Soul is only part of the full picture. Their actions also play an important role in how I judge their character. I am inclined to lend grace to someone who has saved my life."

Jirina looked pointedly at the carnage around them. Most of the bodies suffered from impalement wounds, slain by their own swords, but an arresting amount had perished from having their vitality stripped from them.

"And what of your fallen knights, who were victims not of the realmdrifter, but blood magic? Would you say the same for them?" *Jirina asked, giving the sovereign pause.*

"Sovereign Jasver, while I appreciate your words of caution, I have no tolerance for the Cosmic Arts nor the patience to hear any pleas for clemency on her behalf," *King Rhys finally interjected.*

He turned his attention toward Haizea and focused on vitality around him, concentrating it around her neck, ready to rip her head from her shoulders. Sovereign Jasver stepped in between, blocking his line of sight.

He could have shoved them out of the way with his telekinesis, but for the sake of their allyship, he chose not to.

"Your knight is correct. She just ripped the vitality out of every fallen knight in the room. Which gives more weight to my next concern. My knowledge of blood magic is very limited, but I have heard many tales, as I'm sure you have as well. Her magic may act to defend her in a similar manner, even while unconscious. You feel the crushing pressure of her vitality, don't you?

"Ultimately, her fate is your decision, but as your ally I must caution you for the safety of your own people. There is no room for error. I may very well be wrong, but if I'm correct, we won't have the chance to respond—every single person standing here will be reduced to ash in the blink of an eye."

The logic in their words gave King Rhys pause. Blood magic differed from transmutation magic, which King Rhys had more intimate knowledge of. Though transporting her back with them presented many dangers, it may be wise to take a slower, more deliberate approach.

Getting his people home was his responsibility, so he would see it through alone. While he still considered the sovereign an ally, the timing of the attack left him on edge. Yet he heeded the sovereign's advice and only restrained the blood mage with a few binds and utilized an otherwise harmless enchantment. He despised the idea of bringing her back to Arcelia, but at home he had more resources at his disposal that were specifically designed for this type of circumstance.

"I need to write home to Mireille," King Rhys said. They carried a messenger hawk on board, which would get home faster than even the steam-powered trolley.

Jirina handed him a pen and paper. He rolled his shoulders in an attempt to dispel the tension. After his injury from the omen, he should be in pain. He should have bled out from that type of strike. But Hai—the blood mage had reached out to him and contaminated his blood with her warped vitality. His body was fully intact, like his throat had never been sliced open. The thought made his stomach contort.

Twisted magic defiled his body. Something he vowed to never tolerate and to never *ever* meddle with again. A Cosmic Arts practitioner slept right under his nose for years. She knew his family, every inch of the palace, and he'd briefed her on her fair share of Arcelia's top secrets.

Someone capable of lying for so long could not be trusted. An *omen* could never be trusted; experience had taught him this.

He needed to warn Mireille. She and the children needed to go into hiding until he could secure the blood mage and safely execute her. But even then, the realmdrifter still loomed.

Where could they possibly run so that bitch of a mage could not find them?

He clutched the pen tighter. It fractured in his grasp.

"If you'd prefer, I can write home for you," Jirina offered, perhaps a little too eagerly.

She was probably concerned that he thought her abilities were inadequate, but King Rhys knew better than anyone how an omen could slip through the cracks. Cosmic magic was an evil that prided itself on hiding in plain sight.

"No, I'll handle this. I need your help with keeping an eye on the other trolley," he said as he brought the pen to the paper.

My beloved Mireille,

There was a surprise attack at the meeting in Llyr by Cosmic Arts practitioners. Please, don't panic. I am fine and fully intact and so is Sovereign Jasver. Regretfully, save for Zander and Jirina, every other knight I brought with me perished. Begin preparations to notify their families on my behalf.

I don't know where to begin or quite how to say this, but during the attack it was revealed that one of the knights in the Royal Guard was also a

Cosmic Arts practitioner. I hate to bring such an abomination within our borders, but I've no choice but to bring it home.

Call a meeting with Ser Bren in my private suite. He helped me prepare for the previous execution, so he knows everything I'll need to keep the omen securely subdued. Currently, she is chained and is under an enchantment. I hope that it is strong enough for the trip, but it may very well diminish as we put more distance between ourselves and the mage who cast it.

Ser Bren will know what to send back with the messenger hawk. Have him begin preparations for the colosseum as well.

My utmost priority is your and the children's safety. I will be home soon. I will clean up this mess.

Your husband,

Rhys

He quickly rolled the paper, stamped it, and sealed it. Next, he penned a letter responding to Sovereign Jasver.

King Rhys expressed hope that they could continue to rely on each other as allies while they dealt with the unprecedented nature of the unfolding situation. He added that Arcelia would be ready to provide supporting resources Llyr might need in the wake of such an upheaval.

"She's awake," Jirina said just as he tied the letter to the Olyssean messenger hawk.

Ice ran down King Rhys's spine. Raging, burning heat quickly followed. The enchantment had weakened already. His stomach tightened with unease; he'd seen for himself what she could do with that power, and those restraints may not hold.

Though he rued putting Zander alone with her, the alternative was seating her with the three of them. At least this way, if worse came to worst, King Rhys and Jirina could escape while Zander held her off for as long as he could. At least then, there would still be *some* survivors.

King Rhys ignored the questions plainly written on Jirina's face. Questions she knew better than to utter aloud: was he at least going to speak with her? Get her side of the story? Delve deeper into her intentions?

The answers to those questions did not matter. There was no place for the Cosmic Arts in King Rhys's world. No explanation the prisoner offered would qualify her for amnesty. The omen had endangered his family, his palace, his kingdom, and thoroughly defiled his body.

Only one path lay ahead for the blood mage: death.

Chapter 10

Haizea swallowed thickly against the deep pang in her chest. Her heart tugged painfully with each beat. Despite her hurt, when she finally found her voice again, her words came to her easier than when she'd first awoken.

She expected to sound thin, but she retained her usual bravado.

"I only used my blood magic to save you and everyone else. It was a last resort in an impossible situation. I would never hurt you, Zander. You *know* that."

He pressed his lips together tightly. "It doesn't matter what I know or how I feel. The only thing that does is what King Rhys thinks," he said.

"And what does he think?"

"You already know the answer to that."

"No. I don't," she said defiantly.

Zander gave her a long, hard look. "He's decided on your execution."

"But I—"

"But *nothing*. You knew King Rhys's stance on the Cosmic Arts. You knew it and you flaunted that power in his face anyway. You say you did it to save everyone but failed to mention what you did to our fallen comrades. What remained of their bodies wasn't even worth bringing home for their families to deliver their last rites." Zander stood up and practically yelled in her face.

He spun away from her, running a hand roughly through his hair.

Haizea flinched when he brought up what she'd done to the wounded Guard members who had survived the realmdrifter's attack. People she could have saved… *should have* saved, but instead used as fuel for her blood magic.

"I'm not saying you should have let him die. I know I'm glad to be alive. But if you could reverse such a gruesome injury, why not let him take the blow and revive him after? We could have come up with something. A believable lie. But now I… my hands are tied, Haizea. He's seen everything, and he's dead set on taking you out."

Tears welled in Zander's eyes.

"I just… I feel so lied to," he added softly, and a piece of her broke.

"I know how the king feels about Cosmic magic. It's why I kept it a secret. But I couldn't just let us all get slaughtered when I knew I could do something about it. Surely, he has enough sense after what's happened to open his mind at least a little."

Zander shook his head.

"You witnessed the execution just like I did. You saw him. There's no changing that."

"Zander—"

Her jaw clamped shut as he cut her off with his telekinesis.

"Listen, I'm not even supposed to be talking to you. Jirina is surely keeping tabs on you, and if King Rhys gets the impression that I'm sympathetic toward you, he'll suspect me as a conspirator. I don't want my head to roll for something I'm not guilty of doing."

And yet the only reason he still had a head now was because of Haizea's intervention. That fact poured yet another handful of salt into her wounds.

"You're in denial if you think King Rhys will be lenient. He says you've tainted his body with blood magic. In his mind, he'll never be cleansed from your filth. He'd rather be dead than touched by the Cosmic Arts," he muttered.

Though she did not want to admit it, it did not take much to imagine King Rhys saying those words. Haizea envisioned his face twisting in anger and disgust, just as he did before in the colosseum.

A momentary slip in her control was all it took for her Cosmic magic to unleash devastation. First with her grandfather, and now with her comrades. Haizea would never be able to atone for either.

She understood the king's rage, and she did not expect forgiveness. But maybe with time, he would instead come to an understanding. At least, she hoped he would.

"Do you think the same?" she asked.

Zander hesitated.

"I just feel hurt. And conflicted. I wish you would have trusted me. But at this point, we both know there's nothing I can do for you that won't result in both of our lives being forfeit."

"I understand. I'm sorry, Zander," she whispered softly.

Haizea bit down on the inside of her cheek, drawing blood. Zander transformed into a glittering figure in front of her. She drew on the power of the vitality in her own blood, draining her own life force to amplify her strength—a dangerous and potentially lethal course of action, but she had no other choice.

This time, the chains did more than creak in protest when she tugged against them; they snapped like a twig. She did not give Zander a chance to react.

Only half a second passed between her being seated and her fist connecting with Zander's jaw, her movements nearly impossible to track with the naked eye. He slumped to the ground and folded over on himself.

Haizea kicked the back door of the trolley off its hinges and tumbled out. She pinched at the remaining bonds on her wrists, and they crumbled into dust. Her entire escape took mere seconds, so she hoped that they would keep rolling for a little while more before Jirina realized what happened. Hopefully, King Rhys would continue toward home and let her be, for both of their sakes.

She took in her surroundings. Her world still teemed with red, but she could tell that greenery stretched far as the eye could see. The peak of Mount Niaby towered off in the distance, the snowpack shimmering like rubies. A little ways ahead, still on the flat land that made up the base, a cloud of smoke billowed toward the skies and the surrounding shapes resembled a cluster of cabins.

By a twist of fate, she'd escaped close to home. Still, she wasn't out of the woods yet. Although the base fell within the vicinity of mountaineer territory, she stood somewhere in the blurred lines of jurisdiction between Olysseus, Arcelia, and the mountain range.

Due to this, it was hit or miss if she'd cross paths with another Bruvian warrior. If she could simply get to higher elevation, she'd securely be in their regular stomping grounds.

No one in their right mind would agitate the Bruvian warriors. While some warriors were powerful mages, by tradition they did not discriminate against people who could not manipulate vitality.

The original Bruvian warriors were non-mages, and in many ways that made them more dangerous than magic wielders. When they forged their weapons, they infused the metal with crushed leaves of a plant called earth's smoke; a plant with resistance to the vitality. It could only be found on the volcanic peaks of the southern mountains—Haligus, Valdare, and Cortara.

Earth's smoke was a tool exclusive to the Bruvian warriors and throughout history had changed the tides of the war in their favor. It was their greatest weapon and their greatest secret.

If Haizea could go even further to Mount Illiniza, she would have the added benefit of being in the jurisdiction of her mother's cohort.

She'd be with people who bore and raised her yet again. The mountaineers would not care about her blood magic.

With her traveling on foot, she'd never make it back to Arcelia before King Rhys did. If she carelessly returned without a plan, Arcelian forces would apprehend her at the border as soon as she arrived. The king would command Jirina to watch her scepter, like a hawk stalking its prey. While Haizea believed she could best them with her blood magic, she would prefer to get her grandfather back to the mountains without bloodshed.

The good thing was, King Rhys didn't know about Grandfather Harzel's relation to her, nor his location. Given the wall of resistance he put up about moving to Arcelia, Haizea avoided bringing attention to him unnecessarily by mentioning him in her application for the Royal Guard.

And because mountaineers passed on their maternal surnames by tradition, it would not be easy to link them to one another. Those two things acted as a safety net. It wasn't foolproof, but it gave her time to figure something out.

The grass crunched beneath Haizea's bare feet as she walked. They hadn't even spared her shoes when they'd snatched her armor. Haizea blinked away the stinging in her eyes. She'd only done what her grandfather had painstakingly taught her to do: use her blood magic when she needed it most.

The image of the slain knights flashed before her.

Their lives had meaning. And I... I stripped so many of them of significance in a single instant, she thought.

Yet her body betrayed her; her fingers trembled, and a deep yearning clenched her chest as she relived the exhilaration and the delirious euphoria. Haizea inhaled deeply and pushed those desires out of her mind, reasserting control over her magic and the enticing high.

The trolley shrunk in the distance. A deep frown curled her lips as she started walking toward the mountain base. She was going back home.

CHAPTER 11

With the rulers of Llyr out of the picture, the empty throne called Kallistê's name. An ample opportunity lay at her feet to put her face in front of the populace. She needed the type of power that came with influence, from forming connections.

But until she had allies, she would have to forcibly turn the tides in her favor. For that reason, she moved the Beast from the outskirts of Zariya into the Capital City of Zemira.

Her favorite Beast was the three-headed *trivialis*. Upper and lower canines protruded from its mouth like sabers. Razor-sharp claws extended from its paws, each attached to four mammoth-sized legs, tall and sturdy like a tree. Rather than ears, it listened to its surroundings by picking up the vibrations in the air. It had a muzzle like a dog and slitted pupils like a snake. A *trivialis* easily towered over the largest of buildings, at times even blocking out the sun.

Kallistê had used the *trivialis* to throw the distant cities of Llyr in disarray. It was what pushed them to reach out to their neighboring kingdoms to begin with.

The presence of a Beast meant one thing: that a realmdrifter had brought it into the realm. With the Cosmic Arts strictly forbidden in the major kingdoms, Arcelia and Olysseus had no choice but to answer Llyr's pleas for assistance.

The *trivialis* opened its massive jaws, and the wind whipped as it inhaled. A roar erupted from its throat and reverberated through the air, bursting the eardrums of hundreds of inhabitants in the vicinity. The walls of the numerous surrounding buildings trembled, and cracks rippled through windows before the glass shattered. The Beast turned one of its heads toward the nearest structure and swung a massive paw.

The ground quaked from the force of the blow, and a chunk of the façade catapulted through the air. Pieces of debris crashed down onto the people fleeing. Bodies poured out of the damaged building: most likely a library, based on the fact that many of them had books in tow.

Now that she'd moved the Beast to the capital, most of the casualties now were aristocrats and bureaucrats rather than everyday commoners.

Kallistê brought her body into the astral plane and watched everything unfold. The Beast struck again as it roared in frustration. Her lips curved upward. A group of telekinetics gathered together outside to keep the falling debris from crushing those attempting to evacuate. A few noblemen entered the fray to investigate, which piqued her interest.

She took in their faces and memorized them. Kallistê would spend much of her time following them throughout the Capital City over the coming days.

A group of knights attempted to engage the enormous *trivialis*. She stifled a laugh at their efforts. They looked as helpless as the Royal Guard had been when she and Tarja had attacked.

The *trivialis* showed no mercy. It swiped at the attacking knights as they charged forward with their swords, sending them flying high into the air before their bodies broke apart upon landing with sickening squelches.

Although their helmets hid their faces, she could still sense the terror emanating from the knights lucky enough to survive; the Beast had rendered their swords useless.

The small squad of telekinetic knights used their collective power to forcibly move the Beast. Their bodies glistened and shimmered as their vitality surged, hurtling toward the Beast in large waves.

The *trivialis* shifted a few inches, like ants trying to lift a mountain. It turned to the offending party and opened its jaws wide. Its three heads snapped downward like a viper, clamping its mouths shut. It cut through the knights' metal armor like butter and impaled their bodies with its saber teeth.

"Shameful," Kallistê tutted to herself, shaking her head.

In the wake of the kings' deaths and with the catastrophic damage the *trivialis* currently inflicted, Llyr's court should have their hands full. As the nobles scurried away and put distance between themselves and the worsening situation with the Beast, Kallistê followed them.

She'd had half a mind to wipe them out, just as she had done their kings. But who would she replace them with? Kallistê needed warm bodies to be her eyes and ears throughout the kingdom. Besides, she desired a bit of thrill from the danger that came from leaving the nobles intact.

She floated in the astral plane to eavesdrop. The nobles jogged a few steps before slowing down to a brisk walk; their labored breathing served as evidence that they weren't fit for prolonged physical exertion. Unsurprisingly, they were at their wits end.

"This is a disaster. The kings had no living heirs. Who is next in the line of succession?" a man wearing a purple hat said.

The woman walking with him wore long, purple robes. "I suppose it would be Regent Kai," she said, her breathing flustered.

The man let out a sound somewhere between a grunt and a wheeze, and the woman didn't look particularly thrilled either. Kallistê tilted her head. Was that simply frustration at their situation or a lack of fondness toward the regent, an opening she could exploit?

The nobles continued into the castle and marched through the long hallways before finally arriving at a large room. Several other noblemen and women stood inside, debating and arguing similar topics.

"We have a regent position in place precisely for circumstances such as this. Regent Kai is more than qualified to take over in the absence of our kings. Why is this even a topic of debate? We should be more worried about the creature from hell destroying our cities!" someone shouted. Kallistê noted that this person wore robes, like the woman.

"Don't you think it's odd? Kings Johan and Arlo died rather quickly after requesting help from Arcelia and Olysseus—both of whom's rulers escaped with their lives. The same two kingdoms that have a history of trying to raze others to the ground, and dragging Llyr into hell with them," one noble shouted.

"They were fools, both of them. Why would they trust those two wretched kingdoms?"

"They may be dead, but they are still your kings. Check your tone when you speak of them," a knight standing in the corner of the room snapped.

Kallistê chuckled as they squabbled amongst themselves. This moment was as good as any to make her entrance. She landed nimbly on the ground, in the center of the ruckus, and brought her body and spirit back to the physical world.

The people nearest her startled immediately. Those in the far corners of the room hadn't noticed yet, but murmurs spread through the crowd and more nobles turned their heads toward the woman who appeared out of thin air.

She fluffed her blue tresses, her bracelets clanging against each other as she basked in the attention. With all eyes on her, Kallistê finally addressed the crowd.

"Your anger, though justified, is misdirected," she said.

A beat of silence.

"Who the fuck are you?"

"Killing King Arlo and Johan was not personal by any means. They were obstacles, blocking the way of a bigger—"

One of the knights swung at Kallistê. She realmdrifted through his body, appearing behind him as his sword sliced harmlessly through air.

"As I was saying. The kings' position made their deaths unavoidable. However, if you are amenable—and you value your own lives—I have a proposition. I can solve Llyr's problems; all I need is your cooperation."

"Did... did she just walk through him?"

"*You!* This is your fault, witch!" someone shrieked.

Two knights had silently converged around Kallistê. They struck at once, but she was faster. She entered the astral plane as they attacked and returned just long enough to shift the angle of their swords so that their blades cut straight through one another's arms.

Kallistê rematerialized beside the robed noblewoman from earlier and smirked, ignoring the pained wails of the injured knights behind her.

The vitality quivered in her vision as the fear in the room became palpable.

"Maybe we should hear what she has to say," the noblewoman said.

"Very astute. I like you. What is your name?" Kallistê said.

The woman raised her chin. "Ivor."

"Ivor. I'm Kallistê. I have a proposition for you to consider. While you all are free to refuse, I'll preface this by saying that rejecting my offer means forfeiting your lives. First and foremost, I want the throne. You can either surrender it willingly, or I'll take it by force. I've already killed the kings.

"You all would just be a few more bodies to add to the pile. Secondly, as queen, I accept nothing less than devout loyalty. In exchange, I'll send the *trivialis* back to the Beast Realm."

A hesitant silence met Kallistê's proposal. Rumblings of dissent quickly followed.

"Did she just say she spilled the kings' blood?"

"Only an omen could have brought a Beast here. Only a realm-drifter can disappear into thin air," hissed one noble.

Kallistê vanished into the astral plane and reappeared by the door, before any of the nobles could run. Her eyes, cloudy and white from her Cosmic magic, landed on the man who'd last spoken. Again, it was the cohort who wore purple robes that had the most sensible opinions.

"I'd listen to him if I were you."

"The kings would be rolling in their graves if we bent the knee to an omen," someone cried.

The knights kept a calculated distance from her this time, but it didn't matter. Realmdrifting gave her unlimited freedom of movement. They could run, but she would catch them all in an instant.

"What other choice do we have?" another person asked.

Another long stretch of silence followed before Ivor, the robed noblewoman, answered:

"None."

Kallistê took her place at the front of the room. With more distance between herself and the door, some nobles tried to flee. Kallistê caught them, brought their bodies first into the astral plane, and then up into the Cosmic Realm and left them behind.

Without corrupted Spiritual magic that would enable them to traverse between the physical and spiritual, they were trapped forever.

"If anyone else would like to leave, you're free to do so. I'm sure they would be grateful to have more company in the Cosmic Realm." She swallowed a giggle that bubbled up, signaling the oncoming high from using Cosmic magic.

She unceremoniously wiped her hands to distract herself.

No one moved. Many of them didn't even dare to breathe.

"Good. I am pleased to see we're on the same page," she looked around, taking in the nobles who stood, frozen in place. "Now, this is certainly no way to welcome your queen. Is it not customary in Llyr to bow in the presence of royalty?"

First, the people nearest to her got down on one knee. Their expressions twisted in a mix of hesitancy and intrigue. When her eyes met theirs, she put on a dazzling smile, eliciting a gasp from many of the nobles, their faces flushing to match.

They leaned forward and put their heads down on the floor. The rest of the room quickly followed suit.

Kallistê twirled one of the many rings she wore around her finger. With the nobles resting in the palm of her hand, she would use them to get the rest of the populace on the same page.

Chapter 12

As Haizea trekked toward higher elevation, her thoughts lingered on the last several hours, struggling to accept just how quickly things had unraveled. Part of her desperately second-guessed what Zander had told her regarding King Rhys's decision on her disposition.

His words repeated over and over in her mind:

"He says you've tainted his body with blood magic. In his mind, he'll never be cleansed from your filth. He'd rather be dead than touched by the Cosmic Arts."

She'd gone to great lengths to conceal her power so that she would never have to divulge that she practiced the Cosmic Arts. With the attack in Llyr, all of her efforts had been rendered useless. Maybe King Rhys would forgive her, maybe he wouldn't.

But if she spoke to him, at least there would be closure. She didn't want to run away just to never clear the air again. Her intention had never been, and never would be, to bring harm to the Royal Family, her comrades, or the kingdom. Surely, given her years of dedicated service in his Guard, deep down King Rhys knew that. He had to.

And yet, Haizea's chest tightened. Alone, King Rhys didn't not give her pause—but his access did. In addition to the Guard, an entire army awaited at his beck and call.

While Haizea could rely on the warriors, she needed to get to them first. King Rhys's resources and allies were immediately available to him. Haizea also had to consider how the warriors' assistance may be impacted by the treaty between the mountains and the kingdoms. Just as it would not have been wise to retrieve Grandfather Harzel by herself, the warriors would have to infiltrate Arcelia without raising any alarms.

Which meant that if Jirina was keeping tabs on her with her clairvoyance, she would need to approach her plea for help covertly. Yet another disadvantage, since King Rhys had the benefit of doing everything out in the open.

The village she'd seen in the distance earlier was several yards away now. She dusted off her pants and gently patted her hair to try to get some semblance of neatness. It didn't work. Between tumbling out of the trolley and walking for miles, only a fresh shower and a set of clean clothes would give her the proper reset she desired.

She quietly made her way through the village's entrance, which was nothing more than a wooden welcome sign with the name worn off from years of erosion. Haizea strode through, her brows rising high at how different it looked from Windhaven, her home village.

Trash fluttered in front of her, carried by the wind. Haizea became hyperaware of her bare feet as she narrowly missed a suspicious-looking mound on the ground. Lacking distinct lines of demarcation, the dirt roads and walkways blended in with the surrounding greenery, a clear sign of neglecting regular maintenance. Even from several yards away, wood rot visibly marred the buildings and homes.

Haizea balked at the state of the village. She wasn't naïve enough to think that poverty did not exist within the mountains, but until now, she'd never seen it with her own eyes.

In higher elevation, the villages clustered closer together, making it easier to exchange resources and lend a helping hand. While the base of the mountain benefited from a warmer climate, many residents had moved away after the past wars, paranoid that they would be wide open should the kingdoms ever attack again.

Fewer people meant that the community here suffered in isolation. By comparison, having multiple neighboring villages to rely on provided a safety net for those living near the summit.

Haizea's stomach growled just as the stench of human excrement assaulted her nostrils. She sighed. The thought of eating here certainly didn't exactly whet her appetite, but she wouldn't make it far on an empty stomach. Another weathered sign stood just paces away from her current path. She squinted her eyes as she tried to make out the faded letters and eventually got an idea of the general direction of the marketplace.

A line of large tents and run-down wooden buildings greeted her. A few noticeable exceptions that stood out: the coin mastery, the jail, and the bar all appeared to be in pristine condition. Money may be scarce around these parts, but it was easy to see where it had concentrated.

Haizea decided to stop at a small bakery, the cleanest-looking shop. As soon as she crossed the threshold, however, she cringed in embarrassment at her unkempt appearance: barefoot and covered in dirt. She ambled through the shop and took stock of what they had available. Closest to the door were a variety of pastries and sweet treats. A luxury.

She made her way over to the plain loaves of bread that would sustain her a little longer. Most of the other patrons had gathered in this section, too.

A man with long hair silently drifted through, his wavy locks billowing behind him like a soft cloud. Haizea couldn't get a good look at his face from this angle, but she most certainly noticed his hand slipping into the pockets of the people nearby.

He moved with smooth, swift precision that was undeniable, even to her. If she hadn't already been looking in his direction, she would have missed it entirely.

Haizea checked for her own coin purse and breathed in relief to find it still there. Instinctively, she patted her neck for her mother's pendant as well. It still rested beneath her shirt. At the very least, King Rhys hadn't *completely* stripped her dry.

When she brought her selections to the counter, the shop owner looked her up and down.

"You're a new face," he remarked.

Haizea nodded. "Just passing through."

The man tilted his head as she handed him her coins.

"Well, just so you know, there's an additional tax to use foreign currency 'round these parts."

She fought the urge to grimace. "How much?"

"One hundred percent."

At this, she couldn't help but balk. "Are you serious?"

He shrugged. "If you have a problem with it, take it up with the coin mastery. Foreigners aren't common, and the few that *do* roll through here can afford it. As a kingdom dweller, you should be grateful that's all I'm asking for."

Haizea leveled her gaze at him, purposefully leaning into the natural hostility of her resting expression. The shopkeeper stiffened and his heartbeat quickened, pulsing against her vitality. But, to his credit, he otherwise didn't budge.

"Fine," she sighed. The amount exceeded what she held in her coin purse.

She could easily strong-arm him, but looking at the state of the village, that felt wrong. Haizea suppressed a grumble of frustration as her stomach growled yet again.

Deep down, she knew this was unsustainable. She would have to think of something so that she could eat. Either a way to earn money or maybe bartering services for food. Healers were rare, so she could almost certainly make use of her magic in that way. She would need to replace her clothing as well. Hiking boots. Long pants. Something durable that would survive a trip through the mountains.

As she turned to leave in defeat, a cool breeze whispered against her skin. A distantly familiar tug accompanied it, one that toyed with the fuse of her blood magic. A chill froze her in place. Jirina?

Several coins plopped onto the counter in front of her along with several more rolls of bread. Haizea looked up to see the man from a few moments ago and got a better look at his face now.

He looked around her age, with beige, sun-kissed skin and pearl-colored hair. Based on the way Haizea had to crane her neck to get a good look at him, he had to be at least as tall as King Rhys. When his eyes met hers, he grinned at her, and faint dimples adorned his cheeks.

His irises twinkled and teetered between baby blue and lavender. Realizing she was staring at him, Haizea forced herself to blink. Even more alarming, her body began vibrating—the rush of her blood magic threatening to awaken.

"Huh," the shopkeeper said as he counted the coins. "Enough for the both of you. Guess it's your lucky day."

Haizea swallowed the call of her magic as the baker placed her loaves into a bag and handed them to her. She turned toward the white-haired man, wanting to thank him, but couldn't quite get the words out, given that she'd watched him pilfer money off the other patrons—one of whom shoved past her to get to the counter.

Haizea didn't let it bother her and simply stepped out of the way before following the man outside. "Thank you," she finally managed to say.

He closely watched her lips as she spoke. Then, he pointed toward his chest before pressing his fingers against his ear.

The movement sent Haizea back to her days at the Illinizan Mage Academy. She recalled one of the earliest lessons she'd learned, right after enduring the lectures about the sanctity of life: healers were most effective when they could communicate with their patients. In many ways, communication was just as important as healing itself.

That notion resonated with Haizea, and she had taken it to heart.

This time, when Haizea spoke, she used her hands instead of her voice.

~Thank you,~ she signed.

~You're not from around here are you?~ he signed back with a relieved smile.

She considered him, both with gratitude and suspicion. Deaf or not, he was still a thief. But he did her a huge favor just now. To her surprise, he didn't squirm under her glare like she expected him to; in fact, his gaze had grown warmer.

~Yes and no. I'm from Mount Illiniza. Windhaven Village. I'm on my way home,~ Haizea signed.

~Illiniza? That's quite far. Doesn't seem like you're really prepared for a trip like that,~ he signed, motioning toward her unkempt appearance.

Haizea grimaced as she mulled it over, making her look all the more unwelcoming. The deeper into the mountains she went, the stronger the blanket of protection the treaty provided. She also needed to find a way to get a message to her grandfather and let him know what had happened, so that he could leave Arcelia before King Rhys discovered their familial link. The man took in her contemplative face.

~In that much of a hurry to get home?~

She hesitated, reluctant to rehash everything that'd happened to a stranger. He had helped her, but... Haizea's attention flickered to the shop as someone left the bakery empty handed. The man shifted ever so slightly and blocked her view.

His own bag practically burst at the seams, packed to the brim with easily more than a dozen loaves of bread. If not for his slight frame, she might have thought him gluttonous; he looked as if he would snap in half if the wind blew too hard.

Perhaps he'd stolen for more than himself. The man nodded, as if she had given voice to her concerns.

His eyes brightened as they held hers. Haizea shifted her weight to dispel how laid bare she felt under his gaze, like he could see right into her Soul.

~I'm Alastair. What's your name?~ he offered.

~Haizea.~

~Haizea. It's nice to meet someone that can sign so fluently. Most people around here only know the basics.~

That didn't surprise her, given the impoverished state of the village. Mount Illiniza ensured that signing was a part of the curriculum for both the mage academy and the school for non-mages.

While Haizea couldn't speak for Mount Niaby with complete certainty, she assumed the same educational policy prevailed in the villages that were better off. While there was always room for improvement, the mountaineers did their best to leave no one behind. They always looked out for their own.

Alastair's gaze roamed over her, first lingering the curls of her hair before slowly absorbing her athletic stature. Haizea flared her nostrils in agitation, but as she observed his expression, it didn't seem invasive, like he was ogling her. A faint pink tint bloomed across his cheeks, replacing the tan undertones of his complexion.

Haizea cleared her throat to break the tension. Then she remembered he couldn't hear it. Without warning, Alastair took her hand and led her through the village.

To her own surprise, she didn't resist him. His physical touch elicited waves of pleasure that thoroughly disarmed her. Alastair had to be a mage—and a powerful one to have such an effect on her. But aside from that, just by looking at him, you couldn't really tell. His hand felt as gentle and soft as he looked.

She remembered the tug on her vitality earlier in the shop, just as she was about to leave. It must have been Alastair who used his magic on her.

As they walked, his long hair tousled in the wind. Alastair had a quick and nimble stride. Aside from the muted clink of coins clashing together with each step he took, his feet hit the ground without a sound.

Definitely a skilled pickpocket, she thought.

Although she wasn't particularly keen on making friends with a thief, her growling stomach was keen to overlook it. If he was going to steal regardless, she might as well see if he could swipe her a few more servings of food.

On the surface, he seemed otherwise harmless, but the way her vitality spiked in his presence made her wonder. She would stay no longer than a day or two so that she could get her bearings and then she'd be back on her way.

Chapter 13

Cacophonous chatter bellowed from the bar as Haizea and Alastair walked past the establishment. Intoxicated patrons spilled outside, holding massive jugs that sloshed and splashed onto the ground with each movement.

~*That's a daily occurrence,*~ Alastair signed.

Haizea didn't want to badmouth his village, even if he did it himself, so she didn't respond.

~*Do you drink?*~ Alastair asked as they rounded past the crowd and neared the entrance.

She remembered the last time she'd been in a bar and the fight that ensued. In the wake of the assassination attempt, the thought of possibly repeating that left her feeling drained.

~*Yes, but not right now,*~ she answered.

He nodded, his eyes lingering on her dirt-smudged pants.

~*You need new clothes,*~ he remarked.

She shrugged. ~*I just need a spot to wash them.*~

~*What are you going to wear while they dry?*~

Haizea sighed, her shoulders slumping slightly. By the look on his face, it didn't take much to imagine what Alastair had in mind to acquire a new outfit. Her gut twisted at the prospect of taking from a village that did not have much to give, but without much money, she didn't have many options, either.

Haizea hung back while Alastair weaved through another cluster of people. If she hadn't been watching him, she'd have never noticed his fingers dipping into the pockets and purses as he passed by.

The man moved as if he was just on a casual stroll, never pausing or slowing. The passersby continued on, blissfully ignorant. He stole from them so smoothly that Haizea suspected that she'd only seen him earlier in the bakery because that's what Alastair wanted to happen.

He'd probably seen her as soon as she crossed the threshold. A new face couldn't be hard to miss here. He'd used his magic on her to get a feel for her and, now that she thought about it, it reminded her of the sensation from when Sovereign Jasver had read her Soul.

Realization dawned on her then: Alastair was a medium, and a very powerful one at that.

A few minutes later, he joined her again and cast her a playful grin. Those faint dimples returned; they would probably be a little deeper if he wasn't so thin and his cheeks filled out more. He motioned for her to follow him, then led her to a plain-looking consignment shop. Alastair nodded for Haizea to take the lead, letting her choose her own attire.

At the moment, she had on the same pair of pants and top that typically she wore under her armor. Since her travels would send her into higher elevation, she opted for clothing that would keep her warm as the temperature plummeted.

She found a pair of fur-lined boots that should keep her toes from freezing while on the long trek. Then a fresh pair of pants and a shirt with a coat to go on top in case she overheated while still in lower elevations.

When Alastair paid the shop attendant with his stolen cash, Haizea remained silent. For whatever reason, the thief wanted to do her a favor.

Haizea would have preferred to bathe before she put on clean clothes, but she frowned at the idea of going into this stranger's home to do it. She'd find a way to wash up later, at the very least in a public washroom. Assuming that the village had any.

Her shoulders slumped again. Going by the current state of things, she doubted they did.

Another thought popped into mind, and she tucked her clothes between her knees, freeing her arms to sign.

~*Do you know where we could get stationery? And a messenger hawk?*~ she asked.

~*Stationary, yes. But a messenger hawk is very expensive.*~

~*Why not just steal the hawk itself then? You seem more than capable of swiping money.*~

His lips quirked slightly. ~*Coins are small enough to fit in my pocket. How the hell am I going to hide a stolen hawk?*~

Alastair had a point, but in the grand scheme of things, Haizea couldn't budge on this. Her nostrils flared as she inhaled in frustration.

She needed to warn her grandfather before she moved on to the next town. The guilt she felt for letting Alastair swipe money from unsuspecting villagers so that she could buy clothes evaporated. If Haizea had to twist a few arms to ensure Grandfather Harzel's safety, so be it.

~*I need to tell my family where I am. They need to know I'm safe,*~ she offered instead. That seemed to get through to him.

~*You're on the run, aren't you?*~ Alastair asked, seeming perplexed.

She didn't respond.

~*You showed up barefoot and disheveled, while talking about going deeper into the mountains. Not a difficult guess to make. You know... if you want... you can stay with my family while you get your bearings. My folks have a big house with lots of people, but there's space for you,~* he continued.

Alastair gave her such a gentle look that Haizea faltered, nearly unraveling and telling him everything right then and there. She stopped short, still reluctant to fully let her guard down.

Instead, she opted for a different angle. Alastair wasn't the only one who was observant.

~You're a medium, aren't you?~ she asked.

Alastair stammered, his arms moving to sign only to pause and start again.

~How?~ he finally managed to get out.

~I'm a healer. I can sense the vitality within a person's body. Mages are always a bit more vibrant.~

When he signed this time, he made smaller movements, like he was trying to whisper.

~No one here knows,~ he said.

~Is it a secret?~

Maybe he was an omen like her. That might be why his magic tugged so forcefully at hers. Though her countenance gave no hint at the paranoia slithering down her spine, Haizea's body tightened.

For all she knew, he could be in line with those who attacked Llyr.

~Not necessarily. I just don't display it openly. It can rub some folks the wrong way.~ he signed.

Just like healers had different levels to their abilities, mediums did as well. The most basic mediums could speak with the Souls of the dead. More advanced mediums could read the Souls of the living. Amongst the most skilled mediums, their magic enabled them to touch Souls far across the various realms.

And for mediums who wielded enough power to be capable of dabbling in corrupted magic, they could raise the dead themselves.

Necromancy. No wonder Alastair kept quiet about his magic. Even if the people at the base tolerated the Cosmic Arts as much as those who lived well within the mountains, even a normal medium mage would make anyone leery. It was a hairsbreadth away from an abomination.

But then again, what Cosmic Art wasn't? Healing gave way to blood magic. Telekinesis morphed into transmutation. Clairvoyance mages could go beyond the happenings of the world around them and delve into the minds of others, hearing their thoughts. Curse magic emerged from enchantments, just as realmdrifting did with astral projecting.

Alastair studied her, appearing to be in deep thought. She shivered as something fluttered deep inside.

~Your Soul is rife with vitality. But it's very...~ he trailed off, trying to find the right words. *~Volatile. Sinister, almost.~*

~If that's the case, why are you clinging to me like a lost puppy?~

~Because oddly enough, you seem equally as gracious.~

Haizea didn't return Alastair's smile, but the usual harshness in her eyes and lips eased ever so slightly. At the very least, she needed his help contacting her grandfather.

For now, she would focus on acquiring a messenger hawk, but Alastair's mediumship could be useful. He seemed hesitant about his magic, but it might be a perfect way to at least try to inconspicuously contact her grandfather. However, she shied away from suggesting it, because while she welcomed Alastair's help, Haizea needed to impress the urgency of the situation on her grandfather. It needed to be her own words.

King Rhys's face, filled with rage as he killed both a child and a man, came rushing back. Haizea shuddered at the memory.

She would not let the same fate befall Grandfather Harzel, but despite the power of blood magic coursing through her, she was still only one person. For whatever reason, Alastair had taken a liking to her.

It would be wise to take advantage of that, because until she could reach the warriors, she needed allies.

Haizea swallowed her trepidations and recounted everything that had transpired. The execution. The trip to Olysseus before the joint excursion to Llyr that ended with the omen attack. She didn't withhold any details. She told Alastair of the duo of omens that took out dozens of well-trained knights in an instant.

She explained how she saved everyone with her blood magic but had inadvertently sacrificed most of the injured knights in the process.

She gazed into the distance as she remembered being chained in the trolley car with Zander and the conversation that followed. How desperately they both wished that things had been different.

His face persisted at the forefront of Haizea's mind when her eyes returned to Alastair's. An emotion bubbled up then. One that caught in her throat and pricked her eyes. She let out a deep sigh before finally telling Alastair how she escaped her planned execution.

Grandfather Harzel was all she had left. Though he neared the end of his time in this realm, she would do everything in her power to ensure he spent his last days at peace. No matter how much she hoped King Rhys would approach the situation with calm and reason, she would be damned to the Demon Realm itself before she risked her grandfather.

Alastair absorbed everything she said in silence. A range of emotions played across his face: shock, fear, concern, but hesitance remained the longest—his lips pursed and his brows knitted together.

He seemed like he was about to sign, and for a brief moment, Haizea thought he might refuse to help her. It was probably the wise thing to do; she had attracted the ire of a king, after all.

To her surprise, Alastair paused, his bright eyes searching hers. His expression softened, filled with compassion. The sight ruffled something inside of her, deep in the pit of her stomach.

Finally, Alastair answered.

~I'll help you.~

Chapter 14

Zander woke up to a throbbing pain in his jaw. He winced as he put a hand up to his cheek. If he could look in the mirror right now, he'd probably see his chin swollen like a bee sting. Or, more accurately, a punch to the face.

Haizea had struck him with the speed of a lightning strike; one moment she had been sitting in front of him with her hands bound, and a split second later, her fist was connecting with his jaw. Far too fast for him to even register her movement, much less react by parrying her attack or halting her with his telekinesis. By the ache radiating through his head, Zander doubted if even his magic could have stopped her.

He took in his surroundings. At some point, Jirina must have realized what happened and moved him closer. He let out a quiet groan as his head protested with each movement he made. With each beat of his heart pumping blood, his head threatened to burst open. Had Haizea been here, she would have put her cool palms on him and soothed the pain by now.

Zander frowned and his throat tightened. He and Haizea had long been partnered in the Royal Guard. Despite his misgivings about the Cosmic Arts and his hurt about her deceit, nothing in his few years of knowing her ever hinted toward her being the evil incarnate that King Rhys clearly thought she was.

Maybe Zander should try to reason with him. King Rhys paced on the opposite end of the trolley, gripping the handle of his sword so hard that it groaned in protest, just a hairsbreadth away from breaking off entirely.

Zander quickly abandoned that course of thought. Best to keep his mouth shut and protect his own hide for now.

"It is well within my power to track the blood mage with my scepter, Your Majesty," Jirina said. Her proposal was an indirect signal that she realized Zander was awake. She'd waited for him.

A visible crack splintered down the handle of the king's sword.

"It's more important that we return home and regroup where it's safest. There's no telling what she'll do. And that's not even accounting for any other omens that may be lurking in the shadows. Just keep tabs on any direct threats on our path for the time being. We'll track her down once we have more numbers."

Zander didn't expect such a measured response, but he did not trust that it would last.

"Are there any preparations to be made upon our arrival?" Jirina asked.

"At the moment, none that concern the two of you." The king's clipped tone brought any further questions to a screeching halt.

Zander desperately wanted to say that Haizea posed no threat to them. He wanted to take King Rhys by his shoulders and shake him until he understood that he was overreacting.

He remembered the family King Rhys ruined not too long ago. Zander had not spoken up then. Zander had said nothing when the king killed a man and one of his daughters and sent the other child to prison. Questioning the king's actions had never even crossed his mind at the time.

Now, the circumstances that led up to the execution filled him with doubt. Could transmutation be equally as vile as it was innocuous, in the same way Haizea's magic had healed the king while extinguishing countless lives in an instant? His own hypocrisy grated at his insides; his concerns only arose now that someone that he knew and cared about was involved. Before, he'd simply gone along with it without a second thought.

Zander peeked out of the window and a dark purple filled the sky as the last of the sunlight slowly disappeared behind the horizon. A few distinguishing landmarks helped him to figure out their current location.

They had already passed through the mountain range and now traversed through the City of Adarlan, which was still at least a day's travel from Ravaryn, but much closer to home than before.

Both he and Jirina watched in a tense silence as King Rhys stomped throughout the trolley. He walked up and down its length with his hand never leaving his sword.

As he passed by, the sound of him grinding his teeth grated at Zander's insides.

Once King Rhys grew tired of pacing, he stood in front of one of the windows and gripped the sill. The vitality within him brimmed at his fingertips, and the metal groaned, on the verge of buckling. When the king finally sat still, he fumed silently for a bit longer before sleep subsequently took him.

Zander strained his ears, listening for the king's light snores before he breathed a sigh of relief. To his surprise, Jirina did as well.

"This whole situation is a mess," he whispered.

Her reply was simple. "True."

"What do you think about it?"

"The king has made up his mind. There's nothing you or I can say that will alter his decision about her execution."

"That's not what I asked."

Jirina quietly searched his face. "I think that we've had an unfortunate turn of events. It's not lost on me that she saved us, so I'm not thrilled about the king's disposition on the matter. But our salvation came at the cost of our comrades' lives. A sacrifice of that magnitude cannot be overlooked.

"In either case, as knights of the elite Royal Guard, we've sworn an oath to protect him and the kingdom. We have a duty to carry out his commands, and I intend to follow them."

"Jirina, you're well on track to become the next leader of the Guard. Surely, you of all people could at least *try* to reason with him," Zander spoke in a hushed hiss.

Jirina quietly contemplated her response. Her scepter glowed as she looked at the king to double-check the depth of his slumber.

"While we were packing our belongings into the trolley, I saw King Rhys speaking to himself while he was alone. He mentioned a name, Mericus, as well as the Cosmic Arts. It's led me to believe that his stance may stem from a long-standing grudge."

His brows rose. Jirina had spied on the king with her magic?

She scowled. "Don't give me that look. It's our duty to look after the king's well-being. Clairvoyance just gives me additional perspective." She shrugged.

"Sure. Whatever you tell yourself. Did your clairvoyance tell you anything more about Mericus?" he pressed.

"No, it did not. I'm not a mind reader. I can only gather insight as things occur in the present time. And I'd need more details than his name alone to track him down with my scepter. If I knew what he looked like or what class he belonged to, that would help me narrow it down, but it's not as efficient as someone I know firsthand because in those cases I can trace them by their vitality. But I have two guesses based on what I know about the king: either Mericus hides himself very well, or he's dead."

Zander sat up straighter, feeling a mixture of horror and intrigue alike. He wanted to know more, but between the two of them, King Rhys wouldn't give as much pushback if Jirina questioned him about his past.

He didn't get his hopes up on that front—for Jirina, her loyalty rested with the Crown. Whatever requests the king made of her, she would fulfill them. If that meant cutting down her former comrade, so be it. It took too much blood, sweat, and tears to be held in high enough regard to serve the Crown so closely. Jirina wouldn't jeopardize her standing for the sake of someone else.

When she put her hand on Zander's shoulder, it surprised him. She gave him a solemn look before glancing over her shoulder.

King Rhys stirred but quickly slipped back into his slumber.

Jirina broke her silence with a soft whisper.

"You should be careful, Zander. And frankly, the same goes for me. Haizea belonged to our troop, and we're the *only* surviving Guard members from the attack. That alone is enough to warrant suspicion. Add to it that her blood magic slipped by undetected by my clairvoyance, and we're lucky to not be in coffins.

"The king's paranoia has already killed one family. Don't let the next one be yours."

Later the next day, the trolley arrived at the Capital. King Rhys no longer paced about, but a taut expression tightened his face, his fury barely contained.

Queen Mireille met them first, with a trio of knights at her side. Zander swallowed against the tightness in his throat. He struggled to wrap his head around the fact that the omens had wiped out nearly half of the Royal Guard—all in the span of a breath.

The queen ran to her husband and wrapped her arms around his neck. For the first time in several days, King Rhys's face melted. He hugged her back just as tightly.

"I'm so relieved you've made it back in one piece," Queen Mireille murmured.

"Me, too. How are you? Where are the children?"

Her worried gaze met his. "I've restricted the children to the palace until further notice. I didn't want to risk it when you said the culprits were omens."

The king stroked her cheek with his thumb.

"It doesn't matter if you sequester yourself to the castle or run away to an underground bunker or flee from the kingdom entirely. One of them was a realmdrifter. Even if you had an army of a hundred knights, if an omen of that type wants you, they'll get you. Let the children roam, but keep them supervised with an escort from the Guard at all times," he said.

The queen's eyes widened in shock. "Bu–"

"Regarding my letter, I presume you contacted Ser Bren. He's begun preparations, correct?"

"Yes, he has, but about the childr—"

"Good," the king cut her off. "There is still much work to be done. Jirina, come with me. We're in a much better position for you to locate the blood mage. Zander, please see to it that the queen remains safe."

And with that, Queen Mireille had been dismissed. She stammered a few moments in disbelief before her husband walked past her, headed toward the castle.

Following the king's command, Zander offered his hand to the queen, casting her an apologetic look. When she knocked it out of the way, he sighed in defeat. Undoubtedly, King Rhys would spend the coming days, if not weeks, sequestered in his wing as he formulated a plan regarding not only Haizea, but any remaining omens responsible for the assassination of Llyr's kings. Zander could only hope that things turned out for the best.

CHAPTER 15

Haizea followed Alastair to a decently sized house. He'd ignored her protests and insisted that she stay with his family. The paint had faded, and the wooden porch creaked under their weight, but aside from that, it appeared structurally sound. A stark contrast from most of the other buildings throughout the village.

Alastair pushed open the front door and immediately met resistance. Dozens of shoes littered the entrance and blocked the door's path. Some were small enough to fit in the palm of Haizea's hand while others dwarfed her own feet. Alastair kicked them out of the way.

Haizea hesitated in the doorway, but he grabbed her hand and gently tugged, coaxing her to follow. She bit the inside of her cheek to distract herself from the resulting jolt; a tingling sensation shot up from where his hand touched hers all the way up to her shoulder.

Haizea only made it two steps before a few children raced past her. One of them stopped in front of Alastair and raised his arms into the air. Alastair bent down and grunted as he picked the little boy up and hoisted him onto his hip.

Alastair's tawny complexion turned to a bright red from the effort. The boy looked like he couldn't have been more than three or four years old, so he was probably a little heavy to be lifting, but not so much that Alastair should have to strain so hard. Again, Haizea noted how much thinner Alastair was compared to the other people she'd seen in his village.

Alastair tickled the little boy with fervor, and his giggles pierced the air, high-pitched and filled with glee. His happiness was infectious and soon, Alastair's own laugh joined him, with the dimples in his cheeks surfacing once more.

Haizea didn't smile, but a tension within eased at the sight. Only after the tickling stopped and the laughter slowed did she hear the boy's stomach rumble.

~Hungry,~ he signed.

He looked up at Alastair with wide eyes and a small frown puckering his lips.

They had the same distinctive features: bright, periwinkle eyes; skin that teetered between a crisp tan and a light brown, with a golden undertone; and a full head of pearl colored hair.

The boy's hair was much shorter than Alastair's, yet his loose curls tousled around like a curtain just the same. Haizea idly wondered if Alastair's hair would curl similarly if it weren't weighed down by its length.

Alastair set the boy down on his feet and reached for his bag of bread. He handed him a loaf, and the boy scurried off for a few steps before stopping to turn around.

~Thank you,~ he signed.

As he sprinted away, another one of Alastair's family members approached. She was older than the kids but definitely a few years younger than Haizea and Alastair, probably in her late teens or early twenties.

~That was my little cousin, Amiri. This is also my cousin, Alina,~ Alastair signed and introduced the both of them.

~Are you planning on hanging around for once?~ Alina asked, grabbing a loaf of bread and taking a healthy bite.

~I'm going to get Haizea set up in my old room. It's still empty, right?~

~Of course it's empty. Your mom won't let anyone touch it.~ Alina paused briefly, her eyes narrowing on Alastair. *~Wait a minute. You——~*

"I thought I recognized that laugh," a woman emerged from one of the adjacent hallways, breaking Haizea's attention away from Alina.

Unlike Alastair and everyone else Haizea had seen so far, this woman had dark, densely coiled hair. Her gray eyes loomed like storm clouds, but she and Alastair shared the same open face and kind smile.

The magical pressure in the room increased ever so slightly with the woman's presence. She must have been a mage, and given her familial link with Alastair, she was most likely a medium.

To Haizea's relief, her blood magic remained silent. This woman's vitality didn't have the same intensity as Alastair's; in other words, it was normal. When the woman wrapped him in a tight hug, her head only came up to his chest.

Alina gave Haizea a small smile and wave before walking away.

~Mom, this is Haizea. Haizea, this is my mother, Nyra. Haizea is on her way back home to Illiniza. She needs a place to stop and rest.~

~She's a healing mage, too,~ Alastair added. He glanced at Haizea and raked his fingers through his hair. A faint pink tint spread across his cheeks.

Nyra studied Alastair before turning to Haizea.

"How long do you need?" Nyra asked. She spoke and signed simultaneously.

"I really don't want to take up any spare space you might have, but Alastair insisted on bringing me here," Haizea said quickly, while also signing. Nyra let out a soft chuckle.

"That sounds like my son. Illiniza is a long way from here. You should stop and rest. You look strong, but you'll need it," Nyra said.

"Really, I just need a place to wash up."

Nyra narrowed her eyes at Haizea in a way that made her feel like she was a young girl again, and she'd done something to thoroughly annoy her mother.

"I could use a day or two," Haizea admitted.

~I'm going to give her my old room,~ Alastair said, and Nyra's brows rose high.

~Nobody's touched it since you left. I thought it would be easier... for whenever you're ready to come back home.~

Alastair's throat bobbed up and down as he swallowed. His mother reached for him, holding his hand in hers.

~I'll show you where everything is,~ he signed after a few moments.

Alastair led Haizea deeper into the house and introduced her to everyone they bumped into along the way.

Most of his family was deaf with a golden complexion and pearl-colored hair, just like him. There were far too many for her to remember all of their names at once.

Haizea gathered that Alastair lived on his own, away from all the ruckus in the overcrowded home. It was much different from growing up in Windhaven with just herself and her parents. Fortunately, she didn't mind the commotion; two years of working in the Royal Guard had forced her to adapt to nonstop activity.

When Alastair opened the door to his old room, it looked untouched, just as his mother promised it was.

A portrait sat atop the dresser, one of the few she'd seen displayed in the house. It displayed a young man, probably in his early twenties. He had a full head of curly hair and rich brown skin. The fabric of his clothes looked stretched and faded, but he was otherwise well put together.

Haizea arched her brow in curiosity. She didn't think he was related to Alastair, as his family had a very strong resemblance to one another and the man in the picture looked nothing like them. But perhaps he was someone important to Alastair if he displayed a portrait of him in his old bedroom.

Alastair walked over and picked it up. He gingerly rubbed his thumb over the glass covering. His eyes turned shiny, and he blinked rapidly a few times.

Haizea inched closer to him but stopped short, fearing she might be intruding.

Alastair set the portrait back down and turned to her.

~Make yourself at home. I'll be back tomorrow with the messenger hawk you need.~

~Thank you, Alastair. It's very kind of you to do this for me.~

Alastair smiled softly at her, lingering in the doorway for a moment before making his exit. Haizea crawled into the bed for some much-needed shuteye.

As promised, by the next morning, Alastair had indeed purchased a messenger hawk for Haizea. Getting a message to her grandfather was of utmost importance. It was a matter of *when*, not *if*, he would eventually end up the object of King Rhys's ire.

Grandfather Harzel had the advantage of blood magic, but he still needed to be warned. Even with this in mind, Haizea frowned as she looked upon the hawk.

With her scepter, Jirina had the ability to watch her every movement, even from all the way in Arcelia. Based on her time guarding the Royal family, signing didn't seem to be part of Arcelia's curriculum. At least, Haizea didn't know either the prince or princess to sign whenever she passed by during their lessons.

Jirina most likely would not understand her conversations with Alastair. But if she wrote a letter now and Jirina happened to be watching, there was nothing to stop her from tracking the animal all the way back to Von Stein.

Grandfather Harzel wouldn't have enough lead time in that scenario.

~Something wrong?~ Alastair asked, brow furrowing.

When Haizea expressed her concerns to him, Alastair gave her a thoughtful look.

~Can it wait until nighttime? I have an idea to get around that.~

Haizea nodded. As she waited for the hours to tick by, she made judicious use of her time and prepared for the trek through the mountains. Haizea visited shops, gathering additional supplies for travel: packs of dried food, matches, a satchel.

She approached the counter to wait her turn in line and a small boy ran circles around her. His mother trailed a few paces behind, her forehead slick with sweat, a defeated look on her face to match.

Eventually, the boy zoomed out the door, right into the path of someone pushing a heavy cart. Even if they'd seen him, there wouldn't have been enough time to stop.

The cart rammed into the boy, sending him flying several feet before he hit the ground with a thunderous boom. A cloud of dirt erupted into the air. Haizea flinched at the sound of shattering ceramics, the splintering of heavy wood, and the piercing scream that followed.

His mother ran over to him. "I told you about running around like that, didn't I?" she chastised, but her voice quivered with panic.

The boy wailed as tears streamed down his cheeks and blood oozed down his forehead, which already had a visible knot forming. Large abrasions appeared on both of his knees and more blood covered the palms of his hands. He held one of his hands at an odd angle, like he'd broken a bone in the fall.

The woman cupped his face in her hands and tore off a piece of his shirt as she dabbed at his wounds. Blood quickly soaked through it.

The woman stood up when she noticed Haizea watching them. She pulled her son behind her and inched backward. Haizea approached slowly and made an effort to soften her expression.

"I'm a healing mage. If it's alright with you, I can mend your son's wounds," she said.

The woman's brows rose in surprise before she brought her son in front of her. Haizea crouched down to his level, and the boy whimpered as she pressed her hands against his forehead where the gash bled most profusely.

She ignored the call of her blood magic roiling in the back of her mind and focused on moving and weaving the vitality within him, rather than taking it for herself. Haizea held his tiny palms in hers and shifted the vitality in his body until the open cut on his hands had melded shut and the bones in his wrists wove back together.

When she followed by doing the same thing for his knees, the little boy had calmed considerably. He reached up and caught the chain of her pendant, which was poking out from her shirt collar. Before he could yank it, she gently unwrapped his fingers and went back to healing.

Haizea finished and her lips curved upward, flashing the boy and his mother her rare smile. It altered her aura entirely, morphing her from uninviting and austere to warm and welcoming.

The tension in the woman's body evaporated as she visibly relaxed in front of her. She leaned down and whispered in her son's ear.

"Thank you," he said, and his damp cheeks glistened as he beamed back at Haizea.

"You're welcome."

"This village hasn't had a healer in years. The last one that lived here moved away. Said life was more prosperous deeper in the mountains and left us behind. Thank you, again," the woman said, before taking her leave.

Haizea turned back to the shop owner's counter to see them staring at her.

"Consider it on the house," they said with a grin.

She gave them a grateful nod before making her exit. This meant she had more money to work with as she prepared for her trip. As Haizea made her way from shop to shop, she couldn't help but notice the destitute state of the village.

Many shop owners had a persistent cough. In addition to that, just about every person she'd encountered so far appeared generally unwell: pallor skin, sunken cheeks, and circles under their eyes. Alastair's thinness especially concerned her. While the other villagers looked underweight, he seemed emaciated by comparison—even despite his thievery.

Haizea meandered along the walkway, long overtaken by grass and weeds. Someone eventually tapped on her shoulder, and she turned around to see the woman and her toddler again, this time with an older gentleman in tow behind them.

"This is my father. He's been sick for so long, and you healed my son so quickly... I'd regret it if I didn't at least ask if you could heal him, too," the woman said, appearing abashed.

Haizea paused to take in the family in front of her. She may no longer be a knight, but her sense of duty had not wavered. Healers were incredibly rare. Haizea couldn't fix all their problems, but this would help ease some of their pain.

At the very least, it wouldn't hurt to help them until she put her letter to Grandfather Harzel securely in the sky.

While some shops were located within wooden buildings, many of them were nothing more than oversized tents, with tables and stands on the interior containing merchandise.

Haizea found an empty spot next to a tent and made space for healing the older gentleman. She approached this the same way she did the young boy and sensed the vitality coursing through him with her base magic. The vitality was scarce in his lungs, and the little that remained had warped considerably.

She instructed him to remove his shirt and put her bare hands on his back. Her palms cooled his warm skin as she guided strong vitality from other areas of his body into the depleted section. Afterward, she prescribed him a simple potion made from readily available plants within the village. It wasn't a miracle cure, but it would help promote the regeneration of new vitality within his body.

"Drink this once a day for the next two weeks. It should clear up the rest of that cough you have. If you skip out on the potion, it'll come right back," she warned.

When he thanked her, tears welled in his eyes.

Word spread quickly after that. By the evening, she had a waitlist of villagers begging to be seen. At some point, Alastair had caught wind, and she convinced him to get a proper tent and make runs for her, gathering components of various potions she needed to prescribe.

Well, 'gather' was a generous word for it. He most definitely stole anything he came back with. If Haizea hadn't already seen him pick-pocket so flawlessly, she'd be certain that people watched him do it and simply turned a blind eye to it.

Although it would aid her journey, Haizea didn't feel right charging people who were barely scraping by to begin with. Fortunately, a few of the villagers kindly left small tips behind and a few rations of food, all of which would be helpful for traveling up the mountain. Naturally, she gave half to Alastair.

When he refused, she insisted. *~When's the last time you had a full meal?~*

As he stared off into space in thought, his stomach grumbled loud enough for Haizea to hear. She gave him a stern look.

~Exactly. So, eat. Now.~

Alastair took the portion she'd offered.

~So bossy,~ he signed, flashing a smile at her.

Unsurprisingly, he inhaled the food in front of him. Haizea was still chewing when he tapped on her leg to get her attention.

~What are you going to do once you contact your grandfather?~

Although she didn't need to use her mouth to communicate with him, she still instinctively swallowed before answering.

~I'll stay a few more days for the people that could benefit from additional healing sessions. Use the time to collect more supplies.~

~Seemed like you were in a rush when you first got here.~

~I'll feel more comfortable once my letter is in the sky. But I can tell your people need help.~

~And your grandfather doesn't?~

~He does, but not in the same way. He's stubborn and not the type to accept help so readily. A little extra time here won't hurt anything. He'll take a few days to get his ducks in a row, and then he'll be on his way. Knowing him, he'll leave a trap or two behind, as well.~

Haizea almost chuckled but sobered instantly. Unlike her, Harzel had no qualms about killing bystanders. A chill raced down her spine.

How many of his neighbors would be caught in the crossfire once the Arcelian knights found his residence? She'd decided against retrieving him from Arcelia herself precisely because she wanted to avoid that exact predicament.

Haizea huffed through her nostrils. If people were going to die regardless, should she change course and go back to Arcelia now? She was still close enough to the border to turn around... As she weighed the stakes, the memory of the attack in Llyr resurfaced, and she relived how she'd inadvertently drained the injured knights around her to fuel her power.

If she had to fight off a platoon of King Rhys's forces, she would have no choice but to unleash her blood magic. What if she succumbed to the high again? What if the tight leash of her control snapped? How many bystanders would perish then?

Grandfather Harzel's scheming paled in comparison to the carnage she could leave in her wake. Although the strength of his blood magic had diminished since their training accident, for any non-omens, Grandfather Harzel was still a force to be reckoned with. That meant that if she went back, the inhabitants would be caught between not one, but two blood mages.

While Haizea had no reservations about using violence to protect herself, she could not justify such an astronomical level of collateral damage. Only if it could not be avoided would she allow a bloodbath of that degree to occur by her hand. The situation did not call for such measures—at least, not yet.

Alastair tapped her again, pulling her out of her thoughts and back into the conversation.

~*What about your old friends?*~ he asked.

~*They'll do as their king commands,*~ she signed, bitterly thinking of her last conversation with Zander and the subsequent events that followed.

Alastair shuddered as her anger spiked. He didn't prod her any further. When the sun began to set, he stood up and offered his hand. Haizea took it, and he helped her to her feet. It was more of a kind gesture on his part than anything useful; she had at least thirty pounds on him, nearly all of it muscle.

~I have a spot I like to hide out at when I have a close call during my... excursions. There's someone there I think may be able to help you.~

Haizea nodded and followed Alastair. They meandered past the outskirts of the village before they reached his hiding place: a sequestered grassy area, concealed between a gap in a cluster of trees. The setting sun painted the horizon in an idyllic mix of warm oranges and yellows.

The dense foliage camouflaged a small wooden stool by Alastair's feet. He bent down and offered it to Haizea, but she declined. He plopped down instead and let out a long sigh as he gazed up at the sky. The dwindling sun rays hit his face, making his light eyes glint.

~How did you find this place?~ she signed, but Alastair didn't respond.

His blue-lavender eyes had glazed over, no longer looking at the sky. Instead, it was as if his mind had teleported somewhere else, maybe outside of this realm altogether.

Haizea allowed her own magic to rise to the surface. As a Spiritual mage, his vitality had a wispy quality about it, but it also contained a vibrancy that burst at the seams. It reminded Haizea of a storm cloud that you could never touch, but carried an overbearing presence before unleashing a torrential downpour.

Alastair's vitality swelled around her, and he began signing unintelligibly. He'd start a hand movement only to abruptly cut off and move onto another. This went on for several minutes before the glaze in his eyes faded, and he finally returned. He gave her a wry smile.

~Did you call a Soul?~ she asked.

~I knew this Soul when they were alive. They keep watch over this area since it used to be their spot. They call to me whenever I visit.~

~Is it always like that when the dead speak to you?~

He shrugged.

~Sometimes they come in dreams. It feels like a real conversation, but when I wake up, the vision evaporates, and so does my certainty of the memory. This is the only Soul that reaches out to me whenever I come to this particular area.~

Haizea looked around. She could sense Alastair's vitality, but if the Soul was truly present, it existed beyond her reach as a Physical mage.

~Do you mind if I take a drop of your blood?~ she asked Alastair.

Alastair frowned. It didn't take much for Haizea to imagine the reason for his hesitance. He'd listened to her story about how she cut down other omens, but to willingly let her use that same power on himself probably—rightfully—gave him pause.

~How much do you know about the Cosmic Arts?~ she asked, and Alastair stiffened.

Haizea interpreted it as a sign that he did not know.

She continued, *~Blood magic runs in my family. It's good to have a healthy respect for the Cosmic Arts. But you don't need to be afraid of them.~*

Alastair dipped his chin in a slight nod but otherwise did not respond.

~Cosmic magic has its uses. It extends vitality beyond the boundaries set by nature. It exploits the various qualities of vitality that different mage classes and subtypes have access to. It also opens your eyes to the vitality in the world around you, even making the Souls you speak with visible.~

~But warping and corrupting vitality in such a manner comes at a price. The decision to practice the Cosmic Arts is not one to be taken lightly. It brings on an addictive euphoria, whose call is impossible to resist. As your body replenishes the vitality you use—in the same way your body creates more blood—this new, normal vitality competes with the old, corrupted vitality and loses. The end result is magical wasting, which is unequivocally fatal. The only way to prevent the disease is to continually fortify your body

with the corrupted vitality that comes with Cosmic magic. So long as the balance within tips toward the corruption, magical wasting will never set in.~

~Magical... wasting?~ Alastair asked, expression growing troubled.

~Yes. If you take up the Cosmic Arts and change your mind, the imbalance within your body will slowly kill you. I use animal blood works to stave it off with my blood magic, and I had a trap set up outside of my home that was just the right size for rats. But after that assassination attempt, I feel... well, let's just say I think it'll be a while before I absolutely need to use my blood magic again.~

Alastair stared off into the distance, deep in thought. His already thin cheeks looked particularly gaunt at that moment.

~So Cosmic magic for healers manifests as blood magic because healing naturally focuses on manipulating the vitality within the body. And as a medium, my magic would extend or corrupt the vitality that lets me communicate with Souls. Which would be raising the dead,~ Alastair stated. Haizea nodded.

Alastair breathed out a long exhale, and silence fell between them. Haizea waited and let him take the time to digest what she'd told him.

~You need my blood to see the Soul, correct? Use my hand,~ Alastair finally signed.

Haizea unsheathed her blade and gave him a small prick on the tip of his finger. A few drops of blood emerged. She'd learned her lesson from her ordeal with Grandfather and had it reinforced with the attack in Llyr; even with the control that came with experience.

If she didn't want to kill a person, then the opening needed to be miniscule and act as a bottleneck to resist the tug of her power.

The vitality in Alastair's blood diffused across her skin and into her vessels. Haizea's vitality wrapped around it like a cocoon, giving her access to his medium magic. When her brown eyes melted into a bright crimson, Alastair gave a startled yelp.

~Your eyes may do something similar should you take up necromancy,~ she signed.

Within a sea of red, the Soul sparkled like a clear diamond ball as it entered her visible perception. The stark contrast made it easy to identify, but without Cosmic magic, a normal mage's eyes would be closed to the vitality, confining them to merely feeling the Soul's presence in the general vicinity. That's how it should have been for Alastair, but Haizea found herself wondering about that.

~Do you see anything?~ she inquired, trying to keep her face as innocuous as possible. It took quite the effort, given the glacial nature of her typical resting expression.

Her efforts probably did more harm than good given on the way Alastair intently studied her face before shaking his head.

~This is my friend, Haizea, and she needs help. She needs to get a message to her grandfather, but there's a clairvoyance mage watching her,~ he told the Soul.

Although Alastair signed, Haizea could tell he did not need to. She felt the Soul's understanding directly, without it ever uttering a response. It turned its attention to her.

"You are an omen. You can see the vitality," it stated.

"Yes."

Again, they understood one another through feelings and intent. The language of the Soul was not limited to the human tongue.

The Soul briefly turned to Alastair, and a swell of affection and longing passed between them. Haizea wondered who the Soul had been to Alastair prior to its death.

"And your grandfather, he is the same?"

"Yes."

"Good. I will use vitality to write your message for you. Only eyes that have been opened may read it."

The Soul branded her message to the letter paper with its vitality. As an omen, Haizea could see the entire process, but Jirina did not possess the same ability to see either the Soul or her message.

A wave of reluctant optimism washed through Haizea when the Soul flew away. Her letter should make it to Von Stein undetected. She silently thanked the Soul.

~Do you know why it chooses to stay here?~ Haizea asked as she and Alastair walked away from the meadow.

He paused for a few beats before answering.

~They're waiting for their family to join them.~

For all beings with a Soul, they went to the Soul Realm as their final resting place. Souls that lingered in their home realm usually remained because they desired resolution for a conflict that occurred during their life. But loneliness was reason enough as well.

Alastair wore a troubled expression as they walked. Maybe seeing her blood magic unnerved him. He had nothing to worry about, though; the power in Alastair's magic pulsed with each step they took.

Based on what she'd observed so far, he'd never been properly trained at a mage academy, much less in the Cosmic Arts. And yet, Alastair's vitality surpassed anything she'd ever encountered before, even having grown up in the mountains, where the dense concentration of vitality spawned the most powerful mages in the realm.

Haizea rubbed at her pendant. She couldn't shake the tightness in her chest. She and Grandfather Harzel had never been apart before.

For as much as she hated that he'd followed her to Arcelia, she always found comfort that he'd always been within arm's reach. Now that very decision had put him in harm's way. Haizea blew out a long stream of air to keep herself calm and tried to find solace in the fact that, for now, she'd done the best she could for him with the resources she had.

Chapter 16

The *trivialis* stood behind Kallistê, her astral projected Soul intertwined with the Beast's. It bared its saber teeth, which spanned easily as long as she was tall, dwarfing her in size.

The onlookers before her leaned back, their eyes wide with terror at her display of power. In reality, she barely held control over the Beast, but they didn't need to know that. Should she lose control, the city and its inhabitants would be trampled into dust. She'd rather that not happen—at least, not unnecessarily. However, if the nobles refused her demands, then she would make good on her earlier threats.

Upon Kallistê's request, the nobles of Llyr had called an assembly with Zemira's commoners. They met inside the cathedral, as it was the only building able to hold the number of people expected to attend. With its high ceilings that yawned for the skies, it was also the only building that the *trivialis* could fit in.

She took a seat at the front of the room, gingerly crossing her legs and placing her hands on her lap. People began filing it, questions floating to and fro as they took in the surreal scene before them.

Beasts only existed as myth and legend for most people in the Human Realm. The same could be said for the Titans, Angels, and even the Demons—believed to have restored magic to the realm after millennia lost. The sight of a Beast in the flesh elicited dropped jaws and innumerable gasps, and quite a few artists in the crowd pulled out their sketch pads and began drawing this strange woman and the Beast beside her.

It quickly became evident that the masses were not going to settle down by themselves, so Kallistê waved at the nobles to get them under control. Several moments ticked by before a silence fell throughout the cathedral.

Kallistê rose to her feet and addressed them properly. As she smoothed down the front of her gown, a low, guttural growl rumbled from the *trivialis*. Every eye in the room shifted nervously between her and the great Beast.

"I'm sure many of you are wondering who I am and why you've all been called here today. I'm also certain that those of you that travel in high circles have heard rumors about my presence already. I'm here to set the record straight," she announced.

She fluffed her dark blue hair, and the bracelets on her wrists made soft chimes as she did so. Her eyes settled on the many faces in the crowd, absorbing the wide variety of skin shades, eyes that ranged from warm browns to sparkling amethysts to vibrant topazes, hair textures of all types from straight to coils, from long to short, from thick to thin.

"I want my reign to begin with honesty. So, the first matter of concern that must be addressed is your former kings. I am the one responsible for their deaths," she said evenly.

Humorously, the crowd did not share her calmness. When shouts and cries erupted in the cathedral, Kallistê relinquished just a modicum of the hold she had on the *trivialis*, and its roar erupted through the building.

Kallistê's inner ears vibrated from the sound. The walls shook, and the glass chandelier that swung from the ceiling shattered, shards raining to the ground. Every person stopped in their tracks, and the room fell silent. She cleared her throat and stood straighter, looking down her nose at them.

"I deposed your kings, and I'll be taking their place on the throne. You're free to pry it from my grasp, but you'll have to get through the *trivialis* behind me first. I'm sure if you all work together you could accomplish such a feat. But by the time you do, I'll have brought at least a dozen more from the Beast Realm."

"Murderous witch!" someone shouted in the crowd.

This time, Kallistê did not hold back her laughter. A beat of stunned silence followed. Then, the people burst into another fit of outrage.

She dabbed the tears from her eyes with a handkerchief before snapping her fingers at the nobles, signaling for them to bring things back under control. It took several moments before the noise died down enough for her words to be audible again.

"If the kings could die so easily, were they really fit to rule? I am but one person, and yet your kings were two. I slipped past every knight and every defense they had in place. I killed them with such ease it almost filled me with the same guilt one should feel when stealing candy from a child.

"You all decry their fate, but it was their own weakness that led to their demise."

"You are no person. You are an omen. Your magic has been tainted by the Sins of the Demons!" another voice roared.

Kallistê realmdrifted the short distance from where she stood to the dissenter's location. She materialized behind the woman and curled her fingers over her shoulders as she whispered in her ear.

"Tell me, you are a mage, no?" Kallistê drawled, although she knew the answer already.

The woman nodded, her head bobbing up and down nervously.

"The Demons are the ones who brought magic back to our realm. Anyone who can wield the vitality, Cosmic Arts or not, has been touched by them. Just because you refuse to accept the truth does not put me beneath you."

The woman froze as Kallistê delved into her Soul, weaving it with her own. Kallistê strained under the added weight of balancing a human Soul with the *trivialis*, but she managed.

"Do you know why the Demons chose to return magic to our realm?" Kallistê asked, her voice loud enough for all to hear. The woman said nothing, so Kallistê gripped onto her shoulder, digging her fingers until she drew blood.

"No," the woman sputtered.

"That is no way to address your queen."

"No, Your Majesty," she said, earning a smile from Kallistê.

"No one gives up that much power out of the kindness of their hearts. Look at the feats human magic can accomplish. There is not enough generosity in the seven realms that could prompt such an act of benevolence, unless they had something to gain from it.

"And you know what I think? If it was the *Demons* who returned our power, then it was the *Angels* who stole it to begin with."

Kallistê released the woman and floated to the front of the room.

"You all spurn Cosmic magic, but no one knows if it's the result of their meddling or if this is how humanity's magic has always been. I believe it's the latter, though there's never been a mage in who could turn back the wheels of time to confirm it. Anyone care to guess why?"

She sat back down in her seat and willed the *trivialis* to bow its head to her level. The crowd remained silent, so she kept going.

"Every realm in existence is connected by the Cosmic Realm. We are all birthed from its power and in turn, we add to its obscurity. One cannot exist without the other," Kallistê said and locked eyes with the woman again. "It matters not how you obtain power, but what you do with it once it's in your hands. There are seven known realms, and most of mankind will never see anything beyond this one in their lifetime.

"For too long now, the continent has been too afraid to accept that the natural order of things is chaos. The Cosmic Arts dismantles the constraints on our magic, breaking barriers that should not exist in the first place.

"And as queen of this realm, I will guide us into a new era. One where, through Cosmic magic, we will reach for the skies and surpass its boundaries. This leaves you all with a choice: either you follow me into the new world or find yourselves destroyed in the old one."

"Who are you?" another voice in the crowd shouted.

"My name is Kallistê. Newly exalted Queen of Llyr. Born and raised in the Three Corners, but I consider Kestramore my home."

The mention of Kestramore sent a jolt to the crowd, many of their faces blanching in fear, while others twisted their expressions into fury.

Despite their isolation from the continent, it was no secret that the island of Kestramore was a breeding ground for omens. They embraced the Cosmic Arts primarily to act as a deterrent to the continent from dabbling in expansionist or colonizing expeditions.

Kallistê knew her ideals would be a source of contention for the people of Llyr.

Some of them seemed intrigued by her words, but many of them looked upon her with disdain, undoubtedly plotting to unseat her.

But how would they defeat an omen without learning corrupted magic themselves? How many of them would travel down that path, while the others insisted that they could resist through purer means? They would splinter and tear themselves apart while trying to take her down.

She smirked, amused at the prospects of rebellion.

"Any more questions?" she asked, but the people gawked at her, stupefied.

She waved her hand for the nobles and Guard to evacuate the cathedral. Some of them would come for her head. And when they did, she would make an example out of them for all to see.

The islanders of Kestramore lived peacefully in their isolation, openly embracing what the continent considered as unorthodox and taboo. They were self-sustaining, though far from wealthy.

Although she had grown bored of her newfound home, Kallistê had love for the people who had taken her in and trained her in the ways of the Cosmic Arts, and she had every intention of leveraging her new position in Kestramore's favor. Not to mention, with the deaths of her allies who'd traveled with her, it left her very much alone.

Even though the gift of realmdrifting would make assassinating Kallistê difficult, she was exposed in a foreign nation with zero allies.

Her first order of business was to write a letter home—abiding by Kestramore's customs of submitting a written request for an audience with their leaders. Kestramore did not have a monarchy like the continent did, but instead had an appointed leader called a premier.

The premier held significant power, but their position required the cooperation of elected dignitaries, who acted as the voice of the people. Years ago, Kallistê's enthusiasm for learning the Cosmic Arts had caught Premier Eryx's attention, and she introduced Kallistê to the mentor who taught her realmdrifting.

Given their camaraderie, the premier would certainly lend Kallistê a listening ear, but to get any kind of official backing from

Kestramore's government, Kallistê would need to convince a majority of dignitaries as well.

Based on her past encounters with them, the dignitaries were much too risk averse to appreciate her vision. They would shy away from stoking the flames of war, even though victory and greatness awaited them on the other side. She penned the details of her recent excursions, choosing her words carefully in hopes of convincing them to provide aid.

Kallistê warned of the possibility that at least some of the inhabitants of Llyr would cross the ocean in pursuit of vengeance. However, they would be in a rude awakening. If they ever arrived, that is. Any seer worth their salt would hear the hostile thoughts of those approaching miles before they reached Kestramore's shores.

A mage wielding curse magic could make them jump overboard, drowning themselves in the ocean.

Now that one of their own kind sat on the throne, she had more confidence that they would be willing to offer a listening ear. Kallistê chose an angle that the dignitaries might be more open to endorsing.

The continent utilized technology the island did not have. Specifically, the newly developed steam power that fueled Llyr's cities. Kestramore's isolationist policies meant the absence of knowledge exchange which put them decades behind, but their people never went without. The island's rich source of minerals allowed for lush plant growth.

Kestramore grew more food than it could ever use, overflowing their storage reserves year after year. The climate of the island offered a wider variety of crops than the continent could ever hope to cultivate.

Kallistê proposed a trade relationship to officially establish the two nations as allies: Kestramore's crops for Llyr's technology. She knew that Premier Eryx would see the hidden opportunity within the message. Kallistê still had every intention of wiping out the remainder of the kingdoms' rulers, and Premier Eryx particularly loathed Arcelia most of all.

Helping Kallistê meant getting her long-lasting revenge, a chance she would never pass up. When Kallistê sent the hawk on its way, she expected that she would have to make a second appeal, perhaps even a third.

Roughly two weeks later, she received a response.

Kestramore would send a diplomat to discuss her proposal further in person. She couldn't help the grin of defiance and pride that spread across her face. Plan A had come to a ruinous end, but Plan B was charging full steam ahead.

CHAPTER 17

Alastair watched as Haizea arranged her supplies for the day on the table. She ended up staying a little longer than she originally told him she would, and they had quickly fallen into a routine since then.

~I'm planning on leaving soon. Either tonight or tomorrow. There are a few people I promised another session with. I'm going to try to fit them in today so that I can get going,~ she signed.

Alastair frowned as he handed Haizea one of the many plants she used to make potions with. His disappointment didn't necessarily surprise him, but the intensity of the feeling caught him off guard.

~Why not leave tomorrow? I can make you a home-cooked meal to send you on your way,~ he offered.

~Alastair, you don't have to do that.~

~There's plenty of money to buy what we need. Plus, my folks would appreciate it if you let them see you off properly before you go.~

He chose his words meticulously. Haizea had set up a hammock in his meadow, opting to sleep there rather than Alastair's old room. She stored the supplies she'd gathered at the house, but aside from that, she avoided spending time there.

They always set aside a plate for her, and although Haizea wouldn't let it go to waste, she would use some of the money she made to reimburse them the next day. His family didn't see her as a burden, especially not after her doing so much for their village.

And he didn't either. Besides, Alastair loved cooking—when he had enough food to do so, at least.

~Okay. A home-cooked meal before hitting the road sounds really nice. Thank you, Alastair.~

Haizea's piercing gaze softened, and her eyes became light and sweet, luring him in. She didn't smile at him—she never did—but this was the closest she had gotten, and it took him longer than it should have to realize he was standing there with his mouth slightly ajar.

He composed himself and tried to think of something to say, but his arms and hands wouldn't move, words unable to form. She turned away from him to continue setting up her stand. A few moments passed before he had the presence of mind to get back to helping her.

Once they finished getting their supplies in order, he made his way to the marketplace.

With money in his pocket that for once *wasn't* obtained through ill-gotten means, one would have thought that Alastair would take his time as he shopped, but he couldn't kick his thief instincts so easily.

Other villagers perceived his deafness as a vulnerability, which often meant that whenever he wasn't targeting someone else, another person was targeting him.

In his peripheral vision, Alastair caught a man watching him. He held some sort of flier in his hands, but every few moments, he glanced around the shop. When their eyes met, he glared at Alastair.

Alastair made a wide loop, hastily putting more distance between them.

He continued along the crumbling walkway to the butcher shop. The merchants tended to be more fluent in signing than everyday villagers because they had the incentive of making a profit. The rest of the villagers didn't know much besides the basics; not quite conversational, but enough that Alastair could get what he needed to across, so long as he slowed down and gave them time to think.

Most people were too preoccupied with trying to put food on their tables for proper mountaineer education. And given Goldenleaf's small size, most of the deaf community outside of his kin were older folks.

Alastair was waiting for the butcher to cut his order of meat when an icy chill raced down his spine. The sensation clawed at his insides, too intense to ignore. Like someone was watching him. Someone, or maybe *something*, wanted his attention.

He double checked the change purse in his pocket—still there. Alastair looked around. He didn't see the man from earlier, but his gut tightened, nonetheless.

He surveyed the room again before locking onto a sheet of paper hung on the wall by the door. He frowned and moved closer to it, and a cool breeze prickled over him as he did so.

A portrait of Haizea greeted him, unmistakable and disturbingly clear. It depicted her from the shoulder up. She wore armor and her voluminous hair was in its signature style: neatly woven braids that fed into a thick ponytail.

The words 'WANTED ALIVE' in all capital letters blared at him above her image. A bounty.

Alastair nearly fell down in the middle of the butcher shop when he read the amount. His breathing hitched, and he had to catch himself by placing his hand on the wall. His periwinkle eyes widened in disbelief.

One million dollars.

The money would be paid in the person's native currency by King Rhys of Arcelia.

The average person in the village was lucky to bring in a thousand dollars a month. A million dollars would be life-altering.

There was no way there wouldn't be bloodshed as word of this spread. Even the first person to capture her wouldn't be safe; people would crawl over themselves as they stabbed one another in the back to get to her.

His mind raced a mile a minute as he imagined how different things would be for him and the rest of his family with the bounty.

Only a fool would come back to the village after receiving it. He'd leave altogether and buy a house no closer than on the opposite side of the mountain. Maybe he'd go as far south as Mount Cortara, clear on the opposite side of the range, where no one would recognize his face.

Alastair began calculating and strategizing like Haizea was a sack of coins in an unsuspecting person's pocket. He had unrestricted access to her, unlike the rest of the villagers.

Anyone else would have to make up an excuse about needing to be treated, but she would easily see through that with her healing magic. All Alastair would have to do is knock her out and keep her that way as he transported her back to Arcelia.

Of course, as soon as the plan had formulated in his mind, it began to crumble. According to Haizea, King Rhys had tried that himself and she'd woken up and escaped.

If she'd wanted to kill her former comrades, she would have. Haizea had simply let them be. She was more preoccupied with her grandfather's safety, and even the wellbeing of the villagers, than her own.

She could have left a while ago, and probably *should* have, but she was still here.

Alastair internally kicked himself at how quickly he'd been willing to turn on her. They'd only known each other for a short time, but

Haizea had been nothing but kind to him. He hadn't missed a meal since she'd been here.

Even if he could figure out a way to turn her in, would he really go through with it?

His eyes flickered back down at the price. A *million* dollars.

It took great effort for him to divert his attention away from that amount. Alastair altered his course of thought as he took in the rest of the poster. Smaller print divulged information that Haizea was a blood mage.

He'd missed it the first time. That was likely a feature and not a flaw. Anyone with even a crumb of knowledge about the Cosmic Arts would know the dangers of going against an omen, so telling people may have an undesirable effect.

But the king probably didn't want people going in unaware and unprepared either. So the smaller print was likely a compromise between having informed bounty hunters and not immediately scaring people off.

If people saw a million dollars before they read anything else, they'd be more likely to take the risk, even after realizing what they were up against.

It had worked on Alastair. Surely, the rest of the village didn't have the self-control he had to think this through. And why would they, when most of them had no idea how they were going to feed themselves from day to day?

The fact that turning Haizea in was wrong wasn't alone a full deterrent. The fact that betraying her would be idiotically dangerous also wasn't reason enough alone to ignore the bounty. A million dollars was still a million dollars. But combined, both of those facts stilled Alastair.

He believed that Haizea had been truthful when she told him about saving the king, though it came at the cost of her comrade's lives. He'd read her Soul plenty of times, and each time something nefarious flowed beneath the surface.

But her actions told another story; she didn't seem like the type of person to intentionally do something so heinous. If Alastair could see that, then surely the king—who'd known her for much longer—could see it too. There must be a deeper reason behind the king's persistence, but they would have to address that matter later.

The most pressing concern was what would happen when—not if, but *when*—the village she spent so much time helping betrayed Haizea? What then?

Goosebumps rose on Alastair's skin as another breeze ran over him.

He's watching.

The words silently echoed within him and his vitality thrummed in tandem. It was a message from a Soul, one that had most likely drawn his attention to the poster in the first place.

Alastair ripped the paper from the wall and jammed it in his pocket. He snatched his order from the butcher and raced back to their makeshift healing tent, placing the meat on a pack of ice that was intended to keep some of the potions cool.

When Haizea protested, he shoved the poster into her hands.

To his astonishment, she read it and seemed entirely unfazed.

~I figured he'd do something sooner or later. Just wasn't sure what. A bounty is pretty tame. At the very least, it means his eyes still are on me and not my grandfather.~

~I really think you should get going. Now. You've been here long enough, and everyone knows your face. You've healed enough people.~

Haizea's brows drew together, as if she didn't like the prospect of leaving so suddenly. She was likely thinking of the last few people she'd promised final healing sessions with and how she didn't want to take back her word.

~A few more days or even hours could be the difference between an angry mob cornering you and you making it back home unimpeded.~

Now she visibly bristled, as if Alastair had insulted her.

~I'm a blood mage and a trained warrior. Angry mob or not, there is not a way in the seven realms that this village could subdue me.~

Her arm movements had a certainty about them, and her expression had solidified into steel, which made her words feel like she was merely making a factual statement rather than an arrogant claim.

That didn't stop Alastair's hands from gripping at his hair, nearly ready to pull it right out of his scalp. Haizea absorbed the movement, an impassive glower etched onto her face as she considered him. Her chest heaved up and down, most likely sighing.

~Okay. You're right. I'll leave now. I need to collect my belongings from your family's home,~ she signed.

~I'll come with you.~ Relief flooded through Alastair in an instant.

They made the long walk to Alastair's family home. He went to unlock the door, but to his surprise, the lock was busted, and the door swung right open.

The sight and stench of blood invaded his senses as soon as they crossed the threshold. It was splattered on the ground and streaked all over the walls. The table in the kitchen had been toppled, and a massive crack split down its center. The items within the cabinets lay strewn across the floor.

A fight had happened here—no, a massacre.

Alastair's heart sank into the pit of his stomach as he assessed the carnage before him.

Haizea moved in front of him but stopped short as they passed the kitchen and went into the living room.

A hand rested on the ground behind the crouch, disturbingly still.

Alastair's chest vibrated as his voice caught in his throat—a scream, a cry. Haizea put her hand on his arm and shook her head, telling him not to come any closer.

He stood there, frozen as she stepped into the room. Her vitality spiked, and he hoped that she'd find a heartbeat or any sign of life with her healing magic, because his own magic told him that there wasn't a living Soul here.

He could sense his parents, his cousins, his aunts and uncles as they passed through him one by one. They'd waited for him to say goodbye before departing to the Soul Realm.

But Alastair wanted them to stay.

He so desperately wanted them to stay.

Please don't leave me, he thought.

Alastair had meant for it to be a plea, but his medium magic transformed his words into a command. The Souls of his slain family members stopped in their tracks and wrapped around him like a cocoon.

Haizea had told him that mediumship gave way to necromancy. Alastair kicked himself for not taking her up on her offer to teach him the basics and learn how to wield his abilities properly.

He could bring them back. He could undo this. Alastair raised his hand up, prepared to force his family's Souls back into their broken bodies. Haizea could heal them afterward.

But he paused as a vision appeared in his mind, a memory he'd spent years doing his best to forget.

Only once before had Alastair's magic thrust his mind from the Human Realm. It was the day he'd lost Rey, his beloved. To this day, he kept a picture of him in his old room. Grief and desperation consumed Alastair. He begged and pleaded for Rey not to leave him, but in turn, he had inadvertently called with his magic, and to Alastair's bewilderment, someone—something—had answered.

One moment, Alastair was firmly rooted in the Human Realm and the next, he stood in a dark and gloomy area that stretched on as far as the eye could see.

He turned to see a hooded figure looming over him. It pulled its hood back, revealing a face that was nothing more than a skull. Realization dawned on him then: Alastair was in the Soul Realm, and before him stood the Soul Reaper.

Haizea tapped Alastair's arm, bringing him back to the present.

~Alina's not here.~

Alastair reached out with his magic. Haizea was right; he couldn't sense Alina's Soul. Had she somehow managed to escape this unprecedented violence?

A heaviness settled on his shoulders, and his stomach twisted into knots. He was vaguely aware of Haizea rapidly packing her supplies. He clenched his fists.

Her presence here had brought ruin upon his family. But it was only a small part of his mind that carried that thought, that blamed her for this. The larger part of Alastair's mind focused on his fellow villagers, the people he'd spent his entire life with. How could they do something so heinous? Then again, how could they not?

Although he pickpocketed to keep his family fed, Alastair had always feared that one day it would come back to hurt the people he cared about.

Maybe this was penance for his actions, for selfishly taking from people who had nothing to give.

But couldn't they have taken him? Unleash their wrath on *him* instead?

He couldn't wrap his mind around the violence that had transpired here. A lightheaded fog spread on the edge of his vision, and he clutched his head. Gods, how much kindling he'd have to gather to burn them properly.

If his fellow villagers would slay them like this, they wouldn't take the time to properly tend to the bodies.

A trail of blood out in the hallway caught his attention. Against his better judgment, Alastair followed it with his eyes. He squinted against the shadows obscuring a small form on the ground.

Alastair froze in place.

Eyes swollen shut and bruised a deep purple. White tufts of hair matted with deep red. A tiny hand curled into a fist.

Amiri.

Alastair planted his hand on the doorway as his stomach lurched. He only managed to dry heave; it was still early in the morning, and he hadn't eaten since the night before.

His vision blurred, and the room spun. This wasn't real. It had to be a dream.

Blazing hot fury seared into his Soul and blanketed the room as it clashed against his vitality, making him still. The emotion didn't belong to him. He turned toward the source.

The scowl on Haizea's face as she zipped up her pack sent a chill down his spine. She rifled through a box that had clearly been broken open. Her mouth moved, and although he couldn't hear her, based on her body language, he assumed she said at least one expletive.

Alastair went over and tapped her shoulder. *~What is it?~*

~My mother's necklace. I take it off during the day because people bring in kids and they always end up trying to play with it. I kept it locked in a box under the mattress. But it's gone. It was the last gift she ever gave to me.~

Haizea's eyes grew glassy as she signed. But then her vitality shifted. It tugged forcefully against Alastair 's Soul. Their magic intertwined and her anguish, her remorse, and her unbridled wrath poured into him, lighting his Soul on fire.

Alastair tried to lean into that, because if he didn't, if he allowed his eyes to wander, he would see... he couldn't look again. He refused.

Haizea's head snapped toward the front door. He followed behind, and she put her arm out, guiding him behind her as she peeked out the window. When she leaned back, Alastair inched forward.

A mob of people carrying daggers, torches, and a variety of other weapons had gathered outside. Their lips moved, and their faces twisted with anger.

Haizea's hands patted at her hips, grabbing at something that wasn't there. Alastair peeked back out at the angry crowd and couldn't help but to move closer to her. An imminent threat loomed outside, and his every instinct told him to run.

This was like if he'd been caught red-handed with his hands in a man's pocket and a solid right hook was barreling toward his face.

Haizea's scowl disappeared when she turned to him, replaced by an expression of sorrow.

~I know an apology won't fix this, but I am very, very sorry, Alastair. I won't let them get to you. I won't let anything happen to you.~ Her hands trembled ever so slightly as she signed.

Haizea inhaled deeply, and her Soul stabilized. Her fury became more pointed.

Alastair held his breath as she put her hand on the knob and swung the door open.

CHAPTER 18

The door flew off the handle despite Haizea pushing it gently; the hinges had been brutalized during the break-in. She stood in front of Alastair, shielding him from the mob's line of sight.

A few mages stood amongst the crowd. Four of them gathered in a group as they held their hands over their heads, working together to levitate a heavy piece of equipment. It looked like it could have been an oven from the bakery.

Haizea couldn't help but scoff at the sight, noting the flimsiness of their magic—undoubtedly weak from lack of training. It took four people to clumsily lift an object that King Rhys and Zander could each carry singlehandedly.

She addressed the crowd while signing at the same time for Alastair.

"If the people responsible for this slaughter step up now, I will let the rest of you leave unharmed."

The mob's circle tightened around them, and the heat from their torches billowed through the air, coming dangerously close to the wooden façade of the cabin.

When Alastair pressed into Haizea's back and one of his hands almost painfully clenched around her arm, she straightened up to stand at her full height, intentionally taking up as much space as she could.

She yearned for her swords. She'd spent so much time here chasing after her father's legacy as a healer that she'd neglected her mother's. Her first order of business should have been to gather materials and forge her own replacements. She was in this situation because she'd prioritized the wrong things.

Healing was a thankless job. Given the village's struggles, she hardly expected anything in return. But that didn't negate human decency. The carnage they had unleashed... she could not allow it to go unanswered.

"There is a family dead, and a young woman is missing. I won't repeat myself again. Whoever is responsible can come forward, and the rest of you will live."

"Why? You're as good as a walking corpse. What would we bother to tell you anything?" someone shouted.

The sweltering flame from one of the torches flickered perilously close to her arm. Another person held a pitchfork at her eye level.

So many people stood in front of her. Men. Women. Children, even—their presence made her falter in her resolve. Yet her stomach twisted into knots at the sight of Alastair's family.

They were innocent in all of this, bystanders caught in the crossfire. Her fault.

The matter of her pendant—the last tangible possession that tethered her to her mother—gnawed in the back of her mind. Her world tilted under the added weight, and Haizea could do nothing more than watch, because if she reached up to stop it, the globe would break.

She blinked away the stinging in her eyes and balled her trembling hands into fists. A red haze flickered along the edges of her vision, and the crowd in front of her looked less like people and more like glistening targets.

Haizea tensed, ready to unleash her power, but she stopped herself in her tracks. If she stayed any longer, there would be violence and bloodshed of innocents, children who had no control over their parents bringing them here.

The haze receded, revealing an opening that she and Alastair could weave through to escape. She started to discreetly sign as much to him, when the large piece of equipment the telekinetic mages had hauled went hurtling through the air toward them. Haizea dived to the left while Alastair dodged to the right.

The house caved in under the weight of the oven, and that single move incited the savagery of the crowd. A group of men jumped on Alastair, pummeling him with a barrage of kicks and punches. One of them slammed the blunt end of the pitchfork into his stomach.

Alastair's cries of pain lanced through Haizea, but she had her own assailants to deal with. She dodged most of the blows aimed at her, but a woman with a torch took advantage of her divided attention and set the flames on her sleeve. It raced from her fingers up to her shoulder and neck.

A sharp, stabbing pain seared up her arm as the flames cooked her flesh. Her skin began to bubble and darken from the heat, and Haizea gritted her teeth against an agonizing howl.

Her healing magic quickly rose to the surface, stitching the wounds closed just as quickly as they ripped open, but so long as the fire was on her, the pain would not subside. Haizea reached for the woman and easily overpowered her, plunging two now-blazing fingers into her eyes. The woman's hands flew toward her face, first patting, then slapping, and finally clawing at her orbitals. As her fingernails raked against her own skin, Haizea sensed the first drop of blood as soon as it hit the air.

Instinctively, she seized the vitality as it emerged, drawing it into her own body. The woman's skin sunk into itself, and her full-throated screams hollowed out, becoming thin and airy.

In turn, Haizea gained strength, speed, and resilience. She patted at her arm and used a handful of damp dirt to choke out the last of the flames.

When a man holding a pitchfork tried to attack her, she reached out and snapped the sharp end off with a flick of her wrist. Then she wrenched the wooden handle from his grasp, twirling in her hands so that when she struck, the jagged edge jammed into his throat.

The man tumbled backward as he tried to free himself from the staff lodged in his airways. Blood oozed from the wound in his neck in rivulets.

Haizea blocked out his gurgling groans as he fought for air. She held on until she decisively subdued him before setting her sights on the others around her.

Alastair's cries echoed in the background, and the concentration of his own vitality was increasing by the second. She needed to get to him, but it felt like hundreds of people stood between the two of them now.

Haizea had already killed two people. If she was going to help Alastair, who was only being beaten because of his association with her, she may very well have to kill several more.

They deserve it, she thought bitterly, her lips curling into a snarl.

She made it as quick as possible. Not to spare them from pain, but for speed and efficiency. She took note of the people in her immediate vicinity and estimated two dozen.

Haizea yanked the jagged edge from the man's throat and spun the handle like a staff. The sharp edge swept through the air and scraped anyone within arm's reach, creating an open source of blood for her to draw from. In a single instant, she depleted their lifeforces with her blood magic and, finally, the surrounding survivors hesitated.

Haizea used the opening and ran to Alastair, pushing, shoving, and even full-body throwing people in her way.

He lay on the ground, his eyes bruised a dark purple. His lips were swollen and bloodied.

In the air, his thin arms signed in a repeated, silent plea.

~*Help me.*~

Haizea's heart dropped into the pit of her stomach.

Before she could react, a breeze ran through her and a wall of his magic slammed into her. In the tint of red that made up her blood-fueled vision were clear, sparkling figures racing toward her.

She braced herself for impact, but it never came.

Instead, the Souls of the dead passed through the bodies of the living. She watched in awe and horror as people in the mob dropped to their knees while they clutched their heads.

Something was happening to them on a level she could not fully comprehend. At least, not without access to the blood of a Spiritual mage.

But whatever the Souls had done to them, the people collapsed to the ground, catatonic.

They laid prone, eyes open and unmoving as their breaths slowly came to a halt.

She knelt down beside Alastair and used her healing to make him whole before helping him to his feet. Her vision still shimmered with red, so Haizea couldn't be certain, but she could have sworn his eyes sparkled.

She gave him a pointed look, as if to ask, 'Are you okay?' and Alastair nodded.

With him stable, she addressed the mob once more, whose numbers had markedly dwindled; at least fifty corpses littered the crowd, half of them ruined by her magic and the rest felled by Alastair's hand.

Many people fled, but several others remained, their expressions dumbstruck.

"Where is Alina?" she snapped to those remaining.

A nervous murmuring rumbled through them before one person finally answered.

"I saw someone with her a few hours ago, leaving the village. They mentioned something about Three Corners."

The blood drained from Haizea's face. Never mind the fact that if her necklace ended up in that hellhole, she'd never get it back. Haizea didn't want to think about what fate awaited Alina there.

"What did they look like? Who was it?" she pressed.

Silence was her answer.

"I said, who was it?" Her crimson eyes flashed as she raised her voice.

Again, Haizea longed for her swords. This was no small slight. If this were her home village of Windhaven, and someone had done something of this nature, heads would roll until the Bruvian warriors identified the culprits.

They called it a cull. Sometimes, the warriors made their deaths quick and efficient. Other times, they made an example of the offenders.

If they felt especially vicious, they'd even hack off a part for each lie they'd been told.

For something of this magnitude, the warriors would bring the entire village to heel. A determination settled deep in the pit of Haizea's stomach as she readied herself to take on such a task alone.

She stepped forward, her blood magic brimming beneath the surface, but she startled herself when she laughed. Cackled, really. Tremors wracked through her body, and a fuzziness blurred the edges of her vision.

She couldn't tell where the adrenaline rush ended and the Cosmic high began. Engaging in combat would be unwise right now.

How auspicious for these people. Or maybe, just maybe, they would find themselves wishing they had died today compared to what would come for them.

"I will be sure to tell my fellow Bruvian warriors what has happened in his village. You may live today, but rest assured, your days are numbered. This tragedy will not go unpunished."

Their faces turned ashen. The Bruvian warriors did not take perceived slights lightly, much less actual crimes. They did not take prisoners, and it would be in the best interest of these villagers to make themselves scarce before they caught wind of what transpired here.

Haizea turned to Alastair and wrapped his arm over her shoulder. She adjusted as she led him through the crowd; he weighed more than she expected.

Once she reached Windhaven, her missing necklace would raise questions. All warriors received it upon initiation into their cohort, and they never went anywhere without it. Even though she could lie to protect the village, they had done nothing to protect her.

These people did not deserve mercy. Not after what they'd done to Alastair's family.

But Haizea alone would not decide their fate. The warriors would.

Once she and Alastair put a good amount of distance between themselves and the crowd, she let him stand on his own and took a closer look at his injuries.

Although she had healed him, he was still clutching his head. His legs shook beneath him, but he looked... denser. His cheeks seemed fuller, and his hands were thicker than she remembered. Their eyes met, and Alastair's irises appeared normal. She must have been mistaken about the sparkling before. Even his vitality had calmed.

~I'm sorry to have gotten you into this mess. You're more than welcome to come with me, but I understand if you don't want to,~ she signed to him.

Alastair observed the skin on her arm and neck that should have been burnt to a crisp. By every account, Haizea should have smelled and looked like a half-cooked roast, the same roast he'd picked up from the butcher to prepare for them.

~I'm with you. There's nothing left for me here,~ he finally signed

~I'm very sorry I've caused you so much trouble. If I'd have——~

He shook his head, cutting her off.

~They were already dead. There's nothing your healing could have done,~ Alastair signed, his shoulders deflated.

~We should hit Three Corners, and then I'll catch up with Grandfather myself.~

~I thought you wanted the warriors to get him?~

~I do. But your cousin needs help, and it's all my fault. Besides, after today? I know it's risky, but I just want to lay my own eyes on him. He's all I have left.~

He was old and moved at a snail's pace. He probably wouldn't leave his home until at least a week after receiving Haizea's warning. Haizea and Alastair were far enough north still that they could slip through Llyr rather than risk running into King Rhys's allies in Olysseus and Arcelia.

~I can't ask you to risk yourself for my sake. You should go deeper into the mountains where your people are, so you're less likely to have people turning on you for the bounty. Plus, the kingdoms have no jurisdiction deeper within the range's borders. If we run to the Three Corners with a bounty on our heads, it'll be a disaster. You have connections with the warriors, so it makes sense to use them,~ Alastair signed.

~But we're in a race against time. The longer we go without finding Alina, the less chance she'll ever be found again.~

Given that the Three Corners was the black market, whoever had abducted Alina might have swiped her pendant, too. She could kill two birds with one stone.

~I know, I know. I just think going to the Three Corners without any backing is a mistake. You're strong, but you're not invincible. You shouldn't do it alone.~

~I'm not alone. I have you.~

An infinitesimal but sad smile formed on Alastair's lips, and he rubbed the back of his neck.

~When I saw the bounty... when I saw how much King Rhys was offering for your head... my first thought wasn't to warn you. I—it was...~

Alastair trailed off as he struggled to find his words, but his apologetic expression said what he could not.

Haizea's level countenance did not betray the growing tightness in her throat. Both he and his family had treated her so kindly that it never crossed her mind that Alastair might consider the bounty.

~Well, at least I'm worth more than a million dollars to someone,~ she tried to sign lightheartedly.

~Not just more. What you did for my village was priceless. And I hope you can forgive me for my lapse in judgment. For almost betraying you.~

~I should be apologizing to you, Alastair. This is my fault. Besides, a bounty of that amount is life changing, and it's enough to make the average person turn on their own family, much less someone they just met. It means a lot to me that I mean that much to you," she signed.

Alastair's brows shot up, and his lips parted, slightly ajar.

~I'm with you, Haizea.~ Despite herself, her heart leapt as the softness that she'd grown used to seeing in his gaze returned. *~And as your backup, I must reiterate that I really think you should send your*

warrior friends to do this, but I think I understand why you want to move now. You should probably write to your grandfather again.~

~I want Grandfather to keep going toward Illiniza. If I write to him again, he'll try to meet me in the Three Corners. That's why we should meet him at the border crossing.~

~I'm not sure that meeting him directly is a good idea.~

Her brows furrowed. *~Why?~*

~A Soul led me to the wanted poster. It spoke to me. A warning, to be exact: He's watching. You were right.~

~Jirina,~ she signed and hissed her name aloud like a curse.

Haizea kicked herself for staying behind to help the village. She'd fallen in too deep, dreaming of a life where she'd followed her father's footsteps. She had wasted her time in this village. Time that, until recently, she'd thought was well spent.

Mountaineers looked out for each other. But she'd known from that start that Goldenleaf Village did not share the same sense of community.

They would have to find another way to ensure her grandfather's safety. So long as the king focused his efforts on her, it meant Grandfather Harzel wouldn't be the object of his attention. It was safer for him to travel without her being his escort. For now, at least.

~Alright. Well, in that case, I still need to get word to the warriors. Do you think you could call in another favor using your medium magic?~

~I should be able to,~ he signed.

It was a compromise. Haizea didn't want to risk Grandfather Harzel anymore than she wanted to lose the lead they had on Alina. The bounty would be worthless to the Bruvian warriors; the mountaineers had a long history with the three kingdoms, none of it amicable.

Her pendant symbolized their bloody history. Hopefully, they would find both it and Alina in the Three Corners.

With Alastair at her side, Haizea turned her back on her homeland yet again. And for the first time in a very long time, a solemn, yearning feeling emerged within her as she did so.

CHAPTER 19

Fire burned on the bottom of Alastair's feet, and he could feel blisters forming with each step he took toward their destination.

Unlike Haizea, he hadn't grabbed any supplies or travel attire before leaving Goldenleaf behind. He'd never had the chance to. On top of that, Alastair wasn't used to walking long distances either. But that was the least of his worries.

Several miles stood between them and the mountains as they traveled north toward the Three Corners.

At the moment, Haizea and Alastair traversed through wildlife's domain. Due to a history of contention between the mountaineers and the major kingdoms, the population was sparse, with a few small villages and cities located sporadically along the border.

~We should have gotten you better footwear before we left. At this rate, your feet are going to be worn like sandpaper,~ Haizea signed.

~I'll be fine. Just... I–I need a distraction.~

He didn't want to be alone in his thoughts right now. The numbness had passed, and now tears pricked at his eyes, fighting to break out. If he let his grief take him, he wouldn't be able to continue on. He'd collapse to his knees and beg the Soul Reaper to take him instead.

He couldn't let that happen, not when Alina needed him.

Haizea's ever-present frown deepened, but her brows tilted up-ward, more sorrowful than angry. *~I can talk about the warriors?~* she suggested.

Alastair nodded. He had never attended mage school, but he knew the major points of the mountain range's history. It was common knowledge that even prior to the return of magic a few centuries ago, the mountaineers always maintained their independence from the kingdoms.

They did so through bloodshed. People claimed that the Demons returned the vitality to humanity, but Alastair wasn't fully convinced that they would go out of their way to do something like that; in fact, it made more sense for them to do the opposite.

~Warriors have protected the mountains for as long as humanity has made a home here. For most of our history, mountain warriors were non-mages and remained isolated to their respective peaks. It wasn't until the return of magic that a woman named Samira Bruvia united our fighting forces across the range.

~When the kingdoms led their armies into our lands, our people quickly overwhelmed them. The mages worked together to protect the bases and perimeter while the warriors were well adapted to the tumultuous terrain near the mountains' summits. The warriors caught any enemies that broke through the mage's frontlines and, under Samira's leadership, they gained a merciless reputation.

~Although Samira wasn't the first dual sword wielder, she utilized techniques that particularly put an emphasis on brutality. Due to the effectiveness of her methods, they gained traction. We dual wield because having two blades means twice the pain. Why settle for impaling one kidney when you could destroy both? Nearly all our weapon choices reflected this line of thinking: dual daggers, flails, chain blades, barbed arrows specifically designed to expand upon impact and rupture internal organs. Samira

is the one who popularized displaying the heads of our adversaries as a warning.~

Haizea paused, her gaze growing distant. Wistful, almost.

~I had an old friend back in Illiniza. Her name is Shauni. We went to mage school together, but her mother was a warrior too. She had a knack at throwing swords. As long as you were in her line of sight, she never missed her mark, no matter the distance.~

Haizea was the first warrior Alastair had met personally. He'd never seen their savagery firsthand, but he recalled a story his mother regularly told about her childhood. A string of unexplained murders had plagued the village.

Goldenleaf had always been small and fairly poor, yet nobody had been able to track down the culprit. His grandmother had managed to purchase a messenger hawk and sent it toward higher elevation to secretly request help.

The warriors arrived a few weeks later in the middle of the night. His mother told him that she only caught a glimpse of them as they camouflaged themselves in the snow-covered foliage. The screams that followed kept her awake. When she left the house the next day, everyone had gathered around the village entrance.

The warriors had placed the brothel owner's head on a skewer and left it for all to see. They'd also created a funeral pyre for the body, disposing of it so the villagers wouldn't have to.

The would-be victim had lived to tell the tale of how the warriors intervened in the nick of time.

Haizea continued, *~The warriors played an integral role in the war and helped draft the Treaty of Certain Demise. Given the kingdoms' defeat in previous wars, the treaty's namesake was a promise of the kingdoms' fate should they wage war against the Bayeux Mountain Range ever again. It forbids either side from crossing into either lands without explicit permission.*

~For average citizens, there is a kill-on-sight policy. But if the trespassers have any ties to any of the ruling monarchs, or in the case of us mountaineers, any connections to the warriors or their village elders, it is to be interpreted as a declaration of war.~

Alastair looked at her thoughtfully. *~I suppose that's why King Rhys opted for a bounty rather than confront you himself.~*

She nodded. *~Yes, I believe so. And I hope for the sake of Arcelian populace that he thinks carefully before he pushes things much further.~*

Off in the distance, a plume of smoke billowed in the air, signifying human presence. They'd likely reach that village by sundown if they kept their current pace. Alastair frowned at the prospect of encountering more people. He put a hand on Haizea's shoulder to get her attention and nodded in the direction of the upcoming village.

~We should disguise ourselves,~ Alastair signed.

Haizea scrunched her nose.

~I can handle whatever they throw at us. Besides, how would we slip by unnoticed? Shaving our heads won't be enough. At least, not for me. As soon as we cross the threshold, people will see a woman as tall as a grown man, and their eyes will be glued to me the entire time.~

Alastair suppressed a grin. Haizea had captured his attention as soon as she arrived in his village. Although, it was more than just her height that had drawn him in.

~Well, I think we should at least do something. Hiding in plain sight will make things easier. You may be fine, but I got my ass handed to me the last time.~

~It won't happen again. I'll protect you. Just make sure to stick by my side and I'll handle anyone who comes for us.~

Alastair shifted his weight but didn't press it any further. Haizea could take care of herself, but he would rather slip by inconspicuously.

At worst, if he got caught alone, he'd have to finagle his way out. But if they went together, or if Haizea had to save him anyway, and someone recognized her...

A tremor ran through him at the all too recent memory of how they'd subdued the mob. Dozens of bodies on the ground, some by slain Haizea's magic but an arresting amount also killed by Alastair's. Hopefully, things went more smoothly here.

They crossed the village's borders by late evening. Alastair paused, taking in the lively atmosphere. The people's faces were flushed with color, and the children had round cheeks, laughing as they chased one another. The buildings were well put together, and the roads looked well maintained.

This village wasn't destitute like Alastair's home; wood rot didn't mar the buildings' exteriors, greenery didn't protrude from massive holes and cracks in the roads, and the stench of human excrement didn't foul the air.

Back in Goldenleaf, the high price of the bounty combined with their desperation made their violent reaction a foregone conclusion.

But maybe people who weren't starving and struggling to keep a roof over their heads would respond differently.

~We're going to get you better clothes,~ Haizea signed as they walked.

They stopped at a small clothing shop that sold a variety of garments. Alastair picked out a few colorful tunics made of soft fabric. It wasn't something he had the opportunity to buy back home. He turned around to see Haizea shaking her head at him.

~We're here for practicality, not fashion,~ she signed and walked over to a different section.

She picked up a plain-looking shirt with thicker threading. Alastair didn't protest when she moved to put the thinner colorful ones back, but Haizea paused and looked between him and the shirts. She held up one that was a light purple.

~This one matches your eyes. You should keep it. But just *this one, so we can afford everything else.~*

A grin crept across Alastair's face as he absorbed her words, but Haizea had already moved on to the next section before he could respond.

She brought back a pair of boots with a sturdy, solid sole. Haizea hadn't asked him his size, but they fit perfectly. A moment later, she grabbed a jacket in a far corner and handed it to Alastair for him to try on. It clung to his form comfortably and would be perfect to put on and take off as the weather shifted the further into the mountains they ventured.

~We should get you a satchel, too,~ she said, leading him to a different wall that displayed various bags.

When Haizea suddenly stiffened in front of him, Alastair put his hand on her arm. He followed her line of sight to the wanted poster on the wall, plain as day.

Alastair shoved the clothes in the bag and swapped his shoes with impressive speed. He snatched a jacket off a clothing rack and pushed it into Haizea's hands and then motioned for her to pull the hood over her head. She moved to tie her curls back, but the band snapped in her hands. Her mouth moved, and he recognized the swear on her lips.

She jammed most of her hair under the hood but struggled to conceal the last few tufts of blonde. Alastair reached over and pushed the hood back and started from scratch. Haizea held still and tilted her head upward to face him as he ran his hands along her coils, gentle yet firm against the resistance.

He got them smoothed down and contained just enough for Haizea to pull the hood over them. Alastair better understood why she usually braided the front down; it made tying her hair back much easier. The hood instantly poofed up under the density of her strands, making it blatantly obvious she had a lot of hair underneath. Alastair tightened the lace so it wouldn't move. That was as good as it was going to get.

As they left, he tossed a sack of coins in the direction of the cash counter. Fortunately, the shop owner was preoccupied with another customer. For once, or at least for the moment, they had gotten lucky.

Alastair knew this would happen. He glared at Haizea, but she was looking pointedly in another direction and avoided his gaze.

~We should get something to eat. We barely have any rations as is. I think we should save our current supply for travel where food may not be easy to come by,~ Haizea signed once they had walked a little further from the shop.

Alastair desperately wanted to leave. His every instinct told him to run and yet he was letting himself be dragged along. But when his eyes met Haizea's, level and determined, he struggled to focus on his perturbations. *I'll protect you*, her expression said.

They continued down the next road to a farmer's market, rife with every scrap and morsel of food a person could desire. They made haste there; Haizea grabbed an array of dried fruits and canned vegetables that would last much longer than fresh food. Alastair made sure to acquire dried meats, as well as some match sets.

One of the merchants offered him a sample of jerky, and Alastair tasted it eagerly. He swallowed and frowned. It was bland as hell. He spotted herbs and spices a few vendors down.

~You're going to cook dried food?~ Haizea asked, raising a brow.

~I'm going to season this meat to the best of my ability. I'll be damned if I eat nothing but jerky that has no flavor for the next few weeks.~

The corners of her mouth flickered upward, briefly flashing just a fragment of her smile. Alastair smirked, realizing that she was about to laugh but had caught herself.

~We should really get going now,~ he insisted.

She paused. *~You sure there's nothing else we need?~*

~*Positive.*~ He nodded.

~*Alright. Let's go.*~

They were considerably far into the village, so it made more sense to walk to their northern entrance rather than go back the way they came. It also meant avoiding giving wandering eyes a second look at them.

As they reached the border, Alastair's stomach twisted. He stopped in his tracks.

~*You okay?*~ Haizea asked.

He took a deep breath against the discomfort in his gut.

~*I don't think that jerky is sitting with me too well.*~

When Alastair's mouth began to water, he knew he was going to be sick. He shoved everything he'd been carrying into Haizea's hands before sprinting back to one of the restrooms they'd passed.

He barely made it before his stomach heaved and everything he'd eaten violently came back up. The jerky wasn't just bland, it had been rancid, probably not cooked for long enough. Alastair stayed for a few minutes, to be certain he was done. There was nothing worse than thinking the worst was over and having to run back.

His hands trembled and his head pounded. Although his stomach felt far from settled, he thought that had some time before another wave of sickness would hit him again.

He exited the bathroom and practically walked into a group of people loitering outside. Their attention snapped to him, and Alastair stepped backward as they surrounded him. Spittle flung from their moving mouths.

Their faces turned red, and a vein pulsated in the forehead of the person nearest to him. His stomach threatened to heave again.

This was because of the bounty. They'd seen him with Haizea.

Tell her where I am. Tell her to help me, Alastair called out with his magic. The ghostly whisper of the Souls trailed along his skin before they flew in her direction.

With passing each moment, the group in front of him grew more agitated. Someone grabbed him by the hair and shoved their face close to his. The heat from their breath fanned across him as they shouted.

Alastair tried to sign and tell them he couldn't hear them, but they misinterpreted his movements, and the person struck him in the face.

His already pounding head threatened to split open entirely.

Alastair felt Haizea before he saw her. Her Soul and her vitality had a heavy weight to it, like an anchor. He followed that sensation, and his eyes met hers as soon as she entered the fray.

Haizea tore through the crowd, even as multiple people circled her at once. Four men jumped at her only to be beaten back with a flurry of well-aimed strikes. One caught a fist to the eye, and the next a knee to the groin.

When he bent over in pain, Haizea picked him up, and the muscles in her arms visibly flexed as she threw him at the two remaining assailants. A cloud of dust plumed into the air as the man hit the ground. He didn't get back up.

One of the men still next to Alastair noticed the commotion and followed Alastair's gaze. He looked over his shoulder only to be met with a bone-shattering roundhouse to the face.

The tension in Alastair's scalp loosened, and suddenly his hair was free. He dropped to his hands and knees as he coughed up blood.

Alastair looked up to see that Haizea had wrapped her arms around the man's neck, suffocating him. He struggled for a few moments, but she easily outpowered him, and he sagged to the ground. Anyone else left standing ran off while they had the chance.

Haizea helped Alastair sit on his bottom. She gently cupped his cheeks between her cool hands, her expression painted with worry. The throbbing in his head slowly dissipated as her magic healed his wounds.

Alastair searched her eyes for a few moments before a dropping sensation in his gut had him pushing her hands away. He got back on his hands and knees just as his stomach turned against him again. He wished he hadn't tried that jerky.

Haizea held a torn piece of cloth in her hand and gently wiped his face. Then she pulled a container of crushed leaves from her satchel and handed it to him.

~I don't have anything to make a full potion with, but this will at least get rid of the sour taste.~

As Alastair chewed on the leaves and the flavor of mint burst in his mouth, Haizea slipped her hands under his shirt, and the rumbling in his belly calmed.

~How are your feet?~ she asked, but Haizea didn't wait for him to answer as she unlaced his boots.

She pressed her palms against his skin and mended each foot with her healing magic. The blisters shrunk in size before disappearing altogether, and the pain faded away.

~Better?~ she asked.

Alastair was vaguely aware of her question, but every coherent thought he might have formed slipped away before they could take hold. Haizea's dense curls, which they had worked so hard to neatly tuck away, were now flying freely after fighting the crowd of people.

She pushed her hair back so that it no longer obscured her face. He had been around Haizea long enough to see how easily she unsettled people. With the way she towered over others and her consistently icy stare, she had an imposing aura that effectively shrouded the softness buried underneath.

Alastair's gaze lingered on her lips, soaking in their full-ness—plump and soft. Haizea's eyes slowly reeled him in. They were light against the rich brown of her skin, only a few shades darker than her blonde locks.

Haizea had all the features of a beautiful person, but it was wrapped within such a frightening package that it went unnoticed until she let her guard down.

Alastair, however, always noticed it.

Even as she glared at him, he sat there, fixated as if Haizea was the sun and he was merely the moon, caught in her orbit as he reflected her light.

He knew to look further than her scowl—which at times seemed to be permanently etched into her face. At the moment, he didn't sense any turbulence in her Soul.

He almost thought she was waiting for something. For him, maybe. But why? Alastair rehashed the last few minutes to the best of his ability. Then he remembered Haizea had asked him if he was better. He still hadn't answered her.

~Yes, I'm much better now. Thank you,~ he managed to sign.

~I'm sorry.~

That's right, he was annoyed with her earlier. Though he couldn't seem to summon that emotion now.

~Next time, please, let's try it my way,~ he signed.

~If we're being watched there isn't a disguise we could wear that would circumvent King Rhys and Jirina. As long as you're with me, you'll be at risk.~

~Well, there must be some way to minimize that risk, is there not?~ he asked.

~We part ways. I can send you ahead to my home village and have you mention me by name. The warriors will protect you. This way, you won't

sustain any more injuries, and I can still move forward reuniting with my grandfather, and I'll do everything I can to find Alina.~

Her hand rubbed at her chest, where her pendant normally rested.

Her words settled in him before he responded. He'd already known that this would be a risky, dangerous journey.

Alastair knew nothing of King Rhys' wrath personally, but he'd seen the aftermath—tearing whole villages apart with his bounty just to capture someone who, in his experience, spent her time trying to help the people around her.

And even that aside, each time it was Haizea who neutralized the threats they encountered. Each time she'd barely broken a sweat. She was always saving him.

The king likely knew Alastair's face by now. If he was going to run, it should have been when his gut told him to, after learning her story on the very first day they met. Running now probably meant they would come after him to use as leverage, and he didn't have near the fighting prowess that Haizea had.

~That's the only option?~ he asked.

~No. That's the safest *option. The other option is for you to take up Cosmic magic. You're a medium, so that extends into necromancy. You don't need to learn how to fight if you can create an army at a moment's notice.~*

Alastair stared into blank space, images flashing before him.

Rey. The Soul Realm. The Soul *Reaper.*

Haizea's movements pulled him back to the present.

~It's not a choice to be made lightly. But King Rhys is using aggressive tactics because I'm an omen. He has endless resources to throw at me, and by extension, you. So long as we're together, this is what we're going to face,~ she signed.

Alastair wrung his hands together.

~There's something I need to tell you.~

~What is it?~

~You know the Soul I introduced you to? The one that helped get a message to your grandfather?~

Haizea nodded, and Alastair relived the memories as he told her the full story of the Soul formerly known as Rey.

Only a few years had passed since Rey departed this realm. He had dark, curly hair and warm brown eyes. Rey had a smile that never failed to take Alastair's breath away.

When Rey died, Alastair wanted nothing more than to see that smile again.

He'd come by Rey's home to say his final goodbyes; mountaineers burned their dead, usually within the first two days. Any longer than that and vermin were bound to desecrate the body.

As Alastair sat with him and held his hand, he sensed Rey's Soul looking down on him.

It wasn't a conscious decision. The desire for Rey to come back to life consumed every fiber of his being and, before he knew it, Rey's Soul was no longer by his side. When Rey sat up and looked at him, Alastair immediately knew something wasn't right. His beloved's eyes were no longer brown, but now glowed brilliantly, like diamonds.

He did not know how long he stayed in the Soul Realm, but when he finally came to, Alastair was lying in his bed, and his mother sat by his side, her face full of tears.

A few days had passed. They'd burned Rey's body without him. The experience frightened Alastair so much that he decided he would never try to bring someone he loved back again.

As Alastair signed, understanding dawned on Haizea's face. And then, he could have sworn something in her expression fractured. She masked it almost immediately, but Alastair had seen it, he'd *felt* it; her feelings were hurt.

She brought her hands to her chest and curled in on herself, making herself appear smaller. Although Alastair never lied to her, he hadn't been forthcoming either. He never corrected her assumptions, instead letting her think he had no knowledge or connection to the Cosmic Arts.

~*If you don't want to practice the Cosmic Arts, I understand. No one can force you. But I... I can't sit back and watch you suffer from magical wasting. If that's your choice, this is where we part ways,*~ she signed

Back then, he hadn't known enough about the Cosmic Arts to understand the effects of magical wasting. And now that he did, Alastair was terrified that either option would destroy him.

Magical wasting? Or losing his mind and possibly his Soul from necromancy?

For a long time, Alastair had thought he'd made his choice. But as Alastair noted the glassiness in Haizea's eyes and the way she shifted away from him ever so slightly, he faltered.

Why did Cosmic magic come to Haizea so easily while it tortured him? Maybe there was a way to stop his spells, and he just hadn't found it yet because he spent so much time resisting his power. There was only one way to find out, but it frightened him.

It also bothered him how quickly Haizea was ready to abandon him if he refused. Even with her clearly being upset, she had not wavered or hesitated in her decision.

She signed with conviction. Something tightened within Alastair as he imagined the two of them parting ways. All this time, Alastair never imagined that he could ever hurt Haizea, and yet somehow, he had pierced her armor.

Haizea had deliberately chosen to become an omen. Had she never dabbled in the Cosmic Arts to begin with, magical wasting would never be an issue. She'd never have to trap and kill animals as a substitute for killing her fellow man.

Alastair wondered what that was like—to taste a power that was deliriously intoxicating and be able to ignore the foul aftertaste that came with it. Perhaps that was why her Soul had a sinister undertone to it, despite the kindness she'd displayed.

Necromancy was no different. It meant a lifetime of bringing animals back to life rather than defiling a human grave. As far as he was concerned, necromancy was a gateway to Hell, but Alastair brought Hell to his fellow villagers every day.

He made his living as a thief, spending his days skimming the pocketbooks of his fellow impoverished villagers. He justified it by telling himself that his spoils helped his family: a deluge of siblings and cousins and aunts and uncles. In a way, he'd simply transferred the pain from one family to the next.

Every coin he swiped could be a day's wages, a week's worth of meals, the difference between a much-needed dose of medicine and suffering with illness. His actions brought about a different kind of anguish.

Alastair had worked an honest job making an honest wage, but he brought home pennies, putting him in the same boat as everyone else. It was easier to steal. At least this way, he could afford to eat once a day rather than once a week like so many others.

If there was something tainted about Haizea with her blood magic, then something foul lived in him too for taking from people who could not afford to give.

Haizea had told him about her father. More than anything, he related to why she did not want to watch someone she cared about die. With Rey, Alastair had gone through that loss not only once, but twice. Maybe if he perfected his magic, he wouldn't have to go through it again.

Maybe, one day, he could bring someone he loved back to this realm.

Or maybe his magic would drive him mad.

Alastair steeled himself, strengthening his resolve. The gate to Hell had been waiting for him patiently all this time.

He supposed it was best for him to open it on his own terms rather than be forced through it again. He placed his hand on Haizea's and squeezed her fingers lightly before lifting his arms to sign.

~I want to learn.~

Chapter 20

As King Rhys sat alone in his study, a soft knock on the door pulled him out of his thoughts.

"Come in."

Princess Sage's face appeared in the doorway. Her eyes glowed faintly against the dim light as her telekinesis swung the door open without lifting a finger. Although she was the younger of the two royal siblings, her magic had long surpassed her brother's.

King Rhys waved her over and held his arms open. Despite her size and age, the princess crawled into her father's lap and wrapped her arms around him.

"I'm glad you made it back, Papa," she whispered.

King Rhys pressed his cheek against her soft blonde tresses. He returned her embrace, blanketing her with warmth and protection. "Me too, my love."

Princess Sage leaned back to get a better view of her father's face.

"What's on your mind?" he asked.

"I overheard Mother talking earlier. She said you told her that there's no safe place for us anymore. Not even the palace."

"Your mother lacks... full comprehension of the situation. So long as I walk this realm, you, your brother, and your mother will be safe. And I have every tool at my disposal to ensure anyone, omen or otherwise, intending to bring you harm will be swiftly subdued."

She frowned. "Do you really think Haizea wants to hurt us?"

"She's an omen. It's in her nature. Even if she tries to fight it, she'll succumb to her twisted blood eventually. Inevitably, they all do."

The princess picked at the hem of her shirt. The blood mage had always treated his daughter kindly. She would occasionally spend afternoons with Sage while she worked on her schoolwork, or watch as she practiced her telekinesis.

A wave of disgust slithered down King Rhys's spine at how close the omen had been to his daughter. He could not allow their proximity to taint Sage's perceptions.

"I see the doubt on your face. You've never dealt with an omen before. Cosmic magic causes irreversible damage not only to one's body, but their mind and Soul," the king sighed. "Your mother tried to protect you from the execution, but the situation has changed. You're old enough to know why I feel as strongly as I do. You need to know the dangers we face. Listen closely..."

Prince Rhys's parents hoped to pass on a peaceful kingdom to their son. They spent many years on various excursions to warm up relations between Arcelia and its adversaries—from the volcanic, snowy peaks in the Bayeux Mountain Range, to the secluded Island of Kestramore.

While their diplomatic efforts hadn't borne much fruit in the mountains, Prince Rhys made quick friends with Mericus, the son of an esteemed councilwoman in Kestramore.

They were both telekinetic mages and children to their kingdom's leaders, so before long, the two boys were joined at the hip and incessantly badgering their parents for another trip across the ocean.

It was a serendipitous development. Although the council in Kestramore still acted coldly toward Arcelia, the friendship between their future rulers did not go unnoticed. At the very least, a door that had once been tightly shut was now slightly ajar.

Eventually, Mericus's parents agreed to send him to mage school in Arcelia. Prince Rhys's bond with him only grew stronger as a result. They studied the telekinetic arts and received high marks from the magisters. By the age of sixteen, both boys had achieved mastery in their mage class.

It wasn't until after they successfully passed their magical proficiency assessment that Mericus approached Prince Rhys regarding techniques that not even the Grand Magister knew. He told his friend about the dark gift of transmutation: the ability to alter the state of vitality in the world around them and change something from one form to another.

Back then, Prince Rhys had no reservations or hesitation when Mericus offered a demonstration. Mericus had grown up around the Cosmic Arts, and his mother was a transmuting mage.

He knew the basics simply by watching her over the years. Now that he had full control of his telekinetic abilities, transmutation came as easy as breathing.

Mericus started off simple. He took the fountain pen Prince Rhys carried and warped its vitality. It took several minutes and much effort, but eventually the pen transformed into a butterfly, beautiful and harmless.

Prince Rhys's eyes lit up, and his jaw fell slack with awe.

"Show me another." His voice had teemed with excitement.

Emboldened, Mericus used his telekinesis to bring down a golden eagle that had been flying high in the sky. He repeated the same ritual, warping the vitality around the bird until it began to change shape.

The two boys watched intently as the animal shifted and twisted around itself. First its beak separated, the top portion curling upwards toward its eyes and the bottom one down to its neck. A small pink tongue flickered out of the newly formed hole where the beak had been. The eagle's feathers withered before melding with its skin.

Odd shapes began to emerge as its outer skin swapped places with its innards. A strangled, agonizing cry erupted from the eagle's mangled beak.

Mericus dropped the bird. Prince Rhys turned a sickly shade of green, barely clinging onto his composure. A tense silence passed between them before the prince found his voice.

"Mericus, turn it back."

A slow, haunted smile crept across Mericus's face.

"Mericus, turn it back!" Prince Rhys grabbed his friend's shoulders, and his fingernails dug into Mericus's flesh.

The pain cut through the boy's dazed expression. He picked up the bird, but its screams had ceased, and its body had fallen limp. Prince Rhys released him with a gasp.

"Mericus. Mericus, look at me," he urged. His friend's eyes were unfocused as they flickered to and fro, looking everywhere yet seeing nothing.

"Mericus!" The prince slapped him, finally getting his attention. "What you just did... promise me you'll never do it again."

Mericus slowly put a hand on Prince Rhys's. The prince gripped his fingers tightly.

"Promise me."

"I promise," Mericus said.

Time would prove Mericus's words to be a lie. It was a year later, as graduation neared, that the Crown Prince discovered the depths of his friend's deception.

Mericus had perfected his craft, continuing to practice transmutation on inanimate objects and small animals. He allowed the rush that came with Cosmic magic to carry him into the clouds each time.

Then, one day, he felt he was ready for something more. Something more challenging.

Mericus decided to try his magic on human life.

The week before their graduation, one of the magisters went missing. A search was put on for them to no avail. Prince Rhys had joined in their efforts, dragging Mericus along with him. He noticed that distant look in his friend's eyes.

It had felt vaguely familiar, in an unsettling way. But the prince set that feeling aside.

Several months later, they happened upon the magister's wedding ring, but their body was never found.

Three years later, Prince Rhys's father passed away, and his coronation was to be held shortly after. Mericus sat in the front row of the crowd along with the rest of the royal family: Prince Rhys's mother, Queen Cordelia, and his younger brother, Prince Rowan.

The ceremony went smoothly given that the royal family still grieved over the loss of their father and king. A celebration followed, filled with dancing, music, and a variety of foods from the best chefs in the kingdom. As the night carried on, King Rhys noticed Prince Rowan chatting with Mericus.

He smiled, glad that his old friend could be a shoulder to lean on and a listening ear. At the time it was a pleasant sight, but in retrospect it was a nightmare unfolding in real time.

When Prince Rowan did not return home that night, King Rhys did not think much of it. His brother was a young man at the age of eighteen. For all he knew, he could be with a lover or out galivanting with friends. But then a day passed. And then a week.

The king grew worried. He did his best to comfort his mother, but in the wake of her husband's death, it was too much to handle. The healer put her on bedrest until the matter was settled.

Prince Rowan's body was found roughly two weeks later, only identifiable by the emblem on the vest he'd been wearing the night of the coronation. His head had been turned inside out; the lids of his eyes were missing, his teeth had migrated to the back of his skull with his tongue extending out from behind his neck. The rest of his body was a wrangled mess of exposed organs and mottled flesh.

The skin of his arms had a reptilian look to them, green with scab-like scales. A tail extended from his lower back. It had no skin or muscle, only bone. His feet were now webbed, and his legs muscles had been whittled away beneath scaly skin.

This time, when King Rhys's face turned green, he could not hold back the bile that erupted out of him. He dropped to his knees, holding his brother's head in his arms. Grief surged from within, swept him up, and carried him in a deluge of tears before crashing back down to earth.

When he finally regained his composure, understanding dawned on him.

He'd seen this before. Years ago, with the eagle. King Rhys stormed his way toward the guest room where Mericus slept.

"My brother?!" the king snarled.

Mericus jumped out of bed and stumbled to the ground. King Rhys looked in his eyes and recognized that same distant expression from before: the hallmark high from corrupted vitality.

"You promised me," he spat.

King Rhys used his magic to deal a heavy blow to Mericus, but the man was quicker than he expected. They stood there, fighting an invisible battle with their telekinesis. Mericus pushed back against him, rendering him immobile.

The king shuddered when the omen reached out to him, his hand poised to ruin his body just as he had his brother's.

He barely stopped it in time.

"Why?" he managed to gasp, but in Mericus's eyes he saw the answer.

He saw the laughter in his face. The distance in his eyes. There was no reason. Not one that was comprehensible or would pacify him. Mericus had done this to chase after the high that came with the Cosmic Arts.

Prince Rowan had perished for no other reason than an addict needing their fix.

Mericus shoved King Rhys back toward the wall and into several of the potted plants they had in the room. Dirt and particulates erupted into the air. Pain slashed across his face as shards from the shattered vases cut his skin.

He winced as he prepared for the killing blow. A blow that never came.

Mericus was frantically wiping at his face and arms to get the dirt off of him. King Rhys frowned in confusion before he realized that he could no longer feel the pressure of Mericus's telekinesis. In fact, he could not feel his own, either.

The king got to his feet. He reached for the sword still sheathed on his hip. As he approached Mericus, he did not spare him any goodbyes or final words. For the sake of his brother, he ended his best friend's life, slicing his head clean off his shoulders.

King Rhys cleaned the room by himself, eyeing the broken pot curiously. A memory resurfaced from when he was just a boy, accompanying his parents on their first and only trip to the Bayeux Mountain Range, where they met with the leaders of Mount Cortara. They'd been escorted by the feared Bruvian warriors. While his parents spoke with the mountaineers, he and Rowan had wandered off and found a curious-looking plant. It had black leaves, like it had been charred by the volcanic ash and managed to survive.

He wasn't sure why he dug it up and tucked it into his pocket, but he did. He knew better and yet years later, his childish defiance had saved his life.

When Kestramore received news of their newly minted councilman's death, they went from icy to decidedly hostile. They'd even implicated Olysseus, simply for being a close ally of Arcelia. But King Rhys did not care.

He buried his father, his brother, and then his mother—who had died of a broken heart—all within the span of a month. He had no sympathy for Kestramore or anyone who sided with the Cosmic Arts. He vowed to snuff out any sparks of interest of the abominable practice within his kingdom.

The world had no place for an omen.

A few hours later, King Rhys and a select few of the Royal Guard and his advisors conversed in his study. Jirina informed him of everything that had transpired in Goldenleaf village with the bounty.

"It looks like she's heading north, in the complete opposite direction as before."

Zander let out a huff.

"The bounty hasn't done anything but lead to the deaths of regular people. The same thing will happen when she stops at the next village to recuperate, and the people try to chain her down. It's doing more harm than good," he warned.

King Rhys cleared his throat. The room fell silent. Eyes flickered between the king and Zander.

"O-of course, I mean no disrespect or disparagement of your judgment, Your Majesty," Zander backtracked.

"No. You said what you meant the first time. And you're right. The bounty was a mistake. Leaving such a task to civilians was a lapse in judgment on my part. Let's suspend it and replace it with hired mercenaries as a stop gap."

"Stop gap?" Zander asked. The king nodded.

"Yes. I don't expect them to be successful either, but it'll keep the witch on her toes. We can't afford to let her rest and recoup." King Rhys turned his attention to Jirina. "I need for you to look into anything that can be used as leverage. If we can't drag her to us by force, then we'll have her return of her own will."

"She's lost her necklace. I've never seen her go anywhere without it. If we can locate that, then it should entice her to come here," Jirina said with a shrug.

"We'll never get our hands on it. It's long gone by now. Besides, I think that's too obvious of a bait. Too convenient for her to believe. We need something real and tangible in our hands... I know her parents are dead and any other remaining family and friends she has likely live in the mountains. But let's double check anyways. Would be useful if something came up."

"I'll get right on it, Your Majesty."

The king dismissed them all. He would do whatever it took to kill the blood mage, even if it was the last thing he did.

Chapter 21

Harzel Usoro was many things. Old. Frail. Physically, he was certainly a shadow of his former self. But old age had not dulled his sharp mind.

When a hawk landed in his open window, his instincts told him to expect the worst.

He opened the missive only to find it blank. Harzel frowned, perplexed. The only person who had any reason to reach out to him was Haizea, and she'd left on a diplomatic trip with the king weeks ago.

Still, sending a hawk to communicate tracked in his mind. He'd heard whispers that King Rhys had returned with only a fraction of his Royal Guard, but if there were any other details to be known about that peculiar rumor, they had been silenced before making it to Von Stein.

The paper trembled in his unsteady hands. Harzel's body had never recovered after his training accident with Haizea, where she'd permanently damaged and depleted vitality.

Or, at least, that's what he'd allowed her to believe. He knew his granddaughter had not and would never forgive herself for doing it, but the only way to reverse the effects would be to follow the same course of action that had killed his son, Hadyn. And even then, Harzel was not entirely certain if it would be a permanent solution.

Rather than absorb the vitality, Hadyn had wagered that he could reverse the flow—giving instead of taking. His theory had a logical foundation: a blood mage could draw on their own life force for power, but only in minuscule amounts; if the balance tipped too far even once, they would kill themselves.

Hadyn took it a step further by flooding Haizea's mother with vitality, entirely replacing the old with new. When Harzel learned of his son's intentions, he told Hadyn that an exchange of that volume was far too dangerous and too risky.

But his son ignored his warnings. To Harzel's astonishment, it worked... for a little while. But ultimately, Hadyn buckled under the weight of his own magic, and Haizea's mother perished despite his efforts. Harzel would die a thousand times over before he allowed Haizea to take that same risk.

Harzel made many errors with his son and did his best to correct them when it came to his granddaughter. He had gambled that he could avoid scaring her off from her heritage if her first human survived her blood magic.

With Hadyn, Harzel had forced him to kill for his first experience with human blood. Hadyn had been a gentler spirit, and Harzel had ignored it entirely, thinking that if he simply pushed him in the right direction, then he'd accept his heritage. Instead, it broke his son and turned him away from blood magic entirely. Perhaps Hadyn would still be of this realm if Harzel had respected him more.

In contrast, by the time Haizea could walk her mother had her practicing with wooden swords and daggers. She keenly understood violence. But for as many traits she shared with her mother, she inherited just as many from her father.

After shattering his son's innocence, Harzel gave Haizea space to use her own agency on how far she would go with her blood magic. He'd still made errors along the way, but he'd tried his best to improve with her and ultimately succeeded. Even though she still had her doubts, unlike her father, Haizea stuck with her training and her blood magic was a resource available to her in case she ever needed it. And as a blood mage in a kingdom that despised the Cosmic Arts, Harzel was grateful she had listened.

This paper had to mean Haizea was in trouble. She needed him. But why was it blank? The damn thing wouldn't stop flopping back and forth no matter how hard he tried to hold still. In fact, tremors radiated from his fingertips and up to his shoulders. His blood quaked in his veins.

Harzel tilted his head and paused. Then, curiously, he bit the inside of his cheek, drawing blood and igniting his blood magic. His eyes melted into a deep crimson and to his surprise, a message unveiled itself on the paper: words imbued with vitality.

A grin spread across Harzel's lips as he swelled with pride. It was resourceful. Ingenious, even. Only another omen would have seen the hidden message. Haizea had no reason to go to such lengths unless she was being watched.

Harzel had a vague memory of her mentioning working with a clairvoyance mage. As he read the letter, it confirmed his suspicions.

The most important piece of information was that Haizea was well. She was headed deeper into the mountains to send back help, but they both knew Harzel would not sit idly and wait.

A plan had already solidified in his mind. He would need a few days to prepare before he departed on his journey.

Harzel hobbled to his cupboard where he stored a container of ground mirwort, which he took frequently to ease the pain of his unstable vitality. Next, he placed his saltshaker beside it.

Separate, the two substances were fairly innocuous. But combined, they were highly combustible.

The next order of business to prepare for his departure was to collect blood. During his time in Von Stein, Harzel had restricted himself to the blood of animals to avoid drawing unnecessary attention.

Back in the mountains, his endeavors had been less pure and, once a year, he would quench his need for human blood.

The time had come for him to return to his roots.

Harzel kept a mental inventory of the mages who lived in his vicinity. Usually when he needed to replenish his corrupted vitality, one person was more than enough, but for this he needed a variety of abilities in his arsenal.

A family lived about one block down. One woman was a telekinetic while the other was an astral projector. A clairvoyance mage owned the liquor shop that he frequented.

It would be more difficult to hide the disappearance of an entire family, and if word traveled quickly, the clairvoyant mage would be on high alert, making it harder to skirt their perceptive powers. Harzel went to the distillery first and timed his arrival for exactly when they closed up shop.

He entered the store and made a last-minute purchase, using his frail, elderly frame as an excuse when he dropped a bottle. The glass shattered on the ground.

The shop owner gave him a tight smile but otherwise said nothing as they went to clean it up.

"I'm so sorry. Please, let me help," Harzel said.

"No, it's fine."

"I insist," Harzel said as he gingerly bent over to pick up the glass. He hissed when he sliced his hand, and an alarming amount of blood gushed out.

The shop owner crouched down to help him—a fatal mistake. Harzel had drawn on the power of his own life force. Although the strength of his blood magic paled in comparison to his past abilities, he still easily overpowered this person.

Realization hit the shop owner a second later, which was a moment too late. Harzel's hand flashed, and in the blink of an eye he wrapped his hand around the shop owner's neck and squeezed, crushing their windpipe and spine all in one blow. He moved with urgency. Because his vitality had been depleted, his abilities wouldn't last long. Even if he drained this person dry right now, Harzel no longer had the capacity to hold that much power at once.

Harzel pulled a bottle from his satchel. He sat the shop owner upright and sliced his neck open with one of the glass shards lying on the ground.

Using the vials had two main benefits: they were portable, and the amount of blood they held was small enough to avoid overflowing his vessel when he used his blood magic. Once Harzel finished collecting the blood, his knees cracked and creaked as he stood upright. He did his best to ignore the throbbing pain in his back.

Fortunately, his blood magic only caused a muted high. He'd used his own blood, and it hadn't been much, so he still had his wits about him.

Harzel displayed the 'Store Closed' sign and locked the door as he departed the liquor shop, but there wasn't much he could do about the body. Harzel didn't have the stamina for it. If worse came to worst, he would keep an eye on the situation with the blood he'd just gathered.

He didn't expect attention to turn toward him so quickly, but if it did, the clairvoyant blood he now possessed would give him enough advance notice to leave immediately.

As Harzel made his way back home, Haizea's predicament weighed on him. There was very little doubt in his mind about how the situation would play out. He had long ago seen the king's true nature. His granddaughter was intelligent enough to see it as well, but naiveté still hindered her in her young age.

Haizea would be too attached to do what needed to be done. She had always attempted to balance her sense of duty toward the safety of others, with her instinct for survival.

It was why she chose to use rodents to keep magical wasting at bay rather than the blood of her fellow man. She had chosen to be a knight, using a blend of her skills as a healer and a fighter, all while avoiding the regular violence of taking up the Bruvian warrior's mantle.

Some might say this quality was a strength, but honestly, Harzel begged to differ.

A blood mage thrived on the life of others, irrespective of innocence or guilt, and until she rid herself of this softness, Haizea would not reach her full potential.

However, Harzel would never voice that particular thought out loud. It would just be added pressure she didn't need or deserve, a mistake he'd made with his son. His granddaughter would continue to forge her own path, and with experience she'd come to that conclusion on her own.

Harzel spent the next several days laying a trap with the mirwort and table salt compound. It covered every window, every door, and all of the baseboards. He set up lines so that, upon opening a door or window, the friction would light up a series of matches to ignite the compound.

On the night of his departure, Harzel came for the telekinetic family. He whipped through their home like a strike of lightning, draining the two women of their vitality in the same way he had the shop owner. Harzel wrapped a holster around his waist that had multiple slots that could hold vials of blood.

He now possessed enough blood to get started on his journey, but eventually he would need more. A fight that was bound to come to him, and he had done his due diligence to be prepared.

Chapter 22

Beast Realm

The expanse of the Beast Realm stretched as far as the eye could see, a stark contrast from the closed-off environment of civilization back in the Human Realm.

Here, there were no knights or nobles to test Kallistê's patience with insubordination. In fact, she had stamped out any hope of them staging mutiny in her absence by responding to their schemes not with the mighty *trivialis* but rather a fearsome *Great Aiope*.

It was a flying Beast with six horns on its head. Thick, wolf-like fur covered its skin, and large wings protruded from its back. *Great Aiopes* could breathe either fire or ice, depending on which region they originated from. Kallistê happened upon one that expelled a wave of ice.

The nobles had tried to run, but the Beast chilled the atmosphere with its breath, freezing anyone caught in the blast into blocks of ice. Those fortunate enough to avoid a direct hit walked away shivering and frostbitten. They quickly learned that Kallistê did not bluff or mince her words. When she said something, she meant it.

Now, she sat atop a hill in the Beast Realm, watching the various creatures roam. It gave her space and time to think and decompress.

She splayed her fingers into the grass beneath her, lush with cool hues of green, blue, and purple. As the sun's rays heated her skin, it brought out the warm colors of the other foliage around her: trees with bright red leaves and flowers with vibrant magentas.

The crashing sounds of the waterfall several yards away pulled her into a lull. Although Kallistê sought out the largest, most violent Beasts in the realm to bring Llyr to heel, smaller, more innocuous Beasts lived here as well, like the *hydrinidia*. It was a quadruped with translucent skin that reflected the color of the water around it. It had two crisp blue eyes that were large and round. Two antennae protruded from its head, and a long, bushy tail extended from its hind end.

Young *hydrinidias* could fit into the palm of a hand, whereas a fully grown one was the size of a small dog. They splashed and played, diving along as the water fell and jumping high into the air, landing nimbly on the top of the peak to do it all over again. As they did so, their chirps of glee blended with the sounds of the rushing waters.

Of the seven realms, traveling to the Beast Realm always came easiest to Kallistê. It teemed with life, just like the Human Realm. Havoc and serenity coexisted here, much in the way it did back home.

Those similarities laid the foundation of the path that her Soul followed. The Soul Realm was also simple enough to travel to because every human that had ever lived would eventually find their way to the Soul Realm after death.

Unfortunately, that realm was so mind-numbingly boring that Kallistê never spent much time there. Traversing beyond those two realms had proven frustratingly difficult for Kallistê. The more a realm differed from her home, the more she struggled to find the pathway leading to it. Her abilities worked best when a part of her Soul connected with the realm or its inhabitants.

Of the remaining realms, she had visited the Titan Realm, though only a handful of times. On the days Kallistê wondered if she was truly mad, she reminded herself of the Titans.

They were a violent people—if you could even call them that. They towered hundreds of feet in the air, most of them larger than even the *trivialis* she had captured. Kallistê once spent an entire day watching as the Titans slaughtered one another in an endless cycle of bloodshed. They'd gorged themselves on the blood of the fallen. They obliterated the weak and constantly tested the strongest to maintain their status.

Even more unsettling, the realm itself seemed to thrive on death. Wherever a Titan's blood spilled, new life sprang up moments later. Very curious, indeed.

To her shame and frustration, the Demon Realm and the Celestial Realm remained elusive. Kallistê aimed to fix that shortcoming and hoped that her current venture back home would offer enlightenment.

Aaryn and the Demons returned magic to humanity. Kallistê would follow in their footsteps by leaving her own mark on the realm and leading humanity to embrace the Cosmos. Maybe then the pathway would reveal itself to her.

A *Great Aiope* flew overhead, creating a gust of wind with each flap of its massive wings that made Kallistê's long hair blow in every direction. She raked her fingers through it to re-tame her tresses. Her ears popped when the Beast exhaled a scorching ball of fire. It landed on something off in the distance.

Kallistê chuckled to herself at the sight. She had come here seeking a calm environment so that she could focus and escape the turmoil that she'd orchestrated back home and yet chaos still followed her to this distant realm.

She wanted to prepare for the upcoming arrival of the diplomats from Kestramore and put her best foot forward.

As she thought of Kestramore, a wave of homesickness washed over her. A few months had passed since she'd left the island, but it had been several years since she'd been in her old stomping grounds of the Three Corners.

She'd left behind her parents, her meager inheritance that was their shoe shop, and everyone else she knew. But Kallistê didn't regret it. Her life in Kestramore had been fulfilling, and even now she enjoyed the danger and thrill that came from her current endeavors.

But, surprisingly, a part of her quietly wondered about her family's wellbeing in her absence.

Being on the continent was as good an excuse as any to check on them, but it would have to wait until after her meeting with the diplomats. She couldn't afford to be distracted or thrown off-kilter before she met them.

Kallistê nodded to herself. She'd had her fill of the Beast Realm. It was time to return to Llyr.

In order for a human to traverse between the realms, they must make their mind, body and Soul incorporeal and navigate the Cosmic Realm, which connected all realms to one another. The Cosmic Realm was where opposites converged—both reality and imagination, life and death, tangible and abstract, light and darkness, existence and obscurity.

It was where entirely new realms could be born. As purely physical beings, most humans did not have the innate ability to manipulate their own Souls in a way that a realmdrifter could.

If an astral projecting mage tried, they would lose their Souls in the Cosmos because they were limited by leaving their physical bodies behind. Only realmdrifters could traverse the planes of contradiction that made up the Cosmos.

Kallistê entered the Cosmic Realm as she had done so many times before. During her years of training in Kestramore, there were two main periods that weeded out aspiring realmdrifters.

First, those who lacked strong enough power to push their vitality beyond its natural limits. Within the first week, the numbers had been slashed in half, but at least they'd left with their lives. The second major hurdle for realmdrifters was traversing the Cosmic Realm.

Of her classmates that remained, another half lost themselves to the Cosmos.

Once lost, it was impossible to find oneself, and it was extremely difficult for another person to bring them back from the abyss.

The Cosmos enveloped her, bending to her form yet threatening to swallow her whole. Kallistê focused inward, weeding out the noise and latching onto the call of the Human Realm.

It called to her Soul the fiercest; it was always easier to return home than leave it behind. Kallistê followed the pull until she rematerialized at the palace, checking the clock on the wall. She had roughly two hours before the diplomats from Kestramore arrived. Perfect timing.

Kallistê instructed the servants to run a hot bath. She let out a long breath as she dipped her toes into the steaming water before submerging herself. Her hair soaked in the water, washing away the heat she used to straighten her locks and unveiled the wavy pattern of her natural hair texture. Once she cleansed her body and had her fill of the water's warmth, she got dressed.

She moisturized her hair with a homemade mixture of creams before pulling it into a tight bun at the base of her skull. Using a small comb, she left a few hairs out and slicked them down in a neat swoop along her hairline.

Along with her typical jewelry, Kallistê adorned a floor-length orchid dress with a silver mantle over her shoulders to match Llyr's color scheme. Next, she painted her face with makeup, putting a cool purple and glittering silver on her eyelids to match her attire.

Kallistê gave herself a once over in the mirror and smiled to herself, satisfied.

One of the servants knocked on her door and notified her that her guests had arrived. Kallistê instructed them to lead the diplomats to the strategy room, designed for the previous kings and their advisors to deliberate during times of war.

She sat in the chair at the front of the long table as she waited for the diplomats to enter. A few minutes later, the door swung open, and two diplomats greeted her. Kallistê motioned for them to sit in the seats beside her.

They exchanged no pleasantries but instead jumped right into business.

"Kestramore is as intrigued by your offer as they are weary," the diplomat to her left spoke.

It was a woman who went by the name of Lotus. She was a transmuting mage and had magenta hair and similarly colored eyes. Prior to serving on Kestramore's council, Lotus worked as an advisor to the premier.

"What are their concerns?" Kallistê asked.

The other diplomat, Viltarin, spoke next. He had chestnut skin, cascading dark hair, and eyes the color of autumn leaves. He was one of the dignitaries currently serving on Kestramore's council.

He'd earned his position through astute financial ties, operating the largest bank on the island. As both an enchanter and a curse mage, with a single word, Viltarin could attain the same influence Kallistê achieved with her dazzling smile and charming looks.

His magic could twist the vitality in a person's mind and warp their reality, an advantage against Kallistê's Spiritual abilities. As such, she kept a close eye on Viltarin.

"You mentioned that there is a blood mage within the Arcelian king's ranks. This mage wiped out your forces. Given Kestramore's contentious history with the current reigning monarch, for there to be an omen in his midst is... unusual, at best.

"The council would like more information on her true alliances. As things currently stand, the mage is a threat such as to the extent that if we attract her ire, she could bring the entire island to its knees."

"Or, the entire continent," Kallistê countered.

"Or the continent, *if* her allegiance can be shifted away from King Rhys. Per your letter, she was dressed as an Arcelian knight, and her actions signify that she intervened on their behalf. Have you delved any further into the nature of her relationship with Arcelia?" Viltarin asked.

"My first priority was addressing the disorder within Llyr's borders. Searching for the blood mage when the country I am to rule is in turmoil and disarray would have been unwise. The situation is now firmly under my control, so I have a bit more freedom to look for her and discern her true allegiances," Kallistê answered.

"I suppose we should share Kestramore's current disposition, depending on how things fare with the blood mage. At the very least, if she's turned sour against the king, the dignitaries are inclined to offer assistance. If she's decisively on your side, all the better, as it would make a more convincing case.

"But if she aims to remain in the king's good graces, it's not a risk the council is willing to take. Our numbers are too few to make that gamble," Lotus said.

Kallistê nodded. "I understand. However, in my letter I only wanted to establish a trade alliance, not the backing of Kestramore's forces. I do not think something so simplistic will put Kestramore at risk. The kingdoms have a history of turning a blind eye to the black market; the Three Corners is a prime example of this. I'm sure we could establish something of similar nature in the interim that would not implicate the island."

Viltarin gave Kallistê a smug, knowing smile.

"Indeed, you request our food in exchange for Llyr's technology, and it is an attractive offer. But even if you do not say it aloud, you are isolated without any allies and could find yourself overleveraged at a moment's notice. As members of council, it is our job to see these things and preempt them."

She returned Viltarin's grin with a tight sneer of her own. Kallistê had wrenched this throne from the ironclad grips of not one but two kings. She could handle a few measly diplomats.

Although their position irritated her, she understood it. Despite Kestramore being an entire island filled with omens, a blood mage *was* uncommon.

Kallistê knew of a few healers, but only one of them had enough mastery to wield blood magic. It was the elderly mage who'd first given Kallistê a place to stay when she arrived in Kestramore. Given the blood mage's youth and her display of fighting prowess, it would be foolish to employ the old mage against her.

But Kallistê had youth on her side, too. She may not be a trained knight, but she had mastered the Cosmic Arts just the same.

So long as the blood mage did not get access to the vitality in her veins, she would be able to realmdrift to ensure her own escape to safety. And under the right circumstances, she could eke out a win.

Kallistê merely needed to find her, which should prove simple enough. She had established her foundations as a Spiritual mage long before she learned to realmdrift. She knew the essence of the woman's Soul. Not to mention, she only had to search one realm. Kallistê said as much to Viltarin and Lotus and gave them her assurances. She told them to give her two weeks' time and she would contact them with positive results.

Neither Viltarin nor Lotus looked fully convinced, but they had no skin in the game. At least, not yet. At this point, Kestramore's officials still had plausible deniability, so only Kallistê risked demise if things went awry.

The diplomats departed shortly after their conversation concluded. People from Kestramore did not like to linger on the continent, which treated such an integral part of their culture with hostility.

With that behind her, Kallistê set her sights on the Three Corners. Many years had passed since she'd last seen her family. She hesitated to show her face, but at the very least, if she was this close, she could see how they'd fared in her absence.

Kallistê entered the astral plane, but since she was traversing through the Human Realm's domain, she had no need to enter the Cosmic Realm. She found her parents' shop by following the pulse of life in their Souls. While maintaining incorporeal form, she stood just outside the front window. Her mother's dark blue hair had turned almost entirely gray, and her father's limp had worsened; he now used a cane.

Kallistê put her hand on the doorknob, her face contorted with confliction. Maybe—

A shockwave ran through her as a charge rippled through the atmosphere. A chilling breeze followed the sensation. Kallistê's head snapped to attention as she turned to locate where it came from.

Two hues beamed off in the distance; one beaconed a shimmering red and the other glittered with a translucent aura. Even without a clear view of their faces, she knew what and *who* it was. The vitality had bent in Kallistë's favor—the blood mage appeared before once again, and this time with a friend.

She smiled to herself. It couldn't be this easy, could it?

No, it couldn't. She couldn't afford to blunder her chances at getting the blood mage to join her league. Despite the obvious opening, she needed to take her time and plan carefully.

The blood mage had seen her face during the attack. Since Kallistê didn't know which way her current alliances fell and had no way of knowing how she would respond to another encounter, she chose to send knights in her stead to avoid alarming the other omen.

It would be impossible to associate the guards with Kallistê until after they'd already brought her into the fold. Kallistê nodded to herself, satisfied with her decision.

In the blink of an eye, she returned to Llyr. Kallistê called a few select knights, who had shown every sign of falling to her charm, to her quarters and gave them the task. Not wanting to lose any precious time, Kallistê pushed back against the buzz beginning to bud and brought the knights into the astral plane and clandestinely planted them in the Three Corners.

To maintain appearances, she provided a ship for their trip home that would be waiting for them at the harbor of the Sidra River, a major trade route between the Three Corners and Llyr.

She looked pointedly between the three of them before letting them loose.

"Do not disappoint your queen."

CHAPTER 23

Haizea and Alastair arrived in the city in the middle of the night. Despite the Three Corners supposedly being a black market, nearly every shop was closed. Only the bars still had any sort of activity, and as they passed, it became obvious that they were thinly veiled brothels.

Women dressed revealing attire—exposed midriffs, plunging necklines, short skirts, and high heels—wrapped themselves around male patrons. When one of them eyed Haizea and Alastair with interest, she nudged him in the opposite direction, down a quieter street that had closed down for the night.

It may have been a blessing in disguise. With less people around, it gave them a chance to gather the lay of the land with less risk of being spotted and interrupted. Hopefully, the bounty hadn't reached here yet. The last few towns had stretched her patience thin, and Haizea didn't know how much more she could take and still maintain her restraint.

Some of the architecture appeared to draw inspiration from Arcelia's royal palace. White stones with specs of soft blue made up the walkway that meandered through the marketplace. Rather than tents, like many of the merchants in the villages used, each storefront was made of brick and mortar. Located toward the front of the marketplace were more staple items like food, clothing, and basic household necessities. As they walked further, hints of the black market rose to the surface.

They passed a botanical store, which displayed a variety of plants in the front window. Because she often used plants to craft potions, she recognized most of them. She stopped in her tracks as one particular plant caught her eye.

~*What is it?*~ Alastair asked, noticing her hesitance. Haizea shook her head.

A plant with black leaves, charred by volcanic heat, rested in the window. It was wilted and barely clinging to life, but there was no denying it—that was earth's smoke.

Haizea shouldn't have been surprised to see it here in the black market, where a wide array of plants native to the mountains sat on the display, but given the anti-magical properties of earth's smoke, its presence here unsettled her.

Did the merchant know the plant's true nature?

And, more importantly, how did it get here to begin with?

Earth's smoke was one of the handful of advantages the mountaineers had over the rest of the continent. While mountaineers not only had more vitality—which translated to stronger magic—the mountains also held the only known source of anti-magic in the entire realm.

As such, the Bruvian warriors protected it as a precious resource by hunting down and eliminating smugglers attempting to traffic it out of the mountain range's borders. But someone had clearly slipped through the cracks.

Haizea didn't bother answering Alastair. He likely didn't know about the plant because he lived further away from the peaks and closer to the base, where the influence of the kingdoms occasionally interfered. Although she trusted him at this point, Haizea didn't want to risk someone watching and understanding her signs. In the back of

her mind, she considered taking up her warrior's mantle and investigating this further, but the bounty took precedence over everything
else. Instead, if an opening arose at a more opportune time, she would
take care of it then.

She turned her attention away from the storefront, and they continued onward. The rest of the stores were similar in their setup.
Displays in the front window showcased items for sale with various
forms of contraband sprinkled in.

As they passed in front of a weapons shop, Alastair yawned abra-
sively next to Haizea. He gave her a quizzical look when she side-eyed
him, but she let it go. He looked exhausted; dark circles had formed
under his eyes, the wind had blown his hair in every odd direction,
and his clothes hung disheveled on his body.

Not to mention that, unlike Haizea, whose consistent training reg-
imen gave her endurance for physical exertion, the conditions in
Goldenleaf didn't exactly lend itself to the same opportunities for
Alastair. Walking for such a long distance had taken its toll on him.

~*Let's find a hostel and call it a night,*~ she signed.

It didn't take long to find available lodging, however, it did take
quite a while to find a spot that didn't price gouge them. Unlike
pickpocketing, they couldn't just slip by and steal a room. Besides,
here in the black market, the people had a better eye for thieves. Being
scalped for virtually every purchase was just going to be their reality
during their time here.

They agreed to compromise, in that Alastair could lift money off
people since he had a talent at doing so discreetly. Then, they would
use the stolen cash to purchase other items.

However, she refused to agree to him stealing merchandise under
any circumstance. They could quash a dispute over a handful of coins
much more easily than being caught red-handed with hard goods in

their possession. Haizea wanted to raise as little suspicion as possible.

With the bounty looming over their heads, Alastair didn't need a reputation preceding him. Plus, if she managed to find her necklace here, she may need him to retrieve it.

They entered the room they would have to share while they stayed in the Three Corners. Because everything was so astronomically priced, it was all that they could afford. Haizea took the side of the bed closest to the door and Alastair laid down on the opposite end, the bed creaking loudly under his weight.

With a sigh, Haizea sat down and unlaced her boots. She took off her jacket but otherwise resigned herself to sleeping fully dressed.

She checked on Alastair before settling in. He was lying on his side, facing away from her. Haizea started to lean over to blow out the candle when she thought she heard him sniffle.

Frowning, she reached over and put her hand on his shoulder. Alastair sniffed again, but he didn't respond. Haizea got up and walked around to his side of the bed, and her heart broke at the sight of him crying.

She crouched down in front of him. Before she could say anything, he rolled on his back and stared at the ceiling, tears streaming down the sides of his face.

She held one of his hands in hers. For a little while, he cried without acknowledging her. Then, Haizea let him go as he sat upright.

~Do you think we'll find her?~ he asked.

In all honesty, she thought the chances were slim to none, but she wouldn't dare say that. Haizea refused to give up while there was still some hope.

~I don't know. But so long as we try, we haven't failed her.~

Alastair absorbed that for a minute, his eyes red-rimmed.

~I feel like I'm in a nightmare that I keep expecting to wake up from, only to find out that this is all real. Is this what it felt like? With your parents?~

~Yes.~

~How long? How long will it feel like this?~

Haizea paused. *~A long time. The pain doesn't go away, but it gets easier to carry.~*

She could tell that offered him little comfort, but she spoke from her own experience.

~How did you make it easier?~ he asked.

~I didn't. My grandfather did. He took me in. He loved me. He gave me everything he could to make sure I could stand on my own two feet.~

And then I ran off to Arcelia, against his advice, as if he wasn't enough. As if his love wasn't enough. And as a result, I got your family killed, Haizea added silently.

Alastair chewed on his bottom lip as the tears continued to stream down. Haizea climbed over him and sat next to him. When Alastair leaned into her, she wrapped her arms around him and cradled him against her chest until, eventually, she fell asleep.

Alastair tossed about restlessly as the rise and fall of Haizea's chest slowed and she fell into a slumber. As if the loss of his family wasn't enough, sleep evaded him lately.

Despite their travels, once Alastair had committed to embracing the Cosmic Arts, Haizea did not let him slack in his practices. Each morning, she would guide him in the ways of necromancy. She'd told him she mostly knew the basics. Being a blood mage meant having a wide breadth of knowledge, but it came at the expense of taking a deep dive into the different magical classes and subtypes. The first task she'd lead him on was to find a dead body so that he could guide and bind a Soul to it.

Without a trap to use, they'd resorted to pilfering through garbage bins; rodents loved digging through the food scraps that had been discarded by the various eateries.

It had taken a few tries to catch one, but Haizea managed to nab a rat by trapping its tail under her foot before picking it up by the base of its tail. It turned back to gnaw at her fingers, but she wrapped her hand firmly around it, crossing its little arms harmlessly over its body to restrain its movement.

Alastair had hesitated to kill it, so Haizea did it herself before handing it to him. Unlike her sturdy grip, he'd held it gingerly at the base of its tail, wanting to minimize touching it as much as possible. Haizea had talked him through what to do next.

~*You've done this before. It's just a matter of guiding the Soul into the rat's body,*~ she'd said.

His shoulders had tensed as he did as Haizea instructed him and extended his mediumship magic beyond its normal boundaries to bind a Soul into the rodent. It had come disturbingly easily to Alastair. When the rat's lifeless body began to move, he concentrated on maintaining his control.

He had quickly grown accustomed to the high from dabbling with Cosmic magic. In fact, he enjoyed it. But the nightmares that came afterward terrified Alastair; they were what made him run from necromancy when he'd first used that power on Rey.

Each night when he tried to sleep, a massive, suffocating presence gradually disrupted his dreams before dismantling them altogether.

This night was no different. A hooded figure wearing a long robe stalked toward Alastair. As the distance between them diminished, the heaviness in the air increased, and the dreadful sensation of death and oblivion tightened around Alastair's chest, like a snake had wrapped itself around him and was slowly constricting his ribs with each breath he took.

Just like the nights before, Alastair turned to run, but the figure reappeared in front of him. He fell onto his rear end, trembling as the mysterious being stopped in front of him. It pulled its hood back, revealing a face that was nothing more than a skull.

The Soul Reaper. If there was such a thing as a god, then he was certainly the God of the Soul Realm.

Alastair's blood turned to ice in his veins. He screamed for his life, and the vibrations from his vocal cords reverberated through his entire body. He tried to crawl away, but he couldn't move. His fear froze him in place.

The Soul Reaper crouched down and rested his hands on Alastair's shoulders. His mouth did not move when he spoke. Instead, his words transmitted directly to Alastair's Soul.

I am not here to hurt you, child.

Alastair only managed a small whimper in response. The Soul Reaper's presence threatened to crush him right out of existence. The being's expressionless face regarded him for a few moments before he spoke again.

Why are you so afraid, child? Was it not you who called me here?

The world spun and tilted, wild and out of control. If Alastair hadn't already been on his bottom, he would have fallen over.

How? Alastair did not sign his question, but the Soul Reaper understood, nonetheless.

In response, the entity lifted his arm, and the sleeve of his robe slid back, revealing his bony hand. The Soul Reaper pressed it against Alastair's forehead, and his eyes fluttered closed as the entity's power flowed through him.

Something deep within Alastair chipped away. It wasn't large, like a gaping hole, but rather it felt miniscule. Big enough to notice, but small enough that he didn't think it would harm him.

With a start, he opened his eyes and looked at the Soul Reaper.

Most Humans only draw power from their own realm. Omens, as you like to call yourselves, draw power from the Cosmic Realm. But as a necromancer, your power passes through the Soul Realm first. You take from my domain.

~So you... took something from me just now?~

Yes—a piece of your Soul as repayment.

Alastair pressed a hand against his chest. Suddenly, he felt very hollow. What did that mean?

Think of Souls as what you humans call currency. When a being dies, whether from your realm or another, they present their Soul to me as payment, and their power becomes mine. In exchange, I grant them entrance to the Soul Realm. The Souls of the dead add to my domain, but your necromancy takes from it, so I take from you to balance the scales.

Alastair inhaled deeply as he absorbed the Soul Reaper's words. It did nothing to calm the frantic pounding in his chest.

~What happens when... when there's nothing left to take?~

The Soul Reaper regarded him for a few moments before answering.

Unlike the Angels, who unchained themselves from their Souls before their fall into Demonhood, Humans are not capable of living without a Soul. When there is nothing left, you will perish. And without a Soul, there will be no place for you in the Soul Realm.

Alastair instantly thought of his family. His mother and father. Amiri. Alina, whom he desperately hoped to rescue. Rey, who waited in their meadow all these years... if Alastair had nothing to offer the Soul Reaper after his death, he'd never be able to join them in the Soul Realm.

He would be lost forever. At this, his mouth went dry.

I do not give freely. One day, you will understand this. You will come to know what power truly is and the sacrifice it necessitates.

The Soul Reaper could not smile, but the entity emanated an unmistakable satisfaction as it looked down on Alastair.

Alastair trembled as he wrung his hands together, wanting to know what the Soul Reaper meant by that remark yet terrified to know the answer. Before he could contain his nervousness enough to ask, Alastair's mind was thrust back into the Human Realm.

He opened his eyes only to be met with the pitch black of the night. A wave of loneliness overcame Alastair as he thought of everything that had been stolen from him—his family, part of his Soul, and his peace of mind.

He felt the warmth of Haizea's sleeping form beside him and reached for her.

When she shifted closer, the tightness in his chest eased ever so slightly.

Haizea woke up at the crack of dawn. Walking the marketplace before settling in last night had been a prescient choice; she already had a mental map of where to start their search.

Beside her, Alastair was sweating profusely in his sleep, and his vitality threatened to burst at the seams. His magic made her body run hot in response, and she had her own sheen of sweat on her forehead. The fact that he was curled around her, with his arm wrapped over her stomach and one of his legs draped over hers, certainly didn't help either.

Alastair had been restless like this every morning since they'd left the last village. At first, she'd thought he was coming down sick, but perhaps it was simply his grief manifesting outwardly. She'd learned to wake him up very gently, and normally she'd cupped his hand in hers before gingerly pushing on his shoulder.

But she couldn't position herself to do that at the moment. Instead, Haizea ran her fingers through his hair, and his tresses brushed against her skin like silk.

Despite her delicate approach, Alastair bolted awake, grunting as he shot up. He hovered over Haizea, his arms planted on either side of her as she looked up at him.

His irises had lost their normal periwinkle color in exchange for a diamond-like glittering hue. One of his long locks fell down into her face and she pushed it back, her fingertips pulsating from the skin contact.

The sight of Alastair's eyes illuminated with his Cosmic magic lit a fire in her blood. A fantasy formed in her mind, where she ripped the vitality from his veins and absorbed his power for herself. Although Alastair's arms caged her, it was really him who was the prey. Drawing blood would be effortless.

The call of her Cosmic magic nearly succeeded in burying her guilt for having such thoughts. But even now, she could see that the Cosmic Arts were having some sort of unexpected effects on Alastair.

Yet it hadn't deterred Haizea from pushing him to continue. Now that he'd begun, he could not stop without suffering magical wasting.

So far, Alastair had made rather expedient progress by resurrecting a few small animals, but she was curious to see if he had it in him to revive a human being. However, short of defiling a grave, they would need to kill a person to obtain a body for it.

Though Haizea spurned the thought of harming an innocent person, the less rational part of her mind yearned for more bloodshed. Although her priority in the Three Corners was finding Alina and obtaining her necklace—and she certainly wanted to locate both unimpeded—a part of her itched for the opportunity to unleash the full might of her blood magic again.

She could continue to stave off magical wasting by using animals, but it no longer satiated the arousing desire her power elicited. Her body had always had a predilection for human blood, and now that she'd given it a healthy taste, it demanded more.

Haizea could have caved in then, in fact she very much *wanted* to, but her years of practicing restraint would not be erased so easily. And on top of that, Alastair was her friend. Haizea reminded herself of that as she looked at him, warm and soft and alive—just how he should be. She pushed the bloodlust into the back of her mind. Tabled it for later. Took a deep, slow breath. Then another.

Alastair's irises gradually returned to normal. His eyes were more lavender than blue as he looked down at her. His tawny skin had a crisp, golden tone, and his face looked fuller. Even his arms, though still thin, had just a little more muscle to them.

For some reason, the sight made heat pool in her chest.

A darkness painted Alastair's expression. A hunger.

Her gut twisted with sudden vulnerability, a foreign, unfamiliar feeling. Maybe she'd misjudged him. Maybe Alastair wasn't really the prey after all.

Haizea shifted beneath him in an attempt to quell her thoughts, but it did the exact opposite. Instead, it drew his attention downward, and she became hyperaware of just how intertwined they were.

When she looked up, Haizea froze in place, pinned by the blazing intensity of his gaze. Her heart pounded in her ears. Even her fingers were still tangled in his locks. Alastair pulled her hand down and pressed his lips against her wrist, unknowingly adding kindling to the inner flame she was fighting to suppress.

Finally, painstakingly, he got out of bed, releasing her from the cage his arms had made around her. The entire time, he never took his eyes off her.

Haizea sat up properly and scooted to the edge of the mattress to plant her feet on the ground, to regain her balance.

~You know, it's impolite to stare,~ she signed, quietly hoping to release this vex he had on her. Tremors ran up and down her arms. She looked down at her legs and feet and realized with a start that her entire body was shivering.

Alastair grinned impishly. *~You're doing it too,~* he signed.

~It's hard not to. Your eyes are like bright marbles following my every movement.~

His damn grin spread even wider.

~Are you saying you think my eyes are pretty?~

~Yes. No. Wait, I...~ she trailed off. How did they even get on this?

~Yours are,~ he signed. *~They're like honeycombs. You know there's something sweet on the inside, so they draw you in even though you're bound to get stung a few times before you can get to it.~*

Haizea blinked, taken off guard by the compliment, but Alastair quickly moved on without giving her a chance to linger on it.

~Thank you for last night. And for coming all the way here for my sake. I know you're worried about your grandfather, so it means a lot to me that you're doing this. More than I can put into words.~

The mention of Grandfather Harzel added a gust of wind to the hurricane of turmoil already brewing within. As a medium, Alastair had been able to confirm fairly quickly that both her grandfather and the warriors had received her messages, but Haizea struggled to find comfort in that.

She wouldn't feel settled until she saw her grandfather for herself and could hold him in her arms again. That was more than could be said about Alina at the moment.

~You're my friend, Alastair. Of course I would be here. You don't have to thank me. Your family treated me with kindness and generosity. This is the least I can do.~

The brightness in his eyes dimmed, although Haizea could tell Alastair was doing his best not to show it. She let him use the washroom first before she took a much-needed bath.

Her body burned like a furnace. Alastair's magic always left her twisted in knots, and this morning was no different. She scrubbed and let the cold water run over her body until she found herself calm again.

They had their work cut out for them. She needed to stay focused on the task ahead: rescuing Alina and tracking down her mother's necklace.

The first merchant they visited was a jeweler they'd passed by last night. It would be less conspicuous to start off by asking about jewelry and then easing her way into inquiring about Alina. Given that whoever had kidnapped her had most likely also snatched Haizea's pendant, she assumed that at least one jeweler would have seen something.

Haizea described the necklace right down to the centimeter-wide scratch on the back of its pendant. The merchant's stony face rivaled Haizea's own piercing gaze.

He shrugged his shoulders and said he hadn't seen it. She eyed him for a few moments, not fully believing him. She started to press him further, but then she remembered the bounty. No unnecessary attention. Not in a city filled with smugglers; if they caught wind of their pursuit, she and Alastair might never find Alina.

If this jeweler didn't have it, there were still a few others in this section of the market she could visit. As Haizea turned to leave, Alastair nudged her with his elbow before pointing off in the distance. A few men loitered near the entrance as they looked intently at the display case.

Alastair must have alerted her because they weren't really shopping, only pretending to as they watched them.

Haizea fell back and let Alastair take the lead. His gait shifted from the relaxed footsteps of his casual stroll into more calculated movements as he concentrated on losing their tail.

Haizea's long stride let her keep pace with his nimble footsteps. They swiftly evaded pursuit and made it to the next shop—this time Haizea managed to get far enough to ask about Alina, but they denied having seen her—before the men appeared again.

As she debated how to deal with the men, Alastair nudged her. A pair of masked individuals wearing plain clothes stood further down the walkway, but they held themselves with a prideful air that reminded Haizea of how the Royal Guard carried themselves.

Had King Rhys dispatched mercenaries? For once, her resting expression accurately represented her inner thoughts. Maybe running from the bounty had made her paranoid, but regardless, she was growing increasingly annoyed with King Rhys's antics.

If they headed toward the exit, they'd run right into the mercenaries. And if they walked further into the market, they wouldn't be able to avoid the men that had been following them.

If King Rhys had sent the first pair of mercenaries to pursue them in a discreet manner, why bother with this second group? Having so many people involved was bound to draw attention. Haizea must have missed something.

Although she hadn't seen any wanted posters yet, maybe they hadn't been as thorough as they thought about covering their tracks. How long had they been followed?

As she stood there reeling, Haizea missed Alastair's signal. The two men from earlier closed the distance before she had time to react. To her surprise, they held their hands up in a submissive gesture.

"We're here on behalf of Queen Kallistê, ruler of Llyr. In exchange for amnesty within the kingdom's borders, she requests your presence at the palace."

Well, that was unexpected.

Chapter 24

Before Haizea could respond, Alastair pulled her further along the pathway and away from the Arcelian mercenaries. The men followed, but because their body language did not portray hostility and their request was so bewildering, she didn't go on the offense just yet.

"Queen *Kallistê?* Of Llyr?" Haizea asked slowly, while signing at the same time for Alastair. One of the men watched her carefully as she did so and followed suit by signing when one of his partners replied.

"Yes. Queen Kallistê has taken place on the throne to keep the kingdom from falling into disarray in the wake of the kings' untimely demise."

Haizea's eyes narrowed on the men in front of her. They shifted backward on their heels.

"And what was her relation to the previous monarchs?"

"She served as one of their close advisors."

A lie. Haizea resisted rolling her eyes. They told a smart one, given that the identities of advisors weren't always public knowledge, but it was a lie, nonetheless.

She still had not forgotten the realmdrifter who slithered away during the attack at the festival. It wasn't a far stretch for the same person to have successfully accomplished in Llyr what they failed to achieve in Olysseus.

The realmdrifter's parting words rang in her head.

"You are... incredible."

They'd said as much even in the aftermath of Haizea killing her comrades; not exactly the mark of a trustworthy person.

On the other hand, enemies had cornered Haizea and Alastair at every turn, and her home village was half a continent away, near the center of the mountain range. Assuming that accomplices of the realmdrifter stood before her, would it be worth the risk to consider her offer?

She still knew absolutely nothing about the omens behind the attack, and getting to know her enemies by keeping them close held strategic merit.

Haizea flared her nostrils. With each passing moment, the chances of finding Alina dwindled. She and Alastair couldn't afford to be interrupted by whatever the hell this charade was.

"I don't have time for this," Haizea muttered.

She and Alastair moved to go around the men, but they grabbed onto their swords.

"You don't want to do that," she warned. Her magic brimmed beneath the surface, begging for them to give her a reason.

One of the men nodded. "You're right. We're not here for a fight. We're here to extend an olive branch."

"Or shove it in our hands if we refuse," Haizea snapped.

He chuckled. "We'd prefer not to go that far."

Haizea had already taken note of the weapons they carried the moment when they first approached her. Two men each possessed a single sword, while the third carried a longbow. In such a short range, that weapon was more of a liability than an asset, but Haizea wouldn't take any chances.

Going by the increased magical pressure, at least one of them was a mage, but she hadn't pinpointed which. Next to her, Alastair shifted his weight. Between their necromancy sessions, she'd worked with him a little on his self-defense; just enough for him to use his nimbleness to get out of harm's reach, but this was beyond his purview.

Haizea, however, had more than enough skill to take down these men with her eyes closed, armed or not.

"I will not be strong-armed into an alliance with an omen I do not know. I don't give a damn if she's a queen. It's in your best interest to walk away." She cracked her knuckles before curling her fingers into tight fists. "While you're still capable of doing so."

They did not want this fight. They would not win.

Haizea straightened her back, standing as tall as she possibly could.

A peculiar giddiness pulsed through her as the men before her stiffened and froze in place. Her muscles tensed in anticipation, coiled and ready to strike. She watched them with bated breath as she awaited their next move.

Without warning, Alastair clutched his head and sagged to his knees. The movement tore her attention away from the men, and she helped him back up to his feet, but as soon as her skin touched his, a spark zapped her fingertips.

The vitality in his blood roiled beneath the surface, eager to be let out. The sensation made her own vitality quake within.

When his eyes opened, they beaconed like glitter, sparkling and clear. Magic pressure bore down on Haizea, smothering her like the winds of a violent storm.

She gritted her teeth and fought back against the tremors vibrating through her from head to toe. No wonder Alastair had dropped to his knees; it took everything in her not to do the same.

One of the men stumbled backward, most likely the mage of the trio sensing the sudden surge in vitality. The two non-mages looked between them, perplexed.

Haizea kept a hand on Alastair's shoulder, but he didn't react or respond in any conceivable way. His mind and his Soul had most likely traversed beyond this realm. She glanced over her shoulder to see the two Arcelian mercenaries getting perilously close to where they stood.

Haizea hissed out a string of expletives. She paused and took a deep breath to push back against the violence her blood magic desired and think about this logically.

She could stay here and be forced to fight, which would undoubtedly draw attention not only to her presence but also the million-dollar bounty on her head.

In a city full of illegal smugglers, it was the last thing she needed. Could she take them all? With her blood magic, it was possible. Should she bet her life on it? Probably not.

Nobody in their right mind would. Not to mention that she had to protect more than just herself. In his current state, Alastair was defenseless and in no condition to run. Her attention would be divided if a fight broke out.

Although she did not have the power of a medium, she could practically feel the Souls of his family watching her. The weight of their deaths rested heavily on her shoulders. She would never forgive herself if the same happened to Alastair. His safety took precedence over everything else.

Haizea turned to the strangers offering the aforementioned olive branch. Their heartbeats accelerated, and beads of sweat budded on their skin as her eyes bore into them like a hawk.

Alastair slowly slumped forward, and the weight of his head hit her legs as she kept him from hitting the ground. She sighed in frustration.

"Okay. We'll go with you. Help me get him out of here first."

Alastair had grown used to his consciousness getting stuck somewhere between his life in the Human Realm and the call of the dead from the Soul Realm. It usually happened as he slept, when his mind was unbound by the chains of reality and free to roam as the vitality pleased, but this was the first time it had happened while he was fully awake.

He braced himself for the Soul Reaper's appearance once again.

Above all, he would not cower this time.

The Soul Reaper was a being as old as time itself. For as long as there had been life, the Soul Reaper had existed to take it. Although Souls could linger in their homes for a while, in one way or another, they inevitably wandered to the Soul Realm for their final resting place.

The Soul Reaper would then devour and subsequently expel them, after absorbing their power.

What the Soul Reaper called power, the humans called vitality.

Two different words that described the same thing: the building blocks that made up not only life but also the foundations of realms themselves.

To Alastair's surprise, the Soul Reaper did not come—but something else did.

A human-like being that towered several feet over Alastair materialized before him. Their skin and hair were a rich gold with soft white wings, and their eyes the color of amber. If Angels existed, that's what Alastair would call this creature.

His magic instinctively reached out to get a reading on their Soul, but he latched onto nothing, like a hand trying to grasp thin air. His heart pounded in his chest as he attempted to understand through the confusion clouding his mind.

Although the Soul Reaper had no Soul of his own, Alastair could somehow still feel and read him, likely because he existed to devour Souls of others. But aside from that, Alastair had never come across another being, dead or alive, that he could not sense a Soul at all.

Then it dawned on him, and his eyes widened.

This was no Angel.

Never in a million years did Alastair ever imagine he would encounter a Demon. He only *knew* of Aaryn, who claimed to be the Queen of the Demon Realm.

The mysterious being who had restored magic to the Human Realm.

The being before him matched the description of the tales he'd heard over the years. Alastair had never truly believed the legends; it always seemed more myth than truth. With her standing before him now, maybe he should have felt gratitude, but instead he looked at her pensively.

~Did I call you here?~ Alastair asked with suspicion.

It dawned on him then just how little he knew about his magic, not just necromancy but also his medium abilities.

Could mediums call upon the Demons in the same way he'd done with the Soul Reaper?

Could he summon other beings?

And, more importantly, how the hell did he stop it from happening?

In answer, the Demon threw her head back in laughter. Alastair looked around frantically for the Soul Reaper.

In the back of his mind, he knew it was odd to seek protection by an entity that sustained itself on death, but his gut told him that would be his only hope should the situation take a turn. Alastair did not believe his human magic would fare well against a Demon, especially since he was a Spiritual mage and Demons possessed no Souls.

Suddenly, Aaryn stopped laughing and looked at him intently. As shiver ran down his spine, as if she had read his Soul although he would never be able to read hers.

When she outstretched her hand towards him, just as the Soul Reaper had when they first met, Alastair commanded himself to run, but his legs refused to move. She had nearly closed the distance between them when the Soul Reaper materialized in front of him, grasping her hand in his.

Aaryn, he chided.

The Demon bristled. *I heard that you brought a living Human to the Soul Realm. I wanted to see for myself if his Affinity was worthy of such an act,* she said.

That's not for you to decide. This realm is my domain. You have your own.

Aaryn ruffled her feathers. *But he can steal Souls from this realm while all the way from Earth...?* she trailed off.

Aaryn, leave of your own volition. Please. The one thing you did right was restore to humanity what rightfully belonged to them. Has your greed not taken enough already?

She recoiled as if she'd been slapped, and sorrow emanated from the Soul Reaper. Alastair knew nothing of the Demon race, but maybe she had a long history with Soul Reaper.

And by the look on her face, it appeared that she shared his sorrowful sentiments. Aaryn spread her wings, which spanned easily three times as long as Alastair was tall. With a powerful flap, a gust of wind sent him tumbling back, and she flew away.

The Soul Reaper turned to Alastair.

The Demons are a complex race, just as you humans are. But unlike your kind, they seldom lend themselves to benevolence, Aaryn least of all. The Soul Realm is no place for a human. You know the cost of using your human magic to draw power from here. Unless you wish to further loosen your bond with your own Soul, you should be careful, young Alastair.

Alastair's brows furrowed in concern. *~Why——~*

His mind snapped back into the Human Realm before he could finish his sentence.

He caught a brief, blurry glimpse of Haizea quite literally dragging him along with the three men that just a few moments ago she'd refused to join forces with.

Alastair's head spun; the combined weight of the Soul Reaper's and Aaryn's presence took their toll on his body. As his world turned dark, he welcomed the reprieve of the quiescence.

<h1 style="text-align:center">CHAPTER 25</h1>

HUMAN REALM, KINGDOM OF ARCELIA, CAPITAL
CITY OF RAVARYN

Jirina shut her eyes and pressed her hand into the handle of her scepter. The vitality spoke to her, not much different from the way it spoke to a medium, however the link existed within her mind rather than her Soul.

Objects closest in proximity entered her perception first, King Rhys in particular. The vitality rippled, and an image of him manifested in her mind's eye.

He stood with his hands clasped behind his back, his taut jaw stretching the scar on his face. As the scope of her awareness expanded, he fell into the background and others came to the forefront. Each person had a different aura which blended into cities before amalgamating into entire kingdoms.

Jirina searched for Haizea through the populace, honing her focus on the familiar traces of her aura. Normally, her vitality exuded vibrancy yet maintained an undercurrent of calmness, but whatever efforts Haizea had taken to conceal her blood magic before, she no longer bothered herself with now.

Her vitality bombarded Jirina with such intensity that it sent a shiver down her spine. That was the difference between a mage and an omen; by defiling the gift that the vitality bestowed upon them, omens tainted their very essence.

Haizea stood beside her white-haired friend whom she only conversed with using hand signs. Jirina couldn't follow a damn thing they were saying. She could recognize standard salutations in sign language, but that rudimentary knowledge left her wanting as she struggled to follow the speed of their movements. Haizea's fluency shocked her as much as it annoyed her. It was yet another secret in her growing pile of lies.

She shook her head to dispel her frustrations. Perhaps she could not understand their signs, but she could take a step back and look at the bigger picture.

Haizea periodically clutched at her neck; her ever-present necklace was absent. The duo had changed course since the last time she'd checked on them and now traveled farther North.

Naturally, Jirina pulled out a map to try to predict the precise location they headed toward. The Three Corners stuck out to her the most. She said as much to King Rhys, and he dispatched a few mercenaries to cover all their bases.

He also hadn't relinquished his quest to find Haizea's weak spot, as he was certain there had to be something or someone they could gain leverage with. Jirina had done her due diligence in that regard, as well.

"I have an update for you, Your Majesty," Jirina said.

He turned his gaze to her. "Proceed."

"She has one living relative within Arcelia's borders. Harzel Usoro, her paternal grandfather, resides in Von Stein. Records show he relocated there shortly after Haizea's acceptance into the Royal Guard. There's not any available information on him prior to that, likely because it's held within the mountains."

The king gave her a nod of approval.

"Quick and efficient work as always, Jirina."

In reality, it had been quite a task to track Haizea's grandfather. In the mountain range, children customarily took their mother's surname, unlike the major kingdoms.

Jirina didn't have access to Haizea's familial records because that too was retained within the mountain range's borders. She connected Harzel to Haizea purely on luck, by searching for similar first names instead. Within the dozens of potential matches, she narrowed it down by how recently he'd established residence in Arcelia; it lined up perfectly with Haizea's work in the kingdom.

Jirina had sent a few servants to question his neighbors. They confirmed that a woman matching Haizea's description visited quite frequently. In addition to that, their accounts corroborated with the records she'd found. The evidence allowed Jirina to confidently draw her conclusion about the man's connection to Haizea.

"I would like to add, Your Majesty, that Mr. Usoro has not been seen at his home for about two weeks. His neighbors saw him leave on a carriage, purportedly headed southeast."

King Rhys clicked his teeth. "Bastard's headed toward the mountains. I'll send a few knights. Should be more than enough," he sighed.

"Well, if I may, Your Majesty. Given that her father was a healer, it's safe to say Haizea's magic stems from her paternal side. Knowing she's a blood mage, it's reasonable to ascertain that knowledge was passed down to her by family. There's a significant chance that her grandfather is a blood mage himself. Which makes him a formidable threat despite his advanced age."

The king nodded. "Noted. I'll send Ser Bren. I trained him myself on how to subdue omens."

Jirina arched an eyebrow, but King Rhys did not offer any further explanation. She knew better than to probe, otherwise the ire currently directed at Haizea may turn to her instead.

Still, she could not ignore that whenever it came to dealing with corrupted magic, King Rhys always sought Ser Bren's assistance.

First with the execution in the colosseum, then with the note he'd written home to Queen Mireille, and again now. On the one hand, it made sense, given that he was the highest knight in the Royal Guard and had King Rhys's utmost trust. On the other hand, Ser Bren could not wield vitality, so how could a non-mage be of any help against an omen?

"The mercenaries have been unsuccessful thus far, so it seems your choice to manipulate her in other ways was prescient," Jirina remarked.

"Such wisdom comes with experience. This endeavor will be an enlightening task for you, as well as the remainder of the Guard. Once we capture and exterminate the witch, Ser Bren intends to retire. Afterward, I will properly reconstitute our forces and, given your commendable work thus far, plan on appointing you to take his place."

Jirina's brows rose in surprise. She bowed deeply and worked to suppress her smile to keep from appearing overzealous. "Thank you for your kind words, King Rhys. I'll do my utmost to ensure we successfully bring the blood mage to heel."

A light knock on the door interrupted them before they could continue. Zander entered the room. He offered a deep bow to the king before taking a seat next to Jirina. In his hand, he carried a cage containing a messenger hawk.

After she'd informed King Rhys that Haizea was headed toward the Three Corners, he explained that his hands were tied. If he openly pursued Haizea himself, he risked upsetting the delicate balance within the city's borders. Each kingdom had an unofficial '*don't ask, don't tell*' policy regarding the black market. He'd already breached that agreement by sending hired mercenaries, but the bounty provided cover and allowed him to retain some plausible deniability on their direct connection to the throne.

Even if the mercenaries' ties to Arcelia were revealed, King Rhys could argue that they had acted independently in hopes of obtaining the bounty's reward and not by his explicit command.

However, if King Rhys sent knights or anyone else actively serving his court, that was a different story. Convincing Haizea to come of her own volition was now of utmost importance. The king did not want his pursuit of justice to stoke the flames of war.

It was for that reason that he took a risk by penning a letter to the new monarch of Llyr and tasked Zander with sending it. Though she was an omen who had tried to assassinate the king, her motivations remained unclear. Perhaps her lack of success could provide an opening for negotiation.

If not that, then at the very least, her response would serve as a window into her inner thoughts. Jirina never would have deigned herself to do something of this nature, but she didn't dare utter that sentiment aloud.

Zander removed the hawk from the cage and handed King Rhys the sealed letter. He read it aloud.

Dearest King Rhys,

I am writing to you to confirm receipt of your letter and to send my thanks for the act of diplomacy despite our tumultuous beginnings. I would be elated to mediate any peaceful discussions and negotiations between you and your knight, if that is your desire.

With that being said, it needs to be made abundantly clear that Llyr will not be aiding you in this rabbit chase if your ultimate goal is the death of a fellow omen. Any Arcelian personnel caught within our borders—including any claimed and contested territories—will be treated as hostile actors of an enemy nation, initiating an act of war.

I hope you are as shrewd and astute as my predecessor's believed you to be. If so, I eagerly anticipate the amenable relationship between our two kingdoms. If not, then I equally look forward to the day that Arcelia is crippled by such a foolish blunder.

Kindest regards,

Queen Kallistê

The queen's refusal came as no surprise; of course an omen would look after their own kind. He handed the letter to Jirina with a sigh. With the paper in her hands, she let the vitality flow into her mind, giving her insight.

Each person who'd handled the paper left behind traces of their essence. Zander's and King Rhys's vitality drenched the letter because they'd touched it the most recently. But wisps of a third, cacophonous vitality seeped through. Jirina latched onto it and followed its path. With each second that passed, it grew louder, leading her to a maelstrom that left nothing but destruction in its wake.

But even that chaos formed a coherent picture. A woman appeared before her, with long flowing blue hair, vibrant sapphire eyes, and smooth, blemishless dark skin.

Jirina set the letter down. She did not need to be a seer to understand the outcome if this woman ever crossed paths with the blood mage. Her eyes locked with Zander's. He'd always been closer to Haizea than she had been. Maybe...

Zander shook his head as soon as he saw Jirina's expression. But it was too late, because King Rhys shared her train of thought. He put a hand on Zander's shoulder.

"I'm going to be sending some knights on a special mission to retrieve Haizea's grandfather. I'd like you to join them. If we can get the man to return to us willingly, all the better. Your bond with Haizea should help convince him. And you're well-trusted within the Guard. I think you can get the job done, despite the dangers."

Zander blinked as he took a moment to gather his thoughts. He had no choice in the matter, not truly, for the king had spoken. Refusing would be akin to treason, especially since the king had just highlighted his friendship with Haizea.

This was a test of his loyalty. Fail, and Zander's head would roll.

He exhaled a long, beleaguered breath and avoided Jirina's gaze.

"Thank you, Your Majesty," Zander said as he bowed before exiting. The king's wish was his command.

CHAPTER 26

Human Realm, Sidra River

Violent winds whipped about, lifting Haizea's heavy coils away from her neck and shoulders in a gravity-defying manner. A shadow passed over her as a cluster of clouds drifted by. High above, the sky loomed a dismal gray, and the rumbling sound of thunder erupted. The storm was still a ways out, but if the wind kept up, it would overtake them in no time.

The knights from Llyr knew the path of least resistance back home. As a result, Haizea and Alastair were aboard a small ship that followed the Sidra River, which traveled along the border between Olysseus and Arcelia. It snaked directly through Llyr before its estuaries met the ocean on the northern coast.

At first glance, Sidra was epitome of serenity. The waves flowed with a smooth calmness, and the river's depths appeared shallow enough for a quick dive into the water.

But powerful undercurrents ran just beneath the surface, forming tunnels and voids that quickly trapped even the most experienced swimmers. Even the wildlife never fully relaxed as they stopped to drink along the riverbanks; their ears twitched at the smallest sound, and they held one paw of hoof hovering just above the ground, ready to flee at a moment's notice.

Sidra's danger didn't stop human ambition, however. It was too convenient of a trade route to ignore and, with the recently developed steam technology, boats of the old days had evolved into durable ships. They could withstand the powerful currents while their narrow designs gave them the agility required to navigate within the river's banks.

Queen Kallistê had sent her men down on such a ship, which acted as a perfect decoy as they sailed up the river. Anyone looking would simply assume it was a trade ship.

Haizea hated to admit it, but the queen had made a judicious choice. Unfortunately, it didn't account for Jirina's clairvoyance, but Haizea didn't bother voicing that particular concern aloud. Short of killing her former comrade, there wasn't much that could be done about it. She'd have to cross that bridge when she reached it.

The sound of Alastair grunting loudly disrupted her thoughts. He'd been in a stupor for hours, and no one had been able to rouse him. She walked over and nudged him to see if he was truly awake, or still caught in whatever dream he'd been in.

To her relief, Alastair's eyes fluttered open. He shot up, gasping and grunting, almost as if he was trying to speak, but words wouldn't come. Haizea grabbed his hands.

~Use your words~ she signed with him.

It took him a few moments to calm down enough to finally sign an intelligible sentence. He told Haizea not only of the Soul Reaper, but of the Angel—no, the Demon, Aaryn. He'd seen her with his own eyes. Spoken to her in the Soul Realm.

Haizea's brows rose briefly, the only sign of her surprise, before she leveled her gaze once more.

~It's because you lack control. You're like a tankard carrying vitality, but whenever you try to access it, you let it all out at once. I had the same problem when I first learned blood magic.~

She didn't mention that her inexperience resulted in a lack of magical precision that nearly killed Grandfather Harzel. Although the cause of Alastair's problems was easy to identify, the end result manifested differently because he was in a different magical class.

For an undisciplined blood mage, whether they wanted to or not, they drained any and all sources of vitality nearby and ripped the life out of every being around them. By the looks of things, for a necromancer, using too much power meant drawing the attention of the Soul Reaper.

As a Physical mage, she struggled to decipher what specific aspects in which Alastair lacked control. Her training as a blood mage only gave her surface-level knowledge. Grandfather had trained her to use her power as a means to protect herself. She knew enough to overwhelm her enemies and to show Alastair how to do the same, but not enough to teach him the intricacies of what being a medium entailed.

She blew a puff of air, pushing a loose curl out of her face. The queen was a realmdrifter, which meant that she was a Spiritual mage. While not quite the same as medium magic, there should be considerably more overlap between her skillset and what Alastair needed. Yet another thing Haizea hated to admit.

Alastair was a walking liability without control of his magic. Otherwise, Haizea never would have bothered with the queen. She'd nudged him in to pursue necromancy, or, more specifically, *continue* with it.

Even though the choice ultimately came down to him, Haizea still felt some culpability for his struggles. She frowned. Was this how Grandfather felt when he approached her about learning blood mage? Did her father have the same qualms before deciding not to pass on his heritage to her?

Alastair's hand curled around her arm, and he braced himself against her to rise to his feet. Tufts of his pearly white hair sprouted in every direction. Dark circles cast shadows under his eyes, and his cheeks were sunken in.

He stumbled into her before righting himself.

~I think you should take it easy,~ she signed, forehead creased in concern.

Alastair ignored her and stalked toward the railing on the side of the ship. With each unstable step, he nearly toppled over, so she followed just a few paces behind.

But he soon made it to the railing, and his hands clutched onto the metal all on his own. Alastair stared out over the waterfront as the ship sped along. Haizea wondered if a wandering Soul had captured his mind yet again. She walked up and stood next to him.

When he linked his pinky with hers, it reassured her that Alastair still had his presence of mind in this realm. He was just distracted at the moment. They stood together until another roar of thunder clapped overhead and large droplets of rain began pouring down.

~There's another ship coming,~ Alastair signed.

~A Soul told you?~ Haizea asked.

He paused for a moment before nodding.

~How far? I'm assuming they're hostile?~

He shook his head. *~Not hostile. There's an issue with the ship. A school of fish got caught in the propellers. Some of the crew tried to get it out, but they drowned.~*

His hesitation a few seconds ago made sense to her now. It wasn't just any wandering Soul he'd felt, but the people who'd just died had passed through him.

Haizea ushered him away from the railing. One of the knights side-eyed them, while the other two—who, notedly, could not sign—concerned themselves with steering.

He said something to them that Haizea couldn't quite catch over the baleful winds. When she narrowed her eyes at him, he paled and quickly busied himself with something else.

They'd already had two run-ins with people invested in King Rhys's bounty. She refused to make that mistake a third time. A lull broke the winds. If she listened hard enough, she could hear screams in the distance, growing louder with each passing second as they got closer. A chill raced down her spine.

The ship finally came into view. It careened and tilted at a dangerously sharp angle, on the verge of capsizing. The steep incline caused some people to lose their footing, and they slid into the water, where the river's rapid undercurrents consumed them.

Alastair put his hand on her arm.

~This ship should have a spare lifeboat we can send. I know we can't bring them all on board, but at least save some of them…~

Haizea shook her head. Even though one of their escorts was a telekinetic mage, and hypothetically she could use her blood magic to access their power, she had no desire to. She'd been burned one too many times by helping people when she should have kept moving forward.

For all she knew, the wreckage was an elaborate decoy by King Rhys so that she'd let her guard down.

Not again. And she wouldn't let Alastair take that risk and jeopardize himself, either. A loud splash rocked against their ship as the boat overturned completely and took the passengers along with it.

Haizea did her best to block out the sound of their gurgled screams as their lungs filled with water. Beside her, Alastair's face contorted with agony as their Souls bombarded him with each extinguished life.

She comfortingly rubbed his back, and he leaned into her. It brought her no joy, and it went against her every instinct as a healer, but intervening would be foolish.

She found herself wondering what Grandfather Harzel would say right now. And worse yet, she wondered what her parents would have said. Her mother was a warrior. She'd dedicated her life to protecting the people around her. And her father...

Haizea shook her head and dispelled those thoughts. How they felt and what they thought didn't matter. What *did* matter were her own choices and how *she* felt about them.

Like how Haizea could see now that her decision to become a knight was a lapse in judgment. One that her grandfather tried to want her about, but she'd ignored. Now the consequences of that choice had come after her in full force.

At least Grandfather Harzel did not take that choice away from her, like how her father had tried to do with the Cosmic Arts. It finally dawned on her that common denominator between her maternal and paternal sides that seemed to skip her father: survival.

Survival had driven her family to spend most of their lives covered in the blood of others. Some innocent, some guilty, and many somewhere in between.

As the ship full of people drowned in front of her, Haizea realized no matter which way she carved her own path, the end result was still the same. Wherever she went, whatever choices she made, carnage would follow. Coming from a long line of blood mages and warriors, it was written in her blood and entrenched in her nature: her past, her present, and her future.

The only options laid before her was *whose* blood she was willing to spill.

And if she made no choice, then life would choose for her. Like it had her father.

He had tried to resist his legacy, and in the end, he died for it. With time, Haizea had come to understand why he made that choice, but she found no dignity in the way he'd died.

Both he and her mother suffered needlessly because of his failure. They'd perished and left her behind when she needed them the most. She couldn't follow in his footsteps and repeat his mistakes.

Haizea would choose life. She would protect *her own* life. And those that she cared about. She nudged Alastair and coaxed him to turn him away from the devastation. It was easier to let an atrocity happen when you weren't looking at it in the face.

CHAPTER 27

Kallistê stood in front of her bedroom window with her hands clasped in front of her. Absentmindedly, she fiddled with the rings around her fingers, feeling the textures of the gemstones embedded in them.

After sending her thinly veiled threats to King Rhys of Arcelia, she was certain she'd attracted his ire. And if he somehow miraculously managed to keep his wits about him after reading it, then surely recruiting the blood mage to her side would send him over the edge.

Kallistê had inquired about the king's reputation and heard disturbing tales of his treatment toward omens. Anyone with corrupted vitality was a traitor in his eyes and as such, he sentenced them to a traitor's punishment.

She did not fear the king, but something about a normal mage killing an omen unsettled her. It defied the hierarchy of power. It could undo all her hard work and jeopardize not only her throne, but the island of Kestramore entirely. Hopefully, the blood mage would be able to offer some insight into this. Maybe she knew the king's secret.

Fortunately, she wouldn't have to wait much longer. Her window offered prime viewing of the Sidra River, and she watched as a tiny spec in the distance grew larger with each passing second.

Her knights were returning home with her treasure. Kallistê barely suppressed a squeal of excitement.

She had assigned every servant to make the palace spotless. In fact, she'd commanded them to redecorate the entire castle.

The late Kings Arlo and Johan had no taste. They hadn't bothered with any interior design. The furniture had been there for centuries. Even the walls, although pristine, were plain white. They could at least fill the castle with the purple that represented Llyr's flag.

Kallistê took it upon herself to redesign everything. She had lilacs planted around the palace's fencing. Jacaranda trees now lined the walkway that led from the front gate to the castle's entrance, their purple leaves fluttering in the wind. The servants painted the castle's walls a dark gray and lined the baseboards with a lavender streak. She'd taken down the portrait of the fallen kings and replaced it with one of herself.

Some servants would see that particular action as an act of good faith, but Kallistê knew that many would see it as a brazen act of disrespect. A power play. No matter.

She invited either interpretation of her actions. Quite frankly, she welcomed their dissent if it meant they burned their own country to the ground trying to get to her. The less resistance in her way, the better.

In the last few weeks, there had been multiple attempts on her life. A case of poisoned food a few days ago, detected only by her insistence that a servant ate a bite from her plate at every meal. Before that, a knight had raised his sword at her—only to suddenly find himself abandoned in the Beast Realm and torn apart by the creatures there.

She had heard whispers from some of the nobles already about sending a trusted person to study the Cosmic Arts so that they could unseat her, as well.

It did not take much for people to turn to darkness, because most teetered on the edge at any given time. All they needed was a gentle nudge.

With corruption comes power. And with power, chaos is destined to follow. Let them come, she thought as she smiled to herself.

Kallistê dressed in her full regal attire for the arrival of her esteemed guests. She wore a black dress paired with a purple-lined mantle. Her naturally wavy hair had been straightened with a heating element so that it hung down to her hips. She donned a neutral brown lipstick and paired it with a muted purple eyeshadow.

When the front door of the castle opened and her knights entered with the blood mage, Kallistê greeted them with a smile.

She faltered internally for just one moment when she saw the white-haired man, whom she'd forgotten to account for, but set it aside. A friend of the blood mage presented an opportunity, a tool she could use to her advantage.

"It's a pleasure to meet you. I apologize that we haven't been introduced properly until now. I am Kallistê, Queen of Llyr."

The blood mage greeted her with silence, staring Kallistê down with the intensity of a hawk. The man stood behind her and looked around the room inquisitively.

Though his height dwarfed the blood mage's impressive frame, her commanding aura concealed him in a way that made Kallistê's eyes glaze over him. Kallistê glanced at her knights, a silent request. One of them stepped forward.

"Your Majesty, this is Haizea and her companion Alastair. As you can see—"

"What do you want from me?" Haizea said, cutting him off. She moved her arms and hands as she spoke.

Kallistê nodded to her knights. None of them were omens. If this conversation went awry, they'd end up dead with their lifeforce powering Haizea's magic. She'd best handle this alone. Her knights bowed and took their leave.

"You're an omen, as am I, so I believe we have aligned interests."

"You've assassinated two kings and nearly succeeded at killing the other two monarchs." Haizea made a point to take in the room around her, noting the decorations. "Your only goal is to enrich yourself, and that's not something I'm inclined to align myself with."

Haizea's face had twisted into a sneer so fierce that Kallistê froze for a half a breath. She wiped away the surprise in her expression and composed her thoughts.

The blood mage was merely a Beast, and Kallistê was the tamer. She'd done this hundreds of times before.

"And yet, here you are," Kallistê said, motioning her arm around her. "My goal isn't fortune. If that were the case, I'd have simply drifted right into the kingdom's coffers and emptied them myself. I don't need to kill the rulers to obtain wealth."

Haizea hummed lowly in response. Kallistê looked between her and Alastair. The man had not spoken a word and whenever Haizea spoke, he paid close attention to her arms and hands.

He must be deaf, Kallistê thought.

"Then what is your objective? Why kill them, and why find me?"

"I want nothing more than to watch the continent burn to the ground. And I want a world ruled by omens to rise from the ashes."

"So what? Is this some sort of vendetta?"

She almost scoffed, "No. This is about *vision*. I have no personal quarrels with the ruling monarchs or their people, not truly. I just... when I see a pond filled with calmness and serenity, I can't help but throw a rock at it just to see how it ripples."

"You mean to tell me that my life has entirely been upended and my grandfather's life is in peril because of a fucking whim?" Haizea's voice dipped dangerously.

Kallistê let Haizea's tone slide off her this time.

"Your former king has no appreciation for your power, however I do. It's why I extended an olive branch. But you knew this already; it's why you're standing here now. Together, the possibilities for us are endless."

Haizea bristled, and for a fleeting moment, Kallistê thought she was about to pounce on her. But the towering woman took a deep, calming breath, and the threat passed.

"For *you*. The possibilities are endless for *you*."

"A kingdom ruled by an omen is one that would welcome you with open arms. I would never put a bounty on your head for using your magic as you see fit." Kallistê smiled at Haizea, poised and charismatic.

Haizea returned it with an unwavering glare.

"And neither would my homelands in the mountains. Just because someone is a fellow omen it doesn't automatically mean they're an ally or hold my best interests. People are more complex than their outlook on magic."

Haizea paused for a moment as she regarded Kallistê.

"I pledged myself to one monarch and served the throne faithfully. In return, I've been exiled with the threat of execution looming over my head, and the same peril threatens my surviving family. I will not serve another ruler. Whatever this is, whatever you want from me, I will never bend the knee," she continued.

"King Rhys does not understand power like ours. Based on the obsequious letter he sent me, I'm sure he's pissed his pants with fear. If you don't want to join me as a loyal subject, then that's fine. It's of no consequence to me. We can form a partnership as equals."

Haizea signed to Alastair. By the way he glanced at Kallistê before responding, she instantly knew she'd said something wrong, pushed the wrong buttons.

"What do you mean by he sent you a letter?" Haizea asked.

"King Rhys wants your head. And he's willing to bargain with me to get it. But I have no interest in working with him. He thinks people like us shouldn't exist in the world. I would never side with someone like that."

"So, you refused him," Haizea surmised.

"Of course. Omens are rare on the continent. We have a common enemy, so it's best if we watch each other's backs. My intention on killing the king has not changed. Given that you'll be safer with him out of the picture, I assume you would agree with my plan."

But to Kallistê's surprise, Haizea looked uncertain.

"King Rhys has a young daughter that I've watched grow up over the last few years. He has a son, too. I can't in good conscience leave them fatherless. Not if there's a chance we can still resolve this without killing him."

Kallistê huffed. "That's ridiculous. Who cares about his children? The man has put a bounty on your head and chased you throughout the kingdoms. It's either his head or yours."

"No. All I need to do is make sure both my grandfather and I make it to Mount Illiniza in one piece. King Rhys cannot pursue either of us beyond the borders without violating the treaty and stoking the flames of war. His bounty and his mercenaries will all be for naught then. He'll be forced to retreat. That's the only way that everyone comes out of this unscathed."

"King Rhys is unhinged enough to go after you despite knowing you wield blood magic. He's even stooped low enough as to ask an omen to aid him, despite the fact that he's surely well aware that I tried to kill him. I barely know him, and even I can see his desperation to see you dead. You will not have peace until that man is buried beneath the ground. Do you really think the Treaty of Certain Demise will be enough to stop him?"

"No one with obvious ties to the Arcelian throne has tried to touch me. It means that, at least in some sense, despite his desperation, King Rhys is playing his cards carefully. That's why I think he's leery of the treaty. The mountains are my safe haven, but really, I'm more concerned about my grandfather making it back than I am about myself. I can handle King Rhys."

"Ah. I suppose you want my assistance with your grandfather then?"

Haizea's eyes hardened. Kallistê smiled innocently.

"No, I sent word to the warriors. They will help him. They just have to make it down the mountain." A flicker of worry flashed on the woman's face. "If you're serious about wanting a partnership, then how about this: my friend here is a Spiritual mage. He's having trouble controlling his vitality. His mind keeps getting pulled into the Soul Realm. If you can help him, then consider it a deal."

"Why you choose to let him live is beyond me," Kallistê sighed.

"Can you help Alastair or not?" Haizea snapped. "Otherwise, we're done here."

"Possibly. Is he the reason why you were in the Three Corners?"

"Answer the question."

"Well, I need more information before I can be certain if I'll be of any use to you."

"The Three Corners has nothing to do with Alastair. We were there for a different reason."

"Which is...?"

Haizea flared her nostrils, but she acquiesced.

"His cousin was kidnapped. And my family's heirloom was stolen in the process. We heard from the village responsible that they might have been taken there."

Kallistê barked out a laugh.

"I see. Well, you'll never see either of them again by going around and asking like I assume you were. I grew up in the Three Corners, so I know the ropes. I have a better idea. Let's make this a two-pronged approach; I'll track down your cousin and heirloom and in exchange, you help me get the situation stable in Llyr. And if it turns out that I can help Alastair, then I want your assistance with King Rhys."

A few beats of silence passed as Haizea repeated what Kallistê said to Alastair. He shook his head, clearly not a fan of the proposal. But to Kallistê's relief, Haizea seemed more open.

Haizea closed the distance between herself and the Kallistê, extending her hand. Kallistê craned her neck to meet Haizea's gaze when she stood so near.

The two women shook hands, forming a delicate alliance as omens.

Chapter 28

HUMAN REALM, KINGDOM OF LLYR, CAPITAL CITY OF ZEMIRA

Haizea and Alastair followed behind Kallistê as she gave them a tour of the castle and Royal Palace. Alastair was still voicing his disapproval as they walked.

~This is a terrible idea. There's no reason to trust her.~

~I don't. But you collapsed right in the middle of things. I didn't think that I could protect you and fight them off and avoid attracting attention regarding the bounty. Think about it this way: I've been in the dark about the people behind the assassination the entire time. This is a chance to learn more and decide how they should be dealt with.

~Plus, Alastair, you've been having spells ever since we opened the floodgates of your Cosmic magic. She's a Spiritual mage who practices the Cosmic Arts and may be able to help. Unless you'd rather continue to have unexpected visits from Demons and the Soul Reaper?~

Alastair raised his hands, ready to protest again, but stopped short and dropped them by his sides.

~What's the worst that can happen? All I need is a drop of her blood and any advantage she has is lost. And if we can get your magic under control, your connection to not only the dead, but to the other realms may be beneficial rather than a risk.~

Kallistê paused in front of a door and pushed it open, revealing a large bedroom.

"You all look like you can use a good night's rest. And a hot bath."

Haizea ignored her coy comment as she took in the space. Next to the bed stood a display case that stored unmistakable knight's armor. It was a dark gray with deep crimson along the borders.

"If you want separate rooms, there's a spare just across the hall. I wasn't sure. Otherwise, this one is spacious enough for the both of you." Kallistê looked between them, lips quirking slightly. "And it's fairly soundproof."

Haizea blinked once, caught off guard. Then, her shock evaporated, replaced by a fearsome glower. Kallistê's stilled, but she immediately regained her composure and gave Haizea an infuriatingly amused smile.

Haizea flared her nostrils and turned to Alastair to translate. He was standing closer than she realized, and she bumped into him and stumbled slightly. Although she quickly recovered, she felt the warmth of his hand press onto her lower back.

He eyed Kallistê with a small scowl before his attention flickered back to her.

Alastair's hand didn't linger; she knew his intention was to steady her, but her chest and neck flooded with heat. His eyes roamed her entire face before finally meeting her gaze.

~*She said there's a spare room across the hall.*~ No way in the seven realms was she going to translate the last bit.

Alastair nodded, but he raised his eyebrow in a way that told her he wanted to say something. The heat in her neck rose up into her ears, and she turned away before he got the chance to do so. Haizea crossed the room and zeroed in on the case that stored the armor she'd seen earlier.

She ran her fingers across the metal, smooth and cold. Then she lifted it, and her muscles tightened under the burden of its heavy weight. The only thing missing were her swords. She turned around to see Kallistê and Alastair watching her.

Alastair tilted his head in curiosity, while Kallistê's blue eyes twinkled as she smirked. The realmdrifter turned to Alastair.

"I think now is a perfect time for you to show me what you're struggling with, dear."

He hesitated after Haizea translated, still not fully on board with letting this strange woman into his Soul. But after reassuring him that she would be right beside him the entire time, ultimately Alastair nodded. He recounted his experiences in the Soul Realm with the Reaper and the Demon Queen, Aaryn. Kallistê perked up visibly at the mention of the Demon Queen, but quickly composed herself.

"Sounds like you're letting too much in. Your magic is like a faucet that won't turn off. You need a little help getting that extra turn," she drawled.

~How would I go about doing that?~

"Well, for starters, this is going to be tricky. You're a medium, and I'm an astral projector. Your magic blends mental and spiritual, whereas mine overlaps between physical and spiritual. But this all happened when you dabbled with necromancy.

"So, I think the issue may be that because necromancy requires so much power, you're overcompensating and opening the door too wide, which allows too many Souls in. I can tell you how I control my vitality as a realmdrifter, but it may or may not work."

~If it means getting those entities out of my head, I suppose I can try it.~

Kallistê adorned her signature dazzling smile, and Alastair blinked a few times. He shifted away from her and glanced at Haizea. Kallistê followed his line of sight.

"Come," she said, leading them out of the bedroom and into the queen's study.

Kallistê walked over to her desk and pulled a blade from the drawer. Then they all took a seat at the table with a few chairs in the center of the room. Kallistê sliced her fingertip and reached out to Haizea.

Blood dripped onto Haizea's palm, and she opened the gates to her Cosmic magic, allowing Kallistê's vitality to flow into her. Then Kallistê held Alastair's hand, cutting his finger as she had done her own in order to give Haizea access to his vitality. The realmdrifter watched Haizea intently as her warm brown eyes melted into a sparkling crimson.

"Now, I am going to guide you both into the astral plane. Unlike Alastair, I cannot commune with Souls of the dead by simply opening my mind. I cannot call them, nor can I attach these lost Souls to a living body. But within the astral plane, I can see what is not visible in the physical world. It should hopefully give me an idea of what he should be doing differently."

Kallistê and Alastair's Spiritual magic increased, and the pressure wrapped around Haizea like a vice. Kallistê's sapphire eyes transformed into a cloudy white, while Alastair's periwinkle ones shifted into a translucent shimmer.

Kallistê's Soul reached out to Haizea's, aiding her in her entrance into the astral plane. Her body followed shortly thereafter. Kallistê repeated the same with Alastair.

"Alright. Next, I want you to call the dead like you would do normally so that I can see what's going wrong," she instructed.

In the astral plane, Kallistê or anyone else could speak their native tongue without needing a translator. Here, they communicated and understood through their Souls. The Soul could interpret what the body alone could not.

As Alastair's vitality rose to the surface, he brought on a massive wave that nearly knocked them onto their backs. A powerful gale crashed into them, followed by a rush of Souls. They surrounded the trio, filling their field of vision so that they couldn't tell where the Souls ended and the astral plane began again.

The Souls circled closer around Alastair, drawn to him like moths to a flame. Although the Souls spoke in hushed whispers, there were so many of them that it sounded like a crowded colosseum.

Kallistê put a hand on Alastair's shoulder. Once he looked at her, she took a deep breath, and he followed suit. His vitality shrank back, and the Souls followed in kind. They breathed together for several minutes until his magic stabilized.

"Very good. Just focus on breathing. It's easy to get lost in the haze for Spiritual mages. The first time I realmdrifted, I nearly lost myself in the Cosmic Realm. Too much power and you get swept away and find yourself in one of the distant realms. Too little power and you get stuck in the Cosmic Realm, trapped in the veil between life and death."

A cluster of Souls still lingered around Alastair, but they had fallen silent as he gained his calm. Now, they waited to be spoken to rather than calling out to him incessantly.

Haizea's body hummed as she momentarily held the power of two different subtypes of Cosmic magic. But she had years of experience in opening and closing the gates to her power and kept her power in check.

It also helped significantly that Kallistê and Alastair only gave a few drops of blood. Although their vitality drenched her, she still controlled the reins.

"Now that you've got it under control, I want you to open back up slowly. Just enough to let the Souls whisper to you. Nothing more, nothing less," Kallistê ordered.

Alastair did exactly as she instructed, and the voices of the lingering Souls were comprehensible again. A cool breeze blew over them, and for a moment it seemed like more Souls were ready to flock once more, but Alastair kept them at bay.

Kallistê had come around behind him and placed both of her hands on his shoulders. She leaned in so that her lips nearly brushed against his ear.

"Excellent. Spiritual magic is intricately tied to our disposition. When you panic or let your emotions get the best of you, you lose control. But you see what you need to do now, yes?"

He nodded. Haizea's eyes narrowed, watching Kallistê closely as she wrapped herself around Alastair.

"Holding back isn't any fun either, is it? It feels better to let it all out," she purred. Kallistê's eyes sparkled with eager excitement when she looked up at Haizea. A tangible spark passed between them, volatile and dangerous.

Haizea rolled her shoulders as she stood up straighter. Her blood magic burned in her veins, saturated with the vitality she'd acquired from the two of them. Haizea's vitality devoured theirs, shoving them into the background as her power blanketed the astral plane. The Souls, which had gathered around Alastair, retreated.

She delved into her temporary Spiritual power and grasped her body and Soul. Haizea disappeared from the astral plane and dove into the Cosmic realm. Haizea vanished not only from sight but from their magical senses. She intentionally left a vacuum of power behind, just moments after she'd filled the astral plane with her vitality. When Haizea reappeared a blink later, she materialized just a few feet away from where Kallistê and Alastair stood.

She honed her attention on Kallistê but didn't threaten her outright, because that single movement sent a clear message. This wasn't like the attack; for the time being, Kallistê's power coursed through Haizea's veins, her only advantage rendered null.

If Kallistê so much as *thought* to bring harm to Alastair, if she put even a *single* strand of his hair out of place, Haizea could chase her down—*would* chase her down and bring her to a violent end.

"I think that's enough for now," Kallistê said, lightly patting Alastair's shoulders.

Alastair didn't respond, but Haizea recognized the distant look on his face. He was seeing something that, even here in the astral plane, she could not see.

They all sensed it at the same time. A massive entity, with an ominous vitality that sent a shiver down Haizea's spine.

She felt something staring at her back, just as Kallistê froze in front of her.

When she turned around, she saw him: the Soul Reaper. A being as old as time, drawn to the concentration of vitality just as the Souls had been. Haizea kept her expression even, but Kallistê could not hide her shock.

Alastair's nostrils flared, his expression a mix of fear and determination as he struggled to maintain his composure.

The Soul Reaper said nothing as he watched them. He could rip their Souls from their bodies if he so desired, even from Kallistê who had mastered manipulating her own Soul. He was the God of Death, and they were mere humans.

But he chose not to. Instead, he simply watched.

Haizea found her voice first. "Why are you here, Soul Reaper?"

When his skull face turned to her, her heart pounded in her ears.

"You called me here," he said simply.

Kallistê's fingers gripped Alastair's shoulders tightly, her eyes never breaking from the Soul Reaper.

"He may be the key to your necromancy," she whispered.

Alastair stiffened at her words.

~Why do you think that?~

"Every time you open your Soul to the Cosmos, the Soul Reaper is who answers, correct? He consumes Souls from beings across every realm. Ask him. He might provide the answers you seek."

Alastair's brow furrowed and he wrung his hands together in a way that immediately put Haizea on alert. He'd done the same thing right before telling her about how he'd accidentally done necromancy, long before they'd met. He'd told her about getting trapped in the Soul Realm... but he never mentioned the Soul Reaper.

She swallowed against the lump in her throat. The restless nights. His hesitance as they trained. She never would have imagined that the Soul Reaper was behind his struggles. To make things worse, he'd suffered in silence without telling her.

Her eyes met his and something passed between them. It took her a moment to realize that she felt his Soul in the same way he could feel hers.

They splayed one another open. Though she tried to hide her hurt, his magic unveiled it with ease, rendering her efforts futile. His own fear lanced through her heart so sharply that she couldn't tell where his emotions ended and her own began.

Alastair choked his magic off entirely, thrusting himself out of the astral plane and back onto solid ground in the Human Realm. Haizea and Kallistê quickly followed suit.

Haizea found herself questioning if she'd made a mistake in pushing him to embrace his power. A surprising thought came to mind, one that she never imagined she would ever have: maybe magical wasting was a better fate than what awaited her friend if he continued on this path.

CHAPTER 29

Harzel was about twenty miles outside of Von Stein when he first used some of the clairvoyance blood to check on his home. He closed his eyes as the images played before him.

The Arcelian knights knocked down the front door only to get immediately blown to the heavens.

When the mirwort compound ignited, the walls of his home exploded outward, dismembering any person in its path. Flying debris collided with a handful of civilians passing by. Other walls collapsed and crumbled to the ground, crushing the knights who'd been standing too close.

If anyone survived, they were either incredibly skilled or incredibly lucky. Either way, Harzel smiled to himself, satisfied.

That bastard of a king would come after him now. However, Harzel was no fool—due to the impairment of his magic, if it came to a physical fight, the odds were stacked against him. But he would not hesitate to do everything in his power to snuff out the life of King Rhys or anyone else who threatened his granddaughter.

Harzel would do more than simply end lives for Haizea. He would *ruin* them.

For people like Harzel and his granddaughter, they transformed life itself into a weapon. Only a select few lives could hold meaning for them. There were the people you cherished. And then there was everyone else, whose lives held a single purpose: to sustain his own. Harzel's compassion began and ended with his family.

He'd already watched his only son die. He would not allow his granddaughter to follow in his footsteps. If helping Haizea meant the destruction of innocent lives, Harzel would pay the price a million times over.

And if that made him a monster, so be it. He'd rather that than suffer the loss of someone he loved again.

No matter how much Haizea pleaded or admonished him to run, he would not simply look away while she was in danger. Not if he could help it. If the King's attention turned toward him instead of her, at least for a little while, it should give her more time to prepare. This way, she could come to terms with what she needed to do in order to end this.

The border crossing into Mount Illiniza came into view. Harzel reached for the last few drops of clairvoyant blood he had left, keeping an eye on the Royal Guard that had begun trailing him.

Despite his best efforts, he traveled at a sluggish pace and each time he checked, they'd gained more ground on him. Harzel rolled his fingers across his supply of vials; if the knights cornered him, he had plenty of telekinetic blood in stock. Still, he trusted that Haizea had gotten her message to the Bruvian warriors in their homelands, just as she had gotten her message to him.

The trek from the peak to the base was arduous and long, but he knew they would come. If they weren't already waiting for him, they would be close.

The rumble of steam engines echoed like a crescendo behind him. He recognized the model, which he'd seen semi-regularly in Von Stein, but it wasn't their characteristic white or blue. Instead, they had painted over the vehicle with a plain black—just enough to disguise its Arcelian origins.

The steam powered vehicle circled around his carriage and cornered him. The knights stepped out, one by one, and Harzel wasted no time letting his blood magic rise to the surface.

He counted eight in total. He rolled his shoulders. They cracked and popped from the movement.

"All of this for one old man?" Harzel quipped with a grin.

"Preferably, you'll do this the easy way and prove that we've shown up in excess," one of the knights said.

Harzel focused on the man who'd just spoken. He looked noticeably older than the rest and carried some type of container next to the sword on his hip. The other knights emanated high levels of vitality, but this one in particular did not project the same aura. A non-mage. Plus, seven mages.

In his youth, he would have massacred this many opponents in the blink of an eye, trained knights or not. But the ever-present ache in his body cast a shadow of doubt on his ability to fully execute his mind's commands.

"Not a chance in the seven realms would I ever go willingly," Harzel said.

One of the younger knights teetered backward, hesitating before he took a defensive stance. His eyes began glowing a faint blue. This knight's vitality called to Harzel more potently than the others.

He had never met the man before, but his appearance matched a telekinetic mage Haizea mentioned working with closely. Zander, she'd said.

Harzel gritted his teeth against the throbbing pain in his knees. He broke the vial of telekinetic blood and absorbed its vitality. He raised his hand, palm outward, toward the knights and threw them back several feet. Zander and some of the others used their own power to catch themselves, but the senior knight, having no magic to rely on, landed roughly.

Harzel did not give any of them a chance to reorient themselves.

He broke another vial of telekinetic blood to expand and strengthen his reach. His telekinesis directly correlated with the power of the mage he sourced it from and the total volume of blood he used, so he needed to consume the vitality accordingly.

The ground rumbled as Harzel carved out a large boulder. It engulfed the knights in its shadows as he raised it high overhead before slamming it down where they stood. Zander put his hands up and grunted with effort as he slowed down its descent. His heels dragged through the dirt as the force pushed him back, but he managed to bring the boulder to a halt. It dropped it to the ground, harmless.

Some of the other knights tried to close the distance to Harzel, but he put one hand up to keep him at bay. Harzel had no idea what the non-mage was holding, but the fact that he still hadn't drawn his sword did not sit well with him.

Whatever it was, Harzel's intuition told him not to let that particular knight get close. And he would not leave that up to chance.

Two cracks pierced in the air, signifying broken glass. Two more vials of telekinetic blood, and the last of what Harzel had left. He'd wanted to be closer to the border crossing for this, but it would have to do.

Harzel focused his energy outward, homing in on every particle of vitality in his range. He reached high into the skies and dug deep into the earth. The magnitude of his magic seemed to bring the very realm to a halt. All of the knights, even the non-mage who could not sense vitality, stopped dead in their tracks.

A terrible whining sound whipped about as the winds formed a small cyclone. Harzel's red eyes blazed as vibrant as the sun. His winds met resistance as Zander forced the air around himself to spin opposite to the direction. Harzel might have smiled if the young man wasn't here to kill him. For as much as he hated Haizea working with the Guard, at least her comrades were not weak.

Defenseless against Harzel's magical assault, the older knight fell to his knees with his hands clutching at his throat. Zander reached out to help him, but Harzel intensified his winds, forcing the young knight to give up unless he wanted to suffocate as well.

The non-mage collapsed in a heap. His face turned red, then a stomach-churning blueish purple. Harzel basked in the sight, choking back a laugh—part satisfaction, part intoxication. He shifted the whole of his focus on Zander and the remaining knights. They unsheathed their weapons.

"If you all want to live, then we need to end this quickly. Do not let him get even a drop of your blood. An open wound, no matter how small, is a death sentence!" Zander shouted.

Zander continued pushing against the tempest, forcing it back in Harzel's direction. He tried to match the resistance, but already the strength of his blood magic was fading.

The violent gales knocked loose the container on the non-mage's corpse. It flew toward Harzel and cracked open, its contents tumbling out. Crushed black leaves catapulted through the air and landed innocuously on his body, but a few moments later the red glow in his eyes began to falter. Harzel grunted with effort, straining to maintain his connection to the vitality, but his eyes settled back into their normal deep brown.

Harzel crumpled to the ground, his mind overwhelmed with the ecstasy that came from Cosmic magic. His body was worn thin not only from the effort he'd exerted, but also strained from the sudden severed connection from the vitality.

He faintly recognized that somewhere along the way he'd made a fatal error, but at the moment, the mental fog hampered his ability to fully comprehend it.

Haizea's face pierced the haze, clear as day. Memories flashed by. The day of her birth. Her happiness when she passed her warrior's training. Her mother's hard-earned pride and his son's warmth. Haizea's devastation—guarded and private—when her parents died. She never cried openly, but she often disappeared for long stretches of time and came back with red-rimmed eyes. His own heartbreak at knowing he'd never be able to mend that wound for her.

Harzel's fingers curled into the grass, his hands forming a feeble fist. He refused to succumb here. If not for his own sake, then for his granddaughter's because this would shatter her.

She was strong enough to put the pieces back together again, but just like a broken vase that had been fixed, she would never be the same.

He couldn't do that to her. Couldn't let it end this way.

He grunted and strained as he tried to pry open the gate to his magic once more, but his efforts proved futile; the gate did not yield.

His heart sank into the pit of his stomach.

He would never see Haizea again. He would never hold her again. He'd never get the chance to tell her how much he loved her or how proud he was of her or how much her presence healed him these last few years.

Harzel's vision swam, and his hands doubled before him. Small droplets of moisture fell onto his skin.

Clarity. Not *some* substance—he'd seen those leaves before. Back in the mountains. The warriors...

The warriors.

As the knights tied restraints around Harzel's wrists and ankles, a faint glint flashed in the distance. Harzel squinted, peering up the slope of the mountain.

He could make out the outline of two figures, descending rapidly as they raced down the steep incline. One figure moved notably faster, to the point that they blurred against the backdrop.

The last thing Harzel saw before the darkness took him was the shimmering streak of a silver blade barreling down the mountainside, thrown through the air with deadly precision.

CHAPTER 30

Zander and the other knights double checked the knots to ensure they'd adequately restrained the old man. They took care to avoid the crushed leaves, having witnessed it snuff out a mage's magic in an instant.

Zander frowned as he observed the man's frail frame. Maybe he should let him leave unscathed. He was a blood mage after all, so it would be a believable tale that he'd bested the small group.

But Jirina's watchful eye loomed over their every move. Zander didn't trust her to cover for him, especially if King Rhys was nearby. His own head would roll if he miscalculated. He shook off the twisting sensation in his gut. This ordeal wasn't worth losing his life over.

They tied Harzel up, in the same fashion they'd done to Haizea when she'd fainted after the attack in Llyr. A lump formed in Zander's throat. She'd saved them... but she'd killed half the Guard. He—

A sword sliced clean through his hand. Blood trickled down his fingertips. He blinked, too stunned by the suddenness of his injury to register the pain.

Or the danger.

A second sword barreled through the air before it impaled the knight in front of him. The blade entered in the back of their skull and exited through their forehead. Zander's jaw fell slack, unable to fully comprehend the scene unfolding in front of him.

Something in the back of his mind was fortunately still working, because his magic reached out to form an invisible telekinetic barrier around him.

As Zander yanked the blade out of his hand, he looked around frantically.

Where in the realms had that sword come from?

A flash of movement caught the corner of his eye, followed by a loud crunching noise that grated his ears, the sound of metal being torn to shreds.

Blood sprayed onto Zander, soaking him from head to toe. He turned just in time to see another sword exiting a knight's chest and go flying backward. The sword's unnatural movement indicated more than an impeccable aim; someone was throwing them like daggers, aided with telekinesis.

The flying blades felled his fellow knights, and they collapsed to the ground covered in blood and their own innards. It was unorthodox. Barbaric, even.

Something pushed against his telekinetic barrier before overpowering it entirely. He rolled away just as a series of darts landed near him. One of them nicked his foot, as if they'd accounted for his evasive maneuver and went for a wider spray.

His breath hitched in his throat as understanding dawned on him. If he did not move quickly, Zander would not live to make it home.

The Bruvian warriors were close. He was within range of their weapons, but given that none of them were in his direct line of sight, they hadn't closed the distance to launch a face-to-face attack. Not yet, at least.

Zander clenched his trembling hands. He'd sparred with Haizea countless times over the last two years and never won a match even a single time. Now, an entire group of women with the same training and fighting prowess were barreling down on him.

Zander's heart pounded in his chest so violently that his body rocked back and forth with each beat. He hoisted Harzel over his shoulder, and the remaining knights followed close behind. It was a strategic move. The warrior's had come for the old man, so if he used Harzel's body as a buffer, it would hinder their ability to attack. At least, he thought so.

He put up more resistance against another shift in his telekinetic wall, but it crumpled under the pressure. He felt the mage before he saw them.

Zander tracked the resistance to his magic, following as the mage used their own telekinesis to levitate their body high into the air at the same blinding speed they'd thrown the swords with. The mage moved in complete silence, giving nothing of her position away as she used her magic to accelerate her dive back down to earth.

A woman rained down from the sky and landed on the knight beside him. Though her muscles rippled, displaying the physical strength she put in her swing, the magic behind it was what took Zander's breath away.

He stumbled backward from the onslaught of the woman's vitality as she concentrated her telekinetic power into her swords. She brought each blade down with the speed and might of a guillotine, dragging her swords down the length of the knight's body, starting at both sides of their neck and tearing clean through the armor they wore.

When her blades hit the ground, the earth exploded beneath their feet, and a cloud of dirt and rock erupted into the air. His comrade's body fell apart into three vertical pieces.

Zander coughed to clear the dust from his lungs. As the dust settled, he got a better view of the woman.

An animal skull covered her face, and she wore thick clothing: long pants and dense boots. Blood coated the swords in her hands. Zander met her cold gaze; even through the skull mask she wore, he could see the faint glow of her dark violet eyes.

She took note of Harzel in his grasp. The only signal of her incoming attack was her clenching her swords a split second before she charged at him, accelerating her attack with telekinesis.

Zander put his hand up to stop her, but the warrior's vitality crashed into his as if he'd put up a paper wall against a raging bull. He braced himself for impact just as the other knights moved to protect him, clashing their swords with hers.

Three knights against one warrior. It should have been an easy win, but Zander's gut told him otherwise.

"Run!" one of the other knights grunted.

Zander didn't need to be told twice. As he turned, another spray of darts shot toward him and this time, one of them stuck. A sharp pin pricked in his ankle, and it immediately burned. He gritted his teeth but kept moving.

The trolley was just a few paces away now. The burning in Zander's ankle expanded and radiated up his calf. Those darts had to have been poisoned. He had no idea what the agent was, but given the Bruvian warrior's reputation, it was likely fatal.

Was this how he would die? Dragging a helpless old man away from the safety of his homelands? Would Jirina really sell him out if he gave up at this point?

If he was going to die either way, did it matter?

Zander's steps slowed to a limp as he closed the distance between himself and the trolley. He tossed Harzel inside, a bit rougher than he intended, but he couldn't concern himself with that right now.

As he turned the key he caught a glimpse of the second warrior, who shot the darts at him. She stood about a hundred yards behind them, partially camouflaged by the foliage. Instead of a skull, this woman wore face paint.

Between them, the first warrior was finishing off the three knights that had surrounded her. Zander gawked at the display of magic and swordsmanship.

She stopped a blow with her mind alone and plunged one of her swords into her opponent's chest. Then, she turned her attention to the knight on the other side of her and used her telekinesis to drag him into the blade in her other hand. Zander's stomach churned with sickening familiarity as the force of the blow shoved their hearts from their bodies, impaled on the sharp blades.

He turned the dial to move the trolley forward. He didn't need to see any further that the Bruvian warrior closest to him would make light work of the last knight.

And he didn't know what sort of magic the one further back had.

If he was going to escape, he needed to make haste.

As the trolley rolled forward, Zander tensed at the prospect of them giving chase. The only thing that might stop them was the Treaty of Certain Demise.

How much did the Bruvian warriors value it? Did it take precedence over this man's life? As he pondered, Haizea's voice resonated in his mind, something she'd said many times in the past:

"Mountaineers always look out for one another."

A second later, a sword landed exactly where the wheel had just been. It was positioned at an angle to mangle the spokes and, had it hit, it would have brought him to a stop. Zander's hands trembled in the wheel, and he pressed on the accelerator.

The vehicle pulled forward before coming to a screeching halt, its back tires grinding into the dirt while the front end lifted into the air. He looked behind him and saw the warrior in a skull mask with her hand raised in his direction.

She screamed a shrill battle cry as she fought against the engine's pull.

The metal began to shift and bend and buckle around him.

Zander swallowed rising bile. She would tear the trolley apart piece by piece if that's what it took to get to him.

His gaze landed on the charred leaves still on the ground. With his heart still threatening to flee from his ribcage, he reached for them with his magic, but they didn't budge.

The engine sputtered and nearly broke his concentration, but this was life or death. The leaves choked out magic, so he couldn't move them directly with his telekinesis. He followed the old man's lead and manipulated the wind instead, lifting the leaves up with the air and blowing them toward the warrior.

The strength of her magic faded instantly, but it did not fully disappear; many of the leaves missed her entirely, but it was enough. Zander used his telekinesis to level the vehicle back to the ground and sped away.

He was still alive, still in one piece. He'd made it. Barely.

The burning in his leg roared at the thought. Zander removed his armor and used his shirt to tie off where the coolness ended and the heat of the poison began.

Hopefully, it would be enough to keep it from spreading until he returned to Ravaryn.

Zander steered the trolley, keeping an eye on the receding figures of the Bruvian warriors before finally glancing back at Harzel. The old man's head lulled back and forth as he sat there in a daze.

How different things might have been, had the timing been slightly altered. He thought of his fate if the warriors had appeared a moment earlier. If he, Ser Bren, and the handful of knights from the Royal army had arrived a moment later, Zander and Harzel's places very well would have been swapped.

Fortune and misfortune had respectively paid a visit to each of them. And now, as they traveled back to Ravaryn, one thing was certain: with Harzel Usoro in King Rhys's clutches, his fate was sealed.

CHAPTER 31

HUMAN REALM, KINGDOM OF ARCELIA

King Rhys's jaw clenched as he stared at the omen bound and gagged in the holding cell. Jirina and Zander stood a few feet behind him, tightly clutching a scepter and spear respectively.

King Rhys pulled a metal container from his shirt pocket. It was sealed shut and airtight so that none of its contents could escape. The container levitated and slipped through the bars of the holding cell. The anti-magical plant within resisted his power with near impervious force; even that small movement had him straining his arms and a bead of sweat dripped down the side of his head.

He grunted with effort to untwist the seal before dumping its contents on the prisoner.

"How long until it wakes?" King Rhys asked with effort.

"The depth of his slumber is much lighter. He should awaken soon, likely within the next half hour," Jirina answered.

King Rhys nodded stiffly. "Zander," he commanded.

The king and Jirina stood by as Zander entered the cell and removed the gag from the omen's mouth. Unfortunately for Zander, there was no way to retrieve the gag without getting contaminated, but the risk of doing so before administering the plant was too great. He needed absolute certainty that omen could not wield its vile, twisted magic.

King Rhys released Zander from duty so that his vitality had time to recover from the plant's effects. Then, he clasped his hands behind his back and waited for the omen to rouse.

Less than an hour later, the blood mage opened its eyes: brown and harmless, and yet King Rhys recognized a familiar fierceness in its gaze.

He cracked his knuckles one by one as he approached the door of the cell. He glared down at the prisoner. It looked frail as it curled on its side, but he knew better. There was no such thing as a harmless omen, no matter the age.

Whether it was a feeble-looking old man or a teen bursting with youthful energy, all omens brought about death and destruction.

"I'm going to give you one, single chance to make your death as painless as possible. You will answer my questions truthfully, and if my knight here so much as *thinks* that there's a hint of falsehood in your words, I will tear you apart from the inside out. Do I make myself clear?"

The omen returned his glare in silence. Then, to King Rhys's astonishment, it laughed. Jirina shuffled her feet beside him. The omen slowly sat itself upright. Its arms strained as subsequently it tried to get to its feet, but the thing was too weak even for that.

Instead, the omen spoke to him while seated on the ground.

"You're too ornery to value your own life, so I'll put this in terms that you'll understand. If you go through with this, if you bring me harm, the lives of those around you will be forfeit. I know my granddaughter... I was there the day she was born and have been there every day since." The omen had the gall to shed a tear. "I know what she's been through. I know what she comes from. You can use me to get to her and she'll come back, as you wish. But that foolish act will be your last."

Each word grated King Rhys's insides. His frown deepened, stretching the scar across his lips. The omen didn't beg for mercy. It was... it had *taunted* him. It behaved as if *he* was the one in danger, as if King Rhys had not bound it in chains. He narrowed his eyes.

"I told you that you only had one chance."

He raised his hand with his palm facing upward and channeling his magic in his fingertips. King Rhys curled them inward and tore the omen's tongue out of its arrogant mouth. It took more effort than normal; although the leaves had fallen from the omen's body and onto the ground, it still seemed to form some sort of invisible barrier. Jirina flinched when it screamed, but King Rhys drowned out the sound without so much as a blink.

Faces flashed before him. His mother, Cordelia. His little brother, Rowan. Half of his Guard. All dead because of fucking omens.

He'd left that wretched island untouched, even after what they'd done to his family. Mericus, who King Rhys had loved and trusted and who had *promised* to never meddle with the Cosmic Arts again, had taken everything from him. And here Mericus was once again, having returned from the dead.

Each time King Rhys vanquished him, Mericus always managed to slither his way through the cracks. Not anymore. This would be the last time Mericus returned to haunt him.

King Rhys would go further; he would be more thorough and wipe out the Cosmic Arts once and for all. His inaction had given the island space to continue birthing these abominations. Mericus had sent assailants to kill him and the other monarchs.

He would throw everything he had at Kestramore and exterminate them like the vermin they were. He already had the first one in a cage.

King Rhys glared at Mericus through the bars of the cell.

"You promised me."

He fought against the plant's resistance and ripped a fingernail from Mericus's nail bed. It took three tries. He ignored the blood-curdling scream the omen emitted.

You promised me.

King Rhys tore away another.

You promised *me.*

One by one, he sheared the omen's fingernails until there was nothing left to take. Finally, King Rhys swung open the cell door and lifted his sword, prepared to swipe Mericus's head from his shoulders, but he paused. It was too quick of a death. Too merciful.

Rowan had suffered, alone and helpless as Mericus twisted and turned and contorted his body against his will. Mericus had not suffered enough. King Rhys turned to Jirina.

"Stay here and keep watch. Let it scream until it passes out. Inform me when it wakes once more."

Jirina's eyes widened, her face pale and her shoulders stiff, but she nodded.

"Yes, Your Majesty."

King Rhys turned on his heels, with the sounds of Mericus's cries echoing behind him.

Several hours passed before Jirina informed him that the omen was conscious once more. King Rhys took stock of the anti-magical plant in his greenery; it was still the same one from all those years ago.

He'd never been able to figure out how to make it reproduce, but the plant proved hardy and had survived, although its leaves had grown sparse over the years. Between the execution and this stint with the blood mage, this was the most he'd ever made use of it. With a gloved hand, he plucked one leaf and placed it into a container, hoping it would still be enough for the omen in the holding cell.

He would have to save the rest for the elusive blood mage. King Rhys needed to be absolutely certain that he still had enough of the plant to snuff out the witch's magic completely once he finally held her in his clutches.

There would only be one chance to kill her. A single error, a single miscalculation, a single cut on his skin and she would end him before he could even blink.

King Rhys would not give the witch that opportunity.

He made his way to the holding cell where the prisoner awaited him. King Rhys repeated the same as before by exposing the omen to the leaf, ensuring that its magic was subdued.

He opened the cell door and looked into the omen's eyes one last time. Awake and aware of its impending doom. Then, with a single swipe of his sword, King Rhys cleaved its head from its shoulders. He watched it roll a few feet before it smacked into the wall.

With this, the blood mage would come.

CHAPTER 32

"I've always hypothesized that the more a realm differs from our home, the harder it is to find the path there. If I could see Aaryn just once, I'm certain I could find the path that leads to the Demons."

Haizea tuned Kallistê out as she rambled on about realmdrifting. The trio sat at a table for their midday meal. The servants came to serve them, and Alastair's eyes glued onto the steaming plates in hand.

One dish had cooked beef that was drenched in sauce. Alastair scooped a serving and tucked his napkin into his shirt before digging in. He made satisfied noises with each bite. Although he still ate quickly, he didn't inhale his food like when she first met him. His eagerness stemmed from enjoyment rather than starvation.

Haizea subconsciously touched her neck, still missing the weight of her pendant. Her stomach twisted in knots. Not only had she lost a piece of her mother, but Grandfather Harzel had imbued the jewelry with his curse. The magic within the necklace brought constant assurance that he was at the very least alive. She didn't even have that anymore.

Alastair would have sent a Soul to check on him, but Haizea didn't feel right asking him for any more favors. She'd cost him so much already, and after the experience with the Soul Reaper, he deserved to rest.

Her home village, Windhaven, was 13,000 feet above sea level. Enough time had passed for the warriors to have made the descent, but she couldn't shake her unease. She was very fortunate that her cohort empathized with her decision to leave.

By the time her mother died, she had retired from her duties, but her death still affected them too. She'd led their cohort for many years.

Haizea swallowed her guilt at not keeping up with them the last two years, especially Shauni, her old friend from mage school. Shauni knew Grandfather Harzel and would lead the charge to come help him. They just had to make the long, arduous trip down the mountainside.

She pushed her food back and forth on her plate, her brows drawn together and her lips downturned into a scowl, deep in thought.

Alastair tapped her knee, looking between her and the untouched plate. *~You okay?~* he asked.

~Yes. I just don't have an appetite right now,~ she said.

~It's delicious. Much better than jerky.~

Their last stint with jerky had been... messy, to put kindly. At least Alastair found humor in it. Having witnessed firsthand the full extent of Alastair's loss, Haizea was pleasantly surprised to see even the faintest hint of happiness in him.

Grief could breed resentment, but if Alastair harbored any toward her, he hid it very well. Her lips curved upward slightly, and her glare dissipated into a faint smile. Alastair's eyes brightened and flickered between her eyes and her lips. He drank in the change and gifted Haizea with a beaming smile of his own, putting his dimples on display.

Kallistê was all but forgotten until she cleared her throat, prompting Haizea to tear her eyes away from Alastair. Kallistê pulled a sheet of folded paper from her dress pocket and pushed it toward Haizea.

"I received a response regarding your heirloom. It's purportedly been spotted in the Dragon's Den. It's a brothel that sees many, many wealthy patrons."

Haizea read over the note before passing it to Alastair. They still hadn't made any progress regarding Alina, but this was the first piece of good news in a while.

"Given that the Three Corners is your old stomping grounds, I take it you have an idea on how to best go about retrieving it," Haizea said. Kallistê brushed down the front of her dress.

"Yes. I believe that, given the nature of the establishment, there's a possibility that your cousin might be there, and they've simply chosen not to disclose it. I believe we should tread lightly and—" A knock on the door interrupted Kallistê.

Haizea took a moment to translate to Alastair while Kallistê quite literally floated to the door. She returned with a small metal box in hand and a decorative ribbon wrapped around it.

Kallistê shoved her plate out of the way and placed the box on the table where Haizea and Alastair sat.

"I thought it was Kestramore, but it appears that King Rhys has received my letter and sent his response. I think it's best that you be present while I read it so there is no doubt in your minds where my interests lie," Kallistê said, holding up the seal on the unopened letter.

"Go ahead," Haizea replied. Her throat felt dry and tight.

Kallistê unhurriedly broke the seal, taking great care not to damage the envelope. She set the letter on the table. Haizea and Alastair stood on either side of her so that they all could read it at once.

Queen Kallistê

Thank you for your response. It was very eye-opening. Reaching out to you for assistance was a mistake. I should have never expected anything less than depravity from an omen. I've explored other means to reach my desired ends, and I have taken full advantage of them.

I know that my former knight resides within your palace, and I presume that you'll read this letter in her presence. Please do tell her that I have successfully located and apprehended her grandfather, Harzel Usoro. We took special care to capture him within Arcelia's borders when apprehended, so you have no claims regarding any hostile acts committed by my kingdom that would impact the treaty. The realms must be on my side. Not to mention, what a surprise it was to learn that the man was an omen.

Please tell Haizea that things could have been different had she simply looked justice in the face and accepted its judgment.

Regards,

King Rhys.

Haizea had grown eerily still with each word on the page. She stared at the box on the table, her face carefully blank.

"*Was...* he said he *was* an omen." Her rich voice sounded airy and hollow. She walked over to the box and closed her eyes, taking a moment to calm her fraying nerves. "This came with the letter?" Her eyes never left the table.

"Yes, the letter was tied to it."

Haizea took a few breaths to stop the trembling in her hands. She unraveled the ribbon and removed the top of the box. The scent of blood overwhelmed her. The box held a silk sac and although it looked dry, the bag sloshed as it shifted while she untied it.

When the strings came loose and the bag fell open, Haizea's empty stomach was the only thing that kept her from vomiting.

Grandfather's severed head looked back at her, his eyes sewn open and mouth ajar, stiffened from rigor mortis.

Haizea stood there, motionless as her mind tried to interpret what her eyes were seeing. She blinked a few times to bat away the stinging sensation.

Her mind told her that this couldn't be him, but each time she tore her gaze away from her grandfather's face, she found her eyes drawn right back like a magnet. Her voice caught in the back of her throat; a cry that if she let escape would not possibly stop.

Alastair eyed her rigid frame and moved closer. He flinched upon viewing the contents in the basket. Haizea walked past him and began to pace through the room. A single tear sliding down her cheek betrayed her efforts to remain composed.

Haizea knew grief. She'd lived through both of her parents' deaths at a young age. She'd cried then too, but her parents had primarily perished from natural causes.

Her mother died from illness, and her father from magical wasting, which was an illness as well, although self-inflicted.

This was different.

What she felt now was more than hurt, more than sadness, more than the grief that enveloped her when her parents died.

A wall of guilt slammed into her first. In her efforts to avoid the unnecessary bloodshed that would come if she'd gone back to Von Stein to retrieve Grandfather Harzel, she'd failed to adequately protect him.

A part of her had continued to hope that King Rhys would come to his senses and choose a reasonable path. As she stared at Grandfather Harzel's severed head, her efforts felt foolish. King Rhys certainly didn't care about the lives of innocents; if he did, then he'd have never put a bounty on her head, inviting civilians and mercenaries alike to go after her, despite knowing that she was not only a trained warrior, but a blood mage.

Had she behaved like King Rhys did, Haizea would have stormed into Arcelia to retrieve her grandfather and when the army and Royal Guard inevitably stood in her way, she would have slaughtered them all and not given a damn about the civilians who got in between.

Her hesitance, her conscience, had cost her the one thing she cherished the most. It had also cost Alastair his family. It wasn't worth it.

She blinked to clear her swimming vision.

Grandfather Harzel had passed on his knowledge so that something like this would never happen. He'd given her everything, and when he needed her the most, Haizea had failed him.

Harzel's unseeing eyes followed her every move, forcing her to face how absolute and irrevocable and *abject* her failure was.

The edges of her vision shimmered. Her irises melted, blazing red with fire as the call for vengeance rang through her. This sort of violence could not go unanswered. A hate-filled rage poured into her veins, dousing over her like oil on a lit match.

Haizea sank to the ground, and her tears came in full force.

She did not know how much time passed while she wept. Alastair settled beside her, just an arm's reach away, but she shook her head when he tried to offer a comforting touch. She couldn't handle it.

Even Kallistê had fallen silent and made no snarky remarks to get a rise out of her. Her love, her sadness, and her anger were hers and her alone.

When she finally pulled herself together, a newfound determination steeled her.

She had wasted so much time running from the king. And it cost her Grandfather Harzel, the one person she loved and who loved her unconditionally. All these years, he had been her rock, her foundation. King Rhys had reached into her heart and destroyed the one precious thing she had left.

Haizea shuddered in shame. Her willful blindness had caused this. She'd seen the king that day of the execution with her own two eyes, and yet she did not treat him like the threat he was. Kallistê had tried to warn her.

If Grandfather Harzel had been able to speak with her, he'd undoubtedly have shared the queen's sentiments.

She should have rushed back to Arcelia, Jirina's clairvoyance be damned. No, her mistake was earlier than that. When she escaped, she should have ripped the vitality from Zander's body and destroyed the other trolley as King Rhys and Jirina rode away. No... that wasn't right either.

Haizea should have allowed the omens to slaughter them all. Every last one of them. She should have saved herself, *only* herself, and let the rest of them meet their doom.

She wiped the tears from her eyes, rolled her shoulders, and stood tall once she got to her feet. A plan formulated in her mind. Haizea would need every resource available to her. Queen Kallistê and her allies in Kestramore. Alastair's necromancy. And every single drop of her blood magic.

When she turned to the queen, Kallistê looked at her pensively. Haizea had stopped taking care to keep the full brunt of her vitality at bay. She let it rise to the surface and permeate the room. It wrapped around the realmdrifter in a vice grip.

"Where's your nearest forgemaster?" Haizea demanded.

Kallistê blinked, caught off guard by the sudden question.

"The closest one is here in the palace. But the best forgemaster in the land actually lives in a small village a few miles from here. He prefers his solitude."

"That's fine. Tell him to clear out his shop and to leave only the best scrap metals behind. I'll be taking it over for a few days. If he's fine with being an assistant, he can stay. Otherwise, send him home."

"Consider it done. May I ask why you need a forgemaster?"

"The king stole my swords. When I cut out his entrails, I want the satisfaction of knowing I hand-carved the blades I'm going to use."

Chapter 33

Haizea spent three days in the forgemaster's workshop. Kallistê had not given him the option to go home, like Haizea had suggested. Instead, she commanded him to remain and assist Haizea in her efforts, which made forging her swords go much faster.

She hand-picked the strongest and most durable metals he had available. Haizea described to him the exact cut of blade she desired. Together, they heated the metals until they melted into a blinding red-orange color. Haizea worked on one sword while the forgemaster hammered away at the other.

Although she had learned her technique from the Bruvian warriors, the forgemaster did this type of work day in and day out. He worked faster and more efficiently. He finished his sword first and took over the remainder of the work on the second blade.

They placed a strong magnet within each hand handle, enabling her to attach the swords together and form a bladed staff. It would take another day for the metals to cool. Haizea thanked the forgemaster for his time and assured him that the queen would duly compensate him for any lost wages in addition to this service to the Crown.

In the days that they'd worked on the swords, Haizea had time to think. Her anger had not waned, and grief clawed at her heart like a beast anew. Every time she thought of her grandfather, a waterfall of tears threatened to burst through the dam of her austere demeanor.

Once she returned to the palace with her newly forged swords, Haizea made her way to her room but changed course when she saw Alastair's door open.

Because he couldn't hear people knocking, they'd worked out a system where if his door was closed, then people knew not to disturb him. If he left it open, then it signaled that Alastair was okay with servants—or in this case Haizea—entering.

Alastair looked up from his bed as she stood in the doorway and motioned for her to come closer. They'd hardly signed a word since the delivery of King Rhys's "gift" because Haizea had thrown herself into her work with the forgemaster.

Alastair pursed his lips as he absorbed her appearance. Her ponytail was a fraying bush on the back of her head, and her braids didn't fare much better. Scorch marks marred her clothing, and the scent of molten metal filled the room in her presence. She looked exactly like she felt.

Most of the time, Haizea found comfort in Alastair's tenderness; the delicacy of his eyes, the tufts of his hair, his whimsical frame.

But just as compassion lay deep within his heart, a wickedness lived inside of him as well. It existed within everyone if you dug deep enough for it, and Haizea had come here prepared to drag it out of Alastair.

~You're going to kill the king~ he signed, his bright eyes lingering on her swords.

~Yes.~

Haizea leaned her weapons against the wall before moving toward the bed. Alastair crossed his legs to give her space to sit down in front of him.

~I need you to call him. For closure.~

Alastair nodded and obliged her. He placed his hand in Haizea's and didn't so much as flinch when she pricked him with a small blade. They sat together, crossed-legged and hand in hand as he called on his magic.

His face turned dreamy; his eyelids drooped with his lashes hung low against his cheeks.

Alastair's vitality sprang to life as he called out for her grandfather's dead Soul. They did not have to wait long for an answer.

Harzel Usoro was eager to reunite with his granddaughter. When he answered Alastair's call, Haizea first felt his Soul next to her before she saw his form through her blood magic link with Alastair.

"Haizea," he breathed.

"Grandfather, I am so, *so* sorry I didn't protect you." Her voice quivered before she managed to steady herself.

"You followed your conscience. Your efforts nearly succeeded. I was a hairsbreadth away from the mountains. But..." he paused, cupping her face in his hands. "My death is not in your hands; this was the king's doing. He bears that weight."

Grandfather Harzel could certainly feel her inner turmoil now that he was a Soul. He'd only said those things to placate her.

But she hadn't called him to seek comfort. She'd called him for answers.

"I will right that which has wronged you, Grandfather. But first, I want to know what happened. He... he sent us your head in a basket. I need to know precisely the type of violence he forced you to endure before your life was stolen from you."

"Knowing the details will not bring you any peace, my love."

Haizea remembered the last time she'd visited her grandfather. How small he looked. He walked so slow, it might as well have been a crawl. She'd broken his body with her blood magic, and he suffered in pain every day because of it. He died because she'd rendered him incapable of properly protecting himself. Had she never hurt him...

had she simply turned back... had she simply *listened* to him when they left the mountains...

She did not seek answers because she wanted peace. Haizea was beyond that. Peace was a fortune that life was determined not to afford her, from her parents' deaths and now her grandfather's demise.

Haizea had spent many weeks running away from the violence chasing her.

Now, she would embrace it and answer in kind.

"Grandfather, I'm not concerned about that. Not anymore. I need to know what happened because what I intend to do... before I unleash the havoc, the destruction, and the carnage that my anger tells me to, I need to know if it's going too far," she said gravely.

Or if I'm not going far enough, she thought silently.

Harzel studied her, his lips pressed into a straight line.

"Very well then," he sighed.

He recounted everything that had happened after he received her letter. He described the knights that cornered him, eight in total, with Ser Bren and Zander amongst them. Haizea turned to stone when he mentioned a plant that had snuffed out his magic.

"It had charred black leaves. As soon as it touched me, my magic disappeared. I know I've heard of it before, but I can't remember the name. The warrior's use it, right?"

"Earth's smoke," she said in a daze.

It all made sense now. The execution. How King Rhys bested Grandfather. And beyond a shadow of a doubt, how he intended to eliminate her when she inevitably came for him.

Fuck.

"If you do this, you need to go about it carefully. Gather blood beforehand and put them in vials. Use magic that will let you keep your distance in a fight, so that the plant cannot touch you. Telekinesis will give you the widest range, and it's a magic you're well-practiced with. Astral projecting is a close second."

"Realmdrifting," Haizea whispered, thinking of Kallistê. Grandfather Harzel nodded.

Haizea took a moment to consider their strategy. With the Bruvian warriors, non-mages infused earth's smoke when forging their blades. But by the sounds of things, King Rhys had merely used the leaves themselves and did not know the many different ways he could weaponize them.

In either case, the plant's ability to hinder her magic still posed a threat, but a cut from a contaminated blade was much more dire than leaves blowing into the wind. She would be walking into a trap by going after King Rhys, but her risk was a calculated one.

"Tell me what else he did to you," Haizea said.

By the time Harzel had finished speaking, it took every ounce of Haizea's focus to keep herself from hyperventilating. It had been worse than she'd ever imagined. So, so much worse.

She blinked a few times, batting away the tears. A tightness constricted her chest, as if someone had taken a mallet and shattered her heart, and her body was trying and failing to mend the pieces.

"I'm not sure where they took me, but I know it was away from the Royal Palace. We passed some sort of graveyard along the way. I think it was some type of bunker," he added.

Grandfather was in his twilight years. During his time in Arcelia, he'd never used his blood magic against its citizens. And aside from that, he played no role in what had transpired in Llyr. He died for committing the crime of being related to Haizea and embracing not only his heritage, but his culture, which gave him a power that King Rhys loathed.

Her plan of action solidified. Haizea had spent so much time following what she thought was the path that would lead toward peace.

By quietly escaping into the mountains where the king had no jurisdiction, she and Grandfather Harzel would be untouched by his wrath and innocent bystanders wouldn't be caught in the middle of a fight.

Unfortunately, things had played out much differently than she'd hoped.

She felt Alastair's eyes on her as she got off the bed and looked at her grandfather's Soul one last time. Haizea pulled him close into a tight hug and whispered in his ear.

"The king will not go unpunished for what he's done to you. On the blood magic in my veins, on my parents' graves, on yours, on the very existence of the realm itself, I swear it. He will pay for this. He will suffer."

Grandfather Harzel smiled at her. It was small, just barely there, but his satisfaction poured into her.

"You are the descendant of blood mages and warriors. Bloodshed is your heritage and violence is your legacy. Show him, and anyone else who stands against you, what that truly means," he whispered before his incorporeal form faded away.

Later that day, Haizea made her way to Kallistê's quarters. Any sign of the tension the queen felt earlier had disappeared. She greeted Haizea eagerly and ushered her inside her chambers.

Haizea sat on the large chair on the far wall away from the bed. Kallistê stood by the window.

"I've come to a decision. I think it will please you," Haizea began.

"Something more than killing the King of Arcelia?" Kallistê asked. Haizea nodded.

"King Rhys did not act alone when he sentenced me to execution. Sovereign Jasver used their mages to enchant me on his behalf. That slight is not lost on me. I imagine that going forward, King Rhys will continue to call on allies to aid him.

"It is a lingering threat that cannot go unaddressed, so I want you to focus your efforts and resources on Olysseus. Leave Arcelia to me."

Kallistê tilted her head and smirked.

"Delayed, but never denied," she murmured. "Consider it done. Though, it sounds like you want to handle Arcelia all by yourself. Are you sure about that?"

Haizea nodded and leaned forward to rest her elbows on her knees. Her hands clasped together as she looked down at the floor. The image of Grandfather Harzel was seared into her mind.

She relived his account of how he'd died. How the King had tortured him. How he was still very much alive and conscious while they'd hacked away and dismembered him. Her nostrils flared, and her vision tinted with red at the fresh memory.

"I'll handle this alone, but I need a vial of your blood. I would appreciate it if you had a telekinetic mage in your court to donate blood, as well."

Kallistê studied her for a few moments, undoubtedly stewing over Haizea's request and balancing the scales of power.

"King Rhys has an entire army at his beck and call. He's going to throw everything he has at me. If I'm going to live through this, I have to respond in kind," Haizea added. "I want the king to feel everything that I feel at this moment. I want him to see the full might of my power as I cut down his friends and allies and hope that I will come to my senses and choose peace before I reach him.

"I want him to be forced to run, in the same way he did to me with his bounty. I want him to feel the agony of watching everything and *everyone* he cares about perish before him and know that it was me who did it."

With each word, Kallistê's smile grew wider and her sapphire eyes twinkled.

"Very well. I'll leave you a vial of my blood, and I'll ensure you have a telekinetic vial at your disposal as well. Handling Sovereign Jasver will be easy work," Kallistê said. "This will require me to expedite my request from Kestramore. Handling the masses afterward will be much easier if they provide aid.

"They have a way of doing things, decorum and whatnot. I sent them a letter the last time, but I'll have to visit personally and rush them a bit this time around. It may take a few days," she continued.

During her stay here, Haizea had gathered that Kallistê did not like leaving Llyr unattended for too long, given the strife that her current reign caused. However, the queen had gained some ground; numerous knights and servants had obediently fallen in line and followed her like a shadow. Just like their alliance, the balance in Llyr tilted back and forth between her rule and mutiny.

If Kestramore was as reliable as Kallistê seemed to believe they were, then their support would mean any uprisings that sprouted her absence would be thoroughly snuffed out as soon as they began.

Haizea shifted in her seat, looking askance at Kallistê. She knew very little about the island of omens across the ocean. Killing King Rhys would create an opening for them to fill the vacuum and come one step closer to her homelands.

She could very well be solving one problem while creating another. Perhaps their stance on the Cosmic Arts would bode well for cultural rift between mountaineers and kingdom dwellers. Or perhaps their success would embolden them to set their sights on her people.

Another problem for another day. For now, she would sit back and observe.

Kallistê did not wait for Haizea to respond before departing. She disappeared from sight without another word.

CHAPTER 34

Kallistê landed just outside the government building where the dignitaries worked. A golden statue of Aaryn peered down at her, golden skin glinting in the sunlight. She smoothed down her clothes and her hair, meeting the statue's golden gaze.

Kallistê would leave her mark on this realm, just like the Demon Queen had.

The faint sound of muffled screams carried through the air. A person ran along the road with a gag around their mouth. They clawed at their face, trying to rip it off. Another person gave chase, but they lagged several yards behind. Kallistê entered the astral plane to avoid the commotion but remained close enough to keep watch.

"Get out! Get out! Getoutgetoutgetout!" the person shouted once they freed themselves from the gag. Long, scratch-mark-shaped scars marred their skin, from their eyes down to their cheeks.

An asylum was located just a few blocks away. It detained omens of the Mental class who'd lost touch with reality. Whereas realmdrifters risked losing their bodies and Souls to the Cosmos, over time, some seers lost the ability to keep the thoughts of others out of their heads.

Unable to differentiate their own consciousness from those around them, it drove them into a state of psychosis. Curse mages could also go mad in a similar fashion, but rather than inner turmoil, they turned their magic against others, making them much more dangerous. As a result, they were heavily sedated, if not put down altogether.

Given that this person's words had no effect on her mind, the omen running was most likely a seer. Once the other person chasing them caught up, she lost interest and turned back toward the government building.

When Kallistê dropped into the dignitaries' meeting, no one so much as batted an eye. During her formative years on the island, they'd all run into her at one point or another. They'd long since grown used to her presence.

The dignitaries sat around a large, round table. One of the attendants got up from their seat and pushed it out so that Kallistê could sit. It was Viltarin, who had visited her in Llyr.

Premier Eryx stood up to address her. Her skin was a warm terracotta, and she had a head full of gray hair. She wore a headdress made of seashells and gemstones and a red calf-length dress that had off-shoulder sleeves. She was the oldest person there, but the immense density of her vitality distinguished her from the other omens.

"How auspicious it is for you to join us, Queen Kallistê. We were just about to commence our final vote regarding your petition," Premier Eryx said.

"Thank you for your warm greetings, Premier. I have pertinent information that will assuage any doubts regarding your support of my endeavors."

"You have the floor," Premier Eryx said, waving her hand with a flourish.

Premier Eryx held a longstanding grudge against Arcelia after the king murdered her son many years ago. The mere mention of the kingdom often sent her into a conniption fit. The premier would vote in her favor. Kallistê needed the dignitaries, who acted on behalf of the populace, on the same page as well.

"The situation on the continent has evolved considerably. The blood mage, Haizea, has fully endorsed my stance on eliminating the remaining rulers. She intends to take on King Rhys herself and has left Sovereign Jasver in Olysseus to me. With your militaristic support, victory is certain."

"And I suppose she simply changed her mind over a good night's sleep?" Dignitary Quathir all but rolled his eyes.

"The king murdered her grandfather, dismembered his body, and sent his severed head to our doorstep. That type of tyranny will not go unanswered. By aiding me, you have everything to gain and nothing to lose because it is King Rhys who is the sole target of her anger. Kestramore has nothing to fear."

Hushed whispers passed between the council members.

"If we let the king win this battle, sooner or later, he will turn his sights on this island because of his beliefs on the Cosmic Arts. We have the chance now to cut him down with the power of a blood mage on our side. Destroy the root to kill the weed," Premier Eryx said.

"Or, we take out Arcelia's beloved king and now we have the entire populace ready to sail North. While I'm certain we can hold them off for a while, they outnumber us a hundred to one. Our position on Cosmic magic is a *shield*, not a sword. We practice the Cosmic Arts to protect this small island from the powerful magic of the continent, not sail across the ocean to propagate war. If we miscalculate and it is not a quick defeat, then a prolonged battle of attrition will not turn out in our favor," Dignitary Nehemias spoke up.

More fervent murmurings followed. Kallistê had no rebuttal, because unfortunately, Nehemias had a point. They could wipe out the rulers, but even with the help of Haizea's blood magic, taking on the masses of the entire continent was a huge risk.

And by the look on the council's faces, they deemed it an unacceptable gamble—especially when they had played no part in the havoc unfolding across the ocean thus far.

"Queen Kallistê. With your acquisition of Llyr, you have put the continent and our island in a favorable position to form a united coalition of omens. However, what you are planning... we cannot go on record as supporting it. The potential fallout is too great," Dignitary Quathir answered.

Kallistê deflated visibly, but something caught her eye. Premier Eryx had dipped her chin. The rest of the council dismissed Kallistê and resumed their normal business, but she waited outside for the remainder of their meeting to finish.

Sure enough, Premier Eryx approached her and motioned for Kallistê to follow her to her quarters.

"King Rhys took my son from me, and now he's taken your ally's grandfather. We will not be safe in a world where he continues to exist. Whether we help you or not, Kestramore is in a precarious position. I'd rather see you succeed, but my hands are tied. There is very little I can do without attracting unwanted attention from the council, since my feelings about Arcelia are no secret.

"However, I have a proposition. Killing the last two monarchs on the continent should be easy enough with Cosmic magic. Once you confirm their demise, I can more easily sway the dignitaries to offer assistance. It's one thing to usurp a throne. It is an entirely different undertaking to maintain that power," the premier said as put her hands on Kallistê's shoulders. "My son was the victim of an extra judicial killing by a foreign nation.

"I don't want to believe Mericus did the heinous things he's been accused of, but all we have is that bastard king's words to go by. Whatever crimes he may have committed, he deserved a fair trial.

Please, do everything in your power to deliver justice. Kestramore's safety depends on it," she continued.

Kallistê could barely suppress the smile trying to creep across her face. "Of course, Premier. I look forward to returning with good news."

The first step in Haizea's plan was for Kallistê to begin the assault on Olysseus before she and Alastair trekked to Arcelia. She wanted King Rhys to know she was coming for him. The unhinged nature of his response toward omens couldn't be purely anger; at least part of his demeanor must have stemmed from fear. An emotion easily masked by rage.

With Kallistê gone, that left her and Alastair alone in the interim. Haizea stood in front of the large cabinet that held the armor Kallistê had crafted for her. Quite some time had passed since she'd last dressed as a knight.

A loud knock on her door pulled her attention away from the cabinet, and Haizea opened it to see Alastair waiting for her.

He'd pulled his hair into a half ponytail, keeping any free-flowing strands out of his face. He wore a sleeveless, pearl colored shirt which he'd tucked into a pair of dark pants. He donned the same pair of boots they'd purchased at the marketplace prior to coming to Llyr.

Even with the short time they'd been in the castle, Alastair had put on some weight. His arms had more definition, and his shoulders looked broader.

The dark circles under his eyes had lightened to match the rest of his skin tone. Even his hair had taken on a brighter sheen. Part of it was a direct result of him using his necromancy after having abandoned it for some time.

But based on the destitute state of his home village, malnourishment had also played a large role in Alastair being underweight. Here in Llyr's Royal Palace, he certainly hadn't missed any meals.

Handsome didn't feel adequate enough to describe Alastair anymore; he was captivating, majestic even. Haizea inhaled as he closed the door behind himself.

The scent of black vanilla with a hint of spice filled the room; he'd made good use of the colognes the servants provided. Now he stood just a foot away from her, close enough for her to see that the lavender in his eyes had overtaken the blue.

~I'm ready when you are,~ Alastair signed.

~I just need to put on my armor.~

Haizea's stomach churned as she opened the cabinet. A knight held a title of high prestige and represented an oath of loyalty to the Crown. Before, wearing armor felt like a privilege. Now, it felt out of place. She'd erred in her decision to join the Guard.

Serving as a knight went against everything her ancestors fought for. As a mountaineer and a warrior, she was meant to topple kingdoms, not serve them.

Grandfather Harzel had tried to bestow that wisdom on her many times. She intended to correct that mistake today. Haizea would single handedly demonstrate why the Treaty of Certain Demise got its namesake.

She eased the metal onto her body. Whereas Arcelian knights wore armor that covered every inch of their body, from the helmets on their heads to the boots on their toes, this armor had less coverage. It had a breastplate and pieces that covered her shoulders. Save for an attachable metal cover for her forearm, the rest of her arms remained exposed.

There was no cape or flag that hung from her back, like her Arcelian uniform. She sat on the bed and pushed her feet into her shoes.

Rather than metal boots that came up to her thigh, Kallistê had opted for a heavy boot that stopped just at her knee with detachable plates for her upper leg.

Alastair surprised her when he crouched down in front of her and tied her laces. When he lent his hand to help her off the bed, he didn't strain under her weight like before. He steadied her.

Heat bloomed in her chest. Haizea busied herself by bringing her knee up to her chest with each leg, testing her range of motion. The armor's lighter weight translated to more mobility. Kallistê clearly had plenty of time to think about her design choices. In a way, she had been the catalyst to Haizea's life falling apart. Maybe Haizea should have resented her for it, but so much had transpired that overshadowed the assassination.

She didn't trust Kallistê as far as she could throw her, but larger threats loomed over her head; threats she should have addressed long ago.

Haizea walked over to her dresser where she had one vial of Kallistê blood and another of a telekinetic. She'd sewn a few extra pockets into the leather holster around her waist. Haizea slipped the vials inside and sheathed her swords on her hips.

She looked at herself in the mirror and caught Alastair's reflection watching her.

Bringing him with her was dangerous, but until King Rhys was dead, Alastair—and anyone else she cared about—would never be safe. Haizea refused to let him out of her sight.

~We need to talk before we leave. You need to know what to expect once we get there,~ she signed. Alastair nodded.

Haizea told him her plan and the role she needed him to play in it. With each word, Alastair's bright eyes grew wider, horrified.

She knew how much he struggled with his magic. How it torment-
ed him and how the Soul Reaper terrified him. Her request was unfair
to him, and he had every reason and every right to refuse.

She hummed in an effort to dispel the tightness in her throat.

~*Alastair, I can't do this without you. Jirina is watching our every move.
King Rhys is going to throw everything he has at me; he has to, because of
what I am. I can try to do it alone, but I have to manage the high from using
my Cosmic magic and if it overtakes me...*~ Haizea trailed off. ~*I need you.
Please help me.*~

Alastair stepped closer and cupped her face in his hands. He
brushed his thumbs across her cheeks, wiping away a few tears that
had managed to escape.

Her head vibrated from the skin contact, and a blaze burned
through her veins as his vitality intermingled with hers.

Haizea took a deep breath. She found the strength to push back
against the bloodlust and maintain her calm. She wondered if Alastair could sense the intensity of the battle that waged inside of her.

He was her greatest temptation. But he was also her dearest friend.
Haizea couldn't quite place his expression, but it made her feel fragile
and precious. When he dropped his hands from her face, she immediately longed for his warmth to return.

~*You think I'm going to say no,*~ he signed.

Haizea tensed, wanting to nod, but couldn't bring herself to do so.

Alastair flared his nostrils and looked at her sternly in a way she'd
never seen him do before.

~*After what happened in Goldenleaf... it's not lost on me that your
grandfather would still be here if you left me behind. To me, King Rhys is a
distant figure. And while I understand he instigated the chaos, he isn't the
one who murdered my family; my fellow villagers did. If somebody had to
pay for my family's death, it would be them. Deep down, I wouldn't mind*

if they died. But more than that, more than anything, *I wish necromancy could bring my family back without turning them into mere puppets.*

~I know that it's different for you. King Rhys himself killed your grandfather. I felt your bond with your grandfather's Soul. You loved him with every fiber of your being. And despite that, despite the risk to him, you never abandoned me. I won't let you do this alone.~

Haizea's lips quivered. His words touched her, but part of what he said troubled her, too.

~Grandfather Harzel didn't die because I helped you, Alastair. Never ever think that. His death is on my shoulders. I never should have moved to Arcelia, and if I knew then what I knew now, I would have let Kallistê kill King Rhys then and there. But I don't regret our time together. I wish it was under better circumstances, but I'm really glad to have met you.~

Alastair's dimpled smile returned. He raked his fingers through his hair, sending the warm aroma of his cologne toward her. Haizea shifted her weight.

~I appreciate you saying that. I'm glad you stumbled into my village.~ His gentle smile turned playful. *~Disheveled and disarrayed. Bare foot, hair blown to the skies, covered in dirt and yet convincing you to accept something as simple as getting you new clothes was like pulling teeth.~*

~That's because you came out of nowhere and I'd seen you steal just a moment earlier.~

His smile faltered then.

~Sometimes I wonder if what happened to my family was a balancing act from the realm itself. I took from people who had nothing to spare. I never lost sleep over it even though I know it wasn't right. If it meant my family had to go without... I don't think I could watch them go hungry and not do something about it. Even if it meant someone else starved,~

Alastair paused, his eyes searching hers.

~I would do the same for you, Haizea. In a heartbeat.~

Haizea laced her fingers with his as they left the room. She had a king to kill and with Alastair by her side, they would bring Arcelia to its knees.

CHAPTER 35

Haizea and Alastair used a horsedrawn carriage to travel to Arcelia; she wanted to preserve Kallistê's blood and delay the high of Cosmic magic for as long as possible.

Years in the Royal Guard provided Haizea with intimate knowledge of the palace. She knew the location of every bunker, every hidden tunnel, and every last escape route. As a knight, she once ensured the safety of the royal court. Now, she would hunt them down and eliminate them.

She faced several obstacles in fulfilling her objective. Firstly, King Rhys was well aware of any and all information she knew regarding his forces and strategies, because he was the one who briefed her to begin with. Secondly, because of the time that had passed since her exile, it wasn't outside the realm of possibility for King Rhys to have built another bunker as a contingency.

It would likely have to branch off an existing pathway, since building a brand-new one in that timeframe wasn't feasible. That narrowed down some of the possibilities regarding his location.

Thanks to her discussion with her grandfather, she now knew King Rhys did in fact have that prescience. He'd taken Grandfather Harzel to a holding cell near a graveyard. Although there were several bunkers throughout the kingdom, King Rhys would want to remain within a reasonable distance from his home in Ravaryn so that he could still be close enough to lead his people, while secluded enough to contain the damage of a fight if Haizea came looking for him.

Arcelia had a special graveyard for its previous rulers, away from the grounds of the Royal Palace. It had preexisting structures fit to build a branching bunker. While that wasn't much to go on, she was willing to make the gamble about King Rhys's whereabouts. And if she'd guessed wrong... well, it wouldn't matter, because that's where Alastair came in.

A grim satisfaction ran through her, knowing that Jirina was most definitely keeping tabs on her movements. They left the carriage just outside of the Capital City and waited. The fight would come to them. She would soon give Jirina something worth watching.

Beside her, Alastair's head turned to and fro as he absorbed the scenery. Arcelia's calm and clean aesthetic was a stark contrast to the dirt, clutter, and people that littered the poorly maintained streets in Goldenleaf. Although they'd spent time in Zemira, Llyr's Capital City, Queen Kallistê maintained a level of extravagance that made Arcelia's architecture look bland and minimalistic in comparison.

The steady march of footsteps soon echoed in the distance. As they drew closer, a seemingly endless battalion of knights came into view. These weren't her former comrades in the elite and esteemed Royal Guard, but instead soldiers of the larger Arcelian army.

With the insatiable hunger of her blood magic bucking against the gate in her mind, Haizea opened her vials of blood and poured each into the palm of her hand.

Her vision transformed into a glittering red. Haizea crunched the empty containers under her thick boot and homed in on the shards of glass with her freshly acquired telekinesis. She waited until the frontlines were close enough for her aim to be true, yet still far enough away to negate any earth's smoke they might have on hand.

Haizea attacked for the lone opening in their full suits of armor: their eyes. Once the glass pierced their orbitals, she spun the shards in every direction, lacerating them from within and destroying their eyes from the inside out.

Their metal helmets clattered to the ground as they dropped to their knees and clutched their faces. Howls of pain and despair pierced the air. As they bled, their shimmering forms brightened into individual beacons of vermillion sunlight. Haizea called on their vitality and each and every individual particle answered her with zeal.

The vitality sank deeper into her vessels, amplifying her strength and adding to the magic she could harness. She lifted her hand and tested the reach of her telekinesis.

Haizea slowly curled her fingers into a fist as she launched her attack on the next row of soldiers. Their armor bent and crumpled under the weight of her power before crushing the bodies within. Blood oozed through the small crevices within the metal, and the tang of iron coated her throat.

Some of the soldiers resisted with their own telekinetic power and kept pushing forward.

Alastair's magic surged and blanketed the landscape. It enveloped her, wrapping around her body like a cocoon and tightening its grip. His soft, periwinkle eyes morphed into pristine diamonds.

Her breathing deepened, subconsciously trying to pull his vitality deeper into her. With each breath, Alastair's vitality constricted around her, choking her like a snake.

It took all her willpower to concentrate her heightened bloodlust on the soldiers. Those she'd slain rose to their feet: marionettes under Alastair's control. As he took on the next wave, Haizea entered the astral plane.

She floated above the army, realmdrifting undetected before dropping down in the center of the oncoming platoon of soldiers. While still in incorporeal form, she latched onto their weapons with telekinesis. In one fell swoop, she ripped them from their grasps and mustered as much power as she could to shove the blades through their breast plates to pierce their chests.

Bodies dropped around her like flies. Haizea quietly observed as the neighboring soldiers, who stood just outside of her range, frozen in place. Innumerable desecrated corpses filled their immediate vicinity. And then those bodies rose to their feet.

When the surviving soldiers began to break rank, Haizea's blazing red eyes flashed like a wolf stalking its prey. She realmdrifted in pursuit, still invisible to their perception as she floated overhead and repeated her attack.

Haizea breathed in their fear and exhaled violence. Her heart pounded in her chest, her breathing accelerated, and a roar crashed through her ears. A peculiar rush of giddiness came over her. The high from her blood magic did not increase; she did not absorb any more vitality from those she'd just felled. She maintained tight control of her abilities, and her senses remained sharp.

Yet a faint smirk toyed at the corners of her lips, and a long-suppressed satisfaction settled deep in the pit of her stomach. A cloud lifted in Haizea's mind, and a wave of clarity washed through her.

She enjoyed this. *She* enjoyed this.

Haizea landed beside Alastair as she neared her limit with realmdrifting, having burned through most of that particular vitality.

The power in her blood spiked in his vicinity, and his face turned red as she moved closer. Her magic tried to pull the blood from his body, but Haizea forcibly reined in her power. When his eyes locked with hers, Alastair seemed to look through her.

His lips tilted in a faint smile. There was also something more. The very air around them shifted and twisted from the sheer amount of corrupted vitality emanating from their bodies. For a brief, terrifying moment, Haizea could have sworn she saw the Soul Reaper hovering behind Alastair. But when she blinked in disbelief, the image vanished.

Her stomach twisted. There was no way for him to oblige her request and come out unscathed. She'd known this would hurt him and yet she'd asked anyway.

With a small nod, Haizea led him through the city, hunting down the soldiers who initially charged them but now fled from their power.

Empowered by her blood magic, she cut them down with ease.

Haizea slaughtered them only to resurrect them back under the control of Alastair's necromancy.

As they moved forward, the bodies they amassed followed them—mindlessly, yet purposefully. They were bodies that could not be halted by mere swords or spears. Bodies that could fall a thousand times and rise yet again.

First it was a mere cluster. Then a hoard. And finally, as they marched closer toward King Rhys, an army.

Zander and Jirina stood guard in front of the room that held Queen Mireille, Princess Sage, and Prince Felix. His leg had been amputated at the knee and replaced with a stump.

Whatever poison in darts the Bruvian warriors had hit him with had made his leg rot to the point of no return. The only known healer in Ravaryn outside of Haizea was a middle-aged woman who once served as Queen Mireille's midwife during childbirth.

She'd taken one look at his leg and deemed it hopeless. Suffice to say Zander was lucky to be alive and that the poison had not spread any further than it did.

His attention flickered back and forth between Jirina and the royal family. Every time she reached for her scepter to monitor the situation, Queen Mireille interrupted with a mundane request. It didn't help that the teens bickered constantly in the background.

Jirina grew fidgety with each passing second. She had warned them of Haizea's approach to the kingdom to begin with. King Rhys sent his family to safety while he guarded the castle and dispatched the Royal Army to intercept Haizea.

At the moment, they took cover in the one bunker Haizea didn't know about, because they'd built it in the wake of her exile.

Zander intercepted Queen Mireille right as she was about to tap Jirina's shoulder once again.

"How may I assist you, Your Majesty?" he asked.

Jirina mouthed the words '*thank you*' to him. Her scepter glowed a second later.

"It's the middle of the night, and there aren't any pillows. The beds feel like stone. How are we supposed to sleep?" the queen demanded.

Zander frowned, bewildered that she could be concerned about such a thing at a time like this.

He stammered for an answer. "I—"

"She's nearly upon us. We only have minutes to brace ourselves for the attack, if that," Jirina said, cutting him off.

Although they had felt confident that Haizea would not find them, they'd put a plan in place regardless. King Rhys's paranoia paid off.

Per the plan, Jirina entered the room with the royal family while Zander and the others ran to the front of the bunker to barricade the door with his telekinetic magic. Jirina would keep watch over the battle, and if things took a turn for the worst, she would evacuate with the royal family.

Zander's blue eyes glowed as he held the doors tightly shut with his magic. A few of the soldiers joined with him, using their own telekinesis to support the effort. Despite their combined power, a pit formed in his stomach.

He'd experienced this scenario once already and barely escaped with his life.

A deep groaning noise emanated in front of them, and the metal door rippled. Zander shook his head to maintain his focus.

The door would not open. It *could not* open. A breach was an impossibility; the consequences were too dire to entertain any other thought.

The groaning thundered, grating away at his ears and clawing at his insides. Zander gritted his teeth, both from the sound and the effort he was exerting.

Several moments ticked by before the terrible noise ceased. A hand-shaped dent distorted the door. He shuddered. How much blood did it take for a blood mage to be capable of something like that?

Zander did not have much time to ponder that question, as the concrete wall just to the right of the door cracked, following by a teeth-shattering boom. One of the knights turned to focus their magic in that direction. Another boom quaked to the left.

The knights spread out, which effectively expanded their reach but conversely decreased the density of their magic.

The door protested once more and this time the dent stretched out towards him. Zander put his own hand up and pushed back against it, but to his horror it had no effect, and a hole tore through the metal with a voluminous *pop*.

They all took a few slow, retreating steps.

Despite their collective resistance, they had been overpowered.

Zander couldn't tear his eyes away from the break in the door. Two glowing red eyes appeared in the hole, looking directly at him. All of the sounds around him were drowned out by the roaring of blood in his ears and his heart hammering in his chest—both of which would attract a blood mage like a bee to nectar.

He took out his spear as he sent up a prayer not only to the Angels, but anyone or anything in the seven realms that could hear it.

At their peak, blood mages could wield the combined power of every magical ability known to man. Compared to his lone telekinesis, the woman before him was nothing short of a god. It would take an intervention of another god to save them.

CHAPTER 36

Haizea curled her fingers around the hand-shaped hole she'd carved into the door. The metal whined as it crumpled under her strength. She expanded the opening until it was large enough for her to walk through.

Zander and four other knights stood in front of her. All of them were telekinetic mages, which explained why it took so long for her to break through. They'd drawn their weapons: swords, spears and scythes.

Haizea left her own swords sheathed on her hips. She did not need them.

Her blood roared with the lifeforce of the Arcelian army, felled by her hands. As the suffocating pressure of her magic filled the area, the knights shrunk back from her.

She attacked with merciless efficiency, gripping onto their bodies with telekinesis and flinging them into the army of the dead waiting outside.

As their dying screams filled the air, the only person left standing was Zander. Of all the knights on the Guard, he'd always felt like a friend. It made his betrayal hurt that much worse, and in turn her rage toward him burned that much hotter.

Zander's fingers trembled around his spear. His gaze lingered on her blood-coated armor. The corners of her mouth tightened, and her shoulders stiffened, barely containing the scathing hatred boiling within.

"Haizea—"

In a flash, she'd placed the tip of her left sword into his neck.

A major blood vessel pulsed just a few centimeters below the surface. Haizea pressed down until a trickle of blood ran down his skin.

With her free hand, she brought her finger up to her lips in a gesture indicating silence.

Then, she lowered her weapon.

"I don't have the patience for your words. I have no doubt Jirina is watching us at the moment, ready to leave through one of the many hidden exits. That is, if she hasn't made her escape already."

Haizea scanned the room again. Her eyes landed on the door leading to the branching hallways before turning her attention back to Zander. She stepped forward to close the distance between them, and her breastplate scraped against his. Her left cheek brushed against his as she leaned in and spoke into his ear.

"After the attack, when we conversed in the trolley, it hurt to see your complacency with the king's decision to execute me. But I understood your position. I was in your shoes not too long ago; I watched him kill another omen and did nothing to stop it. Then, I had to face that same violence myself. However, my sympathy ended the moment you hurt my grandfather.

"It ended the moment you sent me his head in a basket... and you dared to speak my name like there's anything for us to discuss. You were more than just a comrade, you were my *friend*, Zander." Her voice wavered, and she took a deep breath. "And in the end, when it mattered most, our years together amounted to nothing."

With each word, she slowly drained the vitality from his blood. The more she prolonged it, the longer he would feel the agony of his lifeforce depleting. By the time she finished speaking, Zander's lively olive skin had shriveled and paled into ghostly white.

"I called my grandfather's Soul afterward. He told me how he died. Everything. You captured him and dragged him back here. And Jirina stood by while the king tortured him. King Rhys was never the bigger threat, Zander. I was. And believe me when I say that what I'm doing to you now is an act of mercy," she said.

Zander's knees buckled, and his face smacked against her breastplate before he slumped to the ground. Haizea put the heel of her boot on his chest.

"I'm sure you know well enough what comes after this. Your Soul may linger here, or it might immediately traverse to the Soul Realm. My grandfather will be waiting for you, as well as Jirina, and King Rhys. There will be no peace for you, not even in death."

Zander let out a garbled cry as the last of his vitality exited his body and entered Haizea's.

The rush nearly knocked her off her feet. She'd been managing the high very well so far, but she worried that this would tip her over the edge and send her into oblivion.

She steeled herself, determined to maintain control. There was still so much left to do. Haizea walked toward the back of the bunker, and the soles of her boots clicked against the concrete, echoing in the empty halls around her.

It wasn't until Haizea had passed her mastery test at the age of sixteen that her mother, Ilmare, allowed her to observe a challenge. As the leader of her cohort, Ilmare had to defend her position against anyone wanted the leader's mantle. Challenges only had one rule: leave your opponent in a condition to where they can never fight again.

For some warriors, a devastating injury would suffice. But Ilmare killed every warrior who had ever challenged her. This challenge was no different.

Haizea approached her mother afterward as she washed the blood from her body.

"Mother, how is it that you can kill other warriors so easily? You've known them for years. Why don't you let them live?" she asked.

"I choose to kill them because anyone who wishes to bring me harm does not deserve mercy. It doesn't matter how long we've known each other." Ilmare paused to look at her daughter. Her brown eyes were a few shades darker, but they shared an identically impassive gaze. Haizea hummed thoughtfully.

"Does that mean it makes you angry when they challenge you? Does that make it easier?" she asked. Ilmare shook her head.

"Every warrior has the right to challenge their leader, so it doesn't make me angry. Besides, emotion alone is not enough for me to kill them, although it helps. A strong mental determination is important. Without resolve, you will hesitate.

"Once you swing your sword, you must follow through. It doesn't matter who's on the other side. Hesitation will get you killed—it creates an opening to be exploited. And even if it doesn't come back to bite you at that moment, rest assured the consequences will hit you later, when you least expect them."

The memory faded as Haizea walked down the hallways of the bunker. The power in her blood spiked as she sensed more people hiding nearby. King Rhys's people.

Her body hummed as Jirina used her magic, amplifying her clairvoyant vitality with her scepter. She hadn't entered Haizea's line of sight yet, but Haizea could practically smell her terror. Every escape route led to a dead end; Alastair had surrounded the bunker with his army of the dead.

Haizea turned another corner. Muffled voices carried down the hall.

"I need to make sure it's safe first," Jirina said.

"You've said that at every door! We've passed dozens, I know there aren't any left! What are we going to do if there's a danger on the other side? Turn around where the blood mage is undoubtedly trailing us?" the queen shouted.

Haizea followed the sound.

"I'm charged with protecting you with my life. If this route isn't safe, we'll find another way."

"Jirina, I understand your caution, but I'd rather deal with what's on the other side of this door than face that witch while she's on a rampage. Either we go through this door, or I'm leaving you behind."

Haizea rounded another corner. Jirina, the queen, Prince Felix, and Princess Sage huddled by an exit. She blanched at the sight of the king's children.

The rhythm of her footsteps faltered, but she did not stop. She bristled at Jirina's glowing scepter; she had used it to track down not only Haizea, but also her grandfather. Jirina brushed past the queen and pressed her palm on the door. Haizea unsheathed one of her swords.

Unfortunately for the queen, she stood between her and Jirina: her intended target. Collateral damage. Haizea couldn't shake the wave of satisfaction at hurting the king in this way. An even exchange, the life of her grandfather for his wife.

She gripped onto the hilt of her blade, thinking of her old warrior friend, Shauni, who could throw a sword from the top of the mountain and never miss her mark.

"The horde is on the other side of this door. I'll go first and you all *must* stay directly behind me and follow the path I create."

As Jirina gingerly opened the door, Haizea sent her sword flying through the air, aiming for Queen Mireille's heart. A loud thud followed. The queen cried out as the sword impaled her shoulder, trapping her in place as the protruding end embedded in the wall behind her.

Haizea frowned. She shouldn't have missed her mark, given the short distance between them. Blood poured down Queen Mireille's arm.

"You two must run. Your mother and I will catch up shortly," Jirina hissed when the prince and princess hesitated.

Jirina yanked the sword out of the queen's shoulder to free her from the wall. Blood gushed from the wound. Prince Felix stubbornly did not heed her warning. Instead, he charged past them with his sword drawn.

Haizea stepped around him with blinding speed. She hesitated to block or parry him—terrified that if she drew blood, she wouldn't have the restraint not to drain him dry. Prince Felix righted himself and came at her again, and she dodged. The boy stumbled, tripping over his own two feet. Her magic trembled when he hit the ground, painfully twisting his wrist as he avoided hurting himself with his own sword.

"Do something!" the queen cried as Jirina hurriedly wrapped her wound to stop the bleeding.

Jirina put her scepter in her waistband and unsheathed her own sword. It wobbled in her grasp, looking out of place. Jirina shoved the queen toward the door, and she turned toward Haizea.

Prince Felix was still between them, crumpled on the ground as he howled in pain. Queen Mireille ran past them and wrapped her arms around her son to coax him away.

Haizea's vermillion gaze burned like a flame. She teetered toward an edge, her fingers curled into claws, thirsting for blood while her chest tightened at the sight of the boy and his mother.

Jirina jumped on the opening and went on the offense. Haizea side-stepped her swing and countered with an open palm to her solar plexus that caved in her breastplate. Jirina stumbled but quickly regained her footing, caught off guard by the hit.

By the way she blinked and gasped in surprise, Haizea knew that her movements were too fast for Jirina to follow.

Jirina's eyes widened as her mortal fear painted itself clearly on her face. Haizea slowly and deliberately picked her second sword up from the ground, red with Queen Mireille's blood.

She locked eyes with Jirina and closed the distance between them. Jirina parried her attack, but Haizea overwhelmed her, and her blades sliced clean through Jirina's sword. The tips of her swords scratched against Jirina's breastplate. The metal pieces clashed to the floor.

She swung at Jirina again and Jirina dodged, the dual blades skimming her skin. Her back was against the wall now. In the corner of Haizea's eye, Princess Sage trembled by the door.

An attack came from behind. Prince Felix came at her, holding his sword in his uninjured hand. Her body responded on pure instinct. Haizea's red eyes brightened and turned at the last moment to parry him.

His sword clattered to the ground, but he picked it back up with telekinesis. The sword spun through the air, wild and barely under control, but he used that to his advantage and aimed it directly toward Haizea.

Jirina crawled out from behind her while she was distracted and went to the queen.

Haizea put her hand up. The sword halted.

"You must leave. *Now*," Jirina hissed.

Prince Felix battled against her grip with his own telekinesis.

"Not without my son," the queen insisted.

He buckled under Haizea's power. The weapon flew toward him, slicing his outstretched palm. Haizea inhaled, basking in the vitality as it wafted in the air. Her magic latched onto his.

Prince Felix sagged to his knees under her power, and the room tilted. He morphed before her, and she saw him not as a boisterous young man, but instead like when she first met him: cheeks round with youth, gangly limbs, and bright blue eyes filled with life.

Her heart hammered away in her chest.

"Your son is dead," Jirina snapped.

The queen shook her head, aghast. "No, he's not, he's—"

The smell of urine filled Haizea's nostrils, partially masking the scent of spilled blood around her. Her eyes landed on Princess Sage, who still stood by the door, her knuckles white as she held onto the sill. A puddle had formed at her feet. A bucket of ice slashed through the fiery haze.

They shouldn't be here. Haizea would not allow the king's children to shield him. But the children couldn't stay here. A wave of Haizea's telekinesis shoved the princess out of the door.

She gritted her teeth and used every last ounce of her willpower to lift Prince Felix off the ground and fling him in the same direction. Her chest heaved from labored breathing. A white fog cornered her shimmering red vision.

Her veins throbbed as her magic whipped and lashed painfully at her insides for denying its call. But her refusal was only temporary; she still had every intention of quenching the desire in her blood.

Haizea set her sights on the queen and Jirina before either of them had a chance to react. Her magic enshrined every single one of her senses. Her vision shined a vibrant red, she inhaled the scent of blood with each breath, and its metallic tang coated the back of her throat.

Haizea warmed with the heat of her power and her ears buzzed with just the same.

She craved the relief that came with release, closing her eyes and allowing her magic to rise, intent on giving her blood magic its due.

Haizea dragged the vitality out of their bodies. The high intensified, and a feeling of euphoria pulsed through her with every beat of her heart. She fought to stay grounded.

Queen Mireille and Jirina began to shrink. Their skin dried out, darkening and puckering with wrinkles. When their bodies hit the ground, they looked closer to mummified skeletons than people.

Haizea wanted to break King Rhys before she killed him. Seeing the desecrated bodies of Queen Mireille and Jirina should be more than enough.

Her entire family had been taken from her. Her father. Her mother. Her grandfather, who still had at least a few more years left in him. The unspeakable violence he had endured by King Rhys's made Haizea realize that the king was not only mad, but weak. Incredibly so.

As Haizea made her way back to Alastair, she leaned on her rage so that she could ignore the coiling sensation in her gut and the tightness in her chest.

She'd thrust the princess and prince into a sudden world of solitude.

Was sparing their lives truly merciful? Or had she erred?

She didn't know.

Alastair's face was unreadable as she approached, but he did not pull away when Haizea reached out to him and intertwined her fingers with his.

She steeled herself and pushed her doubts to the back of her mind so that she could finish this. When she faced King Rhys, she would show him the true depths of the darkness he'd been so desperate to erase.

CHAPTER 37

With Jirina's clairvoyance vitality coursing within, Haizea followed the traces of King Rhys's vitality to the Royal Palace, her hair matted and stiffened from dried blood. The scent trailed her every movement.

The rational part of her mind whispered beneath the bloodlust, telling her that taking in so much human blood at once was unheard of. Back in Illiniza, Grandfather Harzel only took one human life a year to stave off magical wasting.

She'd struggled with the call of her magic ever since the attack in Llyr. Back then, she'd absorbed the life force of dozens. Tonight, she'd lost count of how many soldiers she'd drained along the way, though she'd done her best to mitigate the high.

Only her unbridled fury kept her from tipping into oblivion; she could not falter until King Rhys had paid her back in blood.

Alastair walked beside her with his army of the dead close behind. Even he had a dazed expression, with his once blue-lavender eyes sparkling like diamonds from his Cosmic power.

Once at the palace, they surrounded the castle. Light flickered in the window of the king's suite. Haizea's glowing crimson eyes glinted in the darkness of the night. She signed to Alastair, signaling for him to bring Queen Mireille and Jirina forward.

Between the distance and darkness, she couldn't see his face with her own eyes, but the clairvoyant vitality she'd absorbed from Jirina painted a vivid picture.

First, the king's brows furrowed, confused at what he was seeing.

Then, they rose in disbelief. Those broken bodies couldn't be who he thought they were? Could it?

You left me with nothing, so I returned the favor, she thought.

His fist pounded onto glass. A glib satisfaction flooded Haizea at the king's anguish. Her fingers trailed the handles of her dual swords. The king would die tonight. Either by her blade or her magic, Haizea did not care which, so long as he perished.

Alastair put his hand on her arm.

~I don't like you going in alone for this,~ he signed.

~It's too dangerous for you. He has the earth's smoke. The soldiers didn't use it, so he's probably laid a trap inside. I'm going to have to fight him without my magic, but I can handle him. I just need you to stay out of harm's way.~

Alastair nodded, though a frown puckered his lips. Haizea turned to the castle and with a flick of her finger, sent the front door flying backwards.

It flipped through air, making a loud *whooshing* sound as it did so. Finally, it crashed into a wall on the far end of the room and splintered into dozens of smaller pieces. Haizea ignored the spectacle and casually strolled her way up the stairs, her bloodied hand leaving a trail on the railing.

Her boots clicked down the hall as she passed their living quarters. A basket of clothes sat in front of the princess's bedroom door, ready for the servants to launder them. Haizea turned from it, away from what she'd done, and toward what she had yet to do.

The world around her gleamed crimson. The king's shape bea-coned with his vitality, even through the walls and doors that separated them. By holding so much power, her eyes had more than opened to vitality, but her entire body seemed to meld with it. The air around her distorted as it bent to her presence.

Haizea reached King Rhys's suite. She cautiously let the door creak open this time and tensed, leery of the earth's smoke in his possession. The king was sitting in his chair in front of the window. Small candles dimly lit the room, illuminating his red rimmed eyes. Or maybe it was just the red haze in her vision.

King Rhys leaned back, and a frown spread across his face, stretching his scar.

They stood there in silence as they regarded each other. King Rhys got to his feet, towering over even her large frame. He took a deep breath before he spoke.

"What's been done cannot be undone. You must pay the price for your crimes," he said.

Haizea sneered at him. Did not see how he'd brought her wrath upon his own family because of his own recalcitrance? She wasn't here to listen to whatever diatribe he was about to spew.

His final words meant nothing. Only his pain would bring her gratification. Only his death would even the scales.

King Rhys's telekinetic magic awakened, pulsing through the air between them. Haizea reacted without hesitation and reached for her own, but the king avoided her wall of resistance altogether; he didn't attack her directly.

Instead, the door slammed shut behind her. A sharp crashing sound followed, and a cloud of black smoke exploded around her. It coated her mouth and invaded her lungs, and then it choked out her connection to the vitality.

Despite knowing earth's smoke would render her efforts futile, Haizea still instinctively reached for her magic.

She grasped at nothing. She could see it, she could sense it, but she could not hold it. It eluded her like a feather in the wind.

A cloud this thick was enough earth's smoke to kill a non-mage in an instant. And it was very likely a lethal dose that would cause a slow death in a mage. King Rhys intended to kill her while he thought she was down, before the earth's smoke took him as well.

The air swooshed just a few feet away. A swinging sword. Haizea coughed to expel as much of the earth's smoke as she could from her lungs.

"Your kind is a danger to all of humanity. You have no respect for the sanctity of life. Total disregard for your fellow man is the sole quality an omen has. Otherwise, you'd never take a life with your blood magic. You'd never raise the dead with necromancy. Never twist and contort an innocent person into an ungodly creature with the sickness that is transmutation."

She looked around the room to try to make out at least something through the fog. The glistening hue of the vitality dimmed by the second. In a few minutes, she'd be blinded to magic again. There was no telling how much longer she had until the earth's smoke burned through the vitality sustaining her lifeforce.

Haizea steadied herself. She'd known this was coming. She could do this. She had to.

"You tried to run, but there is not a place in the realm where I cannot drag you back. You tried to hide, but I had every tool at my disposal to find you. And now, you try to fight but without your magic, you are nothing."

King Rhys swung again, his form obscured by the smoke, but Haizea sensed his vitality, though just barely. She flared her nostrils. He truly thought he could best her this way. He thought her only strength was her magic.

Haizea was more than a healer. More than a blood mage. And more than just a knight.

She was a warrior. Her heritage had always been more than just magic. She was just as much as her mother's descendent as she was her father's heir.

This time, when metal sliced through the air, her leg connected with the king's wrist in a powerful roundhouse. The sword skittered across the ground. Haizea let the momentum take her, and as her first foot hit the floor, she spun and landed a spinning hook kick with the other.

King Rhys staggered backward, blood dripping from his nose.

Haizea moved again on the offense, but the king pulled himself up at the last moment.

He blocked the punch she'd thrown and grabbed onto her shirt, slamming his forehead into her nose. Stars sprinkled her vision, momentarily blinding her and the last of her connection to the vitality simmered away.

The red hue in her vision faded, and her eyes returned to their natural brown.

As she shook off the blow, King Rhys walked to the wall where he'd stored a variety of weapons. This time, rather than a sword, he wielded a flail.

With his long reach, he could land a blow with the spiked ball and chain from a safe distance. Haizea ducked and rolled to avoid his swing and unleashed her own swords.

She had just barely managed to grasp them when he flung the flail again.

While on her knee, Haizea blocked it by crossing her blades, and the power behind his blow rattled her bones.

She stood up properly and positioned her swords in one of the many Bruvian warrior fighting stances. She held one sword above her head and the other near her waist, providing a wide range of defense.

When the king swung the flail at her again, she slid beneath his trajectory and struck at him. The flail whipped through the air as King Rhys spun around. He manipulated the chain as he did so, extending and retracting the weapon's reach to make it difficult for Haizea to track.

The first strike dented her breastplate. She couldn't help her startled cry of pain when the spiked ball landed a second time in the compromised area of her armor and pierced the soft skin of her collarbone. A visible chunk of flesh and metal went flying when King Rhys yanked it back.

The earth's smoke had suppressed her abilities, but something roiled beneath the surface right then. She couldn't reach her blood magic, but her healing responded—though, not nearly as potently as usual.

There was no telling how much longer until the earth's smoke snuffed that out, too. Either way, she breathed a sigh of relief. For at least a little while longer, she could take a reasonable amount of damage without too much concern. Her shoulder throbbed, but she ignored the pain and tabled it for later. Haizea focused intently as King Rhys poised his next blow.

The flail whipped through the air in a silver blur, but her swords matched its speed.

With one hand she sliced through the chain that connected the spiked ball to the handle and the sphere went tumbling.

Using her other hand, she thrusted her blade forward and grazed King Rhys's abdomen, just a few millimeters short from contact.

As she righted herself, King Rhys snatched another weapon from his armory. He donned a pair of brass knuckles in addition to the battle axe. He charged at her like a wild boar, fast and ferocious.

Haizea blocked his swing with one blade and landed a solid swipe to his abdomen with the other. The bottom half of the metal plate protecting his chest thunked to the ground.

She went on the offense, linking the magnetic handles of her swords together into a bladed staff that transformed into a silver streak she spun towards him. Although to the untrained eye it looked like she was twirling aimlessness toward him, she attacked with methodical intention.

King Rhys continued swinging his axe, but Haizea kept her eyes on him at all times. One rotation blocked his blow, the next, her blades swiped at his throat.

She spun her swords high over her head and flowed behind her back to keep her movements less predictable. Haizea rotated around the king's axe and brought her swords back up overhead to feign an attack at his eyes before rapidly unlinking them.

She thrust one blade toward his exposed abdomen while swinging the other across his chest, detaching the remainder of his chest plate.

King Rhys grunted as her blade pierced him, digging in at least an inch before she retreated. He took advantage of her forward movement, dropping his axe altogether and putting all his strength into his fist. The brass knuckles connected with the left side of her face, leaving puncture wounds from her eye down to her cheek.

Haizea swallowed the pain. She felt the welts already forming on her face as her eye swelled. Her vitality tugged in response, but her healing responded so sluggishly that the effects were nearly indistinguishable from healing within a non-mage's body.

She yearned for her blood magic. The wound on King Rhys would have been enough for her to end this right here, right now, but her

Cosmic magic was blocked off by the anti-magical properties of the earth's smoke.

She weaved around the king's following punch and answered with a right uppercut to the chin. There was a satisfying crunch as his teeth slammed together, some of them cracking under the force.

As King Rhys recoiled, she hit him with rapidly successive punches to his sternum, carefully aiming with the joints of her middle fingers. She did not stop until she felt the bone shatter.

King Rhys wheezed and fought back against the slouch that his body wanted to curl into from the pain. He grabbed Haizea by her long hair and slammed his fist directly into the injured spot on her face. She reached up and wrapped her fingers around the pressure points in his joints, forcing him to release her. King Rhys fell back before kicking Haizea in the gut and she crashed into the massive window he loved to stand under.

The glass cracked under her weight and with it, a wisp of wind entered the room. Haizea breathed, and her vitality quivered within.

Fresh air. She needed fresh air.

It would push out the contaminated air in the room that had saturated her lungs and her magic would return.

Haizea let King Rhys corner her against the window. She swiveled her head to the side, dodging his fist so that it would connect with the glass. The crack deepened. Again, her vitality hummed and by the look on his face, so did the king's.

King Rhys was no fool. There was no scenario where he had access to his magic and Haizea did not reach for her own and instantly overpower and kill him.

He lunged forward and wrapped his broad hands around her throat, strangling her. Her brown skin brightened from the blood pooling in her face. Already, she felt light-headed. Haizea had to do something—and fast.

The glass continued cracking behind her head, threatening to let more air in.

King Rhys squeezed and pressed against her windpipe, pulling her away from the compromised window. An opening.

Haizea thrust herself forward to match his momentum and throw him off balance so that she could trade places with him against the glass. He held her just far enough away that her arms couldn't reach his body, so instead Haizea brought her leg up and planted her foot on his chest. His grip weakened immediately.

There was no time to pause and catch her breath. Despite the stars in her vision Haizea moved with the speed of a viper. Her muscles rolled as she unleashed a barrage of punches on King Rhys, aiming at his face, his throat, and his chest.

She took special care to slam into his fractured sternum again and again. Even with her blood magic snuffed out, her movements blended into each other, fluid and impossible to follow.

With each blow, the glass crunched and protested behind him, until finally it shattered and rained down on them. She ignored the pinpricks of the shards that pierced her skin and tackled the king, bringing him down the several-story drop to the ground.

As they plummeted, their connection to vitality returned. King Rhys's vitality fluctuated as he used telekinesis to try blunt their speed, but it was still too weak to have any meaningful effect.

Haizea assaulted him with blows, even as they fell. Her blood magic was still silent, but her healing abilities emerged. The smaller wounds began to shrink, but the pain from her larger injuries still remained; her magic addressed her afflictions much slower than normal.

Haizea wasn't entirely sure why her magic returned so much faster than his. It could have been her mountaineer lineage, which provided her with a limitless amount of vitality compared to the king. Maybe it was the vitality of others that she'd consumed beforehand that padded her reserves. Or maybe a little bit of both played a role. In either case, she thanked the vitality for blessing her just this once.

They hit the ground with a loud thud, and her bones rattled and cracked from the force. One of her arms bones burst through her skin, visible to the naked eye. She gritted her teeth and remained motionless on her hands and knees for several long moments as her healing magic fought its way through the suppressive effects of the earth's smoke.

Her gaze fell to the king. His magic could not heal him. His labored breathing rattled against her ears, and blood pooled around him. Finally, his chest stopped moving.

Movement in the corner of her eye caught her attention. She looked up to see Alastair running towards her, his tan face now pale and his eyes wide. Haizea tried to stand up properly but couldn't muster the strength to do so.

Unable to sign, she held her broken arm out to Alastair. He held it in his hands, and his eyes flickered between her face and the injury. Haizea nodded to him. When he pushed her protruding bone back into place, she was grateful he could not hear her scream.

Alastair removed her armor, piece by piece. Every few moments he would glance at King Rhys's body—bloodied and shattered—and reposition himself away from the sight.

As her bones settled into place, Haizea braced herself to stand once more, but the effort immediately drained her. Depleted by the earth's smoke, her body had to divert more energy and resources than normal to healing itself. Had the fight lasted just a few minutes longer, the exposure to the plant most likely would have been fatal.

She was lucky it had been airborne and she'd been able to escape and physically remove herself. It was why the warriors infused it in their weapons rather than merely use its leaves; once earth's smoke entered the bloodstream, it would run its course.

No one, not a healer or a blood mage, could do anything to help.

Those afflicted could only hope that they hadn't received a lethal dose, but the warriors took special care in calculating the amount needed to kill.

Alastair helped Haizea onto his back, and she hooked her legs around his waist and wrapped her arms around his neck. He grunted and readjusted under her added weight, but to her relief, his strength had increased enough to carry her.

As Alastair walked, his army of the dead parted ways to make space for them. Haizea rested her head against his shoulder. For once, she did not feel the buzz of her blood magic at his touch. It did not fill her with bloodlust or attempt to cloud her judgment.

She looked at the reanimated corpses around them.

Zander. Queen Mireille. Jirina. And the royal army who had done King Rhys's bidding.

Somewhere, buried deep inside, guilt ate away at her. But at the moment, the ache she'd felt in her chest all this time had disappeared. Hollowness replaced it, a void that was incapable of holding the pain she once felt.

However, that emptiness made space for understanding.

With her blood magic rendered completely silent, Haizea knew beyond a shadow of a doubt that this, this unfettered violence, was her. All of it was her.

CHAPTER 38

Haizea set a letter from Alastair on her dining room table. She'd returned to Windhaven several weeks ago, while he continued his search for Alina in the Three Corners. Alastair had refused her help, which made her think his choice was less about searching and more about coming to terms with his loss.

Haizea pulled out her stationary and wrote to him, reiterating once again that when he was ready to leave the Three Corners, he had a home in Windhaven.

She couldn't fathom him returning to Goldenleaf after everything that had transpired there. She'd even gone so far as to lean on her alliance with Kallistê, instructing her to use her connections and ensure that Alastair didn't go without during his time there. She sighed as she set down her pen.

She still hadn't visited Grandfather Harzel's old home. The thought alone pained her, just as much as it filled her with shame. Haizea took over her parents' cabin instead. Those wounds didn't pierce her heart nearly as much.

The Bruvian warriors kept the crippling guilt at bay. They'd welcomed her with open arms. The leader, Vendela, had been in her mother's cohort. She recognized Haizea right away, and they both caught each other up on what had happened.

Vendela told Haizea how they'd narrowly failed at saving her grandfather. The fight broke out as he approached the border crossing. They'd seen him put up a valiant effort. He put up a formidable offense despite his age, but unfortunately, by the time they'd closed the distance, the warriors were just a little too late.

"I can't apologize enough, Haizea," Vendela said gravely.

The difference between her grandfather living and dying a violent death had been mere moments. Help had been so close, and yet so far.

If the blood of innocents hadn't already sullied Haizea's tongue, it would have left a bitter taste in her mouth.

Instead, she shared her story of how she sought her own form of justice in the aftermath, holding nothing back. She told Vendela of how she'd leveled an entire army and how she'd defeated King Rhys even in the absence of her magic.

"The same thing happened to Shauni. If not for the earth's smoke, she would have saved him. I've sent a message to the leaders in Haligus, Valdare, and Cortara about possible smuggling, but they've yet to reply," Vendela said with a frown.

Haizea fell silent, fantasizing what it would feel like to drain Vendela's vitality. She wasn't sure why it came to her mind right then. As a non-mage, Vendela's vitality wasn't particularly vibrant. Haizea's vitality had long replenished itself from the earth's smoke attack.

Not to mention, she'd used her blood magic on a rat just a few days ago, so it wasn't a physical need. The desire originated in her mind, not her body.

Vendela lightly punched her shoulder, pulling her out of her thoughts.

"A true warrior takes no prisoners. You do your mother's memory well. And from what I knew of your grandfather, he would have been pleased."

Neither of them mentioned Haizea's father, who would not have wanted his daughter to do what she'd done. But she'd run out of the energy to care. If someone dared to push her again, she would break far sooner than what she'd allowed herself to endure from King Rhys.

"I should have killed the king the moment he decided to execute me," she said plainly. Vendela nodded.

"Better late than never. In the end, you did as a warrior would. It was hard, but you did what was necessary. Come now. The others want to reunite with their lost sister," she said.

They spent that evening sitting around a campfire to keep warm in the crisp mountain breeze. Each woman carried a pair of dual swords on their hips, just as Haizea did during her time as a knight. As she saw the pendants around her fellow warrior's necks, she lamented and brushed her collarbone.

"So, are you here to stay?"

Haizea sat next to Shauni, her old friend whom she'd fallen out of touch with after her move to Arcelia.

Shauni had passed her mastery test a few years after Haizea, around the time her father died. She kept her black tresses trimmed short, just long enough to form a semblance of a curl against her scalp. Her eyes were a dark violet, set against light brown skin.

"I don't have any plans to leave." Haizea shrugged.

Shauni smiled and raised her flask into the air.

"Good. I left the same day we got your message. Vendela nearly tweaked her bad knee trying to keep up with me. I'm sorry I didn't save Mr. Harzel. I know how much he meant to you," Shauni whispered, placing an arm over Haizea's shoulders and giving her a tight squeeze. "We have a lot to catch up on. I'm really happy you're back home—where you should be.

"Besides, it hasn't been the same without you in our ranks." She took a swig and passed the flask to Haizea.

Some of the other warriors nodded.

"Ilmare was one of our best. She would have wanted you to take her place."

"Having a healer nearby makes a world of difference. Not to mention, your blood magic will prove useful on culls."

Haizea's brows rose in surprise. She'd spent so long hiding her true power that it felt odd to talk about it openly around others, especially with so many new faces in the group.

But the mountains had never taken such a staunch stance against the Cosmic Arts like the kingdoms. A people who welcomed and embraced a group as violent the Bruvian warriors would never shun corrupted magic.

Haizea looked to Vendela. Taking her mother's former place on the leader's mantle required challenging her. She would have to prove her fighting prowess without her magic by suppressing it with the power of earth's smoke; though not nearly as much as what King Rhys had unleashed on her. A challenge only ended when one person was dead or injured beyond recovery.

It meant that anyone who wished to challenge their leader would have to think carefully before doing so. It also meant that the leader would have to stay on top of their game. Leaders could resign when they deemed themselves no longer capable of holding the position, but pride kept many from doing so.

Haizea's mother, Ilmare, had ended the life of the previous leader and killed anyone who had challenged her afterward. She stepped down in the final months of her life, when her illness became too much. Because of that, the succession had been more democratic. Their cohort had appointed Vendela, and she'd maintained her position by defeating every one of her challengers over the years.

Vendela had trekked down the mountainside to save her grandfather. She'd done everything she could to help Haizea in her time of need. Haizea had no desire to challenge her.

Besides, she wasn't ready for leadership. And as the days passed by, Haizea wasn't sure if she ever would be.

Two months flew by with the warriors. During her first few weeks, the physical exertion had worn on her as she reacclimated to the high altitude. Windhaven was about 13,000 feet above sea level, and although she'd grown up in the mountains, Haizea's time in Arcelia had taken its toll. She made her way to the training grounds to get her assignment from Vendela.

"When's the next patrol?" Haizea asked. Shauni and a few other warriors had gathered around the leader.

"Actually, I'm sending you and Shauni on a cull tonight. Received a report about a smuggling ring that needs to be dealt with," Vendela said.

A cull meant they were hunting down a person who'd committed a crime deserving of death: murders, assault, smuggling protected resources, such as earth's smoke.

Haizea kept her face neutral, but deep down she ached for the rush that came from absorbing human vitality.

Shauni's violet eyes considered her carefully. She didn't practice the Cosmic Arts, but she was no stranger to its corruptive effects. Shauni stewed for a moment before a devious grin spread across her face. She would never experience bloodlust in the way that Haizea did, but she was a warrior and more than anything else, a warrior understood the thrill of a fresh kill.

Warriors decided when a cull needed to take place in a variety of ways. Sometimes, word came from the village leaders. Other times, they saw someone suspicious on their patrols and, after further investigation, decided it needed to be addressed.

The warriors' primary duty was to protect the mountains. In times of war, that usually involved fighting outside invaders. In times of peace, it meant cracking down on the pockets of crime that bubbled up between their routes. Most were smart enough to avoid the warriors' patrol, but word always got to them one way or another.

As mages, they each donned a skull mask: a mountain lion and deer respectively. Haizea spotted the targets first, and her blood magic spiked. At least one of them was a mage.

She pointed in their direction and let Shauni take the lead. Shauni pulled out her swords and made a slow, cautious approach. When they were in their vicinity, Shauni's telekinesis reached out and wrapped around the group, holding them in place. Then, the two women attacked.

Their swords flashed under the moonlight. Haizea took two people and Shauni followed right behind her. She locked eyes with one of the targets, and the blood in her veins boiled so intensely that it roared in her ears. They were the mage she'd sensed. Their mouth moved, saying something, but Haizea didn't hear it. The desire within drowned out their cries m.

She closed the distance in two strides and cleaved the mage's head from their shoulders in one powerful swing. The blood sprayed on her body, soaking her from head to toe.

She absorbed the vitality through her skin and with it, came their power. The mage had been an enchanter; that was why their lips had moved in those final moments. Their corpse hit the ground and disintegrated into a cloud of dust. Odd. That had never happened before.

As Shauni finished off the last of the group behind her, Haizea eagerly welcomed the high setting in. She hummed to herself in a daze as she followed behind Shauni and collected the heads of the culled.

They displayed them on stakes at the village entrance: a warning for anyone else to come.

"All done?" Shauni said.

Enthralled with the growing red tint in her vision, Haizea didn't respond. She looked at the bodies on the ground and found herself shoving the severed heads into Shauni's arms. Blood, *human* blood, surrounded her.

When she raised her hand in front of her, it wasn't a conscious decision. Her body trembled as she absorbed the vitality, voraciously filling a bucket that should have already been overflowing, but somehow seemed to never completely fill.

The bodies shriveled into husks before disintegrating altogether.

Haizea hummed to herself, a bit from intrigue and a bit from the high. Her hands vibrated as she rested them on the hilts of her swords. She turned back to Shauni.

"Now we're done."

CHAPTER 39

HUMAN REALM, THE THREE CORNERS

A crowd of people in tattered and disheveled clothing rushed past Alastair as he made his way back to his hostel. He held a flier he'd picked up while he was out at the market.

According to the headline, Vadronia, Olysseus's Capital City, burned to the ground in a massive fight between its inhabitants and the invading omens. Thousands of people perished and those that survived fled. It concerned him, but he had more pressing matters to attend to.

He'd spent the last few months in the Three Corners searching for Alina. Kallistê had given him plenty of money and supplies, so he hadn't spent a penny of his own since being here, but aside from that, she didn't bother with him too much. Alastair suspected Haizea had something to do with that; Kallistê did not do things out of the kindness of her heart.

He didn't like the way she looked at Haizea, like she was some grand prize to obtain. He didn't like how, in the end, both he and Haizea had played into Kallistê's plans, either.

Well, the more he thought about—and Alastair tried very hard not to—he understood that what transpired in Arcelia had been Haizea's decision. And that he'd chosen to follow her.

That night, he'd tortured the Souls of countless people with his own magic, forcing them to bend to his will. Acquiescing to Kallistê and her schemes was a secondary byproduct. In the end, their interests just so happened to align.

He and Haizea had kept in touch through a few letters. She'd invited him to live in Windhaven after his time in the Three Corners in her most recent letter.

My home is your home, she'd said.

Haizea was not the type of person to say something she didn't mean. But he wondered if 'home' meant something more.

A lot had happened between them, but there hadn't been much time or opportunity to talk about it. Plus, it didn't feel right to put it in a letter either.

Alastair tabled it for later. Right now, he needed to hone his energy on getting closure with his cousin.

He'd gotten a few leads, but nothing had panned out.

It could mean two things, either Alina wasn't in the Three Corners, or... or...

Alastair didn't want to think about any other possibility than Alina being alive. He'd lost the rest of his family to the angry mob back in Goldenleaf, and he didn't want to live in a reality where his hopes of saving his cousin were dashed with the same finality.

But as the weeks turned into months, he finally came to terms with what he needed to do.

Alastair cleared his mind and let his Soul call out for her. Alina's Soul appeared beside instantaneously, confirming his worst fears.

Alastair.

Her words resonated through him and tears welled into his eyes, obstructing his view. Alina's Soul wrapped around him in an embrace.

~I looked for you. I'm sorry I—~

I know. It's okay. I can tell you what happened, if you want.

Alastair wiped away his tears and nodded his head. For Alina to have died, it meant that she suffered more than the rest of his family–alone and without any help. The very least he could do was listen.

The mob had taken his family by surprise in the middle of the night, just a few hours before he and Haizea had gotten their tent set up. As they attacked, a man used the chaos to his advantage and snatched her away. The black market had a high demand for someone young and beautiful like Alina. She quickly realized what his plan was but couldn't find the means or opportunity to kill him until after they arrived in the city.

Alina took him down, but not before he stabbed her. She died alone in a busy street, and her body had quickly been disposed of—just one of many on any given day in a city like that. Very few people had seen her alive.

Alastair wept as he listened to her story. The only thing that gave him solace was that as she spoke, her Soul grew more peaceful. Alina had gotten closure from this. That's what was important.

They burned the bodies. And punished everyone responsible, she added.

~They? Who?~

The warriors. Someone must have told them what happened. They came in and burned everyone's bodies properly. Then they rounded up the villagers and questioned them. Naturally, everyone pointed fingers at one another, so they took different measures to get a confession.

By the realms, it was terrible, Alastair. But they got answers. They spared the children and the elderly, but everyone else from the mob that attacked us... the village it's... it's gone.

Alastair blinked, absorbing the information. Here in the Three Corners, he was far removed from the Bruvian warrior's justice, but after his time with Haizea, he could easily imagine the rampage they'd unleashed upon the village. They'd repaid in kind what the mob had done to his family.

A weight lifted off of his shoulders. Relief. No, not relief. It was more than that. He felt... vindicated. And Alina did, too.

I'll always be with you, Alastair. We all will. You're a medium, so we're only ever a moment away.

He tried and failed to find comfort in Alina's words. Knowing that his family was in the Soul Realm did not ease the pain of his loss. It didn't erase the violence they had endured.

Alastair wanted them back, alive and whole, in the Human Realm, where they belonged.

But his internal desires had power over the Souls and if he let his sorrow carry him away, he'd thrust his family back into this realm, against their will.

Alastair bid Alina goodbye before that could happen. As her Soul departed, another one approached. Kallistê appeared, running her fingers through her dark blue tresses as she strolled toward him. Alastair sighed. By the way her brows rose incredulously before regaining her composure, it must have been loud.

~Hello Alastair,~ Kallistê greeted him, but her signing was rudimentary at best. They would have to speak someplace where their Souls communicated instead of their voices.

As she closed the distance between them, Kallistê reached into her pocket before placing something in Alastair's hand. He blinked as he looked at his palm.

~Haizea's pendant? How did you—~

~May I?~ Kallistê interrupted, but they both knew it wasn't really a request. He braced himself as she brought him into the astral plane.

~Why are you here?~ Alastair asked.

"My contacts finally got back to me about the pendant, and I figured I'd check in on you with your progress. Besides, I'm sure Haizea would appreciate it if you returned her mother's necklace. I think you'll find she misses your company."

~You want something more than just this.~

"I just want to remain in your good graces. I made a promise that I would help both of you. As allies. Friends, even. Please send Haizea my best wishes."

Alastair narrowed his eyes. That wasn't the whole truth. He wondered if spending all this time in the Three Corners was a mistake. Maybe he should have kept an eye on the realmdrifter instead.

He tucked Haizea's necklace safely away and kept careful watch on Kallistê.

~I'll do it, but this counts as another favor.~

"Of course."

He paused.

~It'll be faster if you take me there.~

At first, Alastair couldn't tell if his nerves stemmed from fear or excitement. Months had passed since he'd last seen Haizea... since they'd laid waste to an entire army and killed hundreds, if not thousands of soldiers.

But as Kallistê held his Soul, he listened to the frantic beating of his heart, which told him this was what he wanted, to follow Haizea right back into Hell again if it meant being back together.

CHAPTER 40

HUMAN REALM, MOUNT ILLINIZA, WINDHAVEN VILLAGE

A violent pounding on the front door jolted Haizea from her slumber. She rubbed her eyes and groggily dragged herself out of bed and wrapped herself in a robe.

Why was someone knocking so hard in the middle of the night? Haizea yawned. Maybe one of the warriors had gotten injured during their patrols tonight and needed her help. She opened the door and was greeted by a cloud of soft white and a pair of periwinkle eyes that took her breath away.

Haizea blinked, and her jaw fell slack. She'd almost forgotten how beautiful Alastair was. His hair had grown a few inches longer. He looked like he might even weigh more than her now; and even with her athletic physique, given Alastair's height, he should have. When Alastair smiled his same old smile, playful and warm and alluring, tears welled into her eyes.

Haizea closed the distance between them and wrapped her arms around his neck in a tight hug. Alastair encircled his arms around her waist, and she had to get on her toes to maintain their embrace.

She nuzzled her face in his hair and breathed him in. His essence enraptured her: his warmth, his scent, his softness, and his magic.

She braced herself to let him go but ended up clutching him a little tighter. Alastair didn't pull away from her either; his hands were warm in the cold night air as he rubbed them up and down her back.

He was safely within arm's reach. She could feel him teeming with life. He was close enough that she could protect him.

Haizea let out a soft sigh and her voice quivered from the swell of emotions roiling within.

It took another breath before she finally managed to loosen her grip on him. She slowly leaned her head back, just enough so that she could look at him again, and Alastair's bright eyes pulled her into a trance. The collar of her robe shifted with their movement, but she was engrossed by the buzz of her vitality responding to Alastair's touch.

Months had passed since she'd last felt the pull of his magic, but the effects had not faded. Haizea's fingers trembled as she rested them against his arms.

He enveloped her with his warmth and pinned her with his gaze. Absent were the stolen glances he took when he thought she wasn't looking; unabashed yearning colored Alastair's expression. His eyes lingered on her lips before flickering back to meet hers. An unspoken question.

In answer, she lifted onto her toes, first nuzzling him with her nose before brushing her lips against his. With her magic brimming within, Haizea had only intended for it to be a quick, gentle kiss, but Alastair's grip on her waist tightened and he deepened it, his lips feverish and hungry.

She melted into his embrace and entangled her fingers in his long hair, sleek and smooth in her grasp. His vitality crashed against her like a wave, and each kiss pulled her further into the sea of his essence. She drowned in his vitality, in *him*.

Haizea lifted up for air, tilting her head ever so slightly, and Alastair trailed kisses along her jaw.

When his teeth grazed the soft skin of her neck, Haizea nearly unraveled as the lines between her blood magic and physical desires blurred.

She pulled away as much as she pushed Alastair back, gently yet in earnest. But not even the strain of her magic could dull the joy she felt in this moment. Her lips tilted upward into her rare smile, radiant and genuine. Alastair's breath hitched in his throat. Before he could test her control any further, she pulled him inside.

The cold mountain air caught up with her, and a shiver raced down her spine.

Alastair's eyes raked over her, and only then did she realize how disheveled her robe had become. Her collar had shifted, teasing her curves lying underneath, and the bottom had risen up, revealing the musculature of her legs.

Alastair reached back outside and brought a bag in with him.

Did that mean that he intended to take up her offer to stay? With her?

A splash of red spread across his cheeks. His nose was bright red, too. She wasn't the only one freezing. He had on pants and a long-sleeved shirt but no other layers. How long had he been standing outside in the cold without a coat?

~Here, come sit,~ she signed.

Alastair laced his fingers with hers as she led him to the living room. She got him situated on the couch near the fireplace and draped a blanket over his shoulders.

~Better?~ she asked.

Alastair nodded.

~I'll get you something warm to drink. I have tea, apple cider...~ she trailed off as she thought through her pantry's inventory.

~Warm apple cider sounds lovely.~

Haizea put some on the stovetop and added a dash of cinnamon like her mother did when she was a young girl. Once it was warm, she brought the cup to Alastair. He grabbed it with one hand and used the other to tug on her fingers, coaxing her to sit beside him.

He took a small sip at first before going back for a larger gulp.

~How was your time in the Three Corners? Did you find Alina?~ she asked.

Alastair's face fell. *~No. I—she didn't make it.~*

~I'm so sorry Alastair,~ Haizea signed. She placed her hand on his leg, and Alastair squeezed it before signing again.

~It's okay. I talked to her. She's with the rest of my family now.~ His eyes turned glassy, and he wiped his cheeks. *~Kallistê brought me here. She gave me this.~*

He reached into her shirt and pulled out a small purple bag. When he opened it, her pendant clanked onto the table. Haizea reached over and snatched it up, her eyes widening in disbelief.

~She found it.~

Alastair nodded.

~You should know that the continent is in disarray. Kestramore sent some of their people to assist Kallistê. It's caused a rift in the neighboring kingdoms as a result. They want the Cosmic Arts coalition off the continent. Uprisings have been a frequent occurrence.~

~Well, that was always a foregone conclusion. What did she think was going to happen?~

~Oh, I think she's enjoying it. But I think she realized she needs us again. I don't know why, but I know I don't like it.~

~Whoever she has from Kestramore might not be enough to get it under control. She probably wants to keep her options open. We'll just have to wait and see,~ Haizea said.

Whatever happened, she didn't want to get involved in the kingdoms' politics again. If these uprisings escalated, the people may flee even further and seek out the mountains. As a warrior, she had to prioritize the safety of her people above anything else.

While the mountains weren't quite the breeding grounds for the Cosmic Arts that Kestramore was, she didn't have to worry about being executed for embracing her power. If the kingdoms began waging war to snuff out the Cosmic Arts within Arcelia and Olysseus's borders, it made no sense to let their civilians take refuge here. Haizea would not allow them to bring harm to herself or to her people in the way King Rhys had done.

Whatever else Kallistê had brewing on the rest of the continent wasn't her problem anymore. Until Kallistê came to her directly, or unless her machinations infringed upon the mountaineers, Haizea had no reason to concern herself.

Alastair wrapped his arm over her and covered her with the blanket, bringing her out of her thoughts. He planted a kiss on her forehead, warm and soft.

She rested her head on his shoulder and relaxed into his warmth.

Haizea refused to fail him like she had her grandfather. She would do whatever it took to keep Alastair safe. Haizea would never shy away from her power again. The next time it called to her, she would not hesitate in her answer.

Epilogue

Kingdom of Arcelia, Unknown

Princess Sage pulled her hood over her head as she followed her brother into the tavern. The last few months on the run had been taxing, both mentally and physically. She'd only ever known life in the Royal Palace, with her mother and father and her brother.

And now... now, she had no home. Felix was all she had left. Her parents were gone. *Gone.*

Felix flopped down into the seat across from her in the booth. He clenched and unclenched his hands. He waited until the server came and went before he spoke.

"We can't do this forever, Sage. Omens are rampant here. One of them is bound to figure out who we are. All it'll take is one of us catching the attention of a seer and we're done for."

"What else can we do but run and hide?" Sage asked, brows furrowing.

"We fight. Except we won't die like Father. They fight dirty, then so do we," he hissed.

The server returned with their drinks, and Princess Sage used her telekinesis to lift them from the tray to the table, ignoring Felix's earlier warnings about minimizing the use of her magic in public.

While she had never faced the populace as much as the rest of the Royal family, it was still a lurking danger for her to be recognized. And with the newly seated omen on Arcelia's throne, they may very well finish what Haizea had started by hunting them down.

There was wisdom in Felix's words of caution, but at that moment she didn't care. She felt powerless and with the way things were going, the only way to regain her strength was through her magic.

"What do you mean by fighting dirty?"

"By taking up the Cosmic Arts."

Sage blanched.

"How will we learn without getting caught?"

"Not we. *You.*"

Her eyes widened. "But—"

"Sage, you've always been naturally gifted with telekinesis. I'm certain there's a learning curve to this stuff, and I'll never overcome it because I've never been that great at magic. But you've been strong from the very start. You have it in you to take back what's rightfully ours. To rid our home of these omens."

"Felix... I-I don't know if I can do it."

"You're just as strong as Father was."

"I'm not. I'm—"

"Sage, there is no future for us unless we carve it out for ourselves. We will never know what peace is again unless we retake the throne. And the only way to do that, the only way to defeat them, is to meet them where they're at." He slammed his fists on the table.

The princess fell silent then. She understood the danger they were in. But to embrace the Cosmic Arts, which had destroyed multiple generations of their family, seemed a bridge too far.

She had not forgotten the story of Mericus, her father's childhood best friend. Her father had particularly despised transmutation magic, but the realm was different back then. Omens hadn't flooded the continent. They hadn't usurped every throne in every major kingdom.

Her father had tried to take the pure path, and he'd lost. Twice, King Rhys had lost his family to Cosmic magic, but what if there was no path forward without stooping to their level? Would their father still be alive if he had learned the Cosmic Arts? Could he have defeated the omens?

Would he have still been himself?

"Father would have killed you for what you're suggesting," she grated out.

"At the rate we're going, the omens will do that anyway. I'd rather go out fighting than cower behind them. The throne is mine, and mine alone. And there is only one way to get it back. And it's not just the Cosmic Arts coalition I want to take down. It's Haizea, too. We have to kill her and the witches that joined her in her charge. It doesn't matter that she spared us. She killed *everyone*. You saw it with your own eyes. We cannot let that go without retribution."

Sage fiddled with her fingers. She didn't know if her magic was strong enough to defeat the blood mage. Pensively, she looked at her brother, who was watching her as well. Felix and Sage only had one another. Whatever they did, they needed to stick together, and she feared what he might do if she refused. What if he abandoned her?

Finally, Sage nodded in agreement, and relief flooded Felix's face. She would learn transmutation. She would kill the blood mage. And she would reclaim the throne for her brother.

THE END

Afterword

I want to thank each and every one of you from the bottom of my heart for reading this story. If you enjoyed The Crimson Knight, I kindly ask that you please leave a review about your reading experience on Amazon, Goodreads, or whichever platform you purchased from. This will help this book find a home with readers who will enjoy it, which in turn helps me as an author.

If you'd like to stay updated on future works, you can find me at: zetakpierce.carrd.co Here, you can sign up for my monthly newsletter, as well as connect with me on social media (@zetakpierce on all platforms).

ACKNOWLEDGEMENTS

There are a few people I'd like to thank.

Ty. My buddy. You're the first person I ever told about this story. Your excitement along the way helped me stay motivated.

My beta readers. Xander, Menaka, Marten, and Bree. Your feedback helped me shape this book into what it is today. I would also like to extend a special thanks to Jesse for taking the time to critique my opening pages when I applied for a mentorship.

My editor. Ashley Olivier at Enchanted Author Co. You gave this manuscript the polish it needed.

My readers. I hope you've enjoyed this story. I appreciate each and every one of you.

About the Author

Zeta K. Pierce is the pen name of the fantasy/science fiction writer behind The Crimson Knight. In her spare time she enjoys gaming, anime, and spending time in nature. She is also an amateur self-taught artist. You can connect with her on zetakpierce.carrd.co

www.ingramcontent.com/pod-product-compliance
Lightning Source LLC
Chambersburg PA
CBHW030119310726
48970CB00004B/1321